From the reviews of *The Ice People*

'Excellent ... intelligent, driven, imaginative, obsessive yet still gracious, one of our best ... Exciting stuff.'   Fay Weldon

'Ambitious and subtle ... She writes elegantly, unsentimentally, expertly ... *The Ice People* works persuasively as science fiction, and is truthful about our emotional lives.'   Nicolette Jones, *The Independent*

'Infused with poetic intensity ... this is a gripping fictional realisation of what we fear: the death of civilisation. Maggie Gee achieves her apocalyptic vision without the clank of hardware and intergalactic wars. Her detail is precise and controlled and her beautifully orchestrated whisper of redemption is rooted in eternal myth.'   Elizabeth Buchan, *The Times*

'An intriguing novel of ideas, fully fleshed out ... Classy science fiction.'   Judith Cook, *Mail on Sunday*

'Not one to shirk the larger issues – gender segregation, racial divisions and environmental catastrophe – Maggie Gee has gone straight for the jugular in her latest novel. Set in a cold and brutally Darwinian future ... Gee's tale shifts seamlessly between the close and dawn of the next century ... Gee has deftly thrown the inhabitants of our future into a game of survival in which every human tension is accelerated ... Gee's futuristic backdrop allows her to stretch her creative wings beautifully.'   Tanis Taylor, *Time Out*

Maggie Gee

The Ice People

TELEGRAM

London San Francisco Beirut

Copyright © Maggie Gee, 1998 and 2008

First published in 1998
by Richard Cohen Books, London
Reprinted 1999

This edition published by Telegram, London, 2008

ISBN: 978-1-84659-038-2

A full CIP record for this book is available from the British Library.

Manufactured in Lebanon

TELEGRAM
26 Westbourne Grove, London W2 5RH
825 Page Street, Suite 203, Berkeley, California 94710
Tabet Building, Mneimneh Street, Hamra, Beirut
www.telegrambooks.com

For Richard Cohen
and for my beloved husband,
Nick Rankin

Acknowledgements

The author would like to thank the Society of Authors for their support and Christine Casley for meticulous editing. Grateful thanks also to E. J. Scovell (Joy Elton), Barbara Goodwin, Roger Pemberton, Fatima Bellacosa, Caroline Winterburn, and Moris and Nina Farhi.

About five million years ago, our ancestors were arboreal, apelike creatures contentedly going about their business in the forests of East Africa. Then, for reasons that are still only partly understood, the Earth entered a series of recurring Ice Ages ... typically a little over 100,000 years long ... separated by interglacials about 15,000 years long. We live in an interglacial that began about 15,000 years ago ... Even during a full Ice Age the forests of East Africa do not freeze ...

John and Mary Gribbin, *Watching the Weather*

... during most of the last half million years the climate was ... considerably colder than now ... The term *interglacial* is used to describe major warm phases, each of which ... lasted 10,000 to 15,000 years ... We are now living within a major warm phase, which has so far lasted about 10,000 years (the warm-up began as early as 13,000 years ago.) It compares closely with previous interglacial periods ... and ... it seems likely that colder conditions will return ...

Anthony J. Stuart, *Life in the Ice Age*

The great glaciers of the Ice Age will return ... the four previous interglacials lasted between 8,000 and 12,000 years, and the present one, called the Holocene, has already endured a little longer than 10,000 years.

Windsor Chorlton, *The Ice Ages*

... the detail of the ice-core record has also revealed short-term periodicities [which] occurred very suddenly and may have been important in stressing populations ... The Younger Dryas has now been recognised world-wide as a sudden reversion to glacial conditions following a generally milder phase of the Late Glacial. After a 'false dawn' of warmer conditions, the world was plunged once more into relative dryness and cold.

Andrew Sherratt, *Climatic Cycles and Behavioural Revolutions*

The Belgian botanist Genevieve Wollard examined the pollen in layers of peat that were deposited in what is now Alsace, in north-eastern France, some 112,000 years ago, in ... the last interglacial epoch ... Within the space of a mere twenty years, pollen from the temperate climate trees had vanished altogether. Just two decades had been sufficient to transform a balmy climate into one as frigid as Lapland.

Adrian Berry, *The Next Five Hundred Years*

Europe should prepare for temperatures to fall to Arctic levels, even though meteorologists have declared 1997 the Earth's hottest year on record, an American scientist says. Wallace Broecker, of Columbia University, says ... winter temperatures in northern Europe would fall by at least 10°C within a decade. Britain would be as cold as Spitzbergen, 600 miles inside the Arctic Circle ... the consequences would be devastating.

Nigel Hawkes and Nick Nuttall,
reporting in *The Times,* 28 November 1997

PART ONE

I

I, Saul, Teller of Tales, Keeper of Doves, Slayer of Wolves, shall tell the story of my times. Of the best of days, and the end of days. Of the new white world that has come upon us. For whoever will read it. For whoever can read.

I am sitting in the halfdark by the fire. A circle of eyes reflects the firelight. The wild children, surrounding me. Not a circle, really. Too regular. They crowd, and bulge outwards, and fight, and crow. Kit, and Jojo, and Fink, and Porker, and some who have roars and grunts for names ...

They are eating something. That familiar smell. Delicious because all food is delicious, then fatty, sweetish, sickening.

They see I am writing. Their eyes flicker. Beyond them, it's black to the horizon, where the afterglow of sunset is brighter than before. The unearthly radiance beyond is coming closer, like the deep new cold. A ring of fire from a ring of ice.

I'm an old man now – old for these times, over sixty. Not long ago, people lived more than twice as long, if they were rich and lucky enough not to be terminated. In the easy days, the long hot days when there were so many human beings ...

I'm not afraid to die. This morning I saw it coming, or did I dream it? – the white bear with a cub beside it, lolloping, joyful, glassbright in the sunlight.

Why should I be afraid? I have lived through interesting times. I have been loved, by a woman and a child. I have seen the world change utterly, perhaps for ever. I have had a son, who is now a god. I have lived through great adventures. I have crossed the Pyrenees in deep snow, fought off the wolves side by side with my son; I rode across Spain on the waves of blossom, from north to south, from winter to spring. I have seen almond blossom, cherry blossom, orange blossom, whitening the blazing skies. Following the seasons down to the sea.

No, I'm not afraid to go. Yet I shiver a little when their eyes turn on me. Writing fascinates them, and makes them jealous. Sometimes they pretend to copy me. A few of them can do it, clumsily. Jojo can do it, and speak in sentences, he lived Inside till he was twelve. More of them can read, perhaps six, a dozen, though I doubt if they've ever read a book, they wouldn't even know the word. They look at me expectantly, waiting for me to tell my story. They like stories about love and adventure, and my story's full of love and adventure ...

But how can they ever understand?

I shall tell this story for myself. And for Luke, perhaps, should he survive. If these packs of wolves let their gods survive.

For Sarah; yes, dead or alive.

I tell this story because I must.

– The wild boys dance between me and the fire, and the cold increases, suddenly. I am an ancestor, to them. Quite soon now they will – celebrate me.

But perhaps my story will keep me alive. Perhaps they will let me finish my story.

They want me to tell them about the future. I tell them I'd better stick to the past. Human beings have always foretold the future. Self-deluders. Wishful thinkers. I used to do it all the time, obscenely self-confident, a tech teacher ... I told my pupils about global warming. I told them why we were so hot, why despite all our efforts it could only get hotter –

Well, as I say, let's stick to the past. Let's hear how the old world turned into this. Me and the wild boys shivering here in the shell of an abandoned airport. The fires that keep us warm are steadily burning their way through the airline's abandoned fixtures. Old desks and partitions collapsing like foam, carpets unravelling in thick black fumes.

By day we don't need them. By day we keep busy. If you're not busy, these days, you die.

We share this airport with hundreds of Doves. Maybe no one in the future will know what they are.

Our mechanical friends. Our robot loves.

My Doves, my dears. How you once obsessed me. My love of machines drove poor Sarah wild. Once I thought their descendants would outnumber ours ... and who knows? They might do, one day, in Euro. We know how many Doves escaped, and some of the escapees must have survived.

Mutating, as they were designed to do. Maybe the Doves will have the last laugh yet, out in this strange new frozen world. But I don't think so. They ... have their limits.

And here in the airport they don't look good. They crouch in rows, looking dull and lifeless, so the wild boys grow bored with them, and I am too tired to maintain them all.

Fleets of them. Quiet now. Heads bowed, wings back.

But if you had seen them in their heyday. Those amazing, brilliantly successful inventions. *'DOVES – The Wings of a Brave New World.'*

And me, white-haired Saul, when I was dark and dashing.

And beautiful Sarah, with her waterfall of hair ... .

Time to begin at the beginning.

I, Saul, Teller of Tales, Keeper of Doves, Slayer of Wolves, bring you the story of my glory days.

2

I was born in 2005, in the country on the edge of London, when the Tropical Time was just beginning, what we look back on as the Tropical Time.

Things changed for me early on. All my life I've remembered the beginning, though. Green fields, a sandy track, conkers, the low *whirrclap* of a wood pigeon's wings. Black and white cattle. A slaughterhouse, a blank brick building where animals moaned. Climbing a hawthorn and spiking my hands. Cow parsley heads like plates of frothed cream, rising to meet me as I fell from above. Thrashing the long wet grass with a stick.

Then fences went up with cartoonlike speed, there were months of dust and hammering, the neat pink houses rose one by one, and when the dust settled, we were in London.

My mother was a loving, worried woman, softly spoken, but a terrier. Almost everything about her was a faded beige, her tired mouth, her pleated cheeks. She read me poetry at bedtimes, watched every move, and denied me sweets, but she was very loving, when she wasn't tired, and my school shirts were always white. She liked reading, she made me love reading, and yet her jobs were never with books. There were too many jobs; she was often exhausted. She was a care assistant in a Last Farewell Home, where people over a hundred were 'termed' unless they had family to take them in. I'm sure she did the job kindly and cleanly. My dad made jokes about her terminating him. Her other main staple was oneoff assignments driving huge haulers for a teleshopping firm, roaring up the emways in the middle of the night. And yet she was a slight woman, not that strong.

My father liked quiet, but he worked for the police, as an enforcer for home prison contracts. His hair was curly, scattered with grey. His face was strong and grave, heavily lined, with big dark eyes, and his voice, heard rarely, was low pitched and slow. It made people listen, that quiet voice. Perhaps it helped him in his job. In those days London had a public policeforce, though the days of public prisons were over. He was also a general law enforcer. If he saw something suspicious, he would go straight in. Most policemen didn't, according to Samuel. 'The police have become a bunch of cowards.'

(Dad taught me to be brave. I've tried my best. And my son, his grandson, has his brave blood.)

Dad talked less than Mum, and I'm not sure he listened, which must be where I got it from, for Sarah said I never listened ... He was a big man. He had high standards. He drank too much. He was slow to anger, but sometimes – Yes, he had terrible rages. I still don't like to think about them.

But he was a good man. They were good parents. They loved each other, and me, and my sister.

Samuel and Milly. So far in the past. They seem so little now, so innocent, and the time they lived in so safe and tidy. My photos have all gone, of course, but they sit imprinted in my brain, posing for the camera, holding hands and smiling. While I'm alive, they are not forgotten.

All they ever seemed to talk about was the shortage of water and the heat.

I was muddled about it, aged twelve. On the one hand there was never enough water, and watering your garden from the tap was a crime. On the other hand, sea levels were rising, and the white cliffs of Dover had to be shored up after part of them toppled into the sea.

Then the crumbling cliffs and the endless money the government paid to underpin them grew confused in my mind with foreigners. People from even hotter countries were always trying to get in to Britain. The screens showed pictures of the eroded white cliffs, then scenes of dark people, sweating and furious, bullying the immigration officers, shouting and swearing, their black mouths open. Often the army would be called in.

I started to hate these foreigners. There wasn't enough to share with them. We lived in a threebed brick twentiethcentury cottage with plasterboard doors that never quite shut, and my parents worked harder than anyone.

One day when my mother had come home exhausted from an allnight run to Edinburgh, I told her I hated black people. She came into the garden in her dingy pink nightgown, and begged me to stop slamming my football against the shed. I did three more kicks, then went and lay down on the prickly yellow lawn, ignoring her.

'What's the matter?' she asked. 'For heaven's sake.'

'I don't like black people,' I said. 'The screen said even more of them are trying to get in.' To me they seemed like liars and scroungers who would keep my family poor for ever. 'I hate black people. Why must they come here?'

She looked at me with a little frown, a puckered white thread in her sunreddened forehead. 'Saul – they're not all the same, you know. You can't go hating black people.'

'It's *true,* Mum. I saw the pictures.'

'You don't understand.' She sounded peculiar. 'Saul, listen ... look ... there's something ...' She stared at the ground, her mouth working.

Then something burst out like a stone at a windscreen. *'Haven't you noticed your father's black?'*

'That's mad,' I said. It hurt my chest.

'Yes. Well – half. Your grandpa was from Ghana. He came here as a student, in the last century.'

'I haven't got a grandpa. Shut up. I hate you. Why are you saying these horrible things?'

'Because it's true. Grandpa died when you were two.'

I stumbled to my feet. She tried to hug me but I broke away and ran into the house.

In the bathroom mirror I looked for the truth. My skin was golden, as it was before, but I watched it change and become light brown. Spots, I saw, and curly black hair, and features broadening with adolescence. My nostrils, flaring. Yes, and my lips. I saw Dad's face behind my own.

She said no more. I was stunned, confused.

I tried to talk to my father. It was never easy. He was a shy man, who preferred to be alone. He liked birds; perhaps that's why he'd gone to live in the country, and until he died he always kept pigeons.

He was throwing them dull yellow kernels of seed, as I tried to talk to him about being black. It was dark in the shed. Everything was dark. There was a dirty little window, high up. But the eyes were bright; so many pairs of eyes, darting about on sheeny silk necks, and Dad and I looking past each other. He didn't say a lot, but he touched my arm. We stood together in the airless darkness, with the warm bodies quivering and shuffling around us, and I thought, this might be like Africa, though I didn't have a clue about Africa.

What did he say, exactly? That I should be proud (but how proud was he? He had never told me about myself). That the first humans were African (but 'You kids are as British as the next person'). That skin colour was not important (and yet it had 'held me back in the force'). That we were 'the same as anybody else' (yet 'people like us always have to watch our backs'). And the sentences seemed to come out muddled, the pigeons pecked, and it was hard to ask questions.

The thing Mum had told me didn't make enough difference. At first I expected the sky to explode and the earth to blacken with astonishment. Thirty years later it would change my life, send me off on an odyssey round half the world – But at the time I just became restless, unsettled, no longer sure I was like my neighbours. Not that I looked particularly different. My sister was darker skinned than me, but her lips, like Mum's, were on the thin side. And yet we shared the same grandfather ... In the end I got tired of going over it all.

Our school had very few black people. Remember, this had recently been countryside, and most black people preferred the city. There were Italians, Asians, Swedes ... And fifty or a hundred kids were probably mixed race, many of them good friends of mine. We hung out together, liked the look of each other, followed Renk and Roots music avidly, but no one mentioned what we had in common. And what was there, really, to mention? We were mostly third or fourth generation British, all with more white in us than black. Yet I think I longed to be recognised. That hidden part of me was waiting to be seen.

Which was partly why I fell in love with Sarah, a dozen years later, when I was twentyfive.

I came to central London when I was eighteen, and lived in a hostel near Regent's Theme Park. It was noisy, but I liked the freedom. Samuel's police career had ground to an end, without leaving him better off or happier. Now he disapproved if I played the wrong music or brought a friend home or used a dreampad to relax after work. Mum, who was retraining as a nurse, explained to Dad that the new way was safer, the little silver pads we stuck on the skin so the drug was absorbed straight into the bloodstream. 'But why do you need drugs?' Samuel would demand, pouring himself another cold beer.

(It's like a dream, to remember those days, when you could flick what you wanted from any dispenser. Now we can't even get hold of painkillers, and one of my teeth has been throbbing for days ... I wish I had one of those old silver dreampads. I'd slip its coolness on to my skin. Then the slow rush, the sweet slide forwards, flying away from stress and pain.

Finished. Gone. There are no more escapes, except through lighter fuel or cleaning fluids, which every so often the wild boys try. Then there is mayhem, fire and death, and Chef and I creep away and hide ... Such beautiful, desirable words: *aspirin, somnifer, paracetamol, diamorphine, tenebrol, heroin, lullane.* Lulling us away from hurt and grief. We grew used to them, and then we lost them.

Now I suppose the only drugs are stories. That's why the kids still look to me. They see I'm writing. They're curious. Don't you see, you boneheads, I'm Scheherezade? I'll spin out my story night after night, hamming, stalling, to save my life –

Scheherezade! Don't make me laugh. None of them knows what I'm talking about. It's a world ago, the *Arabian Nights* my mother used to read to me, the Bible, Dickens, Hans Andersen ... What a waste, what a shame, the old twists, the old tales, all of them lost on these little savages. Vile little shits, ignorant brutes, spitting out their elders like chickenbones, I'd like to kick them to the back of beyond ...

No use, no use. Too many of them.

Now Kit is offering me a leg. 'Take it, old man! Save it for you!' Long, fringed with blackened, gamey meat, glistening in the light of the fire, its shape unpleasantly familiar. Sometimes I eat, but today I'm not hungry. I want to feel human, as I once was. I wave placatingly. Back to my story.)

In the early 2020s I lived in central London. I was happy because it was so different from home. Walking the streets until the cool of the early hours, dancing in the squares, by the river, on the pavements. Teen life had come out of the molelike tunnels where the young liked to hide at the beginning of the century.

My generation did things differently. We travelled everywhere, easily as swallows, we students with money from waiting tables, on cheap, safe airlines that competed for our business. The countries we flew to still had governments. Lisbon, Reykjavik, Beijing – we saw the world, packed in like sardines. Everywhere we danced to the same music. And the smaller towns were even better. There you could dip into the twentiethcentury, a time when each place had its own special taste. That quiet square in Avila. Cool pale beer, smoky black olives. The townspeople were dark like me; there were darkeyed girls in bright satin dresses ...

(Euro got bad in my early twenties. There were three years of plague that closed the frontiers, a new kind of Ebola coinciding with haemorrhagic sleeping sickness; blazing summers when viruses flourished and civil order couldn't stand the strain as hundreds of victims bled to death in their cars, choking the roads to hospitals. Our government fell, and was barely replaced. Looking back, my late teens were paradise.)

We young ones chose to live in the open, though our parents hardly left their homes, hiding behind electronic gates. We ate in the sun; we danced in the sun. We laughed at the old – we called them 'the slows', and sometimes 'the bits', for all their spare parts – with their cautious, waxy masks of whitish suncream. When the evening came, we mobbed the streets.

We liked to be under the orange sky, with the flaring thunder clouds above us. We waited for the little chill of morning, the slight but miraculous lessening of heat that slipped in with the breezes of three or four AM, so that people lying clammy and bare on their beds would reach out in their sleep and pull up a sheet. Outside, the kids drew closer and threw arms round each other, enjoying being young together ... I was happy, whether cool or hot, and slept as little as I could. We were all hotblooded, we were raised on heat. I loved fiery middays and baking afternoons, and the long, familiar nakedness of summer evenings, when no one under thirty ever wore a shirt.

Yet my body was strangely illadapted to heat. I was hairy, unlike my father. I had a thick pelt of curling dark hair which ran down my chest and across my shoulders, and defined the strong muscles of my legs in shorts. Some women were fascinated by it, and would stare, letting me see them noticing. Others were shocked, even a little disgusted, for the fashion was for shaving, of heads and bodies.

Why was that? Hard to recall now, but it lasted for decades, that egglike baldness. Perhaps it was a kind of streamlining, an attempt to keep cool at any cost. And the style appealed to both men and women. The fashion of the time was for androgyny, so hair was suspect, for it signalled gender.

And yet, though our clothes and hair denied it, a great gap had grown up between the sexes. Segging we called it. From segregation. Almost everything we did was segged. Girls with girls, boys with boys, great droves of animals bypassing each other, eyes darting across, wild in the neon, jostling, signalling, twisting through the night, two big streams that couldn't make a river.

The problems with fertility had started to get worse. The screens were full of alarming statistics. They didn't mean all that much to the young, who were too busy having fun to think that having children mattered, but our parents discussed it in solemn voices. They wanted grandchildren. They wanted a future.

I knew, in any case, with that complete confidence that young people have once, then never again, that these reports weren't about me. I wasn't like them. I wouldn't have a problem. I knew I was a man who wanted women. When I had had sex (which wasn't very often because it wasn't easy to get women to have sex, what with segging, and mutant hivs) the pleasure was huge, easy, instinctive. It seemed so natural, like having children.

I felt on the brink of owning the world. I was a man, and human beings ran the planet. There were eight billion of us, though numbers were shrinking, but few other animals were left to compete. Insects, bacteria, viruses. (And cats, of course. Cats everywhere. The city streets were patched with fur, ginger, tabby, blackandwhite. I liked cats though, so that was all right.) I was tall, and strong, and a techie, which qualified me for a lifetime's good money. It was new and wonderful to feel like this; home had too many small sadnesses.

When civil order broke down, over the next few years, I stayed optimistic. Who needed governments? If you were young, you were selfreliant. The plagues passed me by, though I lost several friends. The streets grew rougher, but I stayed away from trouble. In wealthier areas, life went on as usual. I didn't let the newscasts upset me.

I found I had a gift with machines. They were alive to me, and entirely absorbing, like the aphids I once bred in a matchbox. I was fascinated by artificial life, by the huge range of mobots in the college labs, the multitravellers, the swarmers, the sorters, though my speciality was nanotechnics, working with invisibly small molecular machines. I had delicate powers of manipulation that helped me pass out with high honours. Job offers came in plenty from military and security firms. For some reason I found myself turning them down. My father was shocked, but I knew I wasn't ready. Something had to happen first, some great adventure. For the moment I took a part-time job as a tech teacher in a Learning Centre.

One day a week was the teachers' Dee Stress. No pupils came in, and only half the guards were working. The underground trains were back in service, after more than a year of being sealed off. I tubed in, reading a weird story about some people in Portugal living in caves. They said there were hundreds, maybe thousands of them, living as people did in the Stone Age. And they were breeding. There were children everywhere. They looked dark, in the picture, with sparkly eyes. The reporter wanted to know their secret. I thought how much I'd like to go and see for myself. Order in France had completely broken down, but things were still peaceful in Iberia.

The school garden was overrun with big pink mallow flowers like English faces burning in the sun. The litter waved gaily like little silver flags. I remember I felt something good was going to happen.

Three metres away, the front door coded me. I got the normal access signal. The doors opened. The lights came on. The uniformed guard was not in her place, but I was early, and besides, it was Friday. The voicetone welcomed me, as usual. 'Good morning, Officer 102. It is eightothree AM Cooling is in progress. Please specify rooms you want unlocked and conditioned.'

I always said 'Good morning' back, though other teachers laughed at me. They thought I was joking, but I wasn't. It seemed to me anything might be alive. What was the boundary between living and nonliving?

(Now I would give a different answer, as I approach closer to the shadowy line that separates the living from the dead, but then I was besotted with our cleverness.)

I confirmed my code, then asked for the lift, and coffee upstairs in the Dee Stress room. Dee Stress began formally at nine, so there was probably halfanhour or so before the other teachers arrived. I had nothing to prepare; the sun blazed outside the window. And so I requested the day's chillout sounds, sponsored by StartSmart Buildings Inc. 'First up today, we bring you "Nessun Dorma" ...' I never tired of it. 'Thank you, that's great.' When the wonderful music surged up through the silence, it felt as though the building were giving me love.

Behind me, the entrance slid open again. I was waiting for the lift, and didn't look round. The normal welcome routine began, and the music continued more quietly. It spoke of passion, space, grandeur, of hot black windows in high white walls. It made me think with longing of Euro. Mountains. Plains. I should be free ... What kind of life did they live, in the caves?

Then the music cut out. The welcome was repeating. I turned and saw a woman with her back to me, staring mystified at the input by the scanner.

'Just show your coder,' I began to say, but at that moment she raised a pale hand and tried to do something to the input panel. At once the warning buzzer sounded. 'Security,' the building said. 'Security to entrance, please. Security. Security.'

The entrance doors closed firmly behind the woman, who was spinning round slowly, looking nervously upwards, and then the lift doors, which were opening for me, changed their minds, shuddered, closed again. 'Entrance hall sealed,' the building remarked. 'Secur-' But it didn't finish the word.

'Ohgod,' the woman said. I looked at her. She had long hair. Most females under fifty had short hair, unless they were under ten, that is. She was small, slim, in a loose white dress, not fashionable, a 'pretty' dress. What my mother would have called a pretty dress.

'I've done something awful. I'm new,' she said. 'I'm Sarah Trelawney. How do you do.' Her voice was composed, soft, with a burr. A very young voice, despite her appearance.

The voicetone hissed, seethed, strained, as if the building were trying to breathe. Then it suddenly said, in a cheerful voice, 'The emergency has been contained. We apologise for any break in transmission.' I waited for the doors to move, but nothing happened. And the music began to unroll again, wave after wave, into the vacuum.

She walked towards me, and the fog fell away. The sun sheared across her, shining on her hair. She wasn't old. She was younger than me. But how strange she looked, with that loose pale dress, how perversely erotic, when everyone else was wearing clothes that were thinner than skin and clung to the body, to halfglimpse the swell of her belly, her breasts. I tried very hard not to stare at her breasts.

That weird waterfall of hair. Such childish hair. Reddish-brown, shiny, glinting like conkers against their white shell, and her skin had tiny freckles like dots of honey. She looked miserable, but her eyes were very blue. She came closer. The music gathered and poured. My heart swelled absurdly.

'Nessun dorma ...' Let no one sleep ...

Then she spoke, and her firm voice cut through my fantasy. She had sharp small teeth, which caught the light. 'I seem to have locked us in. Sorry.'

'I'm Saul,' I said. 'Don't worry. The others will be here in ten minutes or so.' She had a small nose, a square, strong jaw. We shook hands. Hers was mysteriously cool – most handshakes then were a slither of sweat.

'You must be an officer,' I said, 'to be coded.'

'It's a new post,' she said, shy. 'I'm something called a Role Support Officer.'

'What does that mean, then?' I asked her.

'The government's decided that boys and girls have to be taught to get on together. It's partly political, I'm afraid. They're making appointments all over the country. Because the fertility figures are down again, and they have to seem to be doing something. Elections next year, of course.'

'How do you mean, get on together?' We were leaning side by side against the desk where normally the guards were posted. I noticed her nails: very white moons. Small freckled hands. No rings. A chain. She wasn't pierced, or tattooed. I wanted to get on with her.

(Be honest: I wanted to make love to her.)

'Well – I mean – you know – ' She was intensely embarrassed. 'Live together, I suppose. Try to get them living together again.'

Live together. It was shockingly intimate.

'I bet you got the job because you look like that.' As soon as I'd said it, I knew it was offensive. 'I didn't mean –' I said, then stopped.

But she smiled. 'You mean – I look twentiethcentury,' she said. 'What they used to call feminine. Probably, yes. And I've dressed the part. But I *can* teach. As a matter of fact, I'm good. I've taught Outsiders, you know. I can teach without screens. I even taught for two months in the towers –'

'Wow,' I said. So she was tough. Like everyone else in my year at college, I'd turned down the chance of practice teaching in the towers, despite the huge bonuses they offered and the promise of fulltime protection from zapsquads.

She was staring at me, letting her frank blue eyes run over my neck, my arms – and was she looking at the curly hair on my chest? 'You have a slightly old-fashioned look yourself,' she said, and smiled. 'We could almost coteach.'

Then neither of us could look at each other, but I could feel, a centimetre away, her small white hand beside mine on the desk, burning into me like a naked current. We stood transfixed in a cube of sunshine, saying very little, staring at the glass where hands had begun to wave at us, gesturing, impatient, frustrated, irrelevant. I hardly saw them, because I was with her.

Was it ten minutes, or an hour, before the building yielded? By that time, I was falling in love with Sarah.

And Sarah? I'll never know about her, but she told me later she felt the same way.

We said very little, and a lot. That we both had dreams of escaping from the city. That both of us needed to escape our families. That we both wanted children, and expected them. We couldn't say the word 'children', of course, which would have meant 'sex', to both of us. I said 'I'd like a family of my own, one day,' and she said 'Of course,' and smiled at me.

'I like you,' she said, although it was obvious.

'Why?' I said, feeling happiness spread through my body like oxygen.

'I like the look of you. You're – different. You're not just English, are you? What are you? French? Spanish?' She looked straight at me. Her curiosity was like a kiss. Then she lit up. 'You're *beek,* aren't you. You must be, of course! Tell me I'm right.'

And she had seen the thing that I wanted her to see. *Beek* was short for *bicolor,* the French insult that black people themselves had taken over to mean 'mixed race', and she used it so easily.

'Yes, I'm *beek.* Most people don't notice. My father's halfAfrican, my mother was white.' Had I ever said it straight out before? She made me feel I could be myself.

'That explains why – well, you look good to me.' She finished the sentence in an awkward rush. 'I'm very interested in all that. It was part of my Ethnicities diploma course.'

I'd always disliked the word 'ethnicity' – it sounds like someone cleaning their teeth – but on her lips, it seemed tolerable. 'You're English, I suppose.'

She shook her head fiercely. 'I'm Scottish and Cornish. Not an English drop of blood in me.' (Which must have been nonsense, but it sounded exciting.)

'Did your parents have red hair?' I looked at her hair. It was like some glossy animal fur. What couldn't a man do with hair like that? Wrap it around him, burrow into it.

But something was happening outside the door. Two beings had arrived in brilliant spacesuits. Somewhere to the rear my colleagues hovered, leaving a clear space between themselves and the spacemen. 'The emergency services are going to invade,' I told her, thinking *now it will be over.*

'I hope they don't sack me for crashing the system.'

'Come dancing with me tomorrow night.' I had to say something or lose her for ever.

'Mygod, just look at the size of those vappers!' she said, amused, and then suddenly alarmed. 'Are they going to use them with us inside?'

And then I remembered; it was mirrorglass. We could see out but they couldn't see in. The people outside weren't waving to us, they were simply beating on the glass in frustration. No one would know there was anyone inside. We were in danger; she was in danger.

I tried to sound calm. 'Let's get out of range.' But the spacemen were aligning their vappers with the doors. Something earthshattering was going to happen. Without thinking, I grabbed Sarah by the shoulders, flung her to the ground, and fell on top of her, covering both our heads with my outstretched elbows. She felt soft and small, and smelled of sweat, and flowers, and part of me registered these pleasant things as most of me waited for the end. One second, two, three, four –

I felt her struggling, her small steel fists. 'What the hell are you doing?' she panted, furious. 'You've torn my dress. Get off me, you idiot!'

Then the building spoke. Both of us froze. '...contained,' it said. 'Waiting to code. Waiting to code. Good morning. Please approach and code. Please show all codecards so we can help you.'

It was over. The lift doors glided back like silk. I rolled off Sarah, and patted her placatingly. Outside, the silver spacemen laid down their vappers, and the crowd behind them began to push forwards.

'I was trying to save your life,' I gabbled. 'They couldn't see us. It's mirrorglass.' She was straightening her dress and staring at me. Her pupils were pinprick small with shock, and her skin was webbed with pink where I'd clutched her. 'I was trying to shield you with my body.'

She suddenly stopped frowning and touched my arm. As the entrance slid open, to great whoops and cheers, I watched her pupils expand and darken. 'Why should you?' she said. 'I mean – you've only just met me. I mean, you were *risking your life* for me.'

I thought about that in the split second that was left. I couldn't say 'Because I'm in love with you,' for fear she would think me completely mad.

The thing I did say seemed simple, obvious, though normally I would never have said it. 'Because I'm a man,' I told her. 'Because I'm a man, and you're a woman.'

3

That was the way it began with us. An absolute feeling of rightness together. My colouring, my size, my sex. They all felt right as never before. They married her smallness, softness, toughness. She reminded me a little of my mother, slight but enduring, loving, fierce, good with her hands, helpful, maternal. She was – *womanly,* that was the only word, old-fashioned though I knew it was. So I could be manly, as I wished to be.

'You beautiful man,' she said, when she first saw me naked, not long after. No woman had ever said that to me.

'But I'm so – hairy,' I said, humbly. I did feel humble. She was too good for me. Seeing her like this, it was obvious. Her small sweet breasts. Her delicacy. I was halfashamed of my hairiness. The pressures against it were overwhelming; ninetyninepercent of men were smooth and neat, displaying their gleaming narrow bodies in clubs, corrugated chests that shone like oil and only the faintest grey fuzz on their scalps. I was an ape by comparison, a pelt of blackness from chest to groin.

'Esau was an hairy man,' she whispered, gently running her fingertips through my chest hair, going down, lower, lower, bliss, till she reached the place where I was hard and hairless, and she bent her head and kissed me there, then looked up and smiled – 'See, you're smooth as well.'

Such happiness. Such a time of peace.

Only one thing was less than perfect, and I put that down to my stubbornness, a streak of pride and resentment that had sometimes got me into trouble at school. She was wild about me, everything about me, as she assured me earnestly, running her hands over my lips, my nose, telling me I was the first *beek* she had slept with. (How very dated that slang seems now!) She seemed to think about that more than I did. It must have made me more romantic, my mixed race background, my unusual looks. She wanted me to read the essays she had written for the *Ethnicities* part of her diploma, and I tried, I tried, but it was very solemn, and the language incomprehensible.

She ordered what seemed like dozens of films about black history, and urged me to watch them. *The Black Diaspora, The Black Experience, Caliban in London, African Journey* ... She saw at least half before she got bored, but I made excuses not to watch them with her, I didn't want her telling me stuff, *teaching me* stuff, about my past, I wanted her to love me for myself, I didn't want to be part of black history, I needed to be myself, her man. 'I'll use them later,' I said, meaning never. And she sulked a bit, but then she gave up. We made love so much, there was no time to quarrel.

Never, never ...

Never say never.

For a while we were everything to each other, Sarah and I in a box of a room. (Property, of course, was insanely expensive since the government had stopped all further building to protect the last socalled green spaces. But the illicit shanty town still grew, though every day police tore it down. And in the centre of London flybuilders slipped buildings into every tiny gap and garden.) We were grateful for our sweaty box, though it was on the third floor and had no aircon, no voice response, no autoservice. It was primitive, but so were we.

We made love on the floor, which was cooler than the sleepmat, and in the showerroom, and in the kitchen. We slept intertwined, in a slipknot of sweat. That amazing heat of that first summer.

It was always with us, like a third person. If we hadn't been so madly in love with each other, hungry for each moist salty centimetre of skin, we couldn't have borne to share that space. The middleaged, the slows, the bits, rarely seemed to touch each other. By June or July, handshakes had shrunk to a tentative tap inside the wrist.

But to us that summer was like a mother, holding us clasped together in the heat. Deep down we were very different people, but for months of bliss we lived like twins. I made iced coffee; she made iced coffee. I showered; she showered. We made love again.

The first time we did it, she said, insanely, 'Come on, Saul. Let's make a baby. I know I'll get pregnant. I just feel it.'

I was naked and stiff in the candle flame (which was strictly illegal because of the fire risk). My sweat ran down like melted wax, but a cold little voice from somewhere else hissed in my ear, escaped my lips.

'But if we want to travel, Sarah,' I said. 'You thought, in a year ... once you're established in the job. We talked about going to the ends of the earth ...' I felt as if our dream might slip away, but perhaps I was looking in the wrong direction. 'But never mind,' I added, hastily. I would have done anything she wanted.

I was too late. Her fluid mouth, which had been like an anemone, red and inflamed and fully open, instantly hardened. 'Of course you're right. I'll fix myself up.'

Regret hit me like the back of a spade. I knew I should have trusted her instincts, and we would have made a baby at once, a bouncing, beautiful, healthy baby.

Then she came back towards me, with her copperred hair running in heavy streams across the apples of her breasts, her eyes cast down, her eyes on my penis, and her fingers touched my neck, and I groaned, and forgot.

'There'll be other times,' I said, when we'd finished, and lay entwined in the airless night. All the windows were open, but the breeze never came. Below in the street, car doors slammed, sirens wailed in the distance, a drunk was singing a sentimental song about tomorrow, a can clattered and crumpled underneath a car wheel, a couple continued a distant row – but the sound of her breathing, loud and real in the foreground, turned the sadness of the city into perfect contentment. Or almost perfect.

'Are you awake, Sarah? There'll be millions of times –'

'What?' she asked me, sleepy, happy. 'What are you worrying about, Saul?'

'We'll have lots of babies, like you said.'

'Oh that. Thankgod you were sensible.' She yawned, turned over and fell asleep.

At first we seemed to want the same things. This life in a high poky room in London was temporary, we agreed. We dreamed of making for the last open spaces. Our private mantra was 'the ends of the earth'. We imagined raising a family by the sea, with forests, fields, clean bright water. The children were running, shouting, towards us.

But two years went by and they had run no closer. Sarah was getting more involved in her job even as she began to find its premises 'simplistic', as I heard her tell a colleague in the lift. She was one of the most vocal of the first group of Role Support Workers to be appointed, and because she talked well, and looked good on the screen, she began to be looked on as a spokesperson.

She talked about it to smug presenters. How the children resisted her, how they jeered. The tactics she used to make them take her seriously. How the boys reacted better if she presented herself in a more androgynous way; otherwise they tended to fall in love with her, though of course she didn't put it like that. (I burned with jealousy when she told me about these great lustful adolescents, staring at her.) On the whole, though, the boys were more receptive to her message. They saw great advantages in the old roles, in having women to love and support them. The girls, on the other hand, were not all that excited about developing their nurturing sides.

She came home very thoughtful after one discussion. She described it to me as she made supper. 'I want to look after kids,' one girl had said, a big, loud creature who spoke her mind. 'I worry in case I never have them. But why should I want to look after a man? They're not babies. And most of them are hopeless. That's what Mum says, anyway.'

'We only want them for one thing, eh girls?' her friend had shouted, 'and they're not much good at that, either,' and all the girls shrieked with crude laughter, while the boys sat sullen, their faces burning. 'Slags,' one shouted. 'Lesbians.'

The girls were often hostile to Sarah, too. 'It's because you're so beautiful,' I suggested. 'They're jealous'. But 'Women are more complex than you think,' she replied. 'They don't know how to relate to me, that's all. I'm not like their mothers or their sisters. I'm telling them things they don't want to hear. But they're halfafraid I'm on to something.'

'Well, you're the right person to be teaching them,' I said. 'You do love a man. And live with one happily.'

There was a little pause before she said, 'Yes,' and when I glanced across at her, curious, she left the washingup and came and sat on my lap, looking over my shoulder at the square of night sky.

'Indifference is the danger,' she said after a while. 'And boredom and resentment and a faint sense of guilt that the other sex exist at all. It's as if we would be happier –' She paused and tried again. 'As if they would be happier if the whole of life were segged. Boys feel safe with boys, girls with girls. The downside is, the girls want children. And the boys still want the girls to love them. But they don't, and so they try to ignore them.'

There had been a lot of shuffling and giggling when she showed them old films about love from the Learning Centre's midtwentieth-century collection. It was true that they tended to go silent by the end, and she could tell quite well that a lot of them enjoyed it, but they were sheepish about saying so. 'Boring,' they chorused, when the lights went up. And yet perhaps this part of the course was not a failure, for they always showed up in strength for the films.

She'd begun to get on better with the girls as she started to understand their point of view. 'They're not just yobs,' she told me. 'I used to be scared of them because of their violence, the way they beat boys up outside the gates, but they're quite thoughtful, when you listen to them. I think they have a point about housework, too.'

'But you enjoy it,' I said. 'Partly because you're so good at it. Your food always looks so beautiful. I mean, you turn that side of things into pure pleasure. I wish those girls could see what you do.'

She didn't smile, but nodded slowly. 'It takes a lot of time, though, Saul, you know.'

'Time well spent,' I said, kissing her.

(I was a fool. I didn't spot the signs.)

She let me kiss her, then pushed me away. 'I've got to get on. I must finish my work.' She was preparing one of a series of reports for the government on the success of the project, which would help them to decide on further funding. Each night she was working till the breeze began to stir, long after I had fallen asleep. I would bring her iced coffee as she bent over her screen, though she started to reject it in favour of water.

'But you love iced coffee,' I said to her, hurt. 'And you know I like to look after you –'

'Why don't you, then?' she cut me off. 'I used to like iced coffee. But people change.'

And she began to change more obviously, wearing trousers to work instead of dresses, which she said antagonised the girls, and trimming her hair 'because it gets in the way'. In the way of what? She was going somewhere.

Meanwhile I was online whenever I was able, to update on the latest tech data. Teaching for me had been a temporary plan; now it was time to move back into research, where there was more money, and freedom, and travel. The room seemed smaller when we were both working, two screens like two extra living things in the space, two busy, whispering, hurrying voices. Even so, it felt companionable. I was sure we were working towards the same end, the imagined future of shared freedom. A beach, sanddunes, small feet running.

She made the food; I ate it, gratefully. She washed the clothes; I put them on. I never really noticed that she was doing more (but she could have spoken; she could have complained) until one day we had our first quarrel.

She was standing by the window, drying her hands, preparing to sit down to work after supper. I remember there was a bright sunset. I couldn't see her face, but the new short shape of her hair made her head sharp and black against the scarlet light.

Something was beginning, something very important, but I

didn't understand it, nor anything else. 'There's some weird data here from the Antarctic,' I said. I was reading from the net about the rate of melting of the icecaps, and the various tech fixes trying to slow it down. 'Some of these results are coming out skewed.'

'What do you mean?'

'They seem to show the ice is getting thicker. I wish I were out there. This woman must've left out some of the variables.'

'What if it's true?' she interrupted. 'I'm sick of this heat. I wish it were true. Imagine it. Having fires in winter like my grandmother did on the island ... This cold fog used to roll in from the sea, it was like walking through clouds, it was marvellous.' After Sarah's violent father left, she'd been sent to stay quite often with her grandma in the Hebrides. Her memories of Coll were absurdly romantic.

'Or else they're taking samples from the wrong place,' I continued. 'There has to be some obvious error. Why do these people always screw up?'

'Wrapping up in *coats*,' Sarah went on, 'like they did in the last century. Not every day the same in this godawful heat. And this godawful baking city.'

That brought me up short. 'But you like the heat, don't you?' She turned and stared. I knew her. I loved her. My mind went back to the data again. 'It's curious. Her reports seem to show the icecap thickening in different places. You're right, it would be amazing, wouldn't it? I mean, imagine, if global warming ended.'

But a new, unlikeable expression stiffened her face into a righteous mask. 'I wasn't serious, Saul. If it's anything, it's some kind of fraud by business interests. Trying to prove global warming's slowed up. So they can go ahead and crash the planet.'

'It's just a few data, Sarah. Not enough for a fully fledged conspiracy theory. I don't believe it either. We agree.'

'You always think we agree about everything. And could you wipe the bloody table, for once? I've got a headache ... *Must I do everything around here?'*

I sat and gaped. That was just the beginning. She hated our room, and the heat, and the city, and living together, and wished I would die, so she could live in the country, and have a big house, and a life, and a baby, and another man who really loved her, unlike me. By the end she was yelling. Then she was sobbing. She was wildly unreasonable, then contrite.

It didn't mean anything, or so I thought. I made love to her, and her headache went away, and so did that first queer flurry of awareness, light as the first little flutter of snow.

But the ice didn't go away for long. It returned quite soon, like the nerve in my tooth, the ticking of a faulty electric current.

As Sarah had expected, the industrial lobbies were quick to make use of the discrepant data. 'GLOBAL WARMING A BLIP', shouted the newstexts. 'SCIENTISTS CLAIM POLES NOT MELTING'. This was followed by a flurry of denials from scientists and politicians all over the world, worried that this freak bunch of results would undo every hard-won environmental resolution. Then the denials were challenged by a third group of scientists known to be paid by big business. But no one believed them, no one could envisage that global warming was coming to an end. It was too damn hot, and getting hotter by the day, for the news broke in spring, and soon it was summer ... No one took the odd data seriously, and the original scientist who'd published the results kept her head low while she repeated the probes.

Twelve months later it had all been forgotten. We still hadn't managed to escape from the city. I'd been offered several posts in exciting places; I could have gone to the Galapagos, or Lisbon; I was offered a highly paid job in Africa, helping with a nationwide updating of screens in

Ghana. I longed to accept the last job in particular, knowing how proud my father would have been, and knowing I'd been chosen partly for my ancestry, the gift I was so proud of and had never used. The interviewing board had an atavistic sense that my Ghanaian blood made me less likely to cheat them. (They were right. I wanted to pay my dues, and my father's dues, and my grandfather's.)

But I turned them down, and I don't blame Sarah. Perhaps that means I do blame Sarah. She told me yes, of course I must go, use my talents, live my life. 'You've been dreaming of travelling for as long as I've known you. Go, and I'll come out and visit you.'

'Come with me,' I said, but she wouldn't.

She was fronting a screen show called Gendersense, dubbed 'Utter Nonsense' by Conserver pundits disappointed by the way her position had changed from the early days of her Role Support work. Now she saw her mission as 'giving a voice to the different views of men and women', 'exploring the options for separate development' and 'reflecting the range of the fertility debate', to quote from the twopage synopsis for the series she submitted to Brainscreen at the start.

I read it as I set the table one evening. I was heating up some Thai food for her. She had come home late, and I had made an effort. I wanted her to be pleased with me; there were generefreshed snowberries and cream for dessert. 'Darling,' she said. 'I really love you.' But I couldn't understand this thing she had written.

She laughed when I asked her what it all meant. 'Nothing, really. I just have to sound – well – challenging, but not too controversial.'

'Are you going to tell them what you believe?'

'What?'

'I mean, about men and women loving each other. And living together. Then the babies will come.'

She nodded abstractedly. Her cheeks were full of food. 'Mmm. But it has to sound a bit more theoretical than that. I mean, it is

Brainscreen. Look – it's not about us. Please understand, Saul, it's just a job. We're going to live together, and have a child – one day. I mean, I know we shall. But most people don't live like us –'

'When?' I asked, 'when will you be ready? I'd like to try now.' She wouldn't answer.

She looked different these days from when I first met her. More beautiful perhaps, cooler, more refined, the softness leaving her mouth and cheeks, her jaw more pronounced, her nose more sculptured. She hardly had time to teach any more, but she kept a loose attachment to give her credibility. She wore crisp white trousersuits and structured dresses that bared the long neck under her groomed red hair. She was known as a beauty, now, on the screens, though she avoided gossip and photographs, and particularly frowned on any mention of me, or snatched papshots of the two of us together.

'You're not ashamed of me, are you?' I asked her that evening. She was looking like a model, lean and contained, in a pale yellow suit with combat trousers.

'No – of course not. How could I be? But perhaps you could sometimes wear a shirt. I mean, we're not nineteen any more.'

'That's why I think we should try for a baby.'

She looked thwarted, as though I were being obtuse, but surely she was being obtuse? 'I'd just like to earn enough for us to have a house. Move out of the city. Then the child could have a garden.'

'You mean, stay in England?' I was dismayed.

'Don't take me so literally,' she snapped. 'I just think we should be practical. You're a dreamer, Saul. I have to plan for us both.'

'I thought we'd already made plans,' I said. 'Travel, remember. Children. Freedom. I could earn good money with my research.'

'Well, they don't give a crash about gender in Ghana,' she flared at me. 'Have you thought about that? Do you ever think? I couldn't do *my* work in Ghana. I couldn't earn any money in Ghana.'

'Look, I gave up Ghana, you know I did. But I could support you. I could,' I begged. 'It's what we used to talk about. You could be a mother, I could be the man ... I'd really like to look after you.'

To my surprise, she began to cry. 'It sounds beautiful, when you say that. I don't know why I'm crying, I must be going soft ... Of course I want a baby, more than anything.'

'Then why don't we try? Let's try right away!'

Her precise new face was blurred with tears. She stared up at me from her seat in the window. She had tugged her tailored hair out of shape; it looked softer, more human, fraying at the edges. 'I'm afraid, I think,' she said, slowly. 'I don't want to fail, like everyone else.'

And then I was a man, and she was a woman. 'I'll make you pregnant. Of course I will. Just let me finish looking at this data ... I'm tying up loose ends on that hoax last year.'

'Not the Antarctic thing? I thought that was all forgotten?'

'This woman is testing her ice thicknesses again. It has to be done at the same time each year.'

'Don't worry,' she said. 'I've got things to do. We'll meet at bedtime and – have a go.'

Not very romantic, but I didn't care. My heart was singing. Now life would begin. I flicked on my screen and stared at it through a brilliant film of happiness, scanning automatically across the sites till I came to Professor Raven's homepage.

The data was back, I registered at once. Good, so now this thing would be buried. The Globecorps would have to try another tack. The future would be hot; hotter; hottest ... *I hope our baby won't be hairy,* I thought, *particularly if she's a girl* ... Yet something on the screen was demanding attention, pulling me down from my place on the ceiling.

Improbably, it had happened again. Raven's second set of data showed the icesheets still thickening. The results this time were more dramatic, an increased rate of change upon the year before. The report was concise, but Professor Raven had added a footnote. 'I am of course aware that these results will be scanned by screens all over the world and made use of for various ends by the Globecorps. I am not responsible for their interpretations or misinterpretations, but I can vouch for the data's accuracy. Sceptics might care to crossrefer to Achtheim, Dr Gisele, *Alpine Glacial Movement,* and Geronimo, Professor Jean, *A Puzzle for the Icebreakers.'*

When I finally lay naked with Sarah in my arms, more excited perhaps than I had ever been since the first time I lay with her, my love was shivering with nervousness, and as I stroked her arms and breasts and felt the small goosebumps begin to subside I thought about cold, and the sheets of ice, the vast fields of ice where the sun never set, and how strange and beautiful it would be if the great bluewhitenesses were creeping back. The children came running over the ice, shrieking with laughter, clutching each other, sliding down to the frozen ocean. Were they coming nearer? I still couldn't see. The light on their faces was intense, blinding.

'The ice is growing,' I whispered to Sarah. 'It wasn't a mistake. The ice is thickening. Our little boy might even see snow.'

'Our little boy!' She kissed me, tenderly. 'No, you're deluded. We'll have a girl.'

'Twins,' I said, as I pushed inside her. 'A boy and a girl. Snowbabies.'

4

And so we began on our epic of conception. The details blur, but it took ten years. Ten years of learning to eat my words.

It was as if we shared two different lives, one all success, the other slow failure.

In our waking life, we pursued our careers, began to make money, moved from the room to a threebed flat, then a fourbed flat in a better part of London, less fun but safer, a flat where we could finally have a study each, if we managed with only one guest bedroom.

Sarah, after all, had no family to speak of. Her father was untraceable, and she wasn't on speaking terms with her mother, who was on her fourth marriage, to a twentyyearold skater. Perhaps that's why she clung to me. It's certainly why she adored my parents. The guest bedroom was for Samuel and Milly to come and marvel at their son's success.

And I *was* successful, though I felt a little trapped. I divided my time between working on a consultancy basis for the Learning Centre where I first met Sarah, and researching applications of nanotechnology for one of the two big Nanocorps. I felt proud of what we were doing, designing minute immune machines, 'like minisubmarines', I told Sarah, which could travel through the blood and identify and destroy an enormous range of viruses and bacteria. My friend Riswan was the medical star; my part was the protein engineering. True, it turned out later that many of the agents we'd targeted for destruction had benign effects that we hadn't understood, so the application was never used, but those were the early, heroic days.

I earned a lot, but Sarah earned more. Sometimes it seemed she never stopped working. And she made the flat beautiful; it mattered to her. She would come home exhausted from performing, then work for two hours cleaning and dusting till the flat was immaculate. At first I used to try to stop her, but that made her crosser than cleaning did.

'Someone has to do it,' she would say.

'Sure. The cleaner. That's why we have one.'

'But she can't make it look like a proper home. She doesn't *love* it, like I do. It's ... our nest.'

But she wasn't laying eggs. My mind went blank. 'All the same, you're exhausted. Stop.'

'I want it to look nice.'

'What can I do to convince you?'

'You *can't* convince me. I suppose you could help me.'

'Okay then.' I probably sounded reluctant. I'd had a tough day at the office; I wanted to sit and chill onscreen. 'I mean, if I must, but you worry too much. The flat looks perfectly all right to me.'

'You *won't* help me,' she remarked, tightlipped. 'You make me feel bad about asking you to help. So don't pretend to be all concerned.'

She wasn't logical, because she was tired, always hyperactive, living on her nerves. She found it hard to say 'No' to things. Each invitation to write an article, appear on the screens or speak at a conference might be her last, so she never refused. She put her work before everything – she was always exhausted. Perhaps that was why ... Stress *can* make human beings infertile.

(But was I so different? No, just less successful.)

When my parents came, they were amazed and frightened. The way Sarah's phone never stopped ringing, the gourmet food at every meal (when most people in England lived on pills and Fibamix), the huge china bowls that Sarah kept filled with expensive real flowers in the diner and the screenroom, the way we darted around, without a second thought, in taxis and, slightly less often, minicopters (my mother had only taken two taxis in her life, and neither of my parents had flown in a minicopter until we hired one to take us all to a West End lloydwebber, then supper at the Ritz), the way we worked into the early hours, and lived symbiotically with our machines, which responded to our voices, of course, opening doors, cooling, heating, dealing with rubbish, ordering food. It was a different world from Samuel and Milly's.

'It's *very* nice, Saul,' my mother hissed the first time they came to Melville Road, as soon as Sarah had vanished to the kitchen. Mum liked our cats. Two fluffy white Persians. Not practical, really, with the heat. They were neutered males; we couldn't have coped with kittens. They sat and flicked their thick feathery tails as they watched the flies outside the window. 'We couldn't have cats, with your father's birds ... You've done so well. The flat. Sarah. Your dad and I – we never quite managed ...' She trailed away, not wanting to say more. 'But you, the kids. It's what we wanted for you.'

So we were doing something right. My parents loved us, our employers loved us; our friends came round and were hard to dislodge after Sarah's brilliant salads and my chilled wine; minicopters and cleaners enjoyed our tips; the Liblabs courted our donations, especially in election years, and sent us invitations to celebrity events ... In this life we were flying high.

But we had another life that was a secret minefield of rings on calendars, hopes and fears. 'We'll do it,' I told her, finding her in tears after another period turned up to disappoint her.

'We have to have help.'

'No, you have to have faith.'

So when did I start to accept there was a problem? I found it harder to face up to than Sarah. Harder, perhaps, for a man to admit he can't do the thing his body should do. As if that function defines a man.

I blamed myself. I had been so certain I could give Sarah what she wanted.

And more than a family was hanging on this. Sarah had promised to marry me, once, long ago, in our first few months together. Marrying was rare in the Tropical Time (though it came back later, with the Troubles and the Ice.) In the twenties and thirties, only godlovers got married, plus a few old slows afraid of the future.

But I loved Sarah, and feared to lose her. And I wanted to have what my parents had had. It probably all looked different to Sarah, whose parents split up before she was eight. She was flattered to be asked; it was 'old-fashioned' and 'romantic'. Or so she said, but words are easy. Perhaps it simply went well with the self she had invented to go with her job as Role Support Officer, the false new self she so quickly tired of –

I mustn't get bitter. What good does it do?

As Sarah grew more successful and selfconfident, she didn't see the point of marrying.

'It's a vow, that's all,' I tried to explain. 'Who cares whether other people do it? We're not like other people, are we?'

'No,' said Sarah. 'I suppose we're not. But it's a bit awkward, all the same … The paps will come and photograph us, and afterwards they'll never leave us alone.'

'So it's your immense fame, is it, getting in the way?'

I had to tease her, sometimes, or die, and Sarah usually saw the joke. Not this time, though.

'It's *political,*' she said, in that overemphatic, selfrighteous voice she used when I was being thick. 'You never see the political angle.'

'I thought marriage was personal, actually. It's about you and me, and – love and children …'

'Well, *of course* I'll marry you if – I mean, I'll marry you when we have children.'

So that was settled. A compromise that neither of us was quite happy with, but I held it before me like a baton through the tenyear marathon we ran to conception.

Two years in, I agreed to have tests. Sarah was the realist. I didn't want to do it – to join the thousands of anxious couples who flocked to the Batteries every day.

'I didn't mention the Batteries,' Sarah protested. 'I hate that name, in any case … The fertility clinics do their best for people.'

'Eggboxes then.'

'That's stupid too. We just have to ask our own doctor for a few little tests to see what's happening.'

It turned out she was already wellinformed. She had discussed it all with her friend Sylvie, who'd had a successful techfix conception. I was very upset she had discussed it. I didn't like Sylvie, a thin intense woman with too much makeup and strawlike hair. Her threeyearold son was out of control, and she talked on the telephone to Sarah for hours. To me she always looked slightly dirty.

But then I was ignorant, truculent, proud, and wanted no one to know our problems.

I grew humbler later. God, I did. I have tried to forget the humiliations.

I gave them my sperm to be examined.

I felt I was giving them my dreams.

Of course, as the doctor told us, in his lying, caring, professional voice, no tests were onehundredpercent conclusive, and there were many things medicine still didn't know ...

I was angry, and hurt. Sarah claimed I exploded. 'Oh, you don't know it all, then?' I sneered at him. I tore his form in two, then in four. 'Do you think that's a surprise to anyone? Science knows *fuck all* about making babies –'

'He's upset,' said Sarah, preemptively. 'I'm sorry, Dr Um – I can never remember your name. Sorry.'

'Wang. Dr Wang –' (I laughed, rudely) 'we quite understand these are stressful experiences.'

Dr Wang 'understood' – but no one understood. I had just been told my sperm was semifertile. My balls were no good, that was what I heard. They were big and firm, I had trusted them, I'd secretly believed the problem was Sarah's –

I halfexpected her to leave me.

She didn't, though. She comforted me, back in the privacy of home. At least, she tried to comfort me. 'It's normal, now, you realise. The majority of men have semifertile sperm. At least you were brave enough to get tested. Most men won't, which is simply pathetic.'

'Pathetic?' I said. 'You haven't a clue. You don't understand how much it means to men ... everything, really.'

'You've still got me. And your job. And your future. And we'll still have a baby, somehow, sometime. Other people do. So shall we.' She was brisk and kindly, but thought my grief excessive. She always did think me too extreme –

Yet wasn't that part of what she'd fallen in love with, my passionate emotions, my grandiose self? The Saul who was ready to die for her when the spacemen appeared with their huge silver vappers? She was inconsistent, like all women.

But I knew she liked me to make her laugh. I made an effort to stay cheerful.

'I just need more sex. I'm not kidding. I'm not infertile, just *semi*fertile. *Half*, get it? So I need twice as much sex.'

And then she laughed her beautiful laugh, husky, showing her small milky teeth with lower incisors sharp as cats', and we were happy, and made love again. 'Just one more chance and they'll be in like Flynn.'

One more chance, then another, then another, till nine years had gone by, and we were over thirty, and could have afforded another move to one of the smaller houses in the Northwest Enclaves where everyone aspired to live, but she refused, 'until we have children'.

By now it was Sarah who was utterly depressed, though she smiled for the world every week on the screens. She refused sex altogether sometimes, or else was insatiable and desperate. She read baby magazines all night, or couldn't bear to look at children in the street.

I loved her too much to let this drag on. On my thirtyfirst birthday I said, 'That's it. We're going to do this the techfix way. Whatever it costs, whatever it takes, we're going to get the doctors to make us a baby.'

It was easier once we had given in. It was like being on a moving walkway that carried us along with everyone else. But the Batteries did not have a brilliant success rate, though they boasted of 'upwards of twentyfivepercent'. This figure meant conceptions rather than births, as old hands knew, and tipped off newcomers.

'At least we'll make new friends,' Sarah remarked, after a long intense conversation with a woman in the loo. 'At least we have something in common with people.'

'I don't want friends, I want a baby.'

The men sat silent, while the women confided. I switched my phone on to text and pretended to be absorbed in reading.

We had plenty of money, at any rate. We chose the top clinic, the bestknown doctor. Dr Zeuss had a global reputation. We put ourselves in his hands completely. We made love when he told us to; abstained when he told us to; ate and drank and slept to order.

Instead of having two lives, we had only one. We were totally absorbed in the job in hand.

We whizzed through the tunnels nearly every morning before five AM to be injected or tested, making changes of plan at a split second's notice if the doctors told us they needed us, if eggs could be harvested or sperm donated or any other bits of us removed and twizzled. We said 'Yes' to everything. We'd held out too long, and now we yielded our bodies completely, our private parts, our selves, our money.

What Sarah had said about making new friends began to seem more sensible, for those were the only friends we could have, friends who were equally obsessed, who understood why we could never keep a date or drink coffee or wine or go to bed after nine. Our god, who ran the universe, was Dr Zeuss, and we believed in him, however much the Doctorwatch tried to expose him as a moneygrubber or a charlatan, whatever the disquieting stories onscreen about mixups of sperm or eggs or foetuses, however chilling the articles on rates of deformity in techfix births. We thought they were written by jealous hacks, too poor to afford to get help like us.

But Sarah began to have dreams, and delusions. She dreamed she had children who sprouted wings, poor thin things with stunted bodies, and as she tried to take them out in the sun she found they were kept alive by tubes, and when she tried to free them, they died. This dream returned night after night.

She saw women in the hospital carparks with older children she suspected had been techfix births. They were left in the car looking limp and pale, as if they'd been kept too long in the dark. 'Look at that boy,' she would hiss to me, as we passed a Mercedes with gleaming paintwork and a dim blonde head in the back behind glass. 'He didn't look normal to me.'

'You couldn't see him properly.'

'I did see. You're afraid to see them.'

And yet we never consciously believed our own baby would be less than perfect. Successful people had successful babies, even if they needed Dr Zeuss to help them.

It was a good time for us, despite the terrible stresses, because we were focused on the same thing. Sarah took a sixmonth vacation from TV, and I gave up the Learning Centre and concentrated on the nanotechnics, where I could put in the hours whenever I wanted, since the labs were open around the clock in an effort to keep up with the Africans.

I would sit there, sometimes, halfasleep, looking through the electron microscope at tiny machines performing tiny tasks, their incredible completeness, the way they could selfreplicate and grow, and it satisfied me at some deep level, made me feel life was still all right, that men were still in command of things, masters of a friendly universe.

Well, not entirely in command, perhaps, because the best machines evolved and mutated. One day they would matter, those mute mutations. But then I was proud to help them along. I, Saul, was one of the chosen.

'I feel sick,' said Sarah, one steamy morning when we felt too hot to pull our clothes on. We had got up at fourthirty to get to the Batteries.

'Could be good news,' I said, pausing with my purple singlet over my head. 'You never feel sick.'

'I have a bit, lately ... it's the heat, that's all. You know it is. So much for the icesheets. I think it's been hotter than ever this year.'

'It wouldn't get cooler all at once,' I said, emerging from the neckhole, smiling. 'I bet you're pregnant. *Yes.* Must be.'

We held hands even more tightly than usual as we sat and waited for Dr Zeuss.

If a skull could smile, Dr Zeuss smiled. Indeed, he beamed. He gripped our hands. 'I am happy to say we are successful,' he said. 'Ms Trelawney, we have a twin pregnancy. If you'd like to see the images, we have them on the scanner.'

We heard no more. We were in each other's arms, kissing each other, laughing and weeping. Dr Zeuss gave us a moment before he cleared his throat. 'Ahem. If you're ready.'

A silver moonscape appeared on the screen like the ones we had often seen before, empty. He was having a little trouble focusing. The nurse came up and touched my arm. 'Sir, we'd like you to sign a consent form for us to use these pictures in our advertising –'

'In our *educational package,* yes,' Dr Zeuss interrupted, waving her away, 'but not just now, Marietta, please. Conception is a very meaningful moment.'

We soared over craters and silver seas and dark patches where nothing lived. Then suddenly the picture steadied. 'There you are,' Dr Zeuss sighed, content. 'There we are. A fine twin pregnancy. Three weeks postimplantation, I'd say.'

They were two dim swimmers, curled together in the waves. They were moving, languorously, floating towards earth, but it suddenly struck me, they were here already, they weren't up there where Dr

Zeuss pretended, two virtual ghosts on the clinic's screen, they were my twin babies, they were growing in Sarah, and I fell to my knees and kissed her stomach, and felt her warm tears wet my hair.

'Do you want to know the sex of the foetuses?' Dr Zeuss enquired, slightly impatient.

'It's a boy and a girl, I know already,' said Sarah, laughing up at his long thin face.

We enjoyed her pregnancy so much. There was no shadow for the first four months. Sarah relaxed, and slept like a child; we curled like spoons, my hands on her belly. One morning, though, she began to bleed.

Dr Zeuss always shunted his pregnancy successes across to the care of their own doctors, so Dr Wang had to deal with us when we drove to the Medicentre in distress.

'Have I lost them both?' Sarah begged, desperate.

He scanned her, carefully. It took a long time. He remained calm as we demanded information. After an age Dr Wang straightened up and turned towards us, looking sad.

'You have lost one twin, I'm sorry to tell you. But one looks perfectly healthy and strong.'

'Is it the girl?' Sarah asked, and her voice held hope. I knew that she meant 'Did the girl survive?' I think I was hurt. I know I was. *Didn't she want a boy like me?*

Dr Wang had misunderstood her question. 'It's the girl who has died, yes, I'm sorry.'

'Oh,' said Sarah, a cry of pure pain.

'Darling,' I said. 'Sorry, sorry.'

'It's okay ... But I did want a daughter.'

Yet neither of us could stay sad for long. We were expecting a baby, and that was a miracle, and nothing was going to spoil it for us.

'Robin,' said Sarah. 'Like Robin Hood.'

'I prefer Joe, or Sam,' I said. 'Less ... androgynous. A real boy's name.'

We imagined him, against all reason, brown and bonny and merry as Moses, singing in his basket under clear blue sky. We ignored it when a thick package arrived from Dr Zeuss's Fertility Clinic pointing out, 'as a routine precaution', some of the postnatal complications that had been found to occur 'slightly more frequently' with techfix conceptions. There were pages of detail, most of it hairraising.

'This is obscene,' said Sarah, furious. 'That horrid old death'shead wants to frighten us. If there were all these problems, why didn't he mention them when he was monitoring us every day?'

'Because it could have frightened us off?' I guessed. 'Before we had given him all our money? No, it's okay, I'm not serious. It's probably some legal wrinkle. In case you sue. But you're fit as a fiddle.'

The two of us knew better than the doctors. We heard the loud rhythm of hope in our hearts, the rhythm we heard when she took my hand and held it patiently over her belly till I felt the child kicking, quick and strong.

In her last months there was such tenderness between us. I watched her moving, heavy, slow, her words dreamy and disconnected, drunk with the hormones protecting our baby, and I waited on her hand and foot, not allowing her to carry so much as a coffee cup, rubbing her back, massaging her feet, fanning her with a peacockfeather fan as she lay there at midnight sleepless and sweating, getting up in the early hours to bring her iced drinks, and again in the morning to bring her breakfast.

(Did you forget that, later, Sarah? I rose to the occasion then, at least. And I never lost my temper, did I?)

'Luke,' she said one morning. 'I like that name. You wanted

something short. It's – I don't know. The name of a good person, somehow. I'd like our child to be a good person.'

'Save the world,' I mused, half-asleep.

'Might not need saving, if it cools down. I think about coolness with such longing. I think about evenings on Coll, you know. Walking barefoot on the cool white sands. We kids used to run into the sea. It was so cold we couldn't stop screaming ...' She was talking in her new, softer voice.

'I do like Luke ... cool ... lukewarm ... I'd love to go to Coll with you.'

'I wish I could walk around naked all day. It's inhuman, putting clothes on this great sweaty bump.'

Once I sponged her all over with water from the fridge, gently, firmly, telling her I loved her, reminding her that very soon there would be three of us for ever and ever.

She went into labour two weeks prematurely as the early morning breeze breathed in through the window. We lay there, electric with excitement and hope, watching the sky begin to whiten, kidding each other, laughing and panicking, timing the contractions as we had been told. Her bag was packed. We drove in at sunrise, swooping like a copter between the tall towers that fringed the flyover like great black trees. The windows were jewels, red as blood. I felt sleepless, drunk, a demented god watching the creation of the world. I had brought a bag of luxuries, champagne, music, teabags, massage oil, baby clothes ...

Around eleven AM things began to go wrong. The baby's heartbeat was not strong. The doctors needed consent to act 'if it becomes important to remove the baby'. Which meant a caesarean. I refused. We'd agreed to have the baby naturally.

An hour later, I gave my consent. Sarah was in trouble, pale and sweating. Green fluid sputtered from her womb. More doctors began to appear from nowhere. Sarah was taken away from me to a room with an enormous amount of equipment, blinking screens, pulsing xylon. I followed. No one noticed me. She slipped away beneath the anaesthetic, and suddenly things were going very fast, I was pushed to one side by a team of athletes working semi wordlessly to keep her alive, trying to pull something long and dark from inside her ...

I stared at her face, which was tiny and lost, the mouth and chin I knew so well, the high forehead with its sheen of sweat, a lock of damp hair escaping the cap, her eyelids lifting and falling again over eyes that had no consciousness.

'It's your son,' someone said, and placed in my arms for one brief second a slithery thing that was instantly removed again, swabbed, wrapped, rushed away.

So Luke was born, and we hardly saw him for seven or eight weeks while the doctors worked on him. Instead of the three of us being together, Sarah and I were miles apart, for they kept her in for a blood transfusion. Then an infection that could have been fatal struck at her lowered immune system.

She kept on begging me to take her home. I dared not do it, but she never stopped begging, and perhaps she was right, perhaps she would have got better, and once again I should have trusted her instincts, but my own instincts were dulled with fear. I think she never quite forgave me.

'I'm not a doctor,' I entreated her.

'I hate hospitals. I hate doctors.'

'You're not well.'

'No, I've got an infection, which came from this stinking hospital.'

'But Luke's poorly. He needs more surgery. Nothing major, but they say his intestine –'

'Yes, but my child should be with me, not shut away in some sterile tent – I think my body would make him better.'

'It's common with techfix conceptions … so they keep saying. Sarah, darling, perhaps we should have expected this.'

'But we didn't, did we? What fools we've been. Why did I trust you? You promised – you promised –' And she started to weep, she lay there for days, helplessly weeping when Luke wasn't with her, which was most of the time, blaming, blaming, a Sarah I had never seen. Her friend Sylvie was a regular visitor, holding her hand and avoiding my eyes.

I did do my best to protect my wife, as I watched her disappear into a druginduced haze. 'She hates drugs,' I told her consultants. 'She doesn't believe in them. And why does she need them? She's sad the baby is ill, that's all.'

'Mr Trelawney –'

'That's not my name –'

'Mr Um, your um partner is suicidal. We have no choice. We have to treat her.'

'Sarah has never been suicidal.'

'We found her on the window ledge the other day. She was crying, and the window was open –'

'She likes fresh air –'

'She was on the fourth floor. And leaning right out. That's why we moved her downstairs, Mr Um. She denied it, and asked us not to tell you, but I think we must. There's a child to consider … Should he survive.'

That brought me up short. 'Of course he'll survive.'

But the doctor bowed, his face inscrutable, and walked away. So nothing now could be predicted.

It was in those weeks when I couldn't read the papers that more news about the ice began to break. I learned about it later when I went back to work, a very different man from the proud expectant father who had surfed the net while the world was sleeping.

Now people were starting to ask new questions. I suppose climatologists had always known that the temperate climate of recent history was only part of a short 'interglacial' between much longer glacial phases, but climatologists weren't listened to much, except when hacks harassed them for shortterm predictions. On average, I discovered, there were ten to twelvethousandyear warmings between ice ages of a hundredthousand years. And way back at the end of the twentieth-century, the scientist James Lovelock had famously said, in his Nobel Prize acceptance speech, that 'if it weren't for the activities of man, the earth would be entering a new ice age.' But Lovelock was known to be an eccentric, and no one had taken him literally. We were too busy worrying about rising sea levels and the spread of deserts in Africa. Now we began to see the larger picture. Not that anyone was thinking of a new ice age – we just saw the logic in the earth cooling down. As Lovelock had also said, the earth's warm phases, which seemed so agreeable and natural to humans, were more like the planet having a fever.

'It's good news, darling. Don't you see? After all our fears about the future, the climate may go back to what it was in the last century ... *Our son*' (but was he really our son, this long thin creature with tubes in his arms?) 'won't have to live in a desert.'

But she stared at me as if I weren't there, and her wide blue eyes began to water again. 'Why are you telling me all this shit? I don't bloody care. I don't want this baby. Maybe it's a terrible thing to say, but it's true, Saul, *I don't want him* –' And she looked at me, begging me to understand, but I was shocked and became selfrighteous, though I'd secretly felt the same way myself.

'You have to want him. He's our son,' I barked. I was brutal with her because I felt guilty.

'I wanted a daughter. My beautiful daughter.' She lay and wept, and I wanted to hit her. She was the mother. It wasn't fair.

'Don't cry. Get a grip on yourself. You're a mother.'

I didn't see this was the turning point. I thought it was something temporary. Sarah would have to love me again once she and Luke came home together.

They did come home, but things didn't get better.

She was too weak at first to look after the house. Luke seemed to suck up all her energy. I would come home from work and find her exhausted, with milk and avocado all over her blouse, and the floor, and the table, and the chair. Our flat had never looked like this. I got the cleaner to come more often. I did my best, but Sarah glowered at me. She lay with the infant clamped to her chest and watched old films with her friend Sylvie who always seemed to be by her bedside. If I spoke, they stared at me resentfully. 'You never listen,' was Sarah's refrain, but they only spoke to me to give me instructions, to tell me to heat bottles or bring a fresh nappy. And I worked all day. It wasn't easy.

In any case, it was Sylvie she talked to. 'I *know*,' I would hear her cooing, 'I *know*.' Her son sometimes came along on sufferance, and sat picking Sarah's flowers to pieces. They didn't leave when I came home. I found myself unable to be pleasant to them. Sylvie had a patch of eczema by a stud in her ear, which was some kind of stupid lesbian symbol. If she'd been a man, I would have been jealous ...

Then Sarah did find a man who listened. He was one of the doctors who treated her depression. Most of them disappointed her. His consulting rooms were only two blocks away from Melville Road. She went three times a week, and came back pinkcheeked and invigorated. I was happy to stay at home with Luke, glad that something was doing her good ...

(I still don't know what she wanted from me. I only know that I didn't give it. It seems to me that men couldn't get it right – we were either too brutish or too wimpy for them. But we were ourselves, we were *men,* for godsake. What did they think they could turn us into?)

I was slow to resume our sex life after Luke was born. I wanted to be *sensitive.* I spit with derision to think of it now, but I didn't want to hurt her where she had been hurt. If you love a woman you don't want to hurt her.

And then you want to smash her, rape her, kill her.

Another man's hands on her milky breasts. His filthy hands on her tender belly, still soft and stretched from bearing our child ... Did she laugh with him? Did she come with him? That helpless little crescendo of whimpers –

She told me, one day when Luke was nearly a year old, that she had decided to take a lover, 'since you no longer want to sleep with me'.

If Luke hadn't been there, lying sleepless on the sofa, I think I might have killed her, for I still adored her.

'You've slept with someone. You lying bitch ...'

I wanted sex at once, there and then, I wanted to drive that bastard away. I had a right, I was her child's father ...

But she wouldn't. 'I don't belong to you. I'm not your wife. I don't have to. As a matter of fact, I think we'd get on better if one of us moved out. I'll keep Luke, of course.'

She would steal my child! No, I'd kill them both, her and her lying, cheating lover ... but instead I picked up a little chair, a pretty thing of painted wood, blue and gold, some nursery rubbish, and smashed it hard against the wall. I remember hearing her scream insanely. I suppose I may have been holding a chairleg above my head, but seeing her terror I dropped my arm. I felt suddenly tired.

'You're my family,' I said. My voice had gone wobbly. 'You and

Luke. I know things have been ... difficult. But he's getting stronger. So are you. You said you would marry me, remember.'

The odd thing is, she agreed to it, because she had promised, because of Luke. She would marry me, as a pledge to the child, but no longer live with me or love me. 'I'm tired of men, as a matter of fact. They're okay as friends, but I'll live alone. Or else with Sylvie and her child. That would be company for Luke. Don't cry,' she said, seeing my stricken face. 'Get a grip on yourself. You're a father. And you'll always be special,' she added, more kindly. 'It's just ... I trusted you too much. I think that women should be independent.'

And so we got married; a kind of divorce.

And much of it's still a mystery to me. How can I explain it to these crazy kids, who live for food, and fire, and sex? How love was so important to us. How tiny shades of wants and wishes made us fight, and sob, and part. How humans had everything, and valued nothing.

5

Cold, cold, battering cold, cold that howls and bites and burns, cold we shrink from like an enemy, as darkness comes, as the sun slips away. We huddle together round the fire like friends, but can anyone be friends with the wild children? They let me creep close, they tolerate me, because they want the things I have – my expertise with the machines, my stories. They think I am as old as god ...

They have no family, no history.

In the middle of the night, the cold is like stone, black and solid and hard as death, and as the dawn comes it sharpens to pain, as light creeps back with the morning wind. (I loved it, once, that little wind. In the Tropical Time, it came like grace. Now it's the wind that takes the dying. Comes like a blade to finish them off.)

And then the sun. See, it's rising. Our friend the sun, my only friend. The line of white along the horizon, the light reflected off the back of the ice ... It will redden soon, then the sun will appear, and this frozen ball will roll towards it, the sun will climb over the smoking towers (that stain of foul greasy smoke from the chimneys, hinting at a long night's killing and eating), piercing the mesh of the perimeter fence, till the heat begins to melt the grey grass, and a dull soaked greenness spreads in patches, and the torn airport fence begins to drip, glitter and weep as the frost dissolves, and the broken windowpanes catch fire, great burning lakes for a few brief moments, and the human mound starts to shuffle and groan, what looked like a pyre of blackened bodies begins to colour and shift and dissolve into hundreds of moaning, stretching creatures, and my own blood creeps back, slowly, painfully, my aching limbs unclench and stir.

By night I sleep like a nervous cat, waking whenever a shadow moves. That's when it will happen, one icy night when the dark makes me indistinguishable from any other skinful of meat and grease that would make the fires blaze up for a minute, keep a few starving kids alive.

... One night after the lights have gone out. One night when Kit isn't there to protect me. He does protect me, in a way, though he might be rough with me if I'd let him. He is my friend, I suppose, in a way.

His foot prods me in the small of the back. 'Get up, Gramp,' he giggles. 'Here –' He hands me a can of hot water. The edge is raw metal. I drink with care. I don't look at him until I've finished. It's difficult to unlock my neck, to make the effort of looking up. His skin is a windreddened dirty brown, and the one empty eyesocket puckers like an arsehole, but he smiles cheerily, through yellow teeth.

'Writing,' he says, impatiently. 'Finish?'

I gesture feebly at my notebook. 'Just started.'

He points to the book, then his eyes, then back, then pulls a face of animal displeasure. 'Reddit,' he mouths. 'Yerrch.'

'I know, all right, but it gets –'

'Nope.' He mimes tearing my book apart. One of the pages does tear, slightly.

'I'm going to write about the Doves, right. The *Doves,* get me? You like the Doves.'

'Dying,' he says, and crouches down beside me and stares at the floor. 'The Doves, dying.' Kit is actually crying.

'No no,' I say, encouragingly. 'They just miss me. Their Uncle Solly. I've been too busy –' His foot again, propelling me in the direction of the hangar where the Doves are kept.

'You go today,' I say, firmly. 'I go tomorrow. Today, I write.'

To my surprise, he goes off, hangdog. I didn't expect that to be so easy. Normally I don't write by day, but the last two days I have found a hiding place and written as if it would save my life, though I don't suppose anything can save me. I mean to finish my story, though.

I jog away, stiffly, trying to look young, trying to look tough and in command. I defecate in one of the pits. Hard and mingy, not satisfying. It's the diet. Unless the boys have robbed a convoy there's no fruit or veg except potatoes, which these kids can just about manage to grow, but most of them are rotten by this time of year and they come out of the fire either burnt or half raw. At least the cold stops the pits stinking. On the rare warm days, in the old midsummer, the air is suddenly black with flies. Not all the wild boys use the pits, but it's a crime if you're caught fouling, punishable with beating, and occasionally death, because some of the beaters don't know when to stop.

The Doves are supposed to be my daytime job, but for a few days I'm going to neglect them. Kit will cover for me, with some of the boys. They always like to play with the Doves, though play is becoming less satisfying as more of the Doves become ... *moribund*.

(Such a comic word, round as a plum. Not one of these boys would recognise it. I long for someone who knows what words mean. My mother loved them; my father too. In the new Days, people don't risk words. If you open your mouth, the ice blows in, hurting the teeth no dentists care for. Drying your throat. Piercing your soul. Filling your heart with loneliness. Best keep the old words close to your chest ... They don't hurt me if I write them down.)

I jog purposefully over to the derelict shell that was once one of the multistorey carparks. Till a few months ago it was full of wild children shooting down the slopes on homemade skates and skateboards, but too many were killed, or it grew too cold. The winds that howled through became too much to bear, and now the skaters have moved elsewhere. There's a tiny cupboard here, two metres square, smelling of damp, by an empty liftshaft. There is light to see by if I leave the door ajar, but it would be too dangerous to do that. I'm safe in the open, where many people know me, but no one's safe if they're caught alone. I close the door firmly and take out my candle, my treasured grey stump of life and light. Not much of it left, so I'll have to hurry.

I never stopped loving that bloody woman, however angry I felt with her. Of course I was angry; she was insane. How could we get married and live apart? Shouldn't a woman want to live with her man? She lived with a woman, and had a male lover.

I complained to anyone who'd listen. But people didn't understand. It seemed I'd been living in a timewarp.

I tried to take in what was going on. Behind my back, the world had been changing. Once I started looking, it was everywhere. Segging had spread into so much of life. Young women were beginning to live with women; men were trying to live with men. Colonies of men took apartment blocks together. Those with swimming pools were especially popular. For many the choice was homosexual, but others just liked the camaraderie, which made them less lonely than before. This way of living could get competitive, vying with peers for sex or friendship or leadership within the group, so some of those early experiments failed and the men went back to live with their parents. The older generation thought the world had gone mad. Perhaps it had, perhaps it had.

The women lived together for different reasons. Some of them drew up the battlelines around the scarce, precious children. Four or five women would look after one child. Those rare, petted, unhealthy children ... Again this could get competititive, but the childless ones found a kind of fulfilment. Not that all women were domestically inclined. The gangs of girls who roamed the towers were said to be more violent than the men. Some teenage girls found inspiration in older women's groups which mimicked the men's. Their 'sheroes' were hard, fighting fit: musclebuilders, shaved bulldykes who rode big motorbikes and had big arms. Men looked, and giggled, and looked again, and invented new subgenres of sex magazines in which such women were humiliated, or humiliated us, according to taste. But secretly we were afraid. *I* was afraid. Was this the future?

It reminded me of life in the Gendersense programmes that Sarah had fronted on the screens, which had always struck me as too weird to be true. I must unconsciously still have thought the norm was a home like Samuel and Milly's, or mine and Sarah's, as it once was.

I had known a lot of vaguely sympathetic couples who were trying for babies when Sarah and I were, clinging together like drowning people. Now, in my loneliness, I contacted them. But the 'friends' we had made in Dr Zeuss's waiting-room – to be precise, that Sarah had made – had mostly split up since they'd been through the Batteries, whether the treatment were successful or not. Or else, to my surprise, they had never lived together. Some of them barely remembered each other ...

They had all moved on, but I had not.

It took me some while to take this all in. I confided in Riswan, my friend at work. 'Sarah has left me. And taken the baby. I only see him a few times a week.'

'What do you mean, she's left you?' Riswan's big dark eyes were opaque and puzzled.

'For good. She only comes back to visit.'

'You mean, you were living in the same flat?'

'Of course. We've been together for over ten years.'

'You should be glad, my friend, to be free of the woman! Women and babies make a mess everywhere –'

'Well, she did do most of the cleaning –'

'Men should stick with their own kind, actually. No trouble that way. No shouting, no crying. Tell this woman not to visit.'

He was the third person to react this way. I couldn't deny there'd been some shouting and crying. 'But I love my son,' I said, puzzled, and saw the envy in Riswan's eyes.

'You're lucky to have a son. But it's women's business, looking after children.' And then he began to complain incoherently how now there were more and more male nannies, which once again had passed me by. 'They call them "mannies", instead of nannies. *Mannies,* I ask you! It's ... humiliating. One of my best friends is training to be one!'

'It was Sarah who kept me abreast of things ... I love my wife.'

'You mean, you got married? In the twentyfirst century?'

'Well – yes.'

There was evidently little point talking to Riswan.

All the same, he was a loyal friend who had covered for me after the baby was born. And any friend now seemed valuable. When Riswan suggested I go along to his club, the Scientists, I agreed. 'But not just yet, Riswan. I still have a few things to sort out with Sarah.'

In fact, my despair had been premature. Her arrangement with Sylvie was not a success, despite their 'shared aims' and 'deep mutual understanding' and 'desire to support each other as mothers' (to quote from a thinly disguised account of her life that Sarah had so smilingly delivered on her new programme, *Modern Living,* as if it had happened to three other people, as if nobody real had been hurt, abandoned).

Sylvie had wanted to have sex with her. That was the long and short of it. (Whereas Sarah, I suppose, preferred sex with her doctor.) In theory Sylvie respected Sarah's refusal, but in practice she sulked a lot and left the washingup and sat at the kitchen table weeping, while her son beat Luke up in front of his mother in an eager, professional way.

I'd learned my lesson. I listened to Sarah. It took a long time, with a lot of repetitions. Women do tend to repeat themselves, but of course a man must never say that. Her doctor, it turned out, had been 'a control freak'. Well, naughty old him! But I held my tongue. I was kind and thoughtful, and suppressed my glee. I told Sarah she could always come back. In effect, as it happened, she already was back, nearly every evening when she wasn't working, and when she was, she left Luke for the night. A new, muddled happiness descended on us.

Luke hardly slept and was often ill, but he was a startlingly clever, fairylike child, laughing and crying at things we couldn't see, beating his head on the walls, sometimes, his blue eyes suddenly filling with tears, running to either of us equally. Light as a mayfly, up into our arms. He had Sarah's eyes, her mother's blonde hair, my dense curls, Samuel's long limbs, and his lips were full, my lips, our lips ... I sometimes found myself hunting ghosts, searching Luke's face as I had once searched my own, that long ago day, in the bathroom mirror, hunting the hidden lines of Ghana. But he was thin and pale as a child of glass, and his eyes were weak and slightly unfocused. His heart had a defective chamber, which the doctors had promised could be repaired later, and his asthma, alas, was more severe than most children's. And he had allergies, because of all the drugs. But considering everything, he was pretty healthy.

'It's so wonderful to have you back,' I said, lying beside Sarah, hardly believing it, stroking her beautiful chestnut mane, short and thick now as a glossy pony's, pulling its tendrils across her jawline, stroking the long moist curve of her neck, then down to her belly, still soft from the baby, and lower to her tangle of dark red hair, warm and wet where we had just made love, though we'd used contraception, at her insistence. 'My wife,' I tried; I hardly ever said it. 'My darling wife. I knew you'd come back. I think you just went mad with grief. Those bloody doctors, and Luke being so ill.'

'I wasn't mad,' she said, lightly. 'I just felt trapped. No one listened. I didn't know how to get out of there.'

'The window wasn't a good idea,' I said, unwisely. I felt her stiffen: I seemed to have lost my touch with humour.

'This is only temporary, you know,' she said. 'Just till I can find somewhere for Luke and me.'

'Oh,' I said glumly. But I didn't believe her. Melville Road was convenient for her work, and things were going pretty well between us. It felt right, the way life was meant to be, sharing our child, our food, our bed. After a few months she seemed to settle.

There were days and nights of almost perfect bliss. She could not breastfeed, because of the long time when Luke had been too ill to be with her, so both of us shared the bottlefeeding that went on until he was nearly two. I liked to watch as Sarah fed him, the way the level of the milk slowly dropped, and as it dropped, his lids began to flicker, his blueish lids began to quiver and droop, and by the time she finished his transparent lashes were a faint fringe of silver on his sleeping cheek. I liked to hold the bottle myself, to imagine that as Luke sucked the milk my strength went into him, and my love.

Because of his frailty, Luke slept in a cot at the foot of our bed till he was nearly three. I loved to wake up and hear him cooing to himself, and later singing nursery songs in a remarkably clear, steady voice, talking to himself, or counting his toes. Then there was the morning when he managed to climb out, to scale the bars and get on to our bed, a triumphant day because it had once seemed that his arms would always be too thin for climbing, his large heavy head too much for his neck.

'Time for a room of your own,' said Sarah, 'My big strong boy,' and put her head on my shoulder. And the three of us hugged, wordless, proud. She grew her hair again; it may have meant nothing.

Luke made us laugh with his invented words, his invented friends, his bubbly farts, the way he plastered avocado on his eyebrows or used Sarah's makeup bag as a hat. Each new word he learned entered our secret language, became a secret joke and source of pride for a precious few months, till it faded, forgotten. I took so many photographs the camera died.

I wanted this happiness to go on forever. I tried my best; perhaps I tried too hard. I put her work before my own. It was Sarah who gave Luke his regular medicine, sighing, sometimes, as she ticked the chart with its long row of columns every morning. But when Luke was ill it was I who stayed home and cared for our child, fretful, whiney, speckled with fever and frighteningly hot. I stroked the eggshell dome of his forehead, and poured the medicine that cooled him down.

Sometimes she thanked me, more often not. Perhaps I needed her to be grateful. Sometimes she seemed almost angry with me, as if the mere fact of my dogged presence excluded her, or pointed to her absence. Sometimes she swept home from the studio in the middle of the night to find me and Luke fast asleep on our double bed, with the screen still on, 'as it has been all day, I bet it has', though how she knew that was a mystery, the floor scattered with crumpled clothes and toys and halfeaten plates of nursery food, and she'd order me to carry Luke through to his room 'so he can go to bed *properly,* for heaven's sake', while she set about grimly cleaning the flat.

'I mean, do you have to mess everything up?'

'I was looking after Luke. I mean, someone has to.'

'You're trying to say I'm not a good mother.'

'You're trying to say I'm a dirty scumbag.'

'No –' She crumpled, looked ashamed, let me put my arms around her.

'Okay, then. But I'm doing my best.'

'I'd like to look after him. The *sodding* screens ...'

I saw her resentment, sensed the danger.

She said she didn't want another woman in our flat, so I hired a manny, with her approval, one of the new breed of male nannies Riswan had been so sniffy about.

Ash Vijay was a great success with us both, for I had been getting behind with my work, and now Luke was older variety was good for him. He adored our manny from the first, partly because Ash always brought with him the other child he was caring for, a little girl called Polly, slightly older than Luke. Polly couldn't have looked more different. She was dark and rosy with shining skin, unusually sturdy, glowing, lively.

I saw Sarah looking at Polly one morning from our bedroom doorway, her expression thoughtful. There was something avid in her blue eyes.

'A tenner for them,' I said, walking past her. Ash was in the kitchen, making two banana toasts.

'Oh, nothing ... What a goodlooking child Polly is. I bet – well, I bet she wasn't techfix.'

'Lucky them,' I said. 'We weren't so lucky.'

'I sometimes think I'd like another child.'

My heart lifted. 'I'm ready when you are!'

But she twisted her watchstrap, avoiding my eyes. 'It would just be the same old story with us,' she said quietly.

'You can't be sure.'

'You're a dreamer, Saul.'

Lying awake at two AM, I thought about the conversation. I realised she'd given up on me. If Sarah tried to get pregnant again she was going to look for another father.

In the morning, I dismissed it as night thoughts.

*

A few days later, I came in from work to find Luke and Polly in the bathroom, Polly pink and naked and laughing.

Luke was dressed up in her flowered skirt, with the matching top tucked up as a bra.

'He's a girl,' said Polly, laughing.

'I'm a girl, Daddy,' said Luke, excited.

I felt upset, but knew I mustn't show it. 'Have you seen what they're doing?' I called through to Ash, who was taking out the washing in the utility room.

'Yes, aren't they having fun?' he replied. 'Wow, you look tired ... Are you all right? Where have you been slaving today?'

I mentioned the name of the Nanocorp.

Ash's face lit up. 'You must know my friend – Riswan Manao.'

'Goodgod, yes – he's a friend of mine.'

'I'll be seeing him in about an hour – we go to the same club.'

I remembered the club to which Riswan had invited me. 'The Scientists?'

'Yes, the Scientists. . .' Ash smiled a little mischievously, stroking the wet washing. 'Its full name is the Gay Scientists. From Nietzsche, you know. *Gaia Scienzia.*'

'Ah. Sounds like, um, fun.' I backed away. I was embarrassed, and a tiny bit excited. Was it possible that *Riswan ...?* Yes, of course.

I was cheered to think anyone might desire me.

After Ash had left with Polly, when Sarah came home, I told her about the Gay Scientists. I was hoping she would be slightly jealous. 'It's a gay club. I never really realised that Riswan ... Things were awful between us at the time, remember, and I probably confided too much in him ... I thought they were just screen junkies.'

She was only half-listening, riffling through her diary. 'Oh they're all gay, machine junkies. Why shouldn't you go to a club with Riswan? You don't really think ...' She looked up, amused. 'Of course he doesn't fancy you, don't be ridiculous. Did I tell you what's happening tomorrow, Saul?'

'What in particular?' I felt frustrated. Men had to listen, but women didn't bother.

'It's Polly's birthday. She's five, bless her heart. And so I've asked her round for the day.'

'But she comes every day, doesn't she? With Ash.'

'Yes, but tomorrow's Ash's day off. I asked her round with her father instead. I thought I would do a picnic for the kids.'

'I'm sorry, darling, I have to go to work –'

'Yes. Jack and I and the kids will be fine.'

'You're taking a day off? Wonders will never cease. By the way, who's Jack?' I felt at sea.

'He's Polly's dad. He's very nice.'

Which seemed irrelevant then, but not later. I had something else upon my mind.

'Look, Sarah, Luke was wearing Polly's dress.'

'Damn! That reminds me, I've got nothing to wear tomorrow, my linen dress is being cleaned.'

'Sarah, will you please listen to me? *Luke* was wearing *Polly's dress*.'

'And?'

'Well ...'

'Yes?' She was annoyed. 'You're not going to tell me that worries you?'

'Well, yes, it did slightly, as a matter of fact.' Yet it wasn't just that; it was everything, the fact that Riswan was probably gay, that I'd known him for years and noticed nothing, the Gay Scientists Club I had nearly gone to, my sense that everything was changing, crumbling, and nothing was what I thought it was. 'Am I very old-fashioned? Am I just thick?'

'Both, darling. Did you *never* watch my programmes? Gendersense was all about things like that.'

I felt aggrieved, and isolated. Luke had come in and stood there looking worried, clutching his willy in his spotted underpants.

'Are you cross, Mummy?' he asked, gravely.

Which made her crosser. 'No, *Daddy* is cross.'

Luke backed away. He didn't like crossness. But he wanted to charm her out of her mood. 'Luke was a girl today,' he said.

'Very good, darling. Very nice,' she said.

I burst out laughing. I couldn't help it. Her automatic smile, her encouraging voice – it occurred to me, they had all gone mad.

Or else *I* was mad, which was what Sarah thought.

'You've got a problem,' she snapped at me. 'Why shouldn't the child wear a fucking dress? I'm tired out. I'll sleep next door.'

And she vanished, as she did when she wanted to annoy me, leaving me to put Luke to bed.

But he knew something was in the air.

'Can I wear a dress tomorrow, Daddy?'

'You haven't got one,' I pointed out. 'You can't keep taking Polly's, can you?'

'Mummy's got dresses,' Luke said after a moment.

'Yes. Well. You'd better ask Mummy.'

But could I trust Mummy to give the right answer? I thought about it, and tried again. 'Boys usually wear trousers, like Daddy. Wouldn't you like to dress like Daddy?'

'Dress like Mummy,' said Luke, unperturbed.

'Good night, Lukey.'

'I love you, Daddy.' I was tiptoeing out, ready for a giant drink, when Luke's small bright voice began again. 'Will you and Mummy be cross tomorrow?'

'No,' I said, after a small pause. 'I won't be. I can't promise for Mummy.'

I could sense the child thinking. Soon he offered: 'I won't wear a dress if she won't be cross.'

'Deal,' I said swiftly, but I felt dishonest.

Next day, however, all seemed to be forgotten, Luke wore trousers, there were eggs for breakfast, Sarah had slept well, and was friendly, if distant, and told me not to bother with the breakfast washing-up. 'Oh leave it, darling, go to work,' she said, and kissed me, kindly, and waved goodbye.

Then before I knew it she was off with Jack.

She was fucking him, actually, the bitch, the tart ...

This time I really wanted her dead. She was Luke's mother, but I wanted her dead. Shaved. Shamed. Torn apart.

Whereas Sarah just wanted a baby, of course. Let me try to be reasonable – that's all she wanted. And she wanted one the natural way. She thought Polly's dad could do that for her – give her a child as healthy as Polly. Disloyal to Luke, disloyal to me.

For a bit, I started to hate all women. I stopped caring about myself. Why should it matter what I did? I didn't wash, I smoked, I drank. Sarah came and went, and acknowledged no guilt. She slept with me when she felt like it, ignoring my nasty remarks about paternity.

(One day she left a book in the loo called *The Sperm Race,*
describing the positive effect on conception of competition between
males. So my poor knackered sperm had been entered for a race,
brokenkneed in that woman's vile Sperm Derby.)

She still acted as if the flat belonged to her, cleaning it silently,
manically, whenever she arrived. And I admit I let things get dirtier
than usual, I admit that in my anger I let things slide.

I confided in Ash. He was shocked, sympathetic. 'I thought you two
got along all right,' he said. It was as if his parents had let him down.
He must have mentioned it to Riswan, because Riswan asked me to
the club again.

So what if I went? Perhaps I'd learn something. Sarah didn't care;
had never cared, no more than she cared for Polly's father ...

Men, for Sarah, were just something to use. I found myself telling
most of this to the bald and muscular men at the Gay Scientists. They
laughed a lot, and were basically friendly. They liked me, I felt, they
did not despise me, we were all men together, we could be free ...

Richard and Nimit and Riswan and Timmy. Plump pale Billy,
handsome Paul ... Ian with his clique of bodybuilt clones. Too many
new names for me to get right. Bristlescalped, smiling men in leather,
welcoming me to a safe new dream.

And when we were tired of talking, or dancing, or working out in
the fabulous gym, the machines were waiting, infinitely yielding. The
net expanded through the rows of screens. Somewhere we could go
that was always home. A lap, a space beyond time or pain.

6

I push the door open, cautiously. The cold is telling me it's late. (I had a watch until last week, keeping it hidden under layers of shirts and the final semmit of greasy wool, till one of the boys saw me squinnying at it. I miss my watch, yet I still know the time, it's as if it has been tattooed on my skin through all the years of trying to obey it.) Getting dark already, and I've hardly started.

Is something afoot among the boys? I catch them peering, muttering. It makes me feel as though time's running out, and I must write it now or never, so it won't be lost, all that different life, so bright, sometimes, and lucky, and sunny ...

And the people. All the people I loved.

Luke as a boy, like a tall thin colt, a Palomino, pale and golden. Running down the corridor with slightly knock knees, 'Daddy, Daddy!' He sang like an angel. It was a weird gift, absolute and awesome, a voice like a celestial musical instrument, and no one could imagine where it had come from. It seemed unconnected to the child we knew, gawky, affectionate, impulsive, clumsy.

My mother and father, with their unreasonable pride in all our little family did. Sitting round the table with them at Christmas, eating one of Sarah's flaming puddings.

Sarah. Despite all the bitterness, I mustn't lose sight of how much I loved her. I had faults too. I was cruel. I teased her. I often forgot how fragile she was, under her driving, ambitious shell. My beautiful girl, with her small soft hands and her vulnerable, babyblind face in the mornings, before she put her contact lenses in.

Time cantered by. We were in our late thirties, forty, fortyone, my first white hair, and Luke was five, then six, then seven. Sarah came and went, and had other boyfriends. She grew thinner, more thoughtful, and her hair changed colour, though only someone who loved her would have noticed, a more vivid red to hide the grey.

Someone who loved her and sometimes disliked her.

She grew bitter against men, though not always against me. She had a life with women that I didn't understand, didn't want to know about, never asked. Sometimes she stayed away for days. And who looked after Luke, when she didn't come home? Who was always there to make Luke's breakfast?

She came and went, but she cared for my parents. I'll never forget what she did for them.

Neither of them wanted the replacement parts that gave old people the nickname 'bits'. When monitoring made it clear that Samuel needed a new liver, I tried to press the money upon them, and didn't understand when they refused.

'We're not a lot of use to anyone,' Samuel said. Milly nodded.

'I know you never liked the terming programme, Saul ...' Even then, I didn't want her to mention it. It had come as a sickening shock when I learned as a boy what she did at the Last Farewell Home. If she killed old people, she might kill me. '... but you young people can't carry us all. We don't want to live to be daft and helpless.'

'Nonsense. You're not daft. And how about your grandson? Luke adores you. Luke needs his grandparents.'

'I'm tired,' said Samuel. And he did look tired. He worked his jaw; it was stiff, skeletal. 'It's time to go, my son. Only fools think they can live forever.'

It made me feel guilty that they didn't want to live; it must be because I hadn't loved them enough. 'Listen to me, Dad, please. If *you* take a new liver, Mum will take a heart ... Think about her. Think about us.'

But Sarah dug her fingers in the small of my back. 'That isn't fair, they've always thought about us. I understand what you're saying, Samuel. I'll look after you, if you ever need me.'

'You're not old,' I exploded, irritated at the way my father smiled at her. 'You're only ninety! You can't give up.'

Ridiculous, now I think about it: that ninety wasn't old to us. Now people die at forty or fifty, if they survive the cold that long.

And I am the Emperor of Old Age, at sixty. My bones pain me. Crumbling, sliding. Setting into a cage of claws, the flesh contorted by the bars. I suppose it's arthritis, if it's nothing worse. And chilblains, and footrot, and lice, and fleas – and toothache. That nerve, in the middle of the night. And my scalp crawls constantly. Worrying, tickling.

I hope my Sarah, no longer mine – I hope she isn't enduring this. If she still survives, may she be Inside. In some last warm place, out of the wind.

My delicate Sarah, who so loved cleanliness. She cared for my parents without complaining, when my father shrank, and smelled, and was pitiful, and Milly's circulation began to break down, as if she were giving up, little by little. Sarah took eight weeks off, which was risky, with screen work. She moved into their tiny house so they could stay at home to die, and although Sarah said it seemed endless to her, their dying was over in less than three months – they died two weeks apart, after a lifetime together. They stayed the course. And she stayed by their bedside. I did what I could, but it was so claustrophobic, the little overheated house, and I felt embarrassed by my parents' bodies. The thinner they got, the more heat they needed ... And women are so much better with nursing. Besides, I didn't really understand they were dying – didn't understand, couldn't understand.

Nor the curious legacy Samuel left me, death in a bag, unthinkable, tempting. My father, that lawabiding man.

'In case you need them. You're *my son*,' he breathed, that harsh strange breathing he did at the end. 'Under the bed. Be careful.'

I didn't know what he was talking about. The green canvas bag was under their bed, and I made a halfhearted attempt to pull it out. It looked like something for golfing irons, but it was heavy, and I was in a hurry, I had just dropped by on my way to the airport. 'I'm not sure I'd use them, Dad,' I demurred. 'You know, I'm so busy, and I've never played golf.'

His red eyes stared at me, unsmiling. 'Guns,' he said. 'Good ones. You *could* use them.' Each breath was an effort. 'Anyone could.'

That brought me up short, but I only halfbelieved him, he was very ill, perhaps hallucinating. 'What do you mean, *guns?*'

'You're a good boy Saul, but God help you ... Take the bag and lock it away. Times could get hard. After I'm gone.'

I thought I was humouring him. 'Thanks, Dad.'

His lids flickered down, then he was wide awake. 'Remember, be careful. Accidents. They were confiscated. In the line of duty. One day, I thought ... Maybe one day ...'

He had three days left, though I never realised. I was popping across to Berlin for work, and Sarah asked me if I thought I should stay, but I didn't understand her. Deaf, blind. And so I never saw him again.

Why didn't I take him seriously? I think he wanted to say he was dying, to tell me something about life, and death, and what human beings are capable of – and my father knew; he had lived his life. But I looked at my watch, and chattered on, and never looked inside the bag.

'You're tiring him,' Sarah said at last. 'I'd better give him his injection.' I said some nonsense, and left for the airport, so she was left with the hardest part.

I do realise what she did for me.

I thanked her, inadequately, several weeks later, as we stood with Luke and my alcoholic sister, dark glasses shading her raw dark cheeks, beside the muddy stream where they had asked to be scattered. The church where Samuel married Milly had long been abandoned; her parents' village lay in ruins. Brambles ramped over the fallen grave-stones. We took it in turns to scatter the ashes. There was far too much ash, like dirty hailstones, lying on the grass around our feet. I wished they had been buried instead. I didn't want my parents to be crumbs of bone, and this little valley seemed mean and flyblown, though there were some purple irises, and a few rare sparrows hopping about. Then Sarah swore she saw a dragonfly, and when I tried to tell her they were extinct my sister hissed at me to keep quiet.

'I did it for them, not you. *I loved them,*' Sarah tried to say, but she was crying too much, her cheeks wet in the patchy sunlight. 'I wish we'd managed to live like them.'

'What do you mean?'

'They stayed the course. We didn't, did we? They stayed the course.'

Which puzzled me, because wasn't she the one who had wanted her whole life to be different? Hadn't she decided to redraft the rules? The older I get, the less I'm sure of. We argued so much, but does anything matter? Except whether you and your seed survive? It's as if the game were extremely simple, yet we kept on attempting impossible moves, stupidly intelligent, frowning in the mirror.

*

We were in our midforties – that dangerous age.

Sarah had been staying away from the flat for longer periods than ever before. I suspected her of setting up another home, with some lucky bastard who worked on the screens. Some musclebound kid with castiron balls. Whoever he was, he must have slimed around Luke, because for the first time she was taking Luke with her. They vanished for a month, then two months, three. I suspected my son of disloyalty. I couldn't sleep. I dreaded our bedroom, because it was the place where I lay awake and horribly alone night after night. I lived like a slob on chips and beer, online till the early hours, but the pleasures of loneliness soon palled. I had done some new work on self-replication that my Nanocorp was ecstatic about, but I couldn't love the nanomachines: too tiny to love, too predictable. They were fit for a task, that was all, like me.

Whereas Sarah was never predictable.

I began to go to the Scientists more often. It was one good way of devouring time. If I dropped in after work, and took a few buzzers, I could laugh and dance with the lads till ten. And I was no longer embarrassed about dancing. Sarah used to tease me for the way I danced, but at the Scientists, we just did our own thing, flailing, hopping or slinkily erotic, and no one minded, no one mocked. (*Men don't like to be mocked by women.* Bite your tongues, you sour sisters.) Then when the drugs began to fade I would slip into the saddle of one of the computers and ride away into the shimmering screen.

Once or twice I let a sweet young lad called Paul give me relief in the massage room, though it didn't take away the loneliness. I admit I enjoyed it. It was very exciting. He was tall and slender with beestung lips and a mischievous, appealing smile, rather feminine as well as boyish. His hands were marvellous; he understood men. It made me feel that I still had a body. And everyone seemed to be doing it, in those days.

But another part of me felt dismayed. Did I really believe we were all bisexual? The people who said so all seemed to be gay.

The flat got dirtier, felt darker ... thankgod it was a little cooler, at least. Our overheated planet was at last cooling down, with everyone queuing up to claim the credit, virtuous big business, responsible governments. All complete nonsense, but I welcomed the cooling. I started to leave food out of the fridge in a way I would never have done when it was hotter. It still grew blue mould; I tried not to see it. I fed the cats, resentfully (they were getting old; if I neglected them they'd die, and how would I cope with that, without Sarah?) but I never bothered to clean their bowls. The spoons were dark with crusted meat. I ate out every night, and came back to sleep uncomfortably on the screenroom sofa, going nowhere else except the lavatory. I kept the doors of the kitchen and the bedroom closed.

Weekends were the worst, long and empty. The club didn't open till six PM. On Saturdays I usually got up late and cleared out of the flat as soon as I could, putting in laps on the walking track where I had become a regular – of course no one walked outside in the cities. I needed the exercise badly. All day I was hunched over microscopes or screens, earning good money by wrecking my spine. I needed to walk or fight or run, I was a big man with a big man's body ... *And I wasn't having sex, that was the nub of it.* I needed it. Men do need sex. Wanking is nothing compared to sex. It's like packed lunch compared to hot dinners.

That Saturday I got up late as usual, and switched the screen on while I got dressed. I'd never cared much about the news, but now I liked anything that made me forget, like appalling disasters to total strangers.

But that morning's news stopped me in my tracks.

After decades, nearly a century of trying, human beings had succeeded in making 'mobots', cute little domestic animats. Robots available 'to every home'. Robot cleaners. 'Robot friends'. They cleaned, cleared rubbish, walked, talked. The report was long and very exciting, till pundits arrived to pose and drone, at which point I lost interest and began to pull on my skintight orange tracksuit. (I had bought it from the shop at the club. Encouraged by Paul, I must admit. Now it seemed a brighter orange than before, and showed my genitals embarrassingly clearly, but I told myself it was okay, lots of other men wore 'skins' like that.) I walked to the door, ready to go out, swigging a cup of strong black coffee that I meant to put down on the ledge by the door –

Suddenly the key turned in the lock, the door swung open, it was Luke, it was *her*! I spilled my coffee down the front of my suit.

At once I felt naked in my lurid lycra, but Sarah hardly looked at me. Her eyes were red, as if she had been crying, and Luke looked older, pale and tense, though he jumped up at me as if I were a whale, as if we could swim away together ... A scarf of spilled coffee grew cold on my chest, but he didn't care – children never do, it's only their mothers who make problems and fusses. He ran off to the loo, she went after him, and I stood in the window, my heart thumping.

'Daddy!' Luke yelled in his high reedy voice, dragging me out of my brown study, 'Mummy says why is the flat so dirty?' But neither of us listened to my answer, as I hugged and wrestled with his beloved skinny body that still felt as if I could break it in two, if I forgot, and stopped pulling my punches.

I wanted to say how horribly I'd missed him, but instead for some reason I told him the news. 'I just saw something on the screens about some wonderful robots,' I told him, brightly. 'They do all the housework.'

'You're kidding,' he said, and laughed exultantly.

'No, really,' I said. 'I think they were called "Doves". Shall we buy one for Mummy?'

'What's that?' sniffed Sarah, sweeping in at top speed with a bottle of bleach. 'What are you going to buy for me? You forgot to remind me about your birthday.' (She must have felt guilty for forgetting my birthday.) 'This place is *unbelievable*. I don't see how anyone can live like this.'

'Well, you don't live here any more. Do you?'

'I didn't say that,' she said, uncertain, which told me that something might have gone wrong.

'Mum said we were going to live with ladies,' Luke said.

'Shut up,' said Sarah fiercely. 'Go and unpack.'

'Shut up is rude.' Happily selfrighteous, Luke hugged me tightly. 'But she's quarrelled with the ladies,' he finished.

'You're welcome to sleep here, of course,' I said. A tiny blip of happiness formed itself somewhere. I decided not to press home my advantage. 'Will you be staying long?' I called after her, as she started to bash things about in the bathroom.

'I live here, don't I? We never moved out. But *this,* it's dis*gus*ting, it's worse than I've *ever* ... ' Her voice was muffled by the sound of something falling. I realised the curtainrail had fallen on her head. I had meant to mend it; I'd been too depressed. But then, it was Sarah who had depressed me. I decided not to apologise.

She reappeared like an angry queen bee, the blue flowered curtains draped round her neck. 'Why are you sleeping on the sofa?' she said. 'Have you turned back into a student again? You have no idea how odd it looks. And by the way, what on earth are you wearing?'

(From the hall, Luke put in 'Daddy's dressing up.')

People with showercurtains round their neck should not throw stones, but nothing stopped her. 'You look pretty silly yourself,' I jeered. She looked at me with an attempt at scorn. I so much didn't want us to quarrel. 'Sarah, let's not have an argument. It's great to see you. I hope you'll stay.' She paused in her rampage; her expression softened, and I pressed on. 'I do miss you. I have missed you. And Luke. Badly.' Perhaps I should have left it at that, but she'd made me suffer, I'd *pined,* without them, I was her husband, I had been wronged – 'He needs his father. Boys need their fathers.'

'Rubbish,' she said. 'It's been disproved.'

(Did I look like a father, in my orange lycra?) 'Disproved by what?'

'Studies.'

'What studies?'

'I'm not going to argue with you, Saul. You'repickingafightbecause theflatisdisgustingandyoufeelguiltybutwon'tadmitit.' She said that last sentence in less than half a second.

The nerve of the woman! The outright nerve! 'This is nothing to do with the flat,' I said mildly. 'I didn't mind it the way it was, but if you don't agree, just clean it.' I had never tried this tack before. It made me feel calm and surprisingly powerful.

By now she was armed with a forest of brushes. 'I can't be expected –' she shrieked, automatically, peering at me over the head of a broom, when her voice failed, simply trailed away, as she looked at something just over my shoulder, and I turned, rather stiffly and painfully because the sofa had twisted my neck, to see.

Luke.

Standing in the window, the curtains open, the window open. We were four floors above the ground.

My son's thin body outlined against blue sky, the soft shocking texture of the sky without glass, fragile as a spider in the terrible sunlight. He said, in a brave voice, much too high, 'If you're going to have a row, I'll jump. I can't bear it. I'm going to jump.'

Then everything went into slow motion, as we tried very hard to do the right thing. Sarah put down her brushes, one by one. 'Darling –' we said gently, with almost one voice. We bore down on him, excruciatingly slowly, afraid to upset or startle him.

'We're not having a row. See?' said Sarah, putting a shaking hand on my arm.

'Of course we're not,' I corroborated.

'You *were*,' said Luke, and he suddenly crouched down, so quickly that we both gasped with fear, but he had just gone into a foetal position, shivering and staring at us silently. I moved another metre, then grabbed him in my arms (surely he shouldn't be so light, at seven?), while Sarah banged the window shut with desperate force, and said, 'Sorry, *Sorry*.'

I sat down with Luke on the sofa, and wrapped him in the blanket I'd been sleeping under. I held him until he stopped shaking and crying. 'Mummy and I are so sorry,' I said. 'We weren't really rowing. It was just about the cleaning. Not important. Silly old cleaning.'

'You always row about cleaning,' he said. 'That's why I don't want to be alive any more. I'll go somewhere else. I'll get away. I'll go to heaven and live with Grandpa.'

It was so absolutely shocking to hear a child say that. I hoped his mother was listening.

She was. She came and sat beside us on the floor, her crimson head upon her crimsontipped hands, but when she looked up she was white as death, whiter than Luke, if that were possible. She reached out and patted Luke's ankle. 'I promise not to row with Dad any more. I'm … really sorry. It's been a bad day.' Then she took my hand, stroking it with one finger. 'Sorry, Saul.'

'So I should hope.'

Luke saw my smile, and began to relax. He contrived a position where he could hug us both. 'I like it like this,' he announced. He was quick to appreciate a position of strength. 'Can we have hot chocolate, Mummy? And biscuits? Can we all sleep in the same bed tonight?'

'Yes,' said Sarah, 'Yes, my love,' though she usually said 'no' to requests for chocolate. She got up to see to it, leaving us together.

'Will she keep her promise?' Luke asked in a whisper.

'I think so. But never do that again.' I was remembering what happened after he was born, how the doctors claimed Sarah was suicidal. Perhaps it was genetic. (Or was it me? Perhaps I drove everyone near me to suicide.)

She came in smiling with mugs on a tray and a plate of chocolate biscuits. But old habits die hard. 'There's only one plate. Try not to drop crumbs.'

Something occurred to Luke. 'Daddy!' he cried, so sharply that I slopped my drink again. Sarah noticed but managed to say nothing. 'Tell Mummy you're going to buy her a robot.'

'What?' she asked.

I told her as much as I could remember about the Doves. They were dogsized or toddlersized, like household pets. They looked vaguely like stumpy winged birds, but the TV camera hadn't lingered long enough for me to tell. They could dust, wash floors, recycle rubbish ... And the cost was pitched low enough for everyone to buy one (the Outsiders could never have afforded them, of course, but then, they had no homes to clean). No more than the cost of a cheap car. I remembered the slogan: 'A Dove in Every Home.'

'Giant publicity campaign, huh?' was her first remark, made without enthusiasm.

'Well, they did look – remarkable. I really would like to buy you one.'

'What do you mean, buy me one? Buy *us* one. It would be cleaning for both of us. Cleaning is as much your work as mine.'

Feminism can be fucking pedantic, though my heart leapt up at that 'both of us'. Still, I took her words as a 'Yes'. 'Mummy says "Yes",' I said to Luke, and he beamed hugely, showing straight white teeth. His front teeth had grown down while they were away, and his face was longer, more adult, but also more piercingly vulnerable. 'I'm going to buy us a Dove, Lukey. Our own robot. You can play with it.'

'Great!' he said. 'It can be my friend, now Polly doesn't come round any more.' (She didn't come round because of Sarah, who had been dumped by Polly's father – I'd managed to work this out for myself, but Luke was hurt and mystified.) 'Is it really some kind of dove?' he asked, more gravely. 'How do we make it do what we want?'

'It's just its initials,' I told him. 'Short for "DO VEry Simple things". Jolly clever name, really. What's the matter, Sarah? Aren't you happy?' She was discomfited, biting her nails. I couldn't help enjoying her confusion. If she refused, she would upset her son. 'You need never get cross about housework again.'

'Um,' she said. 'I mean, that's good. It just ... doesn't seem quite natural, to me.'

They delivered it while we were out. The guard hailed me when I came home. 'Enormous piece of furniture for you, sir. New screen is it? Feeling wealthy?'

'Not after buying this,' I told him.

I took it up in the lift with me. To my surprise, I felt tremendously excited, though why is that surprising? It *was* exciting. For decades we had been promised this, robots to live with us as friends.

I decided not to open it till Sarah came home, but then Luke was brought back from school by a neighbour, and he saw the big package and could not wait.

'Please, Dad. You said I could play with it.'

'Yes, but we said it was a present for Mummy –'

'But Mummy said it was for you as well.'

He kept walking round it, poking it, till I used his impatience as a cover for my own. 'If you insist. We'll just take a peek. I'd like to see what colour it is.'

We peeled off the rustling recrap that encased it. I halfexpected it to come out moving, but when I first glimpsed a small patch of its side, it looked like grey plastic, anonymous, dead. I went on unpeeling. Luke was mad with glee. Two protuberances appeared from the base that reminded me of the feet of a dodo, leathery, crudely detailed things, quite large compared to what the body must be. One of the cats was watching us, but it ignored the robot and jumped inside the packing, waving its tail disdainfully, or perhaps the white plume was a flag of surrender.

Luke tugged at my arm. 'Daddy, Daddy.'

'What? I'm trying to get this stuff off.'

'Is it a girl or a boy?'

'God, I don't know. What do you want it to be?'

'I want it to be like me.'

I nodded, understandingly. 'Okay, it's a boy. It can be – a sort of brother.' It still hurt me that he didn't have a brother.

'No,' he said, indignant. 'I want a girl.'

'No, you don't,' I said, not entirely listening. The logic of children is often surreal. 'Oh, look, I say ...'

For the head, when I got to it, was really tremendous. Now we saw our robot whole.

It sat there, looking remarkably composed, a robust, short creature around a metre tall, a little less, perhaps, than a threeyearold child. Its head was huge, childlike or birdlike, a baby bird's head in terms of its proportions, its most notable feature two big lidded 'eyes', which were currently turned down on the ground, giving a winning effect of shy good manners. It had stumpy legs and big flat feet; its arms had a softer, velvety texture. There were numerous panels, buttons, indentations, both front and back, suggesting many talents.

'Hallo,' I said. I didn't mean to be facetious. I liked it at once, and wanted to greet it.

'Dad, Dad, why isn't it moving?' Luke was jumping up and down on the spot. The cats were weaving around it, more confident now, tapping it gently with their paws, trying to see if it were dead.

'I don't know how we switch it on,' I said.

But I soon found out; it was delightfully simple. You pressed a little panel marked 'Hallo'.

'Luke, do you want to switch him on?'

'Or her,' he said. He thought about it. I think he was suddenly afraid. 'No,' he said. 'We've got to wait for Mummy.'

The miracle was, Sarah liked it too. It appealed to her love of novelty – it tickled her sense of humour, too, the way they had made it like a cartoon character, its cheeky roundness, its big brainy head. 'It's almost too sweet to be useful,' she said. 'Look at those lovely long xylon lashes. So *cute* ...'

'Luke, switch it on, now Mummy's here.'

Very tentatively, Luke pressed the panel, then stepped away smartly, and we all waited. Nothing happened. He tried again. 'I think you should be firmer with it,' Sarah said.

'You'd know, dear,' I countered, but she didn't hear me. She stretched out her small strong hand, and pressed, and a moment later the Dove quivered, whirred, and set off across the floor with the bandy gait of a drunken toddler, pausing minutely every now and then and whirring more loudly, as if thinking. We watched it, all three of us, as proud as parents. It worked! It walked! We stood and adored.

Then it reached a carpet, and the world went mad. There was a noise like a million electronic saws and the carpet turned into a cross between a flying terrier and a boa constrictor, writhing and hissing like a white tornado, while the Dove stood and fought it, rocking, grinding. Both cats fled yowling into the kitchen.

'Turn it off,' shrieked Sarah above the tumult.

I did. We looked at each other, shaken, but Luke was grinning and shaking his head.

'It's not broken,' he insisted, happily. 'It's cleaned the floor wherever it's stepped.'

We began to laugh.

'It's brilliant,' said Sarah.

Success beyond my wildest dreams.

For a week or two, we were adoptive parents, enchanted to meet the new member of the family.

7

And then the whole of Euro went Dove mad. They were selling a thousand a day, then two thousand, then the figures began to go through the roof and the manufacturers couldn't keep up. The boys at the Scientists voted that the club should buy a fleet of halfadozen for us to play with.

There was a honeymoon of many months. The Doves replaced the refreezing of the icecaps as the chief topic of conversation on trains, in queues at the megamarts, on the net ... They were more popular than Twyla Anders, the most popular child star the world had ever known, as the screens announced when for the first time the Doves' share of chat on the global chatnet exceeded Twyla's, then doubled it.

The Doves were partly inspired by twentiethcentury cartoon figures, Disney characters like Mickey Mouse, with their bigheaded, knowing, childlike charm, and now the process started to work in reverse, as the Doves inspired comic strips, then whole comics, then hundreds of films starring the Doves, and every child (not my poor Luke – Sarah objected to screen spinoffs) had Dove socks, teeshirts, rulers, pens, zedbands, micros, pollution masks.

Speaking as a techie, I was full of admiration for the basic Dove design. Its feet could expand to twice their size when it was cleaning or refuelling. It cleaned ferociously, though slowly, because of the time it took to get its feet across a floor of any size. It dusted with its velvety armpads, using sensors to stop it sweeping things to the ground. If it bumped into walls or furniture, it stopped and restarted itself at a tangent. It 'spoke', a selection of halfadozen messages that were its least sophisticated feature, saying 'Hallo' whenever it came within a metre of a living creature, but unable to distinguish between humans and cats (our snobbish old Persians soon got over their fear and began to ignore it, a little uneasily).

Refuelling was the simplest and most brilliant touch of all. The Doves could run on any organic matter. In a world that was wild about recycling, the Doves arrived like minimessiahs. RefuelRecycle: R and R. All you had to do was put your rubbish on the plastic feeding mat that came with the Dove, perch the machine on the top of the mound, and with a slurping, sucking sound that was unnervingly like a pet eating, the pile of mess began to disappear, and the Dove slowly settled towards the floor, eyes locked on its food, until it sat satisfied flat upon the floor. The mat was usually left spotlessly clean. As a final touch, the machine would say 'Thank you'. Luke loved it when our Dove did that, since he was always being nagged by us to say thank you. But I would find myself thanking it. 'Thank *you*,' I would murmur gratefully. It saved me from emptying rubbish bins.

That first model Dove needed a lot of instructions, unlike later models, that became selforganising, 'selfmotivating', as the admen said. We rather liked following ours around – it was fun adjusting the controls, thinking of new tasks for it to do, enjoying our power and its obedience, as we no longer could with servants or children.

The designers had been cleverer than they knew when they modelled their protégés on humans.

For what was our world short of? Babies. The Doves' inventors were our storks. Looking back, those first models soon seemed crude, quite limited in their abilities, but they fulfilled an essential need, for a small new being to enter our life. Instead of refining the dusting sensors, the inventors should have made them say 'I love you'.

(As they quickly realised. Later models did.)

I think I was a little crazy, at the time. I didn't know where I was with Sarah. She was back, but receiving a lot of phone calls from people whose voices I didn't know. I had changed; I no longer felt able to ignore it. I was fiercely suspicious of frequent callers or anyone whose calls she took into another room.

There were women who didn't sound friendly to me – not that many women did sound friendly, in those days, but these sounded more unfriendly than usual, asking where Sarah was as if I had abducted her. One regular caller finally admitted that her name was 'Juno', which I heard as 'Jeanie'.

'I'll try to tell her you called, Jeanie.' I hoped that 'try' sounded suitably careless.

'Juno, Juno,' she shouted gruffly.

'Oh yes, the goddess.' Perhaps I sneered. Well, perhaps I allowed myself the ghost of a sneer, but that didn't justify her telling Sarah later that I had been 'abominably rude' to her.

It appeared that Luke quite liked this creature. If his mother was out and he got to the phone before I did, he'd talk to Juno for hours. Sometimes he seemed to be singing to her. When I asked him who she was, he said 'Mummy's friend.' Which surely gave me a legitimate excuse, as a caring parent, to question Sarah.

I did so one weekend, at breakfast, while Luke still slept in his room next door.

Sarah prevaricated. I pressed a little. 'She's not some guilty secret, is she?' That led her to inform me stiffly that Juno was the leader of the

'Children's Commune' where she and Luke had been living last year. 'Well, one of the leaders.'

'Who are the other ones?'

'Well ... Me.'

This was something of a revelation. 'You never did say where you two went. I thought you were with some bloody lover!' I found I was shouting with relief, but she looked at me and didn't comment. 'What's a Children's Commune, for godsake? It sounds like something from the last century.'

'It means what it says. You know, a place for children. A place that's run for the children who share it. That thinks kids are important. More important than *anything else in the world* ...' She was going into that overemphatic, intense mode that meant bad faith, or politics.

'Yeah, well,' I said. 'We all think that. Even men think that. Well, I do anyway. So can I join this commune?' I knew perfectly well what the answer would be.

'I don't make the rules,' said Sarah. She looked uneasy; she was circling her head as if an ant were under her ear.

'Thought you said you were one of the leaders? Never mind. But they let boys in. Right? Or wrong?'

'Of course,' said Sarah. She was getting annoyed. 'So what happens when the boys turn into men? They will do, you know. I'm a scientist.' (And I suddenly thought of the club, as I sneered, as I heard my smug, unhappy voice sneering. I remembered the Scientists, and Paul, and my secrets, and I thought, is this what we're coming to? Is this the future for men and women? Are we going to live apart for ever, in endless, wanking loneliness?

Surely not, because I loved her. And I stopped sneering, and tried to be nice.) 'Sarah,' I said, 'don't go back there, please. I want Luke to live with men and women. I want him to know who his father is. How is he going to grow up into a man if he doesn't see what men are like?'

I could see that she halfagreed with me, but she didn't want to admit to it. 'I know the arguments,' she said. 'You're a pretty good father, as they go. I don't want to take that away from you. It's natural that men don't want to lose their children.' (But she said it as though it were inevitable; as if it were natural that the women should steal them.) 'In any case, it's more or less in the past. Juno and I – well –' She blushed. She looked prettier, younger when she blushed. 'We had major policy disagreements. She's a lot more extreme than me.'

She wanted me to feel she was reasonable, that she was still basically on my side, because, I saw later, she needed to stay until she was finally ready to leave.

No, that's not fair, that can't be true. I think she really was divided. I think she did like our little family, our little life, our private life, our life with the son we both adored. I think she found it very hard to decide. And perhaps my stupidity decided her, later.

'Juno has, um, a very stern voice,' I said, and was horribly aware I sounded prurient. I tried to erase a mental picture of a mountainous dyke in chains and leather. I wanted to laugh, but I tried again. 'I mean, are you sure she's good for Luke? He talks to her a lot on the phone.'

'She has a beautiful voice,' said Sarah, blushing again. 'If you heard her sing ... it's an incredible contralto. It's Juno who's been training Luke.'

'I didn't know anyone was training Luke – except his Learning Centre, I mean. They seemed happy with him. Does he need more training?'

Since those early days of singing in his cot before he got up, Luke had always had an exquisite voice. We were accustomed to his perfect pitch and memory for any tune he heard. These days he liked to sing in our bathroom where the echo magnified his liquid soprano.

'Luke has a *gift,*' she explained, too slowly, as if it all had to be spelled out to me. 'The *Commune* thinks gifts should be *developed.*'

It was too priggish for me to endure. 'A commune can't think. Only people think.'

'The Dove can think,' said Luke, who had wandered in silently from his bedroom. His eyes were apprehensive. 'I think it thinks. Does it think, Mummy? By the way. Juno phoned. She wants us to visit.'

We had been much more careful about our quarrels since the terrible incident with Luke and the window. Sarah and I adjusted our faces. It was Saturday; we had a whole day to get through. Luke had begged us to take him on a picnic.

'*Does* the Dove think?' Luke continued, interested.

'Yes–' I said.

'No–' said Sarah.

'– depending what you mean by thinking,' I finished.

'– because it's artificial, not natural,' said Sarah.

He looked despairingly from one to another. 'Can we take our Dove on the picnic?' he asked.

'No,' said Sarah.

'Of course,' I smiled.

With Luke's casting vote, we took our Dove on the picnic, perched on the back seat like a squat second child. Luke even put its seat belt on. How fully we acted our psychodramas out!

Our mood shifted when we left the city, only three hours' drive from Melville Road. It was always a glory, slipping out at last from the covered flyway just south of Duxford and zooming down over the ancient airfield with its twentiethcentury aircraft moored like ships. The traffic speeded up at the last moment, eager to escape the city and its tunnels, zooming through into blue air and light.

That was a lovely day, or most of it was, though it held in its hand the seed of the future. Grass seed, actually. The unexpected.

'We look mad with this thing,' Sarah giggled, as we struggled through the little hawthorn wood with our picnic things and the heavy Dove. Luke had sworn he would carry the Dove if we brought it, but got tired within a few steps of the car, and we were always wary of tiring him in case it brought his asthma on. So I was carrying the Dove, of course. Men were still the people who carried things, and mended them dutifully when they got broken. I wondered if Juno were particularly strong, and tried not to think if she were good with her hands, that little blush, Sarah's sudden prettiness ... The Dove had never seemed heavy before, but I'd only carried it short distances.

She'd made a lovely picnic, just like the old days, hollowed-out baguettes with egg and fishlax, stuffed okra, crystallised grapes, mango juicecubes and breadfruit cookies. Beyond the wood was a little field, one corner of it heavily shaded, the grass, remarkably, almost green, and when we got there we saw it was because there was water running under the hollies.

'Rivers are coming back', I said, smiling at Sarah, who smiled in return. 'The water table might soon be back to normal. Really, you know, it's a miracle.'

'It's almost chilly in this shade,' she said, 'but no, this is perfect, I'm not complaining. It's such a luxury to feel cool.' I put down the Dove with a sigh of relief. Luke ran off and explored the stream, and his singing mingled with the sound of the water, a wonderful sound, a weekend sound, while we bustled about in the picnic basket, clattering glasses and cutlery, the noise of a happy family in the storybooks I had read as a child.

The Dove sat silent, almost forgotten. Sarah poured us both a glass of wine from the wine chiller. We chinked glasses, briefly, looked at each other. Luke's voice wove on, silvery, summery. 'Perhaps it will all be all right,' I said. 'You know. Perhaps – everything's turned a corner. Maybe the earth is healing itself.' I wasn't just talking about our planet.

'I hope so,' she said, and her voice was warm, but her face was a blank against the yellow daze of the sunny field behind her head.

'For Luke's sake, too,' I continued, drinking deeply. The wine had never tasted so good. 'He's only happy when we're happy.'

At that moment he came back, looking unusually boyish with mud on his knees and his shorts half soaked. 'You're wet,' said Sarah with the sharp anxiety she justified as maternal love.

'It's a proper river, not a stream,' he said. 'I climbed out along a branch. It snapped.'

'He's all right,' I said. 'He's having fun.'

'His chest,' she began, then saw me frown, and tried to relax, and almost managed it.

'Aren't you going to switch our Dove on?' asked Luke.

'Actually I did,' said Sarah. 'I've just remembered, it didn't come on.'

'It's out of fuel, then,' said Luke. 'Bother. I wanted to play with it.'

'Wait till after lunch,' I suggested. 'It could feed on our leftovers, surely.'

'You didn't bring the feeding mat,' said Sarah, though it was she who packed the car. Those little unfairnesses you never forget ...

'Probably not essential,' I said.

'After lunch' wasn't soon enough for Luke. 'I want it now. You promised,' he said. 'You could give it some of our sandwiches.'

'You'll just have to wait,' I told him.

'No.' Like his mother, he was obstinate. 'It isn't fair. I hate you, Dad.' He started tugging at the Dove. I went on distributing stuffed okra, bent over the basket, swatting at a fly.

Suddenly I heard a familiar sound, the faint whirring and whooshing of our new pet. Turning, I saw Luke and Sarah gazing at the Dove in astonishment. It was squatting on the grass, and the sound had shifted to the gentle slurping it made when feeding.

'I put it on "RefuelRecycle", said Luke. 'It's doing it. It's feeding off the grass.'

His face was triumphant, but Sarah's was uneasy. 'I don't think you should do that, should you? Go on, switch it off. I mean, it's not our grass.' She appealed to me. 'Saul, it doesn't feel right.'

'I don't see what harm it can do,' I said, though I was shaken, I didn't know why. The Dove powered up in not much longer than it would have taken if we were at home. It tried to stumble up towards the sunlight, but fell on the uneven ground. Luke righted it, and it said, 'Thank you.' Outside in the open, it looked even more real. I made Luke switch it off until he'd eaten his lunch, which he did at a thousand kilometres per hour. Then he dragged the Dove over towards the river. It looked like a mutant, lurching child.

'Be careful,' I told him. 'It's valuable.' Of course it was probably already obsolete, succeeded by a host of more sophisticated models.

Sarah and I sat and looked in silence at the oval of bare ground where the Dove had been. The earth looked brown, and abraded, without a blade of grass. I had never realised their power before. 'Goodgod, Saul,' she said. 'I didn't know they could do that. I thought they only ate the things we gave them.'

'I don't think I ever thought about it. Doesn't mention it, in the instructions.'

'Maybe no one knows.' Sarah said, slowly. 'I mean ... it's not *dangerous,* is it? We had to switch it on before it could do it ...'

I tried to comfort her. She was frightened. It was my fault for saying Luke could bring the thing along. I think I managed to reassure her; but why did I feel so shaken myself?

There was a sudden terrible cry from the river away through the trees, then a sound of cracking branches and a mighty splash, and we were both running, tearing our skin on the brambles as we ran to save Luke. The Dove had killed him, I knew, in that moment –

But Luke was standing on the edge of the river, up to his thighs in brown water, wailing. It was the Dove that had fallen in. 'I was playing,' he sobbed. 'I was playing … I didn't mean to hurt it, Mum. I was pretending we were boys, fighting.'

While half of me was thinking of retrieving the robot, realising it would be completely wrecked, the other part was thinking, he was fighting with his brother, which he'd never done. And needed to do.

'Fighting is *naughty*,' said Sarah fiercely, torn between fury and relief. 'What did we teach you boys, in the Communes? And robots are bloody expensive, by the way. Are you all right? Come out of that water.'

I rescued the thing, to stop Luke crying, but the muddy water ruined it, and not long after we smuggled it away to the garbage hills, though I told Luke we'd buried it. I think he knew the truth, because he never asked where.

That night in bed, Sarah came to my arms. 'You feel so warm and nice,' she said. 'I'm beginning to appreciate warmth again.' She ran her hands over my body. 'Apparently the new model Doves feel warm … That was so creepy, when it ate the grass. I suddenly thought, *they could do without us.* I know it's not true, but it really scared me. Do you know, I think I'm glad the bloody thing drowned.'

'Well, you can't really say it drowned,' I said.

'Let's not get another one.'

'Okay,' I said, for she was stroking my belly, her soft fingers reaching down for my penis, and then it was hard in her small cool hand, and all we needed was each other –

After she had finished, I lay awake, and I found myself thinking of the new models. They had strokeyfeely panels. They could sort and carry. Even more intriguing were reports I had read about research in progress on selfreplication. *Doves that could reproduce themselves ...*

In which case, they'd be doing better than us.

8

'Come, old man. Or all die ...' Kit hissed, then more grimly, *'You die, too.'*

'Middle of the night,' I grumbled, but he wouldn't let me close my eyes. I was lying on the edge of the sleep heap, or else I suppose he wouldn't have chanced it. People who disturbed the sleepers tended to come to sticky ends. But so did anyone who risked it outside, anyone who left the farting herd crammed huggermugger round the ashes of the fire. Kit must be desperate. Shivering, aching, I snatched up a blanket and followed him.

We walked blind through the airfield's shadowy junkyard. Great dark bodies of the airplanes loomed above us, stupidly grounded like gross dead moths. *Darkness has come upon the things of man ...* But far behind the planes there were stars, tiny, frozen, too infinitely distant ever to warm or comfort us, and a queer halfmoon with a halo of rainbow ice glittering and crackling on the black.

'Is bad luck,' Kit said, gesturing back at the moon as we came into the mouth of the shed I call the Dovecote, from which a dull grey glow proceeded.

'No,' I said, putting my arm round his shoulders. He threw it off with savage force. It was the Doves he loved, of course, not me.

I mustn't forget he loves the Doves. And thinks I'm leaving them to die ...

Such a strange sight, in that chilly glow that comes from hundreds of epsilon tubes. No one human wants the epsilon tubes, since it was discovered they caused cancer in young children. *But how do we know epsilon doesn't hurt the Doves?* Perhaps that's another reason why they're fading.

I looked at them in the twilight of the tubes. They've started to resemble a regiment, now most of them no longer have the strength to move from the place where the handlers leave them after their routine RefuelRecycle. A regiment of abandoned babies.

From a distance they still have that compelling look of children just beginning to toddle. But close up you see they're getting old.

Because the routine R and R is no longer routine. There isn't enough waste for them to eat. We couldn't imagine that would ever happen. The elite Insiders produced so much waste, whole meals, whole bins full of fermenting vegetables, rotting chickens, tropical fruit ... (Before the Doves, the Outsiders used to eat it, sneaking into the cities in the long hot nights and rifling the bins and the garbage hills. It got a lot harder for them, after the Doves.)

How well I remember the tropical fruit. How Sarah loved mangoes and yams and pawpaws, custard apples, peaches, grapes. The fruit that fell from the breasts of the heat. Now it seems like a dream, all that amazing ripeness.

Rows and rows of grey crouching birds, with every now and then a twitch, a shuffle, for most of them are selfstarters. Most are selfreplicators, too, but they haven't the energy to do it, and for obvious reasons I've tried to keep nothing beyond secondgeneration replicants. There was no real trouble with the second generation.

'What's the problem, Kit?' I ask, impatient, for I'm an old man and I need my sleep.

He starts explaining in his curious mixture of pidgin English and rapid sign language. So many problems. Mostly my fault. Because I haven't been collecting food from the camp. (I admit it, but also excuse myself. At the moment, every single thing is getting eaten, and some of the boys are still starving. He nods, impatiently. 'If the boys starves, Kit doesn't care. But the Doves don't starve, Sol. I never let them.') And people have been trying to feed the Doves from the fouling pits again. It makes them run fast for a minute or two but then they always have a major malfunction. The Crosbee brothers took two Doves which they insisted afterwards were Category Eight, in other words below salvage quality, and after a wild party in Departure burned them and threw them off the walkway. He suspected Fink and Porker of having sex with two Doves they pretended to be servicing. The small amount of rubbish that Chef set aside for the Doves' R and R had not been sent from the kitchens today. 'Your fault, Sol.' He prods my chest with his finger, but I can hardly feel it through the layers of blanket. 'They know you not here. So Mussyershef feed it to his cats. Bloody cats not need it. The cats eat bloody babies,' and he laughs, quietly at first, then riotously. I see that he's back in a good mood again, merely because I am there to be talked to, and I realise that he's just been frightened, he can't cope with the responsibility for all those hundreds of helpless creatures ... (Of course he can't. He isn't very old. What would he be – twelve, twenty? And he's probably never been looked after himself.)

– *Remember the Doves aren't really creatures.* Machines. Robots. Manmade things. My life went wrong when I blurred the line between living and nonliving.

'The cats eat bloody babies ,' he'd said.

Don't think about that. Have a laugh with him. Cracked and hoarse, but he doesn't seem to notice. I have to keep Kit cheerful, and on my side, for I need a few more days for my writing. I take him by the arm. This time he doesn't throw me off. 'Say after me: *Monsieur*

Chef. Not *Mussyershef.* MuhSyuhShayv. Say it right. You know he likes it.'

(The chef is another oldtimer, like me. He's survived since long before I came here, because he has a skill, because he can cook, and coax the old generator into working. He speaks little English, and pretends not to understand my French. I know it's because he doesn't want to be friends. He has gone beyond things like language and friendship in whatever great suffering brought him here. Now he is dumb, but he's *Monsieur Chef.*)

We begin to walk up and down the rows, and I let Kit report to me as if I were a consultant making my rounds. Praying this charade will be over soon, so I can creep back to my mound and curl up with the others and thaw out enough to snatch an hour's sleep. I need my bloody sleep to write. How long is Kit going to keep this up?

One by one down the rows of Doves, and I pat the heads of some, obediently, the weird felty texture some models had after the first hard models had been superseded but before they had perfected the xylon feathers. Their heads are at the level of my fingertips, about a metre above the ground, just a little taller than a threeyearold ...

'*The cats eat bloody babies*' – No. The cats eat mice and frogs and birds and anything else that's smaller than them. It's the rule of thumb for most living things. You can't eat something bigger without bursting. Kit hates cats, that's all it is. Whereas the Doves in his eyes can do no wrong.

If only we had thought of making them smaller, but we only considered making them more perfect. We wanted them cuter, cleverer, livelier. We longed for them, really, to be alive. We wanted to be god, we wanted to be parents.

*

Dovemania continued unabated with the two or three models after the first, which had major improvements in 'lovability' – the manufacturers actually called it that. And people truly loved their Doves. The new ones could hold simple conversations, personalised with their owner's name, play his or her favourite music on request, sing along with the owner's voice. They could learn the names of up to ten family members, had strokeyfeely panels on their stomachs, hummed and purred in response to being stroked. And instead of needing emptying and cleaning once a month, they had a cute selfcleaning function. When placed upon the rubbish jets, they ejected small neat pellets of detritus from their backs – all this without pottytraining or nappies!

The whole developed world wanted them. Everyone in our apartment block had them. The porter told us about new arrivals. And Sarah, who'd sworn she would never have another one, soon began to feel envious.

She was prone to envy, of everyone. Maybe because as a little girl she was sent to her Scottish grandma once too often. Out there on her own in the icy fogs, dressed in her cousins' handmedowns. There were times in her life when she did feel loved – she knew I loved her, she must have done – and she was successful, on top of the world. But part of her was always left outside, peering into the room where the lights were on and the other children tore open their presents.

We had never moved to the pretty house in the Northwest Enclaves she'd dreamed about. Not because we weren't wealthy enough, but because we had not 'resolved our future as a family', or whatever nonsense Sarah spouted. And yet it began to grate on her that we lived in a flat, however large and comfortable. One of our stuffier dinner guests asked her, 'Is this your *city* base, Sarah?', as if convinced we had a place in the country.

She felt she *should* have a place in the country. She 'loved nature', whatever that meant. I tried to make her see that now nothing was natural, that the flowers she loved had been selectively bred to make them bigger and longer lasting, that even the hills behind the Northwest Borders, which we could just glimpse from our fourthfloor window, were covered with genetically modified crops ...

She stared out of the window while I lectured her, looking resentful, or possibly sad. She waited until I had finished talking. 'It's the colour,' she said. 'That blue. And that yellow.' (It was autumn, and the trees were turning.) 'So beautiful. I love those hills. I'd like my children to live there.' She deluded herself, for she only had one, but she wanted another, so she often said 'children'. Whatever she wanted, she thought she should have. 'You've changed,' she said. 'You've changed completely. You used to dream of living somewhere wild. You used to talk about ... beaches, and forests.'

'It must be middle age,' I said. 'I'm getting fat and old and grey.' I wanted her to deny it, but instead it awoke her tenderness. She put her white smooth arms around me, and pressed my face against her breast, holding my head as if she cared about it, her fingers clinging to my curly hair.

'You're not old, darling. You can't be old.'

But the tenderness did not last very long.

'I shouldn't have to live in a flat at my age,' she said, absurdly, as if it were my fault, as if I had the slightest control over where she spent the night, let alone lived.

'We could afford not to,' I said calmly.

'I would miss my friends,' she snapped at once. Which showed a kind of change in her. Once upon a time she would have cited work, the exact amount of journey time the move would have added. Now work was becoming less central than before. Sarah was in her late forties, after all, and the screens had begun to tire of her. Last year she had twice disappeared for a 'holiday' and returned a little shaky, her skin babypink and covered in cream, avoiding strong light – but despite the peels, she was ageing. She no longer spoke of her longing to conceive, though we still had sex, and without contraception. Our hopes had become too ingrown to risk voicing, not to ourselves, never to each other –

She was my love; my enemy. She gave me great pain, but I still loved her.

'I feel ... I don't have the things I want,' she muttered, frustrated, yet appealing to me, as if I were still the absent Daddy, the one who could have given it all, if he'd cared.

I couldn't ever fill that hole. No one would. No one could.

'I could find a place with a garden,' I said. 'Luke would love it if we had a garden.' Though that was less true than it had once been, for he had become quieter, more nervous, recently, more wrapped up in his music, less boyish, somehow. He spent a lot of time with Juno and the 'Communards'. 'By the way, is he staying the night with the Communards?' It was Saturday, and Luke wasn't at home.

'Don't say *Communards*. It sounds silly.'

'Well, the 'Children's Commune' sounds pretty silly –'

'No it isn't. It's a perfectly good name.'

'Communard comes from commune, Sarah.'

'You're laughing at me. You undermine me. Then you wonder why I want to leave you –'

(Mygod, she'd been 'leaving' me for nearly twenty years.)

'We could buy a house and live together.' I went back to it dumbly, again and again. 'I don't see the problem. You can still see your friends.'

'They're not just some silly indulgence, you know. They matter to me. They're ... my life,' she said. 'And Lukey's life.'

Which made me feel pointless. 'That's stupid,' I said. 'Bloody Juno and her cronies are not Luke's life.'

'How well do you know your son?' she enquired. 'How often does he sing to you?'

This was unfair, but left me winded. 'That's not our thing,' I said, unhappily. 'Luke and me have our own thing, you know. It's ... *father and son.* That matters as well.' (And we did. We joshed. We vegged. We wrestled. We ate the sugarbombs Sarah detested, screaming at me 'He needs fruit, not sweets!')

There was a long pause. It was a lovely afternoon, late October, clear and golden, and the window was open, and by the same magic trick as in the last few years there was something in the air like the autumn chill we used to read about in books.

'Feel the air, Sarah,' I said, touching her hand. She loved things like that; air, water. 'It's wonderful. There's ... an edge. It's cool.' It wasn't much, but I liked to please her. We sat together, taking it in.

'Are you happy?' she asked suddenly. 'I don't know if you're happy, either. We're ... rushing through life, aren't we? Getting older.' And she stared out of the window, as she often did, as if it would eventually give her the answer, that same long view across the aching roads and the rustred suburbs to the sunblurred towers and beyond them the low blue hills she loved. 'I stopped you travelling, I think. You wanted to. To see the world. I do – like you. You're not a bad man. You stayed with me. You stuck around ...' And then she was clutching my hands and crying as if she had done me some massive wrong.

But the tears released some tension in her and within minutes she was herself again, abstracted, planning, chattering, restless, screenwatching, cleaning, talking on the phone, preparing to go away for the night, changing her plans, then again, then again – and it got dark, and she closed the window.

Around nineoclock she called me over to the screen. 'Come and have a look. There's another new range.' She didn't even have to say what of; we were all obsessed with Doves in those days. 'This is absurd,' she said to me, laughing, but she was fascinated, all the same.

Four new types of Dove were coming on the market. All of them had the most popular features of the current mobots, like 'skin' and 'feathers' that felt warm and soft, RefuelRecycle, selfstarting et cetera. But the new models were highly specialised. There were 'Culturevultures', which included a scan of all the books that had ever been written, with universal translation, and a full hive of all Euro music ever recorded, plus the contents of the world's great galleries and the 'World's Hundred Greatest Movies', though these were mostly 'obscure foreign films' from the last century that 'no one has heard of', the TV presenter said, with a contemptuous smile. ('I'd be better than him,' Sarah said, in passing. 'I like old films. They have such great stories.') There were 'Warmbots', whose very existence would have been unthinkable until the last two years. They had furry exteriors and long thick arms and promised to 'keep you warm at nights'. There were 'Sexbots', though we didn't find out exactly what they did that evening because our screen had the automatic KC (kiddiescleanup) function that blocked out any mention of sex, and neither of us could remember how to unlock it before the moron had passed on to the next, but from his face and gestures the Sexbots were on heat. (But I have three Sexbots in my store. They look battered, and used. They look ... *undesirable*. No one would dream of having sex with them.) The fourth variety of Dove was a 'Hawk', a kind of avian guard dog, really, 'for defensive purposes only', he assured us. They had stern beaked heads and watchful eyes. Their defence system sounded unbelievably aggressive. It was called 'SD and R', Selfdefend and Recycle; a high-pitched scream to deafen any 'attackers', an 'immobiliser flagel' to paralyse them, then finally the Hawk would cut up its victims and recycle them in the normal way.

'My dad would be horrified,' I said. Samuel was against private security arrangements. (Or so he said. But what had he left me, what clanking things, in that green canvas bag?)

'I like the sound of those Culturevultures,' said Sarah. 'For Luke, I mean. All that lovely music.'

I'd guessed she would like them. I felt sorry for Luke. 'Don't you think Luke might feel – *got at,* sometimes? He gets a lot of culture, doesn't he?'

She passed on that one, so we didn't have a quarrel. She probably simply wasn't listening to me. 'How about the Sexbots?' she asked. 'Disgusting ...'

'You women will have plenty to say about that.'

I went out to make us a cup of coffee. An hour had slipped away as we watched the screens, riveted. All round the globe it was probably the same. Humans were creating life, at last! It didn't seem commercial, or trivial, or comic. It certainly didn't strike most of us as rash, though the godlovers warned against the sin of pride, and now I'm ashamed of thinking them stupid. 'Everything that lives is holy.' They thought the Doves were creatures of the devil.

Sarah called me back in from the kitchen. 'Listen, Saul, this is interesting.'

The screentalker had moved on into the future; the next expected model was a 'Replicator'. We'd been hearing for years about selfreplication, but to date no actual model had emerged. What he showed today was a cartoon simulation. An adorably chubby Dove sat and ruffled its wings, bounced gently up and down on rubbery legs, cheeping, till suddenly a smaller Dove came wriggling out from under it. The mother, now a little less chubby, began to nuzzle it and clean its feathers.

'Weird biology,' I said. 'Birds lay *eggs,* as far as I know.'

'But it's fantastic,' said Sarah, impatient, interrupting me, 'isn't it? I mean, they were saying it's only months away. These Replicators are almost ready. It can't happen, surely, how can it? Something that human beings have made can't make another of itself, can it?'

She listened to the screens, but not to me. 'I explained that to you years ago, Sarah. Don't you remember that work I was doing for Roche? My nanomachines were selfassemblers. The theory's been around since the 1980s ... Drexler was the guy who started it all. They only need a good source of power and the right kind of molecules. If you can get enough nanomachines working together in parallel, it's perfectly feasible. But well, *wow.*'

'Never mind,' she said. 'Let's listen to him.'

The cartoon Dove and Dovelet had vanished, and the presenter became a little wildeyed, trying to explain the science and making a hopeless cockup of it. After a while I turned it off, and we looked at each other, exhilarated.

'It is amazing,' she said, slowly. 'It's a quantum leap. It makes our old Dove look so out of date. I'd quite like to have one. Godknows why ...'

Her eyes were still large, young, blue, but her hands as she stroked her neck were different, the little hands I had always loved now marked with a delicate delta of veins and a drift of faint brown stains like leaves. Could she be going through the menopause? – Those pills in her bag. I felt a twinge of pain.

'I'll buy you one,' I said, 'for your birthday. The old one was nothing compared to this. Let me buy you a Replicator.'

I hadn't the slightest sense of danger.

We promise for the future, but time moves on, and when the future comes it's different. She had a November birthday, of course, so I always think of her on Bonfire Night; I do even now, when nothing's the same, when the wild boys choose which building to torch and the bodies come hurtling out and screaming, arcing out white from the thirtieth floor like so many flaming Roman candles, and it could be her against the night, I've no idea where she is now, for I hear the Southside is virtually deserted ...

If she survives. My dear, my darling.

Things changed for the worse before her birthday came. Luke was spending the whole week in the Commune, and I found that instead of going to school he was being 'home educated' by the women, though it wasn't his home, for heaven's sake, and I can't believe it was education. He was twelve years old. They were wasting his time.

Perhaps that's unfair. He did sing divinely, and he'd started to do it in public, as well, though it mostly seemed to be at fundraising events for the weird new women's collective, 'Wicca', an outgrowth from the Children's Commune.

Wicca. I still shiver, remembering their name. I confess I occasionally browsed through Sarah's study, when she was away for too long a stretch, just to be sure that her desk was all right, and I found a pamphlet that would have seemed farcical, if it had not included her name, high on the masthead with Juno Jakes's. It was a ghastly amalgam of many things. First, a wacky female nature worship, centring on 'the Hidden Goddess', who apparently 'gave suck' to us all (count me out, I was bottlefed), 'pentagrams', 'equinoxes', 'handfastings'; second, a 'new biology', starring a singlecelled female bacterium which, scientists had recently discovered, had given up sex three thousand years ago; third, a rigid, doctrinaire politics whose central premise was 'separate development' (for women. They didn't mention men. These bitches were too stupid to remember apartheid). The nub of it was, they were through with men. They didn't want us as lovers, or fathers, or friends. The ideas were banal, the logic nonexistent, the rhetoric feeble, laughable ... And yet I was worried, until I saw that the top sheet was scored across by hand with the words 'DRAFT ONLY – SARAH, WHAT DO YOU THINK? J.' It was Juno, of course, with her humourless voice, her heavy black hand, her childish writing. My quicksilver Sarah would see it was rubbish. *Revere the Goddess, and harm none ... We are of the Earth, and of Nature ...* We'd have a jolly good laugh about it together.

But she never mentioned it, so I didn't either, because if I hadn't snooped I would never have seen it. I assumed it had gone into the dustbin of history. No sensible woman would swallow such nonsense. After a bit I forgot about it. And Sarah kept me at a distance from the Commune and Wicca and the whole damn thing, mostly because I was a man, I suppose. It embarrassed her greatly, being married.

There were a few occasions when some of the women – I admit I called them 'the coven', sometimes, mostly to my mates down at the Scientists, but occasionally to Sarah, too, and when she was in a good mood, she laughed, but the old good moods became rarer and rarer – called at the flat to pick up Luke or work through something on Sarah's computer. Sarah usually warned me, and would ask me to go out or keep a low profile while they were there. But occasionally she forgot to warn me, occasionally I didn't obey.

Then she treated me like a dog, for their benefit.

– Not like a dog, she treated me like a piece of wood, a stick, a stone, a broken chair, something she had no further use for. I think she hoped they would assume I was a man who'd come to fix the plumbing, since women hadn't rushed to claim *that* profession, sticking their heads down stinking drains.

I suspect that few of them were fooled, in fact, because they probably had their own guilty secrets. Men hadn't disappeared from the face of the earth just because women didn't want to live with us.

There was many a household where a man clung on in some dirty cupboard to what had been his home. I'd found that out at the Scientists, when the drinks flowed freely and the truth spilled out, and sometimes the men who seemed most staggish, the most determinedly gladtobegay, burst into tears and admitted they were trying to hang on to the remains of their family.

Some of those Wicca women must have seen through Sarah. One I suspected of pitying me, a beautiful young woman with cornstraight hair and a soft country accent – Devon, Somerset? – Briony Barnes. (But I didn't want pity.) Luke made her sound like a sailor: 'Briny'.

The first time I met Briony, she'd arrived early, just as we were sitting down to breakfast, and I had poured a pot of tea, which Sarah virtually snatched from my hand. 'We'll go in my study, Briony,' she said. To me she said nothing at all, not a word, not 'thank you' or 'goodbye', and she didn't introduce me, and the pot burnt my hand as she grabbed it from me, and besides, I was thirsty ... I wanted respect in my own sodding home, but failing that, I wanted my tea.

It was all too much, and I went after them. 'Are you sure the tea is enough for you, Sarah? Wouldn't you like my toast as well?'

She glared at me in stifflipped fury and said 'We're busy. Go away. This is Briony Barnes, Wicca's Weapons Officer.' She obviously thought that would impress me, but I merely thought it ridiculous – how could someone so young and pretty handle weapons? – so instead of shaking Briony's hand, I saluted, and Sarah lost her cool completely and yelled 'Go, you fool!' and actually stamped.

But the beautiful blonde girl caught my eye, and tried to make me like her with a sympathetic look, a selfdeprecating, rather humorous look that surely gave the lie to that 'Weapons Officer'. (A *Weapons Officer*. What the hell did it mean? What was going on with these new scary women?)

Brave sweet Briony. I understood nothing.

Sarah was right; I was a fool. I could never distinguish between true and false, real and artificial, love and hate. And the ultimate folly, the final mistake was to buy her another Dove for her birthday.

She'd said she wanted one, but never mind. One of the very first Replicators.

Both Luke and Sarah were home on her birthday, which made me feel hopeful; a family birthday. I gave her champagne and orange juice for breakfast. Once she had kept our flat full of fresh flowers, but no longer, now she was there so rarely, so off we went to Regent's Theme Park and I took them to the Rosegarden Museum. We pressed all the panels with their heavenly scents, and I called her over to sample one that really did smell of deep red roses and all the memories we shared of summer. 'Red roses for love,' I said to her. She smiled at Luke and patted my arm.

Present giving was to be before lunch. Luke was in on the secret, and tremendously excited. I suppose he thought it might make everything right, finally bring his parents together – or was that *my* problem, did *I* think that? She gasped and blushed when she first saw the box, and unwrapped it in a daze, pink and flustered. I suppose our first Dove was in my mind, which was such a success with her, in the beginning. (I'd given her one child, hadn't I? Was it so foolish to want to give her another?)

The new arrival perched on the carpet. We looked at it. It was extremely pretty, a petrol blue with a slight rainbow sheen on its wings and feet, a fluffy blue head, shallow babybird beak. The detail was about a thousand times better than it had been on our earlier model. I could see Sarah waver between pleasure and guilt, and I said, 'Don't worry. I wanted to buy it. It'll be your slave if I get tired. It will sit at your feet and adore you –'

And Luke, who was watching, suddenly put in, 'Call it Dora, then. That's a good name, Dora.'

'I vaguely thought it was male,' I said. 'What do you think, Mummy?' (I liked to call her Mummy. If she was Mummy, then I was Daddy, and we would always be a family)

'Female,' she said. 'Definitely. Dora will do. Thanks. It's – fine.'

There was obviously something worrying her, but I took it to be the size of the present.

She looked at Dora. Dora looked at the floor. Her head was covered with azure feathers. 'The detail's, well, amazing,' Sarah said, but I could still hear there was something wrong.

'Go on, switch on,' I said. 'Let's see what she can do.'

There was a pause. She didn't move. Then Luke said, 'Mummy, why did Juno say it was wrong to have Doves? It's not true, is it? Say it isn't true, I like this Dove, I want us to keep it –'

She did try to shush him, but it was too late. Things went downhill with bewildering speed. I had been so desperately keen to please her. (My life sometimes felt like a funfair ride, soaring and dipping with nightmare speed. I was sometimes a little highlystrung, though Sarah was wrong to call me manic depressive and vow to get me certified – it was just that I wanted to be happy. I wanted to be happy, and she gave me grief.) I lost my temper, utterly, completely. I remember swearing – about Juno, and the Commune, and women in general, and Sarah in particular, and marriage, and birthdays, and fucking families. I kicked a chair, I threw a lamp – not at Sarah, of course, but at the wretched wall of the wretched flat where we were cooped up together.

It wasn't the row that decided things, though she left with a tearful, anxious Luke without eating lunch or making it up, saying she had to go to a big dinner that her women friends were having in her honour.

They had changed their name now, the witches' coven, they were no longer the Children's Commune. They had taken the name of their political arm, and would henceforth be known as Wicca World, which she assured me meant 'wise women of the world', not 'worldwide witches', thank you, Saul.'

I really had thought that Dora would please her. I think in her heart she had been pleased, and would have liked to keep it, but her politics were stronger ...

It was bullshit, all of it, looking back. No one gives a fig about politics now; we're all too frightened of freezing to death. Animals have no politics, do they? When did we stop being animals?

That awful birthday. I'd so looked forward to it. After they left, I was ashamed and savage. (If I'd held my tongue, it might have been all right. Why were men and women doomed to fight one another?) The flat was too cold, it felt desolate – I switched on the Dove because I was lonely, and watched it stir and melt and flutter, its lids lifting, its big blue eyes ...

I realised too late why I felt so angry. That foolish longing to give her a baby. A second baby, even better than the first one. So I bought her a nice baby, and she turned it down. And that, I suppose, was the end of that.

9

They stayed away for three months or more. I began to wonder if I'd see them again. I thought of contacting them at Wicca World. I practised the phone call many times, and rang sounding sensible and normal – more sensible, surely, than most of their callers – but perhaps they detected I was mad and lonely. I met with a series of fogs and baffles that left me in no doubt that Sarah was a leader. Perhaps *the* leader; it was mystifying.

I was stuck in the flat they'd abandoned, with Dora. I found myself getting close to her. I began to use the 'Sleep' option more rarely, so she was functioning most of the day. She became ... I can only say, a companion. Be honest, go further – she was a friend. And she offered the consolations of words. I'd made sure Dora had Poetryquote, meaning to play love poems to Sarah, but Dora said them to me, instead; she read me Auden's beautiful words – I mustn't start snivelling, someone will notice. (Today I'm writing at the back of the Dovecote, pretending to tally up the stores, and Kit's around somewhere, worrying, fussing. I pretend to sneeze, and wipe my eyes.)

She never lay with me again ... *In my arms till break of day/ Let the living creature lie* ... After that birthday, it was over.

Dora stayed up with me at night through the awful hours before I slept. I was smoking again, which I hadn't done since Sarah's affair with that bloody doctor – and when she came back, I gave up for her. Now I smoked again, and tobacco, this time, fullstrength tobacco, industrial strength, imported stuff which cost the earth since hardly anyone in England smoked tobacco – but I wasn't going to mimsy around with bloody 'green' marijuana, which was one of Wicca's 'pothecary' of 'lifegiving plants'. I smoked tobacco till I pickled myself, snorted like a dragon, thinking grimly of cancer, I'd give myself cancer and she wouldn't care ... but then I'd die, and they would both mourn me, too late they would realise what a man I had been ...

But being a man was the basic trouble. What hope was there, if my sex was all that mattered?

It didn't matter a bit to Dora. I could have been a man, a fish, a clown. She didn't mind if I smoked, or swore, or drank too much beer, or wept, or farted. She ambled about making faint wheezing noises as she cleaned, gently. (They got that right, the new models weren't ferocious cleaners, whereas the first Doves were all too like Sarah, who couldn't clean without screaming and banging about.) So many things were an improvement, though Dora still tended to topple over things and lie there cheeping, her feet in the air. It was worth it, though, for the pleasure you felt when you'd righted her, and she said 'Thank you'. In fact, Dora said 'Thank you. I love you', which I would have thought embarrassing once, but felt quite worryingly touched by, now. (But I couldn't help thinking – would Dora be unfaithful? Could I ever leave her alone with people? Wouldn't she love anyone who picked her up? It was just a legacy from living with Sarah.)

Talking to Dora was very rewarding. They'd added some pleasing extra touches. She said 'Good to see you' if she came into a room and registered a living presence; when a conversation between us ended, she'd say, in a humble, grateful way, 'I've enjoyed talking to you. Thanks.' Once again, it was so different from living with Sarah, who hardly listened to me any more because, she said, conversation caused quarrels. If I tried subjects beyond Dora's understanding (but, of course, she had no understanding: she had a programme – it's not the same thing) she would say, in a respectful, apologetic way, 'I'm afraid you've lost me. Try again, slowly,' and when I tried again, if she did no better she'd say 'I'm so sorry. I'm not up to this,' and this secondstage response was so thrillingly lifelike that I gazed at her, for a second, enchanted, her big blue eyes, pupils permanently wide, expressing innocent affection, her soft adult voice in that cute baby body ... (What would Sarah have said? The first time, 'I don't get you.' Second time, 'You're talking balls.')

That was the point; they were better than us. We wanted them human, but better than us, biddable wives, welltrained children, mothers who never got cross or tired.

And unlike us they would never die. Because of the little 'Replicate' panel. I had looked at it many times already, and felt the electric tingle in my fingers drawing me towards it, tempting me. Of course it was tempting to make another being, to see the miracle before my eyes ...

But you were cautioned against careless use. It was 'extremely demanding' of resources. The Dove would 'suspend normal functions for the duration of the replication process'. Some of her own material would be recycled for the use of her 'child'; you were told to expect 'some longterm lessening of function, change in appearance etc.' after she had replicated. 'This does not indicate a malfunction but is part of the normal lifecycle.'

I looked at Dora, sitting on the floor. She looked so new, so adorable, her feathers gleaming, the down on her crown ... I moved my finger away from the button. It wasn't right. She was simply too young. She should enjoy herself a bit, she wasn't ready for all that yet.

She suddenly chuckled. The 'chuckle' was delightful, one of her most appealing new functions, the irrepressible, bubbly, gleeful chuckle of a happy child, and the clever thing was that each time it happened it was slightly different, so it didn't get boring. It was set on a random programme, so she could chuckle at any time she was switched on, and afterwards she would say, sweetly, 'I just feel happy', or 'Isn't life fun?'

I had never lived with anyone who I'd managed to make totally, completely happy. I have to admit that when Dora did that, with a little shuddery motion of her wings like a child's shoulders shaking with laughter, I felt for the first time in many months that *I* was happy, that life was fun.

I suppose I began to depend on Dora. She wasn't always Dora; her nickname was Dodo, which suited her somehow, less definitely female than Dora for one thing, more playful and loving, a good name for a bird. I switched her off 'Sleep' as soon as I got up in the morning, touched the 'Follow' and 'Conversation' spots, and she would come waddling into the kitchen and talk to me or play me music.

I started to worry about leaving her at home when I went to the nanolabs in the day. There had been a spate of dovetheft; it was the modish crime, for a while, partly because of the manufacturers' cannily short runs of each new adaptation. This increased demand to the point where even quite respectable people turned a blind eye if they could get, say, a Culturevulture in decent condition for a favourite child's birthday.

There were guards, of course, to our building, but all the same, one of them was fairly new, and didn't they say that security firms often recruited criminals?

Every time I left my Dora, I was anxious. She looked so trusting, so vulnerable, as she padded after me to the door, and said, as I stroked the 'Goodbye' panel, 'Are you leaving? Must you go?'

Are you leaving! Must you go! It felt wonderful, but was she getting too attached?

I was getting too attached, that was the problem.

Luke and Sarah came back one midwinter weekend. She didn't ring up. She didn't warn me. Perhaps she was hoping that I'd have gone out, that she could just take their things and go. (Quite a lot of their stuff had already gone, and that in a way was almost a relief, for I could suddenly be reduced to tears by a small pair of sandshoes under the table.)

No, I really think she halfwanted to see me; love doesn't disappear overnight. Or else she'd have rung up and found out my movements, and arrived when she was sure I was out.

They came late. I had had a curious day, the days that solitary people have, when nothing much happens but your moods veer wildly. The weekends could be frightening when there was no work to do and no one to quarrel with. I missed my son more at weekends. I sat in his room for a bit, stared at the wall, at the posters I had given him of footballers and mountaineers, at the little keyboard he had long outgrown, at his narrow bed, which I'd left unmade because it somehow looked more lived in, more as if he'd just left the flat that morning, though I knew it meant that when Sarah came back she would scream at me for being untidy ...

It is a fault in women (particularly 'sensitive' ones, sensitive only to their own pain) that they tend to dismiss men as thickheaded clods, and see all our motives as simple and coarse, just because we don't talk about our feelings. I had feelings for my son. I sat there paralysed. I played some recordings of his voice that she had left lying on his bedside table. His beautiful voice poured through the flat, high, soaring, unforgettable, but I wanted his ordinary daytime voice, asking for a pair of socks, or chocolate.

The morning slipped away like that. Then I spent some quality time with Dora. I was more tempted than usual to use the Replicate function. I even touched it, lightly, very lightly, nothing dangerous, the merest caress ... But she'd spoken, abruptly businesslike, twice, 'Do you want me to replicate? Do you want me to replicate?' And I had answered, rather shamefaced, 'No', feeling I had somehow interfered with her.

By teatime I was extremely depressed. Deciding I should refresh my knowledge so I knew what I was meddling with, I went and scanned through my information about replication and selfassembly in nanomachines. Our publicists had done a preliminary fanfare. 'Nanomachines', which were aggregates, in any case, could certainly 'build in parallel, with many billions of molecular machines working at once.' All that was required was some kind of fuel – of course any organic material could fuel the Doves – and an ability to copy a pattern. If the copies weren't quite perfect, so much the better; that was how life had always evolved, through the random occurrence of mutations, some of which helped the next generation to survive, breed better, faster, multiply. 'The next giant step for machines' would be 'To learn through time, on their own. Not only to adapt, but evolve.'

Not such a giant step, I thought. Computers had been 'Solving Through Evolving' (in my own Nanocorp's slogan) for over half a century, since computer scientists realised artificial intelligence worked better and faster if left alone to race its way through myriad permutations, just like recombining DNA ...

My attention wandered. *I'd* been left alone. I told myself, I must adapt and evolve, I must learn to live in this new lonely world, I must experiment and find solutions, but instead I read on, and dozed and dreamed, till suppertime, and felt a lot better. Then I took a long bath. Dora toddled in behind me and squatted singing in the bathroom. She liked the steam; Doves revived in moisture, it gave their 'skin' a healthy sheen. I felt very glad of her company. On impulse, I sponged her back and feet. She said 'Thank you. That's very nice.' And it did feel tender. It reminded me of something.

The flat was hot because I'd borrowed my neighbour's three blowers to dry a week's worth of dirty clothes (if I had a criticism of the Doves, it was that they had no adaptations for washing. In that way, they resembled modern women. I'd sketched out several letters to the manufacturers.) After soaking in the bath I was too hot to put my clothes on. Yes, simply too hot, whatever anyone said later, I wasn't used to it any more, since the Cooling ... I poured myself a whisky, a very large whisky, and went with Dora into the bedroom.

She hopped on to the bed, as she usually did, though she sometimes missed, and did her piteous cheeping, which made me laugh, as I picked her up, and then she laughed too, which must have been programmed, but I think I only halfbelieved it was a programme, she surely did things that no other Dove did, she was somehow special, she really liked me ...

She snuggled up beside me. Or I settled her besides me. I had a long drink. I wanted a cigar, so I had a cigar, because no one else was there, and I shut out Sarah's voice saying 'No' from my head because she didn't care, had never cared about me.

I had another drink. Dora was very beautiful, her innocent, transparent lashes, the downward, modest cast of her head like the pictures of Victorian women. I tried one or two of our conversations, and I somehow knew, though the words were the same, that more was being said than the actual words, and there was a kind of understanding between us. Then I switched her over to 'Singalong'. We sang long-forgotten rugby songs together. I had another drink, then another, then another ...

Which was why, when Sarah and Luke arrived, I was lying unconscious on the bed 'with a smouldering cigar on the bloody bedspread' (though if I were unconscious, how could it be smouldering? Even I can't smoke a cigar in my sleep), 'buck naked' (a phrase that's always made me uneasy; I was only naked because it was hot) and 'that bloody disgusting thing on top of you' – hold on, if she were on top of me, she had simply fallen over (stability was never a strong point with Doves), and she wasn't disgusting, Dora, ever, even Sarah must have seen that my Dodo was sweet –

I may have briefly wondered whether Sarah could be jealous. This affair was all ridiculous, absurd, but apparently I giggled, which made things worse, and then Dora joined in, which was not her fault, and said 'I feel happy. Isn't life fun?' and although I don't remember very clearly, someone, who must have been Sarah, screamed, and Dora crashed helplessly off the bed.

Next day it all became very serious. I was crippled with headache, and Luke was crying, and saying 'You promised not to divorce Daddy,' which made me realise that was what she would do. Sarah said she would never have believed I could let her down so badly in front of a child. Dora had been banished to a corner of the screenroom. It looked to me as though she were slightly crooked. I suspected Sarah of covert violence, but probably she had just pushed her off the bed. Sarah was packing, with furious energy, such few possessions as she required. Her dyed red hair flew out in snakes, her white arms whipped and thrashed the air as if she would beat our world to death because it had disappointed her. I felt powerless to stop her raging progress, partly because of my hangover, partly because of a sense of unreality, a sense that we were sliding into farce –

But Luke. His pale child's face, lengthening, strengthening towards adolescence, his worried mouth, his stricken eyes – Luke was real.

Luke was tragic. He hardly spoke, just watched us both, his head turning from one to the other, and I thought he looked frighteningly adult till he suddenly said, at some irrelevant moment, 'Can I play with Dora? – I suppose I can't.'

'Juno was right,' his mother was raging. 'They're – completely unnatural. They're wrong. They're perverted. Do you know, *one ate a sleeping cat?*'

'Nonsense,' I said blankly, 'that's utter nonsense.'

'It was on the news,' Luke said eagerly, with a child's enthusiasm for horror.

'I don't believe you,' I said to his mother. 'It's propaganda. It's bloody Juno. It's Wicca World rubbish, isn't it?'

'You were in bed with that thing,' she shouted at me. 'And then you dare to start criticising *us* – '

As if Wicca World were above criticism.

And yet I had a feeling of sick fear. I remembered the day we went out on the picnic beyond Duxford with our first Dove, and how suddenly the grass was bare, that little dark patch of brutalised land. That sudden uneasy sense of its power.

But a cat – a cat. Not possible.

'It just left the collar, because it was plastic,' said Luke, helpfully. 'And bits of fur. And the girl was crying. It was her cat. She couldn't switch it off. The switch had broke ...'

(I thought of our cats' long vulnerable tails, weaving in their wake as they avoided Dora. But Dora was kind. Dora was safe ...)

'That's enough, darling,' said Sarah. 'We're going.'

'When shall I see you again?' I demanded. 'Don't leave in the middle of a stupid quarrel. I just got drunk last night, that's all – '

But she interrupted, before I could explain, 'It doesn't matter, it's still disgusting. I shan't discuss it. He's *only eleven.*'

'Twelve,' I corrected her, I couldn't resist, but it made things worse.

'And you forgot his birthday.'

'I didn't. But you won't bloody give me your address.'

'Because we have a lot of enemies. Wicca World has enemies. Disgusting people. Terrible people –'

Now I had become one of them.

10

Things moved fast after that, in several wrong directions.

Sarah moved out. Although she had been with me so irregularly, the flat felt empty in a different way. Small details hurt; the missing patch of pink where her wrap always hung open on our bedroom door. The bathroom, surgically stripped of all her pretty paints and powders. She took the kettle, and the gilded bowl she once kept piled to the brim with apples, and my favourite mugs, three matching mugs painted with jaunty, impossible bluebirds, which used to hang on the wall in a line.

(One of the cats went missing at around the same time. In my griefstunned state I could never quite remember if I'd let them both out that morning, as usual, or whether one had got left behind. And if he had ... Not a hair remained. His brother, Snowball, grew stout and nervous. We had called them 'the boys', like the original pair we had bought in the early days of our marriage to fill up the emptiness in the flat. Now there was one boy. He mourned, like me.)

I clung to the hopeless phone numbers that never let me through to Sarah. I rang them, often, nevertheless, and doggedly questioned whoever answered. The first time I asked after 'my family', but I could sense the antagonism at the other end, like a knifepoint pressed against my eardrum. I learned I must ask for 'Luke and Sarah Trelawney'.

Mostly the women were noncommittal. Of course they were fine. Of course Luke was well. Happy? 'Of course he is perfectly contented.' I suspect that they took many such calls, from one or other wretched father. After I had phoned I always felt worse.

Then one day I got a familiar soft voice with a strong westcountry tang. I realised it was Briony, the cornblonde girl who had come to the flat, the totally implausible 'Weapons Officer' in whom I'd sensed a certain sympathy for me, a certain reservation about Sarah's manner.

'Is that Briony?' I asked, desperately. 'It's Luke's father. We met. Saul. *Please* can you give me some news of my son. No one will tell me anything.'

There was a long pause. 'Yes,' she said. 'He's fine, and all that.' Another pause. 'But he misses you. Perhaps – have you thought of – You know you can apply to come to see him?'

'I'm banned,' I said. 'You must know that.'

'It's not my department,' she said. 'But there's no formal ban on men. Men are welcome to vote for Wicca ... Some men do support us, you know. We want a better world for everybody –'

I wasn't going to listen to their propaganda. 'I'm not a man, I'm a father. I love my son. Don't you understand? They won't even let me talk to him.'

I heard her breathing. She sounded upset. 'I can't say anything,' she said. 'Sorry.' And then she put the phone down.

It was a Saturday in spring. I was beside myself. I drank four cups of coffee and smoked like a chimney, then opened all the windows and played Wagner very loud, so loudly that I nearly didn't hear the door.

It was Briony with Luke. He fell into my arms, crying 'Daddy, Daddy, Daddy, *Daddy.*' Briony looked pale and apprehensive. 'I've taken a risk doing this,' she said. 'Just half an hour, okay? Then we go.'

She went into the screen room and left us alone. He wore green xylon dungas, the knee-length kind, and was taller, of course, and his hair had grown, curling down almost to his shoulders, and the proportion of his features had changed, or something was different about his face. Did he look somehow more handsome than before? I began to imagine he was wearing lipstick, but of course his lips had always been red. He was kissing me passionately, and I felt confused, his thin bony body was squeezed against mine, loving, needy, like a baby or a woman; but this was my son, my lad, my boy. The tears were running down his cheeks, and I realised they were mine as well.

'Lukey,' I said. 'Lukey, Lukey.'

'Some people call me Lucy,' he said. 'At the Cocoon. It's my new name.'

My heart began to thump with anger, but I swallowed it and asked him quite calmly if he minded.

'First of all I thought it was silly,' he said, 'but now I don't notice. And they don't always do it, anyway. It's because ... I've forgotten what they said. Something about boys being like girls.'

'Your name is *Luke,*' I said. 'You're a *boy.*'

'I know,' he said, as if it was obvious. We hugged again. My heart was still pounding. They were all crazy. The world had gone mad. And what was this 'Cocoon'? Were they turning into insects? 'I did once want to be a girl,' he continued. 'I mean, it's not that horrible, being a girl. Just a bit stupid,' which made me laugh. 'Girls are hopeless at football, and maths.'

It was good to know some things hadn't changed. I was glad Sarah wasn't there to contradict him. 'Do you still play football?'

His face fell. 'Not really. But I still know about it. I'm still good. I watch it on the screens. When they think we're in bed. I practise in my bedroom, nearly every day. I haven't got a ball, but I do the moves.'

Half an hour together. We played a game of Goofball. Sarah never let him play ball inside, but now I let him, now we played, his yellow curls flying through the strips of sunlight, his long shins flashing too pale as he ran, but he was laughing and shrieking, a wonderful sound. He fought with me too, and he was getting stronger, there was a wiry strength in him I'd never felt before. But *Lucy. Lucy!*

Mad evil bitches.

'I'm sorry, but we have to go,' Briony called through from the hall.

She put out her arms to comfort Luke, who stood frozen in his doorway, tense and dejected, and I briefly noticed her wellbuilt muscles, which didn't seem to go with her soft round cheeks.

'Why won't they bloody let me see him?' I hissed, in controlled fury, as they left. 'Don't any of the fathers see their kids?'

'Most of them don't want to.' But she looked uncomfortable. 'Men are sometimes irresponsible. With you, it's more that I believe there was some trouble...'

'With Sarah, you mean? Yes, so what?'

'She's very concerned about male anger.'

She parroted that. I did want to smack her. She wasn't very old, and she knew nothing, and I'd never hurt Sarah, nor my son. 'I've never been violent, if that's what she's saying.'

They were backing away from me down the landing. 'Twelve is an impressionable age ... It's to do with role models, Sarah says.'

'Dad,' said Luke, 'when am I going to see you?'

'You'd better ask your bloody mother,' I said.

Violent? I had never been violent! But as soon as they disappeared into the lift, I nipped back into the flat, got my car coder, and followed. I had to know where my lying wife lived. How else could I launch a firebomb attack on Wicca? It was a tall red building on the Marylebone Road. It burned into my mind like a witch's finger.

Winter lingered into that spring. There were elections in April, and pundits predicted a low turnout because of the cold (yet only five years earlier they were blaming the heat. The fact was, people had lost faith in elections). What was the vote – ten or twelvepercent? Two- percent lower than ever before. Elections of course were already a shadow of what they had been in the twentiethcentury, when the socalled Parliament still played a real role, when there were centralised policeforces, hospitals, schools – but our Speakers still had some importance because of their weekly access to the screens. They could affect people's buypower, and sometimes their opinions.

Wicca World stood in the elections. There must have been money behind them somewhere, because they bought screentime on several channels. Sarah didn't stand as a candidate, but hovered in the background as Mother of the Party. Doubtless her old screen connections helped. She was interviewed several times, very upbeat. We were on the verge of a 'caring revolution' ... Mother of the Party! Ha, I thought. I could tell the world a thing or two about her mothering.

We roared with laughter when one of their campaign films came on at the club. It showed radiant, kindly, softfocus women (I recognised Briony's face among them) dancing in a caring ring, in green fields, around a herd of blonde children. The voiceover spoke about 'revaluing nature', 'nurturing the future'; 'the future is green'. We would 'bloom again' with the 'cooling earth'. We would 'give thanks to the Goddess' for water (some footage of flowing rivers, with laughing women drinking from them), clean air (shots of blue sky, and clouds) and earth (a troop of women digging, with spades, old-fashioned twentiethcentury spades, in rich black earth, among redberried bushes. They looked very cheerful. Had they just buried their husbands?). Then the film came on to that vexed topic, Men. Some men, it seemed, had taken a wrong turning (sinister, repetitive music over shots of bald men in studded leather, bent over banks of flickering screens, blending into shots of other men whooping and yelling with glee as they played on a simulated weapons range – we had one at the club; I was a top scorer – while in a subliminal halfsecond image, two furtive men disappeared round a corner together, and the audience at the Scientists whistled and 'Frohr'ed and catcalled and slapped one another with glee). But Wicca were at pains to say not all men were bad. Men were basically loving (now 'L'après-midi d'un faune' rose tenderly over a shot of Michelangelo's *David,* his penis looking smaller and milder than usual, and another shot of Jesus, surrounded by children, with big kind eyes and flowing hair). Men had a part to play in Wicca too! If we voted for Wicca we voted for a future where contradictions could be reconciled, where hatred could be turned into love, Outsiders (who had votes) could be Insiders (shots of laughing actors playing Outsiders, not dirty and thin, as the real ones were, but brown and happy – thanks to Wicca? – being greeted and embraced on a fat woman's doorstep); where the old could be young, the ill well, black white ... The film returned to its opening shots, the ring of smiling, sunlit women, then panned out to show, all across the meadow, a motley collection of contented people representing every possible voting interest, many of them men, waving to the women (waving their children goodbye, I thought), showing support for the triumphant climax, as chords surged up under that throbbing, urgent, thrilling voice, which I suspected was Juno's, saying 'Vote for Wicca. Wicca Cares' To my horror I realised what the music was. It was 'Nessun Dorma'. Was that Sarah's idea? Had she given away our special music?

Apart from that final act of treachery, I really enjoyed it. It was *gross.* We adored it. Someone pressed the 'Recall', and we watched it again. Only madwomen, we thought, would vote for them.

On Election Day, the *Greek Sheet*'s early headline sneered 'Votes for Wimmin!' over photographs of women queuing to vote. The other parties were the usual crew, venal, arid, selfserving, hopeless. The Liblabs had amalgamated with the Conservers. There was no one to vote for.

Men abstained in droves. We waited for the same grey frauds to be returned.

Something dreadful, mad, unspeakable happened.

The results came in. *Wicca World had won.* I couldn't believe it, but the figures were there. We thought they were a joke, but they had won the election. 'Wacky Witches Win!' shrieked the *Greek Sheet*'s final issue. We weren't quite so clever as we thought.

Sarah was interviewed, looking tired and haggard but flushed with triumph under the lights, gabbling about nurturing nature, and I thought I spotted just a smidgin of panic, as if she hadn't really expected this.

The postmortem told us the turnout was abysmal, ten or twelve-percent, I can no longer remember, threequarters of that female, with women voting overwhelmingly for Wicca. This seemed to me barely believable. I was sure there were still many sensible women who would never have fallen for Wicca's tosh ... Would they? The pundits said women wanted a change. Wicca 'spoke to women's spiritual needs'. They were 'sick of arid materialism'. Yet to me they'd always seemed so practical, noticing that a floor needed cleaning, wiping surfaces, remembering bills, sending birthday presents, flushing loos, knowing from a baby's congested face what type of thing had just leaked from its bottom ... And they enjoyed it, surely. It was what women liked.

Or had men got it all wrong again?

In any case, now we were going to be punished. We were frightened, actually, as well as incredulous, because the Speakers still had some degree of power.

A succession of men went on screen to suggest a campaign of male civil disobedience, withholding communications tax or Comtax (our last remaining tax, which subsidised the net, Leamonline, Speakers' Hour and ScreenRecycle) on the grounds that we had no Speaker representation. But Wicca said they spoke for all, for woman in man and man in woman, the goddess in god and god in the goddess, which wasn't an easy line to argue with. Men held mass switch-offs during Speakers' Hour and swamped Wicca's phone lines with angry phone calls, but the only serious effect of the campaign was the deficit to Comtax. The Witches had announced their intention to raise it by twentyfivepercent, to fund more nursery schools ('Catch 'em Young!', the *Greek Sheet* roared. 'Witches Snatch Our Babies'). But the men refused to pay *en masse,* and as one man remarked of the increases, there were hardly any babies for the witches to school.

And that was at the root of all that happened, of course. That's why men and women hated each other.

The kids had been the glue that held us together. When babies stopped coming, the men got the blame. The women felt thwarted, and abandoned us. And so we moved further and further apart, and turned into parodies of ourselves – the shavenheaded, giggling, machineloving men, the shorthaired, shortfused, furious women, shriving themselves with nature worship.

They didn't want us. We were no good. And we believed them, deep inside.

The women seemed to hate my whole sex, which was hard. The things that made my body a man's, my balls, my penis, my male voice – my size, my sweat, my manliness. The things that had denied them what they craved. And I think they began to hate their sons, the few there were, the weakling boys. They called Luke 'Lucy' ... godforgive them.

I couldn't forgive her that for years.

After the elections, we expected summer, but there was a curious patch of real cold. The summer scanties were in the shops, but people were walking around in coats, some of them heirlooms, twentieth-century furs that hadn't been out of the cupboard for decades, and laughingly showing off the goosepimples they were feeling now for the first time. People began to wish for summer as they must have done in my parents' childhood. We thought it was a little freak, of course, a byblow of the general miraculous cooling that had come to save us from global heat death. And spring did eventually arrive, at roughly the time when summer should have done, and then it got hot, as it always did, and we all forgot it had ever been different.

It was July or August. I had stayed late at work. I was involved in a project to design a mouthwash which was a solution of minute nanomachines, each of which would clean and polish the teeth as it fed off the plaque and gunge on the surface. It would make normal toothbrushing obsolete, and might even make me rather rich if I were lucky enough to scoop that year's 'Hundredpercent Prize', a hundredpecent bonus on salary awarded for 'significant innovation'. I suppose there wasn't that much 'significance' in freeing us from one of our last bits of labour, but I had been told I was in line for the prize. Perhaps they meant, 'makes a significant profit', which this certainly would, if I could crack a few problems. I was having trouble dealing with the chemists who were supposed to be coming up with the flavour, and I'd started to wonder, not entirely idly, if they were being nobbled by toothbrush manufacturers. That evening I was frustrated, or bored ... so I started browsing, which I usually made a big effort not to do, in the lab.

Quite soon I glimpsed the title of what looked like a fairly routine scientific paper, dated that day, 'Development Phases of Climatic Change', and thought 'Why not?' So I started to read it. Two pages in, my heart began to race.

It was a study of the rate at which ice ages came, based on fossil evidence of bands of vegetation, the speeds at which deciduous trees liking warmth were replaced by coldloving conifers, for instance. I had always assumed – hadn't everyone? – that ice ages took hundreds of years to get established.

But the new paper had resurrected an eccentric study from the last century which said it took only *two decades* to move from temperate to permafrost. They had rerun all the data, meaning to disprove it, and found the original conclusions held. So they took new measurements of fossilised pollen all over Europe. The findings were clear. *Twenty years,* that was all it took. Twenty years to slide into an ice age. Two decades. The blink of an eyelid.

I had a sudden feeling that I knew what was happening, I knew what was coming, had foreseen it all, had lived it already as my own heart chilled, as our happiness darkened and began to freeze over.

It got into the news a few days later. 'New Ice Age?', headline after headline enquired. For a few days the screens talked of nothing else.

The sensation would certainly have lasted longer if something hadn't driven it off the news.

One evening I was sitting in front of the screen, feeling relatively happy, since it was Friday. I had done my work and had a pint of beer, eating chicken and halflistening to the news. It was a chicken breast, oval and pink, and I was just thinking that it looked like a face when a voice that had been weaving through my head and somehow becoming confused with the chicken breast suddenly said, quite clearly, 'Tonight the manufacturers categorically denied that a Dove could feed off a living face. A spokesman for the company pointed out that Doves had long been especially valued for their excellent safety record with children. Meanwhile the baby is in intensive care and we await developments. Tonight women picketed ...' Et cetera, et cetera.

Dora was watching the news with me, her large blue eyes flicking from side to side in a parody of animation. Just when it got to the climax of the story – we saw the child who had been attacked, a sturdy blonde baby with crewcut hair, then an 'after' picture, a disc of bloody mess, a featureless horror in a tangle of tubes – Dora chuckled, with her 'random' chuckle, and turned to me, as she often did, and said 'That's funny. I feel happy'. I threw the rest of my chicken away and didn't talk to Dora for the rest of the evening.

I somehow knew at once it was true. I remembered the flayed ground, the vanished cat.

The suspected Dove was a replicant. A thirdgeneration replicant. The screen showed us a picture; it looked innocent, as usual, they'd designed the things to look innocent. Next the manufacturer was brought on, sweating lavishly in a crumpled suit. The presenter asked him questions relating to the model of Dove that had just been shown. Then the manufacturer confessed this wasn't *actually* the Dove that had halfeaten the baby.

'Why not?' the screentalker enquired.

'Because it, ah, cannot be found.'

'Do you mean it has escaped?' The screentalker squeaked. She was a hysterical woman in a wig.

'Doves can hardly *escape,* Miss,' said the manufacturer. 'Gone missing, perhaps. We shall soon find it.'

Dora did her random chuckle again. This time at least she didn't speak, but I took her away into the spare room and left her for the night in outer darkness.

The next few weeks were very fraught. The screens didn't know what to put first, a sudden flood of stories, only some of them authentic, about Doves eating sleeping cats, or a line of sombre, selfimportant scientists wanting to tell us about the new Ice Age. The Speakers came on and tried to calm us, those hideous dykes with their insincere voices, trying to show they weren't panicking, trying to sound in control, and calm.

The men all rallied behind their Doves. Even I did, at first. It was clearly a fluke. The Dove in question had a programming error. We were the machinemen, the Scientists, the Greeks, and the women were trying to take away our machines, our sturdy blue babies with their lowpitched voices and sensitive feathers, the Doves who loved us. I went to the club and raged with my friends and we played with our robots and pined for our kids, and half of us secretly blamed the mothers for not protecting the children they'd stolen.

The fuss died down. It was September now. I settled back into my intimacy with Dora. The screens forgot the savaged baby, forgot the Ice Age, forgot all the horrors to concentrate on the big Tunnelrun that took place every autumn.

I loved the tunnelruns. Everybody bet on them. I bet five thousand on the Russian team. On the big day, I went to the Gay Scientists to watch the race and drink beer with my friends.

Halfway through the race we were shrieking with laughter at an unfortunate Frenchman who waggled his bottom, when they interrupted the programme with a news flash. A Dove in Scotland had torn off the leg of a newborn baby in front of its mother. They switched off just in time to save the baby's life. Wicca World had at once demanded that production of Doves be halted, and all existing models destroyed.

'Was it a thirdgeneration replicant again?' I asked, but everyone was staring at the screen. It was only later that my guess was confirmed. I began to realise that the Doves were mutating.

Back at home, a refrain began in my mind; human error, human error. Mistakes had been made. We must do something. *Human error, human error.*

I was fond of Dora, I said sorry to her, I stroked her soft panels and apologised, but I took out her replicator module, intact. I felt awful, abusive, like a fake gynaecologist, plunging my hand into her cold inner parts, but I persisted, I dragged it out.

And then I broke it up with a hammer in case I should ever be tempted to replace it.

I was thinking of Luke; his long fragile limbs. And Luke as a baby, lying kicking in the sunlight.

If my feelings for Dora changed after that, if some weird deep tenderness was lost, was it because she could no longer reproduce? Did I see her as menopast, like Sarah?

11

Shuddering, gasping with the morning cold that gnaws my lips as I come up for air, driving myself to the jagged window to chip off some ice for a morning drink, I cackle to think how at first we panicked because there was a touch of frost. How we giggled and shrieked at the white on the trees, how we worried when the first cold fogs came drifting in between the towers and fretted at the shortage of blankets and duvets, how the commentators all wrote grave pieces when no one swam in the sea on Christmas Day after doctors advised of risks to the heart.

And the comedy of the heating equipment. No one was making it at the time. A sudden outburst of activity followed, the screens were flooded with advertisements, the new firms were overwhelmed with orders. But so many of these instant systems were rubbish that 'Heating salesman!' became an insult equivalent to 'Thief' or 'Liar'.

Two decades, the paper on the net had said. Our orbit round the sun had lengthened very slightly. Just a small amount further away, and the sun looked just the same size in the sky ...

Twenty years seemed like quite a long time at first. To organise ourselves. To prepare for the ice. The government assured us that scientists would come up with something to prevent it in that time, but scientists themselves were less encouraging. Their ideas required cooperation between international governments that hardly existed, funds they didn't have – If they did, they might be able to increase the amount of sunlight. They could do it by putting giant mirrors into orbit round the earth, or by seeding the icecaps with black material to reduce their reflectiveness, their 'albedo', a word we suddenly got used to hearing, and it always reminded me of my son, the forbidden word which came into my mind when I first saw his tiny white streaks of hair, *albino, albino,* my baby son ... There was no money for science, or support, or time.

Wicca were in an awkward position, having set their face against techfixes. So instead they asked people 'not to overreact' – but how could we overreact to an ice age? They reminded us there had been climate fluctuations in the past that had not resulted in an ice age. Then they pointed out that human beings had survived the last ice age. They harked back to the wars of the last century, and reminded us how people had stuck together – and yet they had done their best to divide us. They asked for patience; donations; calm. They suggested that we needed a mammoth new tax to give 'communal support' in the face of the ice – which they also assured us would not be coming. Two decades, they said, was plenty of time, and yet the Speakers were talking too fast. And Sarah herself had gone very low profile, which suggested she wasn't happy with all this.

I realised quite soon that we didn't have two decades. The original paper had been measuring time from the first slight cooling to maximum cold. But the process was already well advanced. I remembered the steamy, sticky evening in the little room where we had lived first, before Luke was born, before we quarrelled, that normalseeming evening when I found the first queer report of the icesheets thickening, and mentioned it to Sarah, and she didn't understand – how could should she have done? I didn't myself. We had so many other things on our minds, we were sweet young lovers, trying to make babies –

Blindly, blindly through life's night. Missing the landmarks. Missing the stars.

Now at last I see the importance of the stars, as the sun climbs up with that effortless strength above our wasted black horizon. Burning bright, unbearable. Its massive power, so far away, shooting across a million kilometres of icy space to touch my fingers, so early in the morning that I can't feel the warmth, but I watch two fingertips slowly change from frozen yellow to pinkish grey, under the black arcs of my fingernails.

We took the sun for granted, when it was too hot. We began to resent it, it crowded us, but now the ice is all around I start to see it as our god, the blazing face behind the names, God the Father, Buddha, Jesus ... Wasn't it the heat of the sun that made us? Gave us life? Gave us breath?

And then a distance came between us.

*

In fact, we were almost halfway towards the ice by the time the public kerfuffle started. I think it was 2056. Halfway through the century, as well. I was halfway through my life, at fiftyone, yet I began to feel as though it were over. I'd lost my wife, I'd lost my family, and now we were losing all the things we were used to, so familiar we hardly noticed them, hot summer nights, orchids, fruit trees ...

Actually my life had hardly started. I wish I had known that at the time.

The little peach tree on our balcony frosted. I took it in, but it was too late.

Too late to do so many things that we suddenly realised ought to be done. Ever since the state had withered away, nearly fifty years ago at the turn of the century, we'd depended on private contracts for services, some individual – hospitals, learning centres – others bought *en bloc* through our district councils – waste disposal, electricity, gas. Most luxury developments had costlier contracts providing a higher level of service, like London's Northwest Enclaves, for example, where the elite once liked to live –

(It used to look wonderful in spring. Pink villas floating on a sea of pale blossom, and the guards in shirts with goldbraided epaulettes. Children were allowed to play in the streets. It's gutted now, blackened, wrecked.)

Our lives – the lives of the people in work, the people in houses, the Insiders – were a muddle of layered networks of contracts, half of which no longer functioned, since firms were always going out of business. (In a sense life is so much simpler now. Harsher, bloodier, but simpler.) And then there were the homeless – Outsiders, Wanderers, the urban homeless and their rural cousins, who had no contracts, no services, depending on each other, mostly, making their own piecemeal arrangements. Our society was an amorphous pyramid, with the Speakers perched precariously on top, then the relatively successful people, who had jobs and houses and educations and elected the Speakers and contributed to Comtax and paid their district council to keep order. Underneath them were the Outsiders and Wanderers, a great stirring, floating base of people with nothing. The Speakers pretended to address everybody on their weekly show, inserting carefully respectful references to 'fluid lifestyles' to placate the Wanderers, but in fact, what did they have to say to us? For decades politicians had been figureheads, with no money to spend and few legislative powers other than a veto on Euro laws. They vetoed most of them on principle, and Euro didn't care. We were slowly dropping off it, like a tiedoff limb as the blood supply withered.

Now suddenly we needed leaders. We needed something to hold us together. We needed people to take decisions. We needed someone like Winston Churchill, that great British leader from the last century. But all we had got was Wicca World. We needed somebody to save us from the ice. To save everyone from the same disaster, after years of lip service to 'different needs'. We needed decisions about energy, we needed spending on climate studies, we needed decisions about food management, heat conservation, public order ... We needed decisions about healthcare. Who would care for the Outsiders? They had no homes, they would get sick first, with nothing to protect them from the cold. If they got sick, we would be infected. Or perhaps they would want to take *our* homes. We started to realise uneasily that maybe we might need a centralised policeforce. Maybe we would need an army.

We began to see that life would get rough. Fear began to push people together. And fear began to tear people apart.

Fear is also a source of power, and Wicca World exploited it. Because people were afraid of the Doves as well, and that was more immediate, more direct than their misty, epic fear of the ice. And so Wicca ranted against the Doves. More incidents were being reported all the time of what the screens began to call 'grazing' – attacks on living things by Doves, all of them third-or fourthgeneration replicants. Wicca made sure that weeping mothers appeared on the screens with them when they spoke, which helped rally public opinion behind them. I remember one child whose sleeping cat had been eaten, roundfaced, snubnosed, with ginger hair and blue eyes like saucers that filled with tears when she remembered little Tiggs. Marilyn was a propaganda triumph. After she had finished the Speakers came on to promise us that they would 'save us from the Doves', shield our children from 'robot perverts'.

So babyeating robots were a Bad Thing? Well, no one was going to disagree with that. It was all so much simpler than dealing with the ice, and the ice kept coming, slowly, faster; villages in Norway were cut off by the snow, settlements began to be abandoned. A team of scientists taking measurements in the Arctic lost radio contact and disappeared.

Wicca had no statutory powers to make laws, but they could petition the Eurocourt or instruct our own courts to appoint a commission. They announced they were drafting legislation applying to all future robot manufacture. No robot could be fuelled by organic matter or attempt problemsolving through random mutation. But the legal process was very slow. Direct action was easier.

Juno herself appeared on screen, looking heavier, firmer, sadder than before, speaking with the voice of an immensely wise mother (though I happened to know she had never been a mother), and told us that we had a choice to make, between human children and the Doves who were 'stealing the babies and corrupting the fathers'. She cited the 'disgusting' Sexbots as evidence, though they hadn't caught on with the public at all, since their orifices weren't that pleasurable or comfortable or even readily cleanable – (How do I know that? No, truly, I only know because the lads had told me. We talked about every kind of mobot at the club, and maybe some of those men were 'perverted', but that can be a name for loneliness.) I'm afraid I still thought the name 'Sexbots' amusing, particularly when Juno pronounced it with a particularly scornful intonation, looking down her nose like a cow with a cold and spitting out the S's like manure-covered straw ... but the women of Britain were not amused.

The women of Britain rose to Juno's call. They picketed the factories. A fight broke out somewhere in Leicester when the women managed to drag a consignment of Doves off a lorry, and 'tore them limb from limb', as the news put it. In Scotland a fire that started in a Dove showroom and swept through a poor tenement, killing hundreds of people, was suspected to be arson. All over the country windows were broken, salespeople attacked, offices letterbombed, though Wicca World, of course, 'deplored these excesses'. They said they deplored them, but mysteriously active in many of these incidents were the girl gangs who had attached themselves to Wicca, the 'Green Girls', with their greendyed hair and green glass studs in their ears and noses. The Green Girls were very violent.

People became afraid to go out with Doves visible in the back seat after a car was stopped and burnt to a shell with two male passengers and their Dove inside. Sales of Doves plummeted, despite the manufacturers buying endless airtime to reassure the public that the 'problems' with replicants had been 'ironed out'. They added on a 'selfdestruct' programme so replication would only happen once, thus limiting mutation. It didn't help; the market collapsed.

Men weren't rushing out to buy Doves either. Men aren't insensible to pain, the pain of babies, cats, parents ... The faces at the Scientists were grim after each fresh report of a grazing incident. But the men felt more divided, because they really loved their Doves. Dove ownership ran at an amazing sixtypercent of the male population of Britain, which when you consider that at least a third of the population was homeless and without buypower, meant a hundredpercent of the male market.

The Doves weren't a luxury to men, you see. The Doves supplied us with something we lacked. The men who sat talking about their Doves or drove them to the club to show them off had a jaunty, cheerful obsessiveness, a competitive glint, like – what were they like? – Proud fathers, that's the only description. They sat in noisy circles, laughing, shouting, swopping anecdotes about their Doves' achievements. And at home the Doves answered other needs. They were our pets, our kids – our wives. Their docility, their friendliness, the way they served us and seemed to like us, the way they quietly accepted love, whereas women had rejected us –

Not all, of course, I am sure not all. There must have been couples and families who survived, as Sarah and I had once survived the yawning gulf between men and women, and I naively thought it would last, if I gave her leeway, yielded, accepted.

Maybe I don't remember it right. Occasionally she would ring me up, ask how I was, then when I told her – I suppose I sounded discontented – she'd say I was angry, crazy, violent. She said I'd been jealous and unreasonable, rejected her ideas, failed to respect her. She said that I never helped in the house (but I helped with Luke. Didn't that count?). She said she'd never seen me with a broom or duster, and if I cooked, I made the kitchen disgusting (which may have been true, but was surely no problem, with all the machines on the market to help her). She said too much. I couldn't bear to listen.

Till finally she said she must have a divorce. It settled between us, a block of black ice.

*

She sent me a letter, she put it in writing, the solicitor's messenger came to the door and I knew it meant trouble as soon as I saw him. I read all the things she had to say. Maybe there was some truth in them. But then she dared to say I was an unfit parent, and it hurt so much that I had to reply. I went to a solicitor the very same day and gave him instructions to say it all back.

– I didn't really believe what I said. Or maybe I did, but I don't any more.

We had lain on the bed with Luke curled between us, his long white body flushed with fever, and I'd sponged his body all night long with a cool flannel while she kissed and stroked him, loving our son, caring for him. She was his mother. She loved our son.

And yet we called each other unfit parents.

The tie was broken. We savaged each other.

(She'd left me. Why did she have to divorce me?)

I fired off my letter, then felt dreadful. I didn't go in to work that day. I went to the club and talked to my friends. I took a few buzzers to raise my spirits, but they didn't rise. Then I started drinking. I knew that the lads would listen to me. There was a familiar way of talking, where men sat in small disgruntled groups, waving their hands, nodding their heads, vying with each other to tell their tales. They were almost always about women, and the bitterest stories involved children. At first I had felt superior to this, suspecting them of lying and exaggeration, but now I was one of them, the moaners, the loners, the men who felt women had soured the world.

So I told my story, unwillingly at first, then fuelling up with self-righteous anger, and Rob and Rajeet and Jonah and David all said how appalling Sarah had been. I asked them if they thought me unreasonable, and they told me I was too soft on her. They knew she was a power in Wicca World, and started to blame her for its worst excesses, for hating men, for stealing children, for dressing little boys in skirts ... I started to feel uncomfortable; this wasn't making things any better, for they didn't know her, the real Sarah, the girl she had been when we first met – *No one but me ever really knew Sarah.*

The boys raged on, while I grew quieter. I didn't want them to insult her. In the end I drifted away from their table and went to another further down the room – taking in a few more beers on the way, I admit that I took in a few more beers – where halfadozen men sat around a screen.

Billy and Timmy and Richard and Nimit and Ian. I wasn't surprised to find they were watching something about the campaign against the Doves. They were among the most passionate Dovelovers, and two of their Doves were perched on the tabletop, talking at cross-purposes to each other, which would usually have had everyone howling with laughter, but no one was taking any notice of them –

Because for a second time, it seemed, the women were trying to steal what we loved. A draft of the proposed new laws about Doves had been leaked by the courts that afternoon. The women had extended the draft legislation far beyond what we had expected. All existing Doves were to be registered and licensed, Dove ownership limited to one per household, all replicants beyond the first generation destroyed (though there'd been no problems with the second generation), a general ban on sales of Replicators, compulsory removal of replicator modules on existing models, immediate destruction of any Dove found to have taken part in 'unstructured eating', defined as any act of ingestion taking place outside human control and without use of the eating mat ... It was draconian. It went on and on. We watched the screen with increasing indignation.

'They are *mean bitches*,' Nimit said.

'It's grotesque,' said Ian. 'Unworkable. We'll never let them do it. We'll defend our Doves. They depend on us.'

'One per household! How dare they say that.' That was Billy, who had a little fleet of halfadozen Doves, plump, pale Billy with his gentle myopic eyes, a man who never went out of the house by daylight but lived happily indoors with his robot family. 'I love my boys. I won't let them take them.'

'I agree it's way over the top,' I said. 'But we do have to do something, don't we? They were mutating. They still are. What about the ones that have disappeared?' This was another factor in Dove hysteria, the number of Doves who had gone missing. They were all selfstarting replicators, and none of their owners had any explanation. There were probably not more than two or three dozen confirmed cases, hut we all suspected not all losses were reported, for fear of a security hunt to kill.

'Good for them if they have,' said Richard. 'They have as much right to live as those bitches.'

Round the table, several shaved heads were nodding. I thought yet again how dull it was when everyone looked and thought the same. We wore a uniform – bluestubbled heads, lycra vests and calf-length leggings, black cotton jackets with a logo of a Dove and often an 'add-on' artificial fur lining, transparent boots that showed off the toenails, which many men kept brightly painted. (But women, who of course never came here, wore an offputting uniform of short hair and shrouds, long featureless garments, sexless sacks above which their heads looked small and hard. They seemed to be determined we should never see their bodies.) We men went in for desperate display, saying, *Look at our bodies, our buttocks, our cocks, the shape of our balls. You may not love us but you can't unmake us.'* I myself wasn't quite the norm, with my longish curls and my wedding ring, yet wasn't I one of them, socially, even sexually? For Paul was now more than a charming catamite once or twice a year when I was desperate. He was a friend and confidant, he gave me affection, he mattered to me, and I even caught myself feeling jealous when he went into the massage room with someone else. Still, I didn't believe all women were bitches.

'It's just that women and babies are, well – human,' I said, uncertainly. 'They're – natural.' (Goodgod, I was stealing Sarah's word, the one I had so often disagreed with, but it seemed to be the only one that would do.) 'I couldn't put a Dove's life before a human's.' And yet I loved Dora, in a way.

'Women aren't human,' Richard said, and everyone laughed, but I did not.

'So what should we do about the Doves?' I asked.

'No, what should we do about the *women?*' asked Richard. He was slowly getting annoyed with me. 'I'm never going to stop my Doves reproducing. It's a human right – well, it's a right.' He reddened. 'It is a right, to reproduce.'

Yet none of these men could reproduce, because they had no women to carry their babies. And probably our sperm was useless.

I thought of telling them that I had already removed Dora's replicator module, but I realised that they would never understand, they would see it as an act of terrible betrayal. I looked round the table. It was chilly in the club, since the heating system they had first installed had been quickly overtaken by the progress of the cold, but everyone around it had bare brawny arms; a dozen male biceps and six male vests that clung to the curves of six male chests. I thought, *I must get out of here.*

'I see things differently,' is all I said. Perhaps I should have mentioned my devotion to Dora.

'You've been listening to your wife,' said Richard, angrily. And then, indistinctly, into his beer, partly through cowardice and partly through drink, 'Bloody Queen of the Witches herself.' A ripple of laughter ran round the table.

Why did I lose my temper so completely, when I hated Wicca World myself, their crackpot ideas, their lying screen faces, the way they had stolen my son from me? Why did I fight for my wife's honour when she had just told me she was going to divorce me? Whatever the reason, I was suddenly halfway across the table, and both Doves toppled, wailing nasally, their calls of alarm like minisirens, and then I was on top of Richard, crashing my fist into his nose, his chin, his mouth, his teeth, his tongue, and something gave as I punched his face. It was wet, and beer glasses were flying, and plates were crashing to the floor, but I punched his disgusting face again, I knew how to hit, I had boxed as a boy, and gouts of something were hanging off him, snot, and blood, and a tooth on a red string, a little dripping string of flesh (*I hated our bodies, they were stupid and useless*), I wanted to smash him into the ground, and everyone was shouting and pulling at me.

Perhaps I had taken too many buzzers, which didn't always go well with beer. Perhaps Sarah's letter had turned my brain. It took a dozen men to pull me off him, and someone was yelling that his nose was broken and asking which hospital his contract was with.

It was all entirely shaming, later, but at the time I felt nothing but hatred, for the club with its banks of gleaming computers and the gleaming hairless bodies of the guys, for Richard and Nimit and Ian and Riswan and Billy and Timmy and even Paul … Though Paul brought me home in a taxi that night, tenderly wiping a cut on my forehead, delicately picking broken glass from my hair, keeping a protective arm round my shoulder, and came to the door, and wanted to come in, wanted me to want him to come in, I thanked him brusquely and sent him away.

That's what happens, you see, when you lose too much, when too many things all go at once. It happened to me; I had a kind of breakdown, and all over the world things were breaking down, cracking under too many new strains, like hot water pipes in a sudden frost. A hot water pipe! Such a simple thing, one of the million things that we all took for granted, but the world cooled down and everything changed, metal piping soon became something to loot, something to cannibalise, something to fight with, something worth killing or dying for. Not that that means a lot, any more. Hardly a day without a death.

I must watch my back. Good job I'm in trim.

Days draw down to the final battle.

The divorce dragged on. My letters weren't answered, the letters and cards I sent to Luke. I tried not to go into his room. The jumble of toys and tools on his table, the map of the world, the photographs ... One of them was of the three of us, Luke in a red baseball cap, swinging from our shoulders, one arm round each of us, kicking up his feet in baseball boots, and he looked surprisingly sturdy, boyish, not the delicate, gentle boy he was, and Sarah and I both looked happy and proud, our eyes meeting over his head. It was in her second period of longish hair, before she adapted the Wicca crewcut. Her red hair swung in a bob in the sun ... I tried not to look at that photo too often. It was interesting, though, that Luke had liked it and chosen to stick it in pride of place, a photo of a regular, boyish boy. That comforted me, when I thought of the witches.

It was silly, but I brooded about his football. I was never one of those sportsmad fathers, pushing their kids to be great jocks, but when he was at home we used to practise every Sunday, and he had a marvellous eye for the ball. Now he couldn't even watch it onscreen. Wicca weren't keen on anything with balls.

I believed that Luke was still in London, still in whatever lay behind the narrow red frontage of Wicca World's headquarters. It was a tall, slightly grimy nineteenthcentury building with complicated swags of brickred sandstone, rising on the north of the Marylebone Road to a series of sunlit mansard windows. I always imagined a flash of Luke's face, high up in the attics, when I drove past, which I did too often, a hundred times maybe, and always that stupid lift of the heart as I saw the bright windows like living eyes, surely one day he would look out and see me ... Always the blank depression and loss as the traffic swept onwards, time carried me past, and he was inside, changing, growing.

Unbelievably, his birthday came round again. I hadn't seen him for nearly a year. I rang every week, but never again got the soft country tones of Briony Barnes. He would be thirteen. His voice might be breaking ... I hoped his mother understood something, anything at all, about adolescent boys. I hoped Wicca didn't hate them too much. I was smoking like a chimney. I lost weight.

On his actual birthday I rang nine times. It was bitterly cold; it had rained, then frozen. Lucky for them that the traffic swept past in a single snake at two hundred kilometres per hour, lucky that I could only fantasise about crashing my car through their front door with a splintering of wood and screaming women. I drove past mouthing 'Happy birthday, Luke', but I couldn't brake, the road was black glass – I went to bed frantic with rage and frustration.

The creaking ice crawled on towards us. Wicca World decided to evacuate the Hebrides after the supply ships couldn't get through for three months. Great bulwarks of ice crashed straight through the hull of a cruiser bringing wouldbe immigrants from Sweden, sinking it rapidly, with all hands lost, though a fisherman too far away to help described seeing three tall pale figures being carried away on the blue ice floe, floating back north, waving frantically. There had been reports from Hebrideans that some elderly islanders were freezing to death, while others were bringing their cattle or horses into the house and sleeping with them in a desperate attempt to keep warm. However, Wicca World's directive to evacuate was ignored by all but a few young people who were working on the islands on a temporary basis, and they left gratefully enough, spared the trouble of paying their passage. Wicca World got maximum publicity for this, as evidence of their 'Dynamic Caring', the slogan on whose back they hoped they were going to win the next election.

But they couldn't keep up with a tenth of what was happening. Lochs on the mainland began to freeze over, rivers stopped flowing, food crops failed, orchards whitened and weakened with frost, cars wouldn't start, there were endless power cuts from grids that couldn't cope with the surge in demand, deliverymen died in exposed country places, and there was a spate of suffocations in cities among people who had overinsulated their houses.

Yet the pace of change stayed fairly constant. It was getting colder at a rate of one or two degrees a year, but there were still occasional days of brilliant sunshine and balmy warmth, days when we could take our coats off and stand in our shirtsleeves and stare at blue sky. Because certain preparations for the ice were in hand, farmers receiving huge Euro subsidies to switch their crops to frostresistant kinds, computers built to withstand low temperatures, gardeners showing new kinds of plants on the screens – we started to see this as the new pattern, and our basic optimism resurfaced.

Yes, I suppose we became slightly complacent, if a state of controlled panic can ever be complacent.

And then the Indonesian volcano exploded, the one which had been sputtering for over fifty years but had last blown its top in the sixteenthcentury. It threw thousands of tons of volcanic rock and mud and ash up into the air. The world took little notice at first, because everyone had so many worries of their own, so Sumatra got very little international aid, though half its population stifled or starved.

But the world was shortsighted to ignore the eruption as of purely local interest. They soon found they had to be interested – they soon found out they had to be afraid. Because darkness crept across the globe from the thousands of tons of dust and mud. Sumatra rained in millions of pieces upon all the countries who'd refused to help it. There was no spring at all that year in Britain. The temperatures dropped, then dropped again, and the constant grey light was a weight upon the spirit, dull grey light and sharp grey cold. Juno looked tired, grey and tired, and the polls were running more heavily against them. The words of the Speakers seemed thick and slow, as if the cold had reached their brains. Biologists began to talk about extinctions.

The Hebridean islanders were sticking to their homes, but elsewhere in the world people felt less rooted. A great movement of human beings began, from north to south, from the poles to the equator, slowly at first, like the first leaves falling, then more and more, like an autumn storm, like the sky darkening into winter, and the noise was of thousands of running feet, panicking voices, massed birds wheeling –

I sat in our flat like a man of stone and felt the world turning faster and faster. It was true, yes, it was definitely happening, but all of it seemed remote, unreal, I watched them on the screen, great swirls of black ants, crowding the airports, overloading the boats ... They were real people, though they looked like insects, but I wasn't one of them. I was a ghost.

I sat with Dora and watched the screens, and sometimes I stroked her and ruffled her feathers, and sometimes I think I may have been crying, and if her sensors picked it up she would turn towards me, or not quite towards me, for some of their controls were one or two-percent off true, and whisper sweetly to my left shoulder, 'What's the matter, Saul? I'm sorry. Is there anything I can do for you?' But Dora had done all the things she could do.

Perhaps I was what they call depressed. It had never happened to me before, despite Sarah's glib label of 'manic depressive'. It reminded me of something about my dad, that he might have been depressed as well, that sometimes he could not talk to us, that he went out to the pigeons and stayed for hours, just sat and watched them, pecking at the dark. And my mother often said, after the painful day when she told me he was halfGhanaian, 'He's thinking about his father, Saul.' By which I understood her to mean 'about Africa', about being black, that whole lost side of himself, for I never remember him having black friends, nor seeing black family, except one sister, and she was married to a white man ... Perhaps because of his job with the police, who had twentiethcentury prejudices about race, he had simply left that part of himself behind, and I think it sometimes came looking for him, like everything we try too hard to lose.

I know my father was on my mind as I sat and listened with half my mind to an item about Africa on the screens. When I heard 'Ghana' I started listening properly. The pictures they were showing reminded me of something. People fighting to get past a barrier, uniformed soldiers holding them back. The soldiers were black, the people were white. The white people looked desperate, the soldiers bored. Bored and amused and slightly contemptuous. What did it remind me of? Something from the past that upset and disturbed me –

Then I remembered. When I was little, the scenes on the screen that had scared me to death, showing hordes of black people pouring into Britain, coming to take away all we had, with the brave white soldiers holding them back. Only this time, it was all happening in reverse, the negative image of the longforgotten photo. This time the desperate people were white. This time the people with the power were black.

And a long-lost part of me started to laugh: it was *my* turn now. *Our* turn now! *Black man's turn!* – Yet I wasn't a black man.

The report made it clear it had been happening for months, maybe as much as a year. In my strange, suspended state I had taken nothing in.

Each African country was doing things differently, though all were overwhelmed with requests for asylum. Ghana was intending to close its borders 'within six months' to those 'special cases' allowed to immigrate because they had Ghanaian blood. The Cameroons, by contrast, had set no time limit. Sierra Leone would accept no one with any admixture of European blood.

A phrase recurred; the 'ice people'. 'We cannot take in all these ice people ...' 'The ice people are coming here in ever greater numbers ...' 'a growing concern that we shall be swamped ...' 'thousands, maybe millions of ice people ...' *Ice people, ice people ...*

So now Europeans were ice people – perhaps we had always been ice people. (*Yet I wasn't one of them, was I?* That longlost part of me snickered, jeered. *Black man's turn! Serve them right!*)

The rest of the report drifted over me, but I looked with wonder at the pictures on the screen of African scenery drenched in sunlight, a wildebeest quivering behind a thorntree, the canopy of velvety mixed greens in the forest, the bougainvillea, luscious, grape red, and a group of chattering barechested children, sitting in the dust playing music on pipes – goodgod, it was still truly hot in Africa. It might be the last place the ice would come. Indeed where the ice might never come, for previous ice ages stopped short of the equator ...

I began to think, idly, *I could go there.* Halfheartedly, because I'd never gone back, had never wanted it enough, till I was suddenly forty, and it seemed too late. But a buried wish began to stir. *Though no one suspects it, I have black blood, I could just walk in and claim my kingdom* ... 'Look, Dora,' I said, and turned her to the screen. 'That's Africa. We could go there.'

'Is it a tree?' she asked hopefully, which made me laugh, because she had gone into 'Recognition Test' mode.

They were showing the boys by the road again, all clustering round the piper, laughing and clapping, and I thought, they're not so much younger than Luke, I wish that Luke could be there with them –

Then the realisation pierced me, *he could be.* He had Ghanaian blood, his greatgrandfather's blood. He was part Ghanaian, for all his blonde curls. He had a right to be there, in the sunlight. *Stupid, why didn't you think about Luke?*

I started to listen to the programme very carefully. One greatgrandparent was the minimum requirement. If you had one Ghanaian greatgrandparent, you qualified. *Luke qualified,* but I'd neglected him, I'd abandoned him to the clutches of the women. He could have a life, be free, survive ...

But the border would close at the end of the summer. There was not much time left. I got to my feet. Adrenalin, a white electrifying wall of it, lifted me like a tidal wave. I would do it for Luke. I was no longer depressed. I was a man, a father, not some godforsaken wimp. I could suddenly feel the strength in my body, the strength I'd been proud of when I was a boy but had almost forgotten when I was with Sarah, the muscles and tendons I had slowly rebuilt over the last six years' sweating and grunting in the gym.

I was pretty fit. I was going to use it.

Moreover, I had something I had never shown Sarah, never shown Luke, never shown anyone, something that Samuel had left me long ago and I'd never worked out what to do with it, something I went to look for now, locked in a cupboard by the ventilator shaft, wrapped in a bag of stiff green canvas.

Forbidden fruit. Completely illegal. Left me by that careful, godfearing man whose whole life was about upholding the law. 'In case you need them. You're *my son* ...' Dying, Samuel had entrusted me with the cache of shooters he had confiscated over his years as a police enforcer. Instead of turning them in, he'd kept them. So his belief in law and order had its limits. Perhaps he sensed that the sky would fall in ...

There had been a total ban on private ownership of guns in the UK since the massacres of the 2020s, though the licensed policeforces and National Army had sophisticated stunguns and other immobilisers. It was almost the only national law that was still enforced in every council district, since all the police saw it was to their advantage. Domestic manufacture of guns had ceased, and smugglers were gaoled for life or termed, so most illegal guns were twentieth-century metal things, old and heavy, but still dangerous. They were in frequent use among criminals and outlaws, despite a mandatory life sentence for using a gun while committing a crime. If anyone ever discovered my bag, I was planning to say it was a gift from my father, a set of golfing irons, as far as I knew.

When Samuel died we had to burn the mattress, and I saw the bag lying under the bed. Dragging it out, it felt heavy as death. I didn't open it till I got it home, and even then I locked myself in my study. Unzipping the bag and peering inside, I'd felt nauseous, and thrilled, and afraid. It was like looking at a secret part of my father I'd never known before. I'd seen the Speakers' Medal he collected for shooting a maniac straight through the eye in a siege. But now I began to understand that my father must have loved the guns themselves, the weapons with their rich oily sheen. You could tell from the care with which he'd packed this bag, the layers of padding, the swaddling cloths. Down one end were the boxes of ammunition, precisely labelled coloured cardboard boxes packed inside larger ones of clear plastic. There were lubricants, swizzle rods, a set of guntools, magnificent, enigmatic, satisfying gadgets. Down the other end there were halfadozen pistols, and blunter, longer heavier things, wrapped in pillowcases, huge, menacing ... I found myself sweating with desire and panic.

On that first look into Samuel's bag, this was as far as I could bring myself to go. I pushed them back in and closed the zip and locked it away in our security cupboard. Since then I'd been tempted to look many times, particularly when feeling low, but the sheer enormity of it always stopped me. I'd unlock the cupboard, I'd pat the bag, and something would stop me from going any farther. So much power, so much concentrated damage ... Yet I knew I would never hand them in. They were so exciting, so seductive. Their lumpy, masculine shape in the darkness, their rigid bulk, their unspeakable promise.

There was something else to all this, as well. It was a very strange gift that Samuel had given me. He'd given me life, and he'd given me death, because stockpiling guns carried a death sentence.

There was no conscious connection between the bag in the cupboard and my learning to shoot at the Scientists. I didn't even decide to do it. It was just one of the things that the lads all did, like pumping iron, or wanking, or dancing, like every other men's club in the country. We didn't have real guns, of course, just a variety of simulators, and we blasted away at virtual screens, destroying all the people who frustrated us. I found to my surprise I was good at this. I was always the top scorer at the Lonesome Corral, even if Paul occasionally beat me at Red River; I was a crack shot, I had the gene, I was my father's son, though I'd never used a gun.

*

But they were waiting for me, in that cold stiff bag, and I had a little time to get to know them.

My nights were as busy as my days. I had a new, burning interest to catch up on, ironically a bequest from Sarah. She had left the stuff she didn't want behind, including threequarters of her books. Remember, Sarah had passions, then dropped them (as she dropped me; as she dropped men). But when we first met, and she was crazy about me, she'd had that shortlived passion for black history, and I had been grudging, awkward, bored ...

Now, however, I went into her study, the room that had once been my darling's study, knelt down and found them. Two crowded shelves. My orderly Sarah sorted books by subject. *The Black Diaspora, The Black Experience, The Endless Crossing, Black People in Europe, The Colour of the Present, African Journey* ...

The titles suddenly glowed with interest. I couldn't wait to get inside them. Now Sarah was gone, Africa called me. It was there all along, in the flat, in my bones, but it couldn't speak until I listened.

And so a new inner life began. I started to see our family's story as part of something stretching back through the centuries. Shadows and secrets when I was a child, halfheard conversations, began to make sense. And my sister, who I'd scarcely seen in two decades (she had moved to Bristol with her halfJamaican husband; the marriage hadn't lasted, but she had three kids, conceived without problems, my mother hinted) – was the awkwardness between us to do with race? She had drunk too much after our parents' funeral, and I'd heard her say to my father's younger sister, who turned up at the church unexpectedly, 'That boy does not know who he is.' I'd known it was me they were talking about, but only later did I guess what they meant. Many different things began to sink into place.

There were voices, statistics, numbing numbers that I lay awake trying to make real ... If Africa had lost twenty million people to slavery – that's *twenty thousand thousand* people ... My father's father swam out of the darkness, and an endless shimmering continent, and above it beeswarms of unknown people, my own people, being blown away. I scrolled on hungrily, trying to find them. I woke at nine to find the light still on, and the screen glared blankly from the wall, but I made myself get up and get cracking. My days were needed for practical plans.

Luke, my son. We would travel together. Ask the ancestors to take us in.

There was a kind of moral dilemma, which it took me two minutes to dismiss. Should I ask Sarah if she'd let Luke go? Should I give her a chance to be reasonable?

No. She had never been reasonable.

Besides, Wicca World were under huge pressure, the elections were coming in the next few weeks and they were almost certainly going to lose to the Manguard coalition of male liberationists. Sarah had too much on her plate to listen.

Moreover, trouble was expected after the elections. Wicca World were coming under scrutiny for their use of the money they had collected, the fund they called 'People Against the Ice' – PAY, as the newstexts instantly renamed it - which had brought in billions, at least in the early days, before male critics began to suggest they were using the money to promote the party. It seemed likely things would get nasty. Even more reason to get Luke out.

My reasons were good, my logic impeccable. And yet, I took a son from his mother, without any warning. I can't deny that.

Who could I trust? I'd stayed away from the club since the incident when I knocked Richard's tooth out. Paul had rung a few times to see how I was, but I sat alone with the answerphone on.

Now I needed friends. Paul was a friend, and more important, he had hundreds of friends, he was very well liked – well loved, I should say, by most of the regulars at the club. I don't think they had much feeling for me. I was always a bit of an outsider. But on the other hand, I was a man, and a man mistreated by women, at that, and nearly all of them detested women, and especially Wicca World, the archenemy, the witches' coven, the 'Cunts' Coven' as the lads called it, snickering with hatred, spitting at the screen ... It wasn't my scene, but I needed them.

Paul was happy – too happy – to get my call and be asked to the house, after all this time. He came that same evening, smelling of *Le Musc*. (I know because I asked him; it was overwhelming.) He was rather shy with me at first, but after some weed he began to relax. He told me they missed me at the Scientists. 'No one much liked Richard, anyway, she was always being bitchy about people' I had never got used to that knowing way gays had of referring to each other as 'she'. 'You were like a man possessed, you know, it took a dozen men to pull you off him ... Where did you get so strong? I'd never have guessed, you seem so gentle.'

I suppose I realised he wanted me, I suppose I took advantage of him – But I didn't know what was going to happen. How could anyone have foreseen what happened?

I outlined the situation to Paul. I showed him my favourite pictures of Luke. When I talked about Sarah, a frisson of distaste curdled Paul's sensitive, handsome mouth. He said he thought Luke was 'beautiful'. Then I played him one of the two recordings of Luke's voice which had escaped Sarah's furious search. He was singing Mendelssohn, by an irony. We sat and listened to it in silence, that slender thread of filigree wire, singing, it seemed, of some other world where no one would be unhappy or lonely: *Oh, for the wings, for the wings, of a dove ... Far away would I roam, far away, far away ... In the wilderness build me a nest, and remain there for ever at rest ...* His eyes filled with tears. I knew Paul was with me.

The beginning of the plan seemed lighthearted, exciting. Paul had recruited Riswan and Ian and another man, Timmy, whom I hardly knew but am sure must have been a lover of his. Timmy was a specialist in unarmed combat, tall and lean with narrow, sculpted muscles and a wellshaped, blueshadowed naked head which he displayed even when out of doors, unlike most of the boys who by now were adopting little nuskin caps in the face of the cold. Timmy had mixed feelings about me, I think, but his desire to impress Paul must have prevailed over his jealousy. Riswan had known me for over a decade, and understood the situation with Sarah. Ian was friends with all of us.

There wasn't going to be any violence. I was meant to come up with an immensely cunning scheme, though as yet the details weren't quite clear. The guns in my mind were just a kind of backup, in case the women tried anything silly. I knew they would be needed later, when Wicca might come after us, and then as protection for Luke and me on the long drive across Euro. You couldn't fly to Africa without a visa, so my plan was to drive down through France and Spain and make a seacrossing to Africa ...

I meant the guns to come in much later, so why did I show them to the guys, the very first time that we all got together?

Some devil made me go to the cupboard, unlock the door and drag out the bag, heavy and cold, smelling of oil and sour metal. I wanted to impress them, show them I was serious, not just a wild man with a crackbrained plan. Not just another crazy lonely man.

They were sitting round the table in the dining-room, smoking green and drinking beer, a little subdued by the new surroundings. It took all my strength to get the bag on to the table. It landed with a thud, and I didn't say a word. They stared as I unzipped it. We peered inside. They saw the pistols first. There were whistles, and gasps, and a lot of swearing.

I didn't understand it until that day, but guns were made for men to play with. They're the ultimate machine, the perfect toy, and all the guys wanted to handle them. I was first, picking up the .357 Magnum. The hairs on the back of my neck stood up as my hands closed around the wooden grips of the handle. We were all crowding round and reading out Samuel's labels, the ink slightly faded, sellotaped on. I bet he loved the words as well as the guns – 'Heckler and Koch', 'Browning', 'Beretta' ... I got my own love of words from both parents. Dad used to read the Bible to me. *Thou shalt not kill,* pausing between phrases, his dark eyes looking up at me.

The big guns in their pillowcases came out last. There was a 'Chinese Kalashnikov AKM' (I'd thought Kalashnikovs were Russian), which had an ammunition clip that curved like a banana. There was a sawnoff doublebarrelled shotgun, 'Made in Spain', and an antique 'US M1 Carbine 3006', whatever that was, ancient, its wood deeply pitted and scored. (It looked used. How many people had it killed?) There was a 'Tikka Finnish Hunting Rifle', and one or two others I don't remember. At the very bottom was the *pièce de résistance,* a brutal great matt black 'Special Purpose Automatic Shotgun: 15 Shot: Pump Action: Made in Italy'. We looked at that shocked. It was such a bloody monster. It was a few seconds before Timmy hauled it out. Then I took it from him. It was mine; *mine.* It had a hefty pistol grip, and a chunky foldedover swag of grey metal that I worked out must be a shoulder stock. I hefted and swung it; this was the business. I was utterly absorbed. I forgot the others.

Then Riswan brought me back to earth by asking if we were going to take them with us. 'Well, maybe just for backup,' I said, unsure.

'You mean, carry them,' he said.

'Well ... I suppose so.'

There was a silence, while we imagined ourselves, five big men *carrying loaded guns.* It was thrilling. We had seen it in so many old films. It was what men did, in the age of heroes.

'No point taking them if we don't know how to use them,' said Timmy, calmly. 'We might have to use them.'

No one commented, but each of us ran our hands more boldly down the guns' cold noses, and soon we were chattering loudly as we started to work out, in theory, how to load them, opening chambers, sliding levers, clicking triggers ... But I wouldn't let them use the ammunition in the house. I had a feeling this was getting out of hand, but my life was out of hand, and I was going with it.

'Be careful of Dora,' I said, stupidly. She had just bumped into my leg, quite hard, almost as if to remind me she was there. She had been wobbling about in the corner of the room, for once being ignored by everyone, which made her solitary speech and laughter seem slightly vacant, even pathetic.

We drove out of the city the next weekend, five men in one car on a brightish afternoon, looking like five gays off for a Greek party. Or like criminals from the twentiethcentury, when only male criminals drove four or five to a car, so my father had told me, expressing distaste at the new fashion for men driving round together.

Not possible, but we were criminals – when all my life I had been so straight! We were laughing a lot, and drinking beer, and we had the green bag full of death in the back, and we drove deep into the country and found ourselves a wood to muffle the noise. It was the first time I had really noticed what the cold was doing to our woodlands. Some of the trees were brown and dead, others becoming bare in patches. It looked as if something were eating them. I thought, the cold is beginning to bite.

We stretched out a tartan rug on the ground – the remains of a snowfall had frozen hard – got out the guns and spread out the ammo. Then slowly, carefully, we matched them up. Smaller bullets for the revolvers, fine long cartridges for the shotguns. The metal felt cold as ice to the touch, and stuck to our skin. It was almost erotic. Painstakingly, rigid with excitement, we loaded up, growing slowly less clumsy. The enjoyment felt private and intense: the deep delight of perfect machines, of oiled parts clicking in, of something that works – the pleasure a woman could never understand.

Timmy was first to feel sure he'd got it right. I don't know what he aimed at, but he didn't hit it, and the noise was like the end of the world. We all reeled around, shocked and deafened. Paul, thankgod, produced from his bag a fat roll of cotton waste for earplugs.

So we all loaded up, and aimed at the trees, then we aimed at beer cans balanced on trees, and I heard Timmy yelling as he pulled the trigger, 'Die, you witches', which made us laugh, great clouds of frozen steam against the firtrees. Soon we were all joining in the fun, yelling 'Here's one for Juno!' and 'Bang bang, bitches!' There was a kick like a mule after every shot, but after a while I seemed to master it, and it was such pure and mindless pleasure, blasting chunks of bedraggled green from the trees, blowing tins to smithereens ... And we were remarkably successful, considering that this was a first for us all. Most of the cans got holes in them before we decided to hang on to our ammo. We were sweating and redfaced, but I think we felt great.

Then a cat shot yowling and screeching from the bushes, fat and grey and terrified, and that made us laugh even harder, and I had to stop Timmy shooting it. It was a boys' prank, nothing more than that.

(Though it made me think of my poor sad cat, Snowball, who sat alone at the flat and got fatter and fatter till his heart gave out.)

My plan. Though it wasn't much of a plan. Paul and I went off to do a reconnoitre, in dark glasses and the kind of clothes that no Insiders would ever be seen in, layers of rags Paul wore for painting, and two woolly hats Paul had bought from an Outsider – he told me I looked good in mine. We were the same size, though I was brawnier. No one would have looked at us twice, dressed like that. Insiders rarely looked at Outsiders, for fear the Outsiders would ask them for money. We hung around that part of the Marylebone Road, and tried to get an idea of how things were run. We were there for days, shivering, waiting, perched on uncomfortable steps and walls, staring at the fortress of Victorian brick. I envied the pigeons on the window-ledges. Paul patted my arm as I gazed at the glass.

My clothes smelled of him – it felt oddly intimate. We'd never talked at such length before, and I confess I found Paul slightly boring, though it seems unkind to say so now. (He talked a lot about his life; he was an only son. They had wanted him to marry; he had not been forgiven. His violent father had rejected him ... My eyes grew fixed and glazed as he talked. It was *my* only son that I cared about, my beloved Luke in the hands of hags.)

Wicca's leaders, of course, were no longer based here ever since they became the elected Speakers, or we wouldn't have had a chance in hell of getting past the security squads. They'd been doubled, according to the screens, since Wicca had 'lost ground in the polls'. In other words, now everybody wanted to kill them. But the children were still here, some of them at least. On our first morning, around nine AM, two minibuses drove up in convoy and twenty or thirty young children got out and were escorted by female guards into the building. Too young to be Luke, though I scanned them, desperate. The guards were big women carrying stunguns, dressed in greatcoats of violent green. They looked harassed, and moved the children in quickly; the doors closed behind them in a matter of seconds. They were massive doors, which made the people look small. It was like a military operation. The kids were subdued and obedient.

I began to understand this was going to be tough.

As I was thinking that, the doors reopened and a woman with short blonde hair ran out and up to the first minibus, which was just leaving. She banged on the window till the driver stopped. Her body language was grim, urgent, and she dived inside the bus, stony-faced. Was it a bomb scare? we wondered, tensing ourselves. But she emerged again two seconds later, triumphantly waving a large brown rabbit with a floppy pink bow and impossibly long ears. The minibus tooted its horn and left, and she slipped inside the tall front doors, but not before I realised, with a spurt of hope, that it was Briony, with a new short haircut, she hadn't left Wicca World after all. Kindhearted Briony, my almost ally.

It was another week before I managed to follow Briony when she came out at the end of the day. I wasn't used to following women. I moved very fast after she rounded a corner, but to my surprise she was waiting for me there, poised, eyes hard, one knee forward, arms raised, like someone pretending to do karate, but the pose collapsed when she recognised me and anger was replaced by worry. 'Ohgod, I nearly killed you,' I thought I heard her say, then decided she must have said she nearly *called* me. 'Don't follow people, it's dangerous,' she said.

'I'd never hurt you, Briony.'

She looked at me in a peculiar way. Her next thought was a kind one, all the same. She said 'Luke's okay. He's got very tall. His mother sees him at least once a week, even though they're so busy at the moment ...'

I registered that she said 'they' not 'we', as though she and Wicca were separate, but it was probably an accident. 'I have to see him,' I said, hurriedly, walking alongside her down the street.

She stared briefly across at me with solemn blue eyes. 'I can't take the risk of bringing him again. They're not very forgiving to traitors,' she said, with a little shudder that was more than the cold. 'I'm not in as strong a position as I was. I lost my job. Policy disagreements.'

'I have to see him, or I'll kill myself. And everyone else I can get my hands on. I'm *fucking desperate*. I'm not joking.' I hadn't decided what I would say, but the words tumbled out thick and fast.

She looked at the ground and walked a little faster. 'He's still singing. His voice hasn't broken –'

'I shall come back. I'll blast my way in. If you won't do something, I hold you responsible. Help me, for godsake. Just let me see him. I won't make any trouble if you let me see him.'

'I can't. You don't understand what you're asking –'

'I'm not asking, I'm tired of asking, I'm fucking telling you, I'll shoot myself, back there on the doorstep, where the kids will all see it. Do you think that will be good for Luke?'

And so I bullied and lied my way in. I'm not proud of it, but it was for my son. Briony seemed amazingly attached to him (I'd started to find love in a woman surprising). She told me to come back at twooclock on Friday, and she would let me in through the service door. I must be dressed like a delivery man.

Look, I only wanted to save my son. I couldn't foresee ... I didn't imagine ...

The five of us met once more before the day. We considered, and re-jected, perhaps too swiftly, my going in alone and bringing Luke out, depending on Briony's good will ('Never trust those bitches,' said Tim-my). Instead we decided to go in mobhanded as soon as she opened the door to me. So the die was cast. We drank. We were brothers. Paul looked at me with liquid eyes.

The day dawned thinly sunny and cold. I had slept badly, but at least

I had slept. I spent the morning packing the boot with thermal sleep-ingbags, torches, tins, a huntingknife, some of Luke's possessions – his camera, his microscope, his favourite crystals – but would he have grown out of them, and me? What if he'd forgotten me, or hated me? Perhaps the women would have brainwashed him. I packed the guns; of course I did. I was tempted just to take the ones we would be using, but accidents can happen, guns can get lost. Feeling reckless, and dan-gerous, for people were around, I hauled down the whole green bag in the lift and laid it on the floor beside the back seat. Most important of all, I packed our documents. Naturally I hadn't got Luke's pass-port, but passports wouldn't help, the way we would be leaving. I had my copy of his birth certificate, as well as my own, and Samuel's, and by excellent luck *his* father's, my grandfather's, carefully wrapped in tissue paper by Milly. (*Place of Birth*: Accra, Ghana. The keystone of our claim to freedom.) My sister and I had argued bitterly, after Mum and Dad died, over who should have their papers, and thankgod, I had won. Three generations of proof. I slipped them, carefully xylon-sheathed, into Samuel's old brown leather dispatch case. Perhaps my father's spirit might look after us; and my grandfather, who had believed in such things.

I'd decided to leave Dora to Paul. His most recent Dove, Lawrence, had a voice error, so Paul had passed him on to a Learning Centre, but regretted it, and was missing him badly. I knew he would make a kind owner for Dora – I'd never met a man as kindly as Paul. But at the last moment, just before the lads came, five minutes, in fact, before they walked through the door, I realised I couldn't give Dora up.

She'd seemed to be watching me more closely than usual as I threw vests and jumpers into a suitcase. They have big eyes, Doves, with long quivering lashes, and she seemed to stare right into my soul. 'I'm happy,' she claimed – but her voice sounded quavery. And 'Life is fun' – but she didn't sound sure. I picked her up, and her stubby little wings did their 'cling' manoeuvre, which was very like a cuddle. She felt warm and soft. Of course I couldn't leave her, as simple as that – she was family. I was glad to have decided, and I carried her down in the lift to the car, and manoeuvred her sideways into the boot. 'Sorry, Dora.' I switched her to 'Sleep'.

I went back up again feeling a bit better but wishing I had something else to give Paul. Some way of thanking him for all he had done – but then the doorbell rang, it was already twelveoclock, and the boys had arrived. Good boys, right on time.

We had a little whisky to give us courage. Ian produced some buzzers for us all. I did have doubts, but my hands were trembling, and we all took one, and then one more. I thought, my hands mustn't tremble on the trigger. After two buzzers I felt a bit steadier. I played them Luke's recording of 'Wings of a Dove'. *Far away, far away ... in the wilderness build me a nest, and remain there for ever at rest ...*

It was sentimental, but so was I – so were we, we men, we are creatures of feeling, of violent emotion, of love and anger, though some women think that we have no feelings, because we are sometimes short of words ... *Oh, for the wings, for the wings of a dove.*

And then we shook hands, all five of us, quite formally, and silently, and then laughed, and hugged, and went downstairs.

Outside in the street, the mean winter light seemed to make us look smaller than we were. Paul had very blue eyes. They looked worried that day, and perhaps he was not quite as young as I'd thought.

And then we were off. It was only just past lunchtime, and I'd got some sleep the night before, yet I found myself feeling curiously lethargic as the car sped on to the flyover with us all grimfaced, arms touching, quiet, our faces set in the flat white light. Something was going to happen, I knew, that would change everything that had gone before. These men beside me were my allies, my friends, my Roman phalanx, my noble Greeks. Going into battle. The car purred on, with Ian driving and Paul beside him and me in the back with the other two men lest there was a spot road check and I was recognised. The other four had all brought balaclavas; they would burst in behind me with the shotguns. I had the Magnum tucked into my belt, underneath my jacket, relatively light when I looked at the monsters the others would be toting, yet its presence was burning a hole in my jacket, pressing like a hand on my thigh and groin. The traffic thickened at the junction. There had been an incident with a transporter, and road police swarmed around like ants. We had to go slowly, quietly past them in a file of dully normal people, but nothing was normal, we would be too late ...

'Fuck this,' said Ian, and suddenly pulled out and screamed past the queue of cars in our lane. A minute past two. I was cold but sweating, and I smelled the sweat of the others, too, acrid, fresh. Suddenly the building came in to sight. It looked – I don't know – curiously motionless; I had focused on it so hard for so long that I expected it to be living and moving, waiting to confront me, ready for the battle. It stood still and gothic in the afternoon light which made it a different red from normal, rawer, duller, more like ... meat. The windows glittered in the sun. I thought of an animal covered in flies. I wasn't going to kill anyone.

I was breathing hard. My heart hammered. It was three minutes past, no, four minutes past. We screeched on to the pavement by the service door. Then everyone but Ian fumbled their way out, trying not to drop the guns. I felt breathless – and incredulous, because now they were going to put their balaclavas on. I halfwanted to laugh, but this was really happening, and Paul was pushing me towards the door. 'Good luck,' he said, and the little push became a little squeeze at the end, and I halfturned, and he looked at me, and I saw in that split second how much he loved me, and I'd never taken him seriously.

'Thanks,' I gabbled, 'You've done *everything,*' and I think I almost kissed his cheek, which was smooth as a boy's, but there was no time left –

Six steps to the door. My legs were weak. It was fivepasttwo. Just five minutes late. She wouldn't be there. She would be there. Luke would have been spirited away ...

I rang the doorbell. Nothing happened. I felt afraid to ring too loudly, too urgently, lest everyone hear me, but if nobody heard, how would I get in ...? Then I heard the door begin to code, and braced myself, hugging the solid weight of the unfamiliar thing under my jacket.

The building spoke. 'Delivery code,' it said. 'Inform delivery code', but the last word ended in a strangled squawk and next minute the door was swinging open, and there was Briony's frightened face. 'Quick,' she said. 'I've disabled it, but come inside and shut the door behind you.' I'd hoped, I'd expected that Luke would be there but 'He went to the toilet,' she said, 'you're late, and he was nervous, he couldn't wait,' and 'Thank you, thank you,' I havered genteelly, a homicidal maniac grinning at her with four heavies waiting just out of sight, and 'Shut it behind you,' she hissed at me, but I couldn't bloody shut it, though I wanted to please her, though I'd never, ever intended to hurt her – I couldn't bloody shut it, because mayhem, murder – I heard the sound of children singing, in careful harmony, not far off, and I knew all this was a dreadful mistake, that I had to call it off and go away – At that moment all four of them burst in behind me and nearly knocked me over as I stood there frozen; an instant of silence, were we all embarrassed? – and then they were shouting things from films like 'Fucking get on with it' and 'Freeze' and 'Hands up', and Briony was screaming, a thin high scream like the thin skin of something precious tearing, and then I realised it was Luke who was screaming, he stood there above us at the turn of the stairs, framed by a pointed Victorian window, and I leaped up six steps like an Olympic athlete and grabbed him, his boyish, miraculous shoulders, and said, 'It's Dad, Lukey, it's Dad', his eyes were enormous with love or panic, how could he be afraid of me? I pushed him down the stairs ahead of me as I heaved my revolver out of my belt, *no one would keep me from my son,* and then doors were opening off to the right and the guards had arrived in their grassgreen uniform, two of them, *with stunguns,* five, a dozen, running clumsily, pulling down their visors – I saw Timmy spin round curiously slowly and raise his rifle, I knew he would shoot – then the world exploded, I was battered, deafened, but I backed through the door on to the freezing street, clutching Briony and Luke in front of me, Luke seemed nearly as big as Briony, clawing at them frantically with my left arm and waving the Magnum in my right, saying a script that I somehow knew, 'Don't shoot, or both of them will die.' But as I came out there was a little step, I nearly tripped and my finger tightened, I still don't believe I could have squeezed the trigger but a thunderous explosion tore at my arm and a huge red flower, a gout, a flood, a great foul hibiscus of blood and flesh, instantly erupted from Paul's thin chest, stopping him dead as he ran behind us ... Stopping him dead. I think he died at once. He stared for a second, he looked young, he looked startled, he opened his mouth and a plug of thick blood on a stem of red jerked out of it, and Paul went down, I saw him fall, but we went on scuttling back into the car, just me and Luke and Briony, I know I yanked her by the hair ...

The world was ending as we roared away, with Dora bouncing like a ball in the boot.

PART TWO

13

The weeks and months that followed were the strangest of my life. Strangest and most wonderful. They began in chaos, grief, regret. I had killed one man, and possibly more ...

I felt as if I had killed both my friends, for we'd left Timmy in the clutches of Wicca. That green horde closing in from behind, their cruel, identical, sexless faces ... How could I have abandoned him?

You don't know what you can do until you're desperate.

Lucky for Paul that the wound was fatal. They took Timmy alive, and although he was sprung from prison by the Manguard not many weeks later, he'd already confessed at length, on screen, to being one of a highly organised ring of 'pederasts and childmolesters'.

How much torture must that have taken? I have never seen Timmy, since that cold white day, but I think he was a brave man. A decent man, surely. I can only guess how long he was tortured. My mind goes numb when I think about him, when I think of the damage I have done.

My son. What did I expect Luke to feel? We hadn't seen each other for over a year, ever since the farcical evening when Sarah discovered me in bed with Dora. I had no idea what she said to him, or what those other bitches had told him, how much they had tried to blacken

my name ... As I now longed to blacken her name, to try and explain
to him why Wicca were mad, mad and wicked and – *the death of us
all,* for if men and women couldn't live together ...

I looked at Luke. He was thirteen years old. It was hard to believe;
he was still slight and slender, with an almost girlish beauty of face,
smooth pale skin, smooth rounded shoulders – I knew he wouldn't
understand.

He spent a lot of time staring at Dora, though mostly when she was
switched off, his expression a mixture of repulsion and fascination, but
when she was switched on he practically ignored her. He seemed to have
lost his old love of Doves; I suppose that Wicca had demonised them.

He would only talk to Briony. They were the innocent parties
in this. He shrank away when I tried to hug him, and perhaps my
attempt was hopelessly clumsy. Do you hug boys in their early teens? I
didn't know; I had had no practice. Often I caught him looking at me
sideways under long white lashes, broodingly, as if he were trying to
work out who I was.

One night when Briony had gone to sleep, something happened
to give me hope. We were hiding with Eric, a contact of Timmy, who
ran a boys' Learning Centre near Weymouth. He wore nuskin trousers
that hugged his crotch, an unnecessarily bulging crotch, and I'd tended
to keep Luke away from him.

I was lying on the couch in the screen room, netting and dozing,
using my headset, wearing the new pyjamas I had bought against the
cold – expensive fluffy things in real 'natural sheep wool'. They were
white as well; I was a giant lamb. At least, I looked less alarming than
usual.

Luke suddenly appeared, halfasleep in the doorway. He stumbled
through, blinking at the light.

'Water,' he said, a command or a question.

'Of course,' I said, switching my headset off. 'Can't you sleep?' I

got him the water. He took it, silently. He still had no beard, not the
faintest hint of a dark shadow, and his voice was clear, light, high. He
didn't seem eager to go back to bed.

'Am I a prisoner?' he suddenly asked.

It was a reasonable question. I had a gun beside my couch.

'You were a prisoner before,' I said, 'with Wicca. You weren't allowed
out. You weren't allowed to see your father. I did want to see you, you
know.'

He nodded; maybe Briony had told him. 'But now I'm not allowed
to see my mother,' he said. 'Did you two always fight with each other?
I don't remember. You must have done.'

This stung, and I began to deny it, but he shook his head. 'It doesn't
matter. Could I go back if I wanted to?'

He didn't say he wanted to. 'I don't know, I haven't thought about
it yet.' How could I simply let him go back, after Paul had died, after
Timmy had been tortured? I'd risked everything to get him out. All
the same, I was afraid to say 'No' to him.

He said, and for once he looked straight at me, his blue eyes alight
with intelligence, 'I think you're scared to say "No" to me.' This fact
didn't seem to displease him, though.

I nodded. 'I ...' The words stuck in my throat. 'I'm – very fond of
you, you see.' There was a pause. He listened, sipping his water, looking
down at his toes, which I saw were bare. He must be freezing, but this
moment was precious, I wasn't going to tell him to get his slippers.
His toes were long and white, like fingers. 'Look, I don't like guns,'
I stuttered, uncomfortable. 'Or any of this kidnap nonsense. To be
honest, I didn't know what to do ...'

'You aren't going to kill me, are you?' he asked. He must have seen
I was hurt, because he answered his own question – 'I know you aren't.
But where are we going?'

'I haven't decided,' I temporised. 'Partly it depends on you.'

'I want to see my mother. I miss her.'

There was a long silence. I felt like a brute. 'We're going to have an adventure,' I said, trying to work out how to cheer him up.

His eyes brightened. 'I like adventures – at least, I like reading about adventures. I don't think I've ever had one yet.'

'We're going to Africa,' I blurted out.

There; it was said.

'What about Mum?' said Luke, blankly. 'I don't want to go to Africa. In any case, Africans hate white people. They won't let us in. I've seen it on the screen, they're always saying there are too many of us.' He was gabbling now, fully awake.

'Do you remember what I told you when you were little? How I'm partly black? I mean, I'm not all white.'

'No,' said Luke, peering at me. 'You never told me that.'

'I did.' Probably when he was too young to take it in, because I didn't want to leave it too late, like Samuel.

'But *I'm* white,' said Luke. 'I'm white as anything' – Suddenly sounding like a sixyearold. And indeed, he couldn't have looked much whiter, sitting in the light with his brilliant pale curls, the skin on his face almost transparent, his limbs like twigs with their bark peeled off.

'You look it, but you're not. You're my son, Lukey. I'm a quarter black, so you're an eighth –' A look of incomprehension and disbelief. 'Don't worry about it, never mind. But they'll let us in to Africa. If we get there in time. We have to go soon.'

More definite now, his shallow jaw setting. *'I don't want to go to Africa.'*

'We'll talk about it another day. . .'

'Are the Wicca soldiers trying to shoot us?'

'No ... Yes. Not you. Me.'

'Mum wouldn't want to shoot you. She says she's sorry for you.'

'Really.' The tone of my reply was lost on Luke.

'Yes. And that's what the teacher said in the Cocoon. We were meant to feel pity for all the men who like Doves better than anything else. Like you do, Dad.' It was an accusation.

'Actually –' I said, but again, when I needed it, my voice choked up. 'Actually, I love you more than anything. More than Dora. Easily more. Most in the world.' It was something I'd never said before, for always before there were the two of them, Sarah and Luke, level pegging, jostling.

He grinned, and then the grin faded. 'You don't love Mum any more, then?' It sounded as though he had accepted it.

'Yes, in a way, but – we don't agree.'

'It's because of me,' he said, slowly. 'She's sent the soldiers because of me.'

'It isn't your fault. It's our fault, Lukey. One day maybe – one day, who knows.' I spread my arms hopelessly in fluffy white wool, indicating vaguely that things would get better, but he nodded forlornly and rubbed his forehead as if he were rubbing a line away. Without a word, he slouched off towards his bedroom, looking like a teenager at last, and turned in the doorway, not fully towards me, and repeated, softly, 'Don't wanna go to Africa.'

After that night, though, he wasn't frightened of me, and often asked to sit in the front when we drove, and I let him, after dark, when his blonde curls would not be noticed. (I'd suggested a haircut, but he refused, and I wanted to avoid a battle about it.) I hoped he was forgetting the horror of the kidnap, but one day to my surprise he started asking about it, eager to know all the practical details, where we got the guns, how we'd learned to use them, how I had got Briony to open the door ...

I realised, with a little shock of pleasure, that my teenage son had begun to admire me.

The kidnap was a public relations gift to Wicca, who used it to improve their position in the polls by fifteenpercent over the following week. 'MEN KIDNAP CHILDREN' the headlines howled, with details of the incident both real and imaginary. Even I didn't know how much to believe. According to the screens, some children had been shot, not fatally, but one in the cheek, 'threatening her sight', and another in the knee. Hideous, but possible. Timmy had been carrying a heavyduty shotgun, and the pellets would have sprayed, maybe ricocheted, and hit two of the children I'd heard singing next door, so calmly, with such dreadful normality ... Not one of the reports said that I was Luke's father. The kidnap was supposed to be the work of an unspeakably sinister group of perverts, not far away, it was strongly hinted, from the leadership of Manguard.

I'd been following the news obsessively from a succession of safe houses, men's safe houses, mostly Manguard connections, as we drove by circuitous roads to the south, trying to avoid the emways with their constant camera surveillance and unpleasant little sixstrong fleets of bikepolice, cruising up and down like arrows of geese in their dark greased plastics and menacing goggles –

That poor child's cheek. 'Threatening her sight'. Once I woke up shouting, and was instantly afraid the noise had put us in danger. I don't think I ever did that again. Remorse, I learned, is a luxury ...

(And that was a lie. Only yesterday I woke with a thin bony hand across my face, clamped over my mouth like a great spider of ice, and it was Kit, one eye furious in the firelight, hissing 'Shut up, Sol. You was shouting in your sleep. Who this Sarah you keeps shouting about?')

We were an odd crew, odder than I meant us to be, Briony, Dora, Luke, myself. We'd dropped Ian, minus his balaclava, at his mother's house on the way to Bristol. I think he was relieved to say goodbye. But we'd 'done our bit' and 'behaved like men', he said something like

that, something mute and embarrassed, and I nodded, hugging him –
he'd risked his life. We'd behaved like the soldiers we had never been,
never had a chance to be, like outlaws or heroes in a childhood film; we
hadn't been wimps, or panicked like girls ...

In our Days, life wasn't easy for men. It was softer – but it wasn't
easy.

I'd never intended to bring Briony – a *woman,* for godsake! One of
the enemy!

– But she wasn't, really. Nothing was predictable. In those months,
everything was turned upside down. My behaviour to her had been
appalling. I'd lied to her, manhandled her, sheltered behind her
like a coward. I 'took her hostage', in the Wicca's phrase, as though
I were always taking people hostage, that clean little phrase for a
demented cockup, so she started on the screens as a heroine, 'YOUNG
WOMAN SNATCHED AS SHE TRIES TO SAVE BABIES'. But
soon it changed. The police 'had suspicions', there were 'questions to
be answered', 'discrepancies', and before very long they had all decided
that Briony was part of the conspiracy, and she had a price on her head
as well, for Wicca offered hundreds of billions for our capture.

I had done all this to Briony, who had merely been kind, worried,
decent. I expected her to fear and hate me. On that first awful day I
had sat in the back of the car with my Magnum jammed up against
her ear while Ian roared out of London in a frenzy and Luke sobbed
and wheezed on the seat beside us, but she'd suddenly said, some five
hours later, as we drove down a rutted lane through a wood to a safe
house Paul had arranged, 'Could you take that thing away from my
head please? It might go off by accident. Look, I was fed up with
Wicca as well.' And at first I took no notice of her, though Luke said
'Briony's my friend,' but as days went on and her image on the screens

changed from saintly virgin to demonic witch, I saw she had as much to lose as me if we were captured, and relaxed.

I thought about letting her go – I thought about dumping her, to be honest. Three might travel lighter than four, but when I suggested it she said, 'If I get caught, you know they'll kill me. You have to take me with you across to Euro.'

She had a heavy fringe, like a Palomino pony, and her pale blue eyes glittered underneath. I thought that she was going to cry. I'm not very good when women cry. 'How do you know I'm heading for Euro?'

'I'm not stupid. Take me with you.'

And so I did. She was young, calm, kind, and she liked Luke, and she was beautiful, which wasn't important, but cheered things up, and I soon needed cheering up very badly, for it seemed we would never get out of the country.

I hadn't meant to bring Dora, either. She was suffering a little as we kept on the move, unable to stop anywhere long enough for her to have a good slow twelvehour refuel, which all Doves needed as they got older. Nor was she 'happy' travelling in the boot; Doves' mobility and bodytone wane with disuse, all around me now they are failing, waning –

Doves have no concept of the future, although some of them have a time delay. If that isn't in use, they exist in the present, commands, perceptual apparatus, the lot. We were sitting round the table in a safe house near Bournemouth, I'd been drinking I suppose, and feeling expansive, and foolishly I started to explain to Dora, and perhaps to our hosts, who were Dovelovers, that once we'd got to Euro she could travel with us, look out of the window, play with Luke, see mountains, lakes, everything ... But she looked at me with her big soft eyes, a little duller than usual from being switched off, and said, 'This is not a correct message. I see a table, I don't see lakes. I see a red bottle, I don't see a mountain.'

'Tomorrow,' I said, 'or maybe next week. I shall show you and Lukey the lakes, and the mountains.'

'I don't see lakes, I don't see mountains,' she said, and it touched me with foreboding, as if she must be right, as if she were a prophet. But of course she was just a preprogrammed machine.

We were hunted everywhere. I couldn't fix a crossing, all Manguard's contacts couldn't fix a safe boat, no one would risk it, all the ports were watched, or they asked for impossible amounts of money. 'Lie low,' was the advice. 'They'll get tired of watching,' but I knew that Sarah would never get tired of it, I knew she'd stick at nothing to get Luke back.

(Sarah. I couldn't think of her. She'd become a black hole, a ghastly vortex of blame and guilt. Guilt would only slow me up, and I had to be light, fast, hard – I gave curt, repressive answers when Luke asked me about his mother. *I was his father. I too had suffered.*)

Those days were hectic, comfortless, shot through with jolts of adrenalin when we had to leave one hiding place for another, never sure how welcome we would be, for most of our hosts were as afraid as we were ...

Once Wicca nearly caught us, by accident, I think. We were hiding on a wind farm near Bideford in Devon and something woke me in the middle of the night. I crawled past the sleeping body of my son to look out of the window of the outhouse where they'd put us and I saw under the moonlight fifty, a hundred strange figures shrouded in dark capes or blankets passing through the tall silver forest of propellers, seeming to look neither to right nor left, never pausing for a moment, unstoppable. They looked like a company of Amazons, and the great still propellers were a field of spears, stuck into the ground to show their power. They never stopped. They strode over us, or through us, but I shivered as I watched them fade into the distance.

(Perhaps I imagined them; or dreamed them. Perhaps my whole life was lived in terror of women. I think that was true of all of us men. We felt they had everything and we had nothing.)

Then our fortunes changed. The elections came, and our little crew was almost forgotten by the screens. There was a storm of accusations of ballot rigging, falsified votes, intimidation. Ballotboxes – those weird, anachronistic gadgets which required us to go and vote in person, always wooing out a few strange waxen figures who had obviously not been Outside for years, hooded, dazzled, in gloves and dark glasses – were snatched from polling stations, dumped or burned. There were four or five recounts at most stations, although the poll was only fourteenpercent, a pathetic fraction of what it once was, when elections were real, in the twentiethcentury. Everywhere defeated Wicca candidates furiously demanded more recounts, and great batches of votes suddenly emerged from nowhere. The election ended in virtual deadlock, with neither side conceding defeat, though most people seemed convinced Manguard had won.

And then there was chaos. There was still a National Army, which had soldiers of both genders, all nominally loyal to the Speakers. But over Wicca's four years of power, there had been more and more reports of men defecting, whole units joining security firms that were really more like private armies, many of them linked closely to Manguard. And the local police forces were also breaking up as the men and women went different ways. Manguard took over some of the ports, but the coastguards, for some reason, were loyal to Wicca – I imagined brawny women in roaring boats. The screens were completely polarised: Wicca still dominated Nationscreen, Manguard had good links with Euroscreen.

The country teetered on a knifeedge for days as the two sides wrangled tensely for power, while behind the scenes they marshalled their forces. I heard shooting several times in the distance. No one really knew what was happening. We seethed with rumour as we tried to sift the thousand different stories on the net, and we kept our heads down, though we sensed we were becoming a minor distraction from the bigger story of peace or war.

And all the time it was getting colder. This was long after the collapse of the Eurotunnel, twenty years after the great disaster under the Channel when the Euroscept bomb destroyed a crowded train and fractured the walls, which held for a few hours, then cracked catastrophically in a few seconds, so the blazing inferno we were watching on the screens was suddenly doused as the sea flooded in – thousands of tons of black sand and mud, and the screaming died, and the screens went blank ... And hundreds of bodies were never recovered, and the Speakers couldn't raise the money to repair it, and anyway people were afraid to use it, and so it was broken, our link to Euro.

By ferry from a friendly port would have been the obvious way to get across, since flying was out of the question, but the ferry company had just suspended service, announcing it a week after I kidnapped Luke, because the ice floes were heading down from the north in increasing numbers, growing bigger all the time. Though there'd been no trouble in the Channel as yet, the company was reinforcing all its hulls to avoid a repeat of the Scottish disaster when so many hopeful Swedes were drowned.

And so we decided on a small boat, with a gathering sense of excitement on my part. The chaos meant they were available again for the kind of money we could just afford. To be off on the sea in a boat with my son – wasn't this the life I had been longing for? The kind of action I had somehow been missing?

I had to pay the bugger two million ecus, although the boat had come through 'friends', through a Manguard member, Riswan's second cousin. It was nearly a quarter of the sum I'd brought with us – it would have bought me a bloody castle in Scotland, now everyone was flooding south, as I told him, but Kishan insisted the price was cheap. Perhaps it was. The boat would be a writeoff, for he was too cautious to come with us and sail it back across the Channel.

At first I was dismayed that he wouldn't take us, but very soon a sneaking excitement, a sense of wild exhilaration, took over. I would sail the boat. Of course, of course.

I had sailed quite often, with my mother's brother, when we stayed by the sea with Milly's family. My mother had always got cross and worried and nearly succeeded in spoiling it all. I loved it, though. The nautical language, the sense of freedom, the light on the sea, the chance to do something without the women – and my uncle said I was a good sailor. But I hadn't sailed for over thirty years.

Still, anyone could sail a boat. I'd seen endless images of men sailing boats. My boyhood hero, the actor Guy Ball, had sailed a small boat across the Atlantic in *Sea Man,* the film to end all films. I was ten, a very impressionable age.

I had to take Briony along, and Dora, which maybe made everything a bit less romantic ...

Yet more old-fashioned, in a pleasant way. Myself, my son, the wife, the dog. Sailing off together on a Great Adventure. Daddy could do it. Daddy would.

If anyone had watched us setting out, from a Dorset cove near Lulworth, at sunset, they would have seen something from a twentiethcentury picturebook, Briony's blonde head bronzed by the sunlight, Luke's loose curls, Daddy at the helm, Luke with the faithful pet at his side, Dora the Dog, tethered, sleeping, Mummy bending over the picnic things (in fact, she was checking we had the guns), homewardbound as the sun went down, tacking slowly across the V's of red surf as

Daddy got used to harnessing the breeze, and out through the black rocks that guarded the bay, sailing out silently as far as we could before we took the risk of starting the engine.

It began like something fun, romantic, and Luke was grinning with excitement at the bow, leaning back against the pulpit in the last of the sunshine, the red light glazing his face with healthy colour, wrapped up (on my advice) in layers of sweaters that made him complain of being too hot. I was giving him and Briony firm, calm instructions about hauling and sweating up the sails, and all of us were doing awfully well ... But that was at first, before the wind got up, while we were still near the dark shape of the shore, with the ghost nets of light from the little resorts growing brighter point by point as we watched and, Briony and Luke competing to count them.

(Only I knew Briony was afraid. We had had a conversation the night before. She'd been at pains to tell me how tough she was, which I took with a hefty pinch of salt, since she had been crying, one second earlier. 'You won't regret taking me,' she sobbed. 'It's just that I get horribly seasick. And I can only swim ten lengths –' She looked adorable when she cried, her cheeks flushing, her full lips trembling, and I comforted her, till she got very assertive, and pretended she had once been in the Army. But I poured her a whisky, and calmed her down. I felt that somehow we had got closer, and I liked the new feeling of responsibility. It made me feel tender, and – yes, tender.)

Now no one would have guessed she had a problem. Briony was chattering away to Luke, and Dora was perched by my son's knee, and the sky overhead was a picture of heaven, great lakes of wet crimson with gulls flung across it. Sarah would have loved it; I missed Sarah, how very sharply I missed her, suddenly, but that was in another country, and I was here, in the gathering dark. I was Daddy now. I had to protect them.

'Luke, take Dora below,' I said. She was sleeping, but the wind had strengthened a few knots, veering now from south to southwest, and I thought she might slip from her seat in the cockpit. Definitely time to start the engine.

It was an old-fashioned boat, almost a hundred years old, though Kishan insisted he had cared for it 'like my own child' – but he had no child. The engine was an ancient twostroke inboard that you started with an enormous castiron flywheel. I gave Briony temporary charge of the helm (I thought it would give her confidence, though she was already looking faintly green) while I followed his written instructions precisely. First I worked out what everything was. I attached the starting handle, opened the seacock, turned on the fuel, then swung the handle vigorously. And nothing happened. Nothing at all. We thudded into the shortening waves.

I had paid the bastard bloody millions for this. I tried it again, more violently. 'Bastard!' I shouted, 'Start, you bastard –' In response, the motor suddenly backfired, the carburettor spat out fuel and blue smoke and the starting handle kicked back against my shin. From the cockpit my silent crew watched me. 'You'd better calm down,' Briony said. What did she mean? I was perfectly calm. I ran up the companionway, grabbed the helm and lashed the tiller to keep us upright.

'You bloody see if you can do any better,' I shouted, but she took me at my word, went down and started rotating the flywheel, and I must have got the thing ready to go, because her languid turning of the starting handle made it cough into life almost straight away, and there was a wonderful, steady chatter, and then we hardly felt the swell but only the purposeful power of the boat, shooting us out across the blazing water and beyond the brightness to the dark horizon, and on to the point of no return ...

I had killed a man. I could use a gun. I was fifty years old. I refused to be frightened. And steering was easy – wasn't it? Into the wind, straight into the wind, but the mainsail for some reason was flapping wildly, making it hard to concentrate, so I gave my crew orders to get down both sails and secure one to the boom, the other to the guardrails – I was doing okay, it was all coming back. I could hear Uncle Jim's voice, giving me advice, and I loved the way my crew obeyed me, it wasn't a feeling I was used to –

But as soon as I relaxed the other worries came back. I was on the alert for copter patrols. They'd been whining ceaselessly overhead on land since the run-up to the elections, hovering and circling like the last crazed wasps, anything from two or three to a dozen, working on our terror, our sleeplessness. Now I could hear a buzzing in the distance, but the rhythmical thump of the little engine and the wind whistling through the stays and halyards made it hard to hear if it were getting any louder. I could see them maybe ten miles down the coast, their little red nightscopes darting and diving over what might have been Southampton, where Wicca still ruled, so perhaps there was a nest of them ... I almost wished for a few more knots of wind, and then the copters would be grounded.

But the coastguard patrols were a worse danger. Their fast response launches could handle any weather, and their microradar scanners were minutely accurate. The coastguards had been vapping unauthorised vessels on sight, we had been warned, to deter emigration. The coastguards, Wicca's strongest supporters –

I started whistling to keep up my spirits. 'The crossing should only take five hours,' I called. Time to give out some of my bars of chocolate. 'We should be in France by two or three in the morning.' Saying that made me feel a lot better, though I'd plucked the figures from the air.

'Can I muck about on the sand?' asked Luke, excited. 'If I keep my jumpers on. And boots –' He was always anticipating Sarah's worries, and of course when he was little there'd been reason to worry, but now he seemed fit enough to me. If – somehow soft, for a boy of his age.

Then I thought, how often has he been to the sea? We'd taken him to Euro and the USA, but the British seaside was considered unhealthy. There had been too much food poisoning and dysentery and sunburn, and swimmers dying from the faeces in the sea, and nineteenth and twentiethcentury hotels collapsing ... My mother and father always took us to the sea, with her brother there it was convenient, but now it was a place for the very poor, with great camps of Wanderers on the beaches in summer.

At that moment it occurred to me. Luke had not been to a Learning Centre for four or five years, ever since Sarah started taking him to the Commune. Those were the years, between eight and thirteen, when you saw the files of shouting, laughing children gangling through the streets to the Learning Pools. All Insider children were taught to swim. But thinking back, when he was five or six, I'd suggested to Sarah that we took Luke swimming, but she worried about his asthma, and bugs in the pool, she worried that the exercise might overexcite him or hurt his voice or whatever damn thing ...

The lights of shore, faint trails of white, were shrinking, blurring slowly to nothing. The distant copters were tiny red matchheads, then a single pinhead, then they were gone. The wind was getting up, razor-sharp, steelcold, driving into my eyes, nose, mouth, making it a battle to keep my lips closed, and glancing up at the top of the bare mast I saw the windgauge rotating wildly. There was a sudden vibration from the stern and then the angry whine of the engine over-revving. I realised the whole stern of the boat was lifting bodily out of the water – the propeller was beating on thin air. We were pitching forward, headfirst, headlong, sliding down into the abyss – at the last moment, we recovered.

'Luke,' I said, trying to sound calm, 'you can swim, can't you? You have been taught?'

'No,' he said. 'Did you think I could?'

'It's okay,' I said. 'I just – wondered.'

'We shan't sink, shall we? We're not going to drown?'

'Of course not.' I cursed myself for worrying him.

And now we could feel the swell again, even through our speed, even through the engine, like a gentle nudging from a giant beast that was just beginning to get moving, a fluid, easy, enormous something that balanced our littleness on its shoulder, too vast to notice we were there, beginning to stretch out into a lazy gallop, sliding us slowly across its muscles, breathing a great wind into our faces, backs of our necks, ankles, wrists, finding each little nakedness, for the wind had become a steady gale, and we were all at once so small, and the danger wasn't from the copters, the danger wasn't from the coastguards, the danger was an absolute dizziness, the danger was of falling through the world, the danger was of bringing my beloved son into the middle of the ocean, and he *could not swim,* and I was the father, and could not protect him ...

Had not taught him, or thought about him.

'Briony,' I called. They were huddled together at the forward end of the cockpit, their two black shapes like a mother and child, high in the sky, then plunging, plunging, then up again, and someone was shouting – I think it was Luke – with excitement, not terror, but Briony had her arm round him – I couldn't help wishing that it were Sarah: if we had to die, we should all be together – I saw Briony's profile briefly outlined, against the glow that still hung along the skyline, a bar of gold below the indigo, and the sea had turned black, silky, oily, and now it was trying a new little trick, rolling us lightly from side to side even as it pitched us from head to foot, while the whole damn ship, as it pitched and tossed, was rising and falling like a heavy yoyo, and before her face sank into the blind darkness, I saw her small nose, her high forehead, she wasn't as tough, as hard as Sarah – 'Maybe you and Luke should go below.'

'Lukey, go in the cabin,' she said. 'Lukey!' She gave him a little push. And then, as he scrambled noisily through, she called to me, 'I can't go below. I'm going – going to be –'

And then she was sick, with a profound, tearing, retching movement that brought her suddenly to her knees, clutching the side, again, and again, as we surged up and down like a horse at a fair, a merrygoround going round for ever. I couldn't leave the helm to go to her. We had only been out at sea for an hour. Could she stand another four hours of this?

I missed the lights of shore very badly. I should have felt great, for we hadn't been followed, we hadn't been sunk, we had made our escape, we were free of Wicca, and of Manguard too, of the endless men with their shiny heads and sweat and perfume and corded muscles, and free of my silly, homophobic anxiety for Luke, aged thirteen, and beautiful – instead I felt cold and lost and empty, for ahead there were miles of howling darkness.

In those days, none of us were used to it, because, in London, it was never dark.

I had a brainwave. 'Luke, switch Dora on.'

'What for?' He never wanted to.

'Because she'll give you some light. And warmth. We're safe from the copters now. Go on.'

It was good to see her familiar eyes at the foot of the companionway ladder, glowing orange in the night, and to feel her squat friendly presence again. 'Why don't you curl up next to Dora and try to get some sleep?' I shouted to the back of Luke's blonde head, illuminated in the cabin before me.

'I'm worried about Briony.'

'She's all right ... she'll be down in a minute.'

'She's claustrophobic,' he said.

'What?' He didn't usually use words like that.

'You know. She doesn't like being shut in. She can have one of my jumpers if she likes.'

He suddenly sounded so grownup. I realised that he was not a child, not just someone I had to look after. And he wasn't scared. I could hear that too.

'You're a good kid,' I yelled. 'Keep that lifejacket on. I know it's uncomfortable, but keep it on.'

'You don't have to worry,' he replied. 'I'll come and help you sail the ship,' but as he said it, I lost concentration and let the wind take control away from me, pushing the bow round as we hung on the top of yet another wall of water. Sideways, sideways, we were slipping sideways ... what did Uncle call it? Something deadly, *broaching,* mygod, we were definitely broaching ... Clutching the tiller with one desperate hand I grabbed for Briony with the other. She was vomiting in that strange attitude of prayer, 'Hang on!' I yelled to Luke, 'Hang on!' There was a sickening sense of time stopping as we plunged down, down, we would never come up, down, down, I started praying *please no further,* and then in an instant the whole cockpit was filling with water, we were going under, *oh, pleasegod,* I'd forgotten the washboards, if the cabin filled –

All of a sudden we were shooting up like a flea on the back of an enormous dolphin, then slowing towards that horrible pause, that queasy second or two of stillness – but somehow, before we plunged again, I managed to wrestle her round head to wind, and the danger was over, for the moment.

I looked for Luke, and was instantly afraid. He was face down on the floor of the cabin, twitching – he had had convulsions when he was a child – then I realised he was actually *laughing* with pleasure, and Briony was shaking herself like a dog, trying to get the water out of her clothes, till she slipped on the wet floor and fell over.

And then I started to smile myself.

Then Luke came staggering through into the cockpit, and put one arm out to help guide the tiller. His hand touched mine, hesitated, stayed. Shoulder to shoulder, we faced the waves, bracing ourselves for the next rollercoaster. His shoulder was not a lot lower than mine.

I know I felt better with him there.

Somewhere over our heads, to our left, then our right, then sweeping above us in a sickening arc as I tried to peer out and see what was happening, the moon had come up, and was streaking the waves with wild cracked filaments of silver. We slapped the water, we spun like a top, we were skimmed like a stone, we were flung and pounded, and I let Luke hold the tiller with me, I felt the surprising strength in his arms, and I tried to explain, as the storm roared on, how the tiller was connected to the rudder, how the rudder deflected the power of the water, how important it was to keep the head of the boat pointing into the oncoming walls of water – but I'd left it too late, he could not hear, the black O of his mouth saying 'What? What?'

I gave him more chocolate. My child, my son. I crammed black chocolate into his dark craw.

For three or four hours, or what might have been days, we battered on through the bruising cold. My lips were splitting with salt and tiredness, my hands were raw and stiff from clutching the tiller, my arms were almost wrenched out of their sockets, my neck ached horribly from peering forward. I heard my bones start to crack like chalk, breaking, crumbling like cuttlefish corpses ...

I must have fallen asleep at the tiller. Luke was suddenly tugging at one of my arms, then beating my side like a faithful horse, and I registered that he trusted me before I heard what he was yelling, 'The sun's coming up. Dad, it's the sun!'

Luke must have taken the helm for me. I pulled myself up. My legs complained, my arms were shaking, I was soft as a baby –

Now I am hard and dry as leather. Now I no longer yield to pain.

But the boy was right. As I heaved myself up above the level of the window of the cockpit, I saw a faint glimmer over to our left.

'And I counted ten seconds between the last two waves,' he said, as we began to plummet again. Sure enough, we didn't dive so far, and halfasecond or two later we were on our way up, and I hugged him, he hugged me, we rose into the air, we hung there, together, a boy and his father, and in the last moment before dipping again I could see the pink and yellow line of sky above the water and a thin edge of white coming slowly closer, 'It's France. It is. It's France. We made it.'

'France!' he yelled over the wind, ecstatic, jumping up and down, hugging himself, 'I'll go and tell Briony! Dad, *you did it!*' And he briefly, fiercely headbutted me, dug his forehead excitedly into my side.

'We did it together, Luke,' I said. He looked up and grinned, a big boyish grin that I couldn't remember him having before, and staggered away to wake Briony.

He was back in a second, pulling at my jacket. 'She's not dead, Dad, is she?' he yelled at the wind.

'I'll go and see, but you'll have to take the helm,' I said. For a moment, both of us hesitated. The swell had quietened, though the sea was still lively, shaking and worrying us like a dog, but he was thirteen, and if he felt he could do it – 'I can do it, Dad,' he said, and I went.

The cabin was sloshing with icy water. The morning sun had just cleared the window, and glittered in a thousand pieces through the glass, on the frill of Dora's feathers, a seraphic azure, on her great soaked feet like plates of black meat, and Briony was slumped against her –

Her matted blonde hair, her wan white face, the greyblue shadows under her eyes, the bloodless, beautiful curve of her mouth. I knew nothing about her, but she had come with us, had risked her life on the sea with us. She had cared for Luke. She was – what was I thinking?

'Briony,' I said. 'Wake up. We've made it.'

Her xylon jacket was dark with vomit. One of her gloves had fallen off, or she'd pulled it off to look at her watch. I looked at her watch – it was fivetosix – and one eye opened, puzzled, startled, wide and frightened, pale blue as the sky. 'Where am I?' she said.

'Nearly in France.'

She put up her hand to touch my face. I saw her do it, but I couldn't feel it; my face was like a block of ice. We had never touched since the day of the kidnap when I'd mauled her around like an enemy. I watched the slow movement of her white hand. It was amazing, wonderful. 'Thankgod,' she said. 'I thought we would die.'

'I'm so sorry,' I said, 'that you were frightened.'

'Is Luke all right?'

'He's steering the boat.'

She smiled. The blood came back to her face.

'He'll like that,' she said. She tried to sit up, but the boat lurched and she collapsed again. I took her hand and pulled her up.

'Hadn't we better switch Dora off?' she asked. 'She's been on all night, and we can't refuel her.'

I bent to do it, but touched the wrong panel, and got 'Voice' instead, which we often turned off, because her giggles didn't help when our nerves were bad. 'I have a water malfunction,' she announced, in her little voice, which sounded slightly smug, slightly too sure of herself, perhaps. 'I have a water malfunction.'

'You're wet,' I told her, and switched her off.

'There's France,' I told Briony, pointing to the band of whitening sand a mile or so away. 'I'd better go and help Luke bring her in.'

'Do you think ships are female?' she said, eyes sharpening.

'No ... Yes. What does it matter?' I gave up explaining, justifying. 'Luke wouldn't be here if it weren't for you. I'm – very grateful,' I said, quite humbly.

I felt that I loved her, deeply, adoringly, I wanted to take her in my arms, I wanted to shout and dance and drink, I wanted to kneel down and worship the morning –

Instead I went back and took the tiller from my son, and he sang as he guided me through the shining rocks to the deserted beach where we ran aground.

It seemed to me, as we rested on the sand – halfprotected by the lip of an enormous dune, its spiky green crest sticking over us, and under its fringe, the brilliant sea, still streaked across with racing whitecaps, but blue as air underneath the foam, a holiday sea that meant no harm – it seemed to me that we were coming home, me and my son and this kind tired woman who dozed between us in our nest of blankets, and Luke chased a sandfly from her hair.

That morning was so bright, so unforgettable. I thought, *A new life, away from Sarah. Hope. Joy. Another child ... ?* Because Briony was young, and I wasn't old, and perhaps it was Sarah, after all, who had the problem. And since Briony was sleeping, and could express nothing beyond what the curve of a cheek seemed to say, I could dream whatever I wanted to, I could feel like a god or a happy hero relaxing after an epic battle ...

Of course, she woke up, and Luke was hungry, and all of us were cold, and we had to get moving. Reality struck me like a wet sandbag, every joint and muscle of my body ached, and we had no car until I'd bought or stolen one –

But I had eight million ecus in my pack, I had my son, I had Briony, and a little song of triumph rang out in my brain. I had escaped, I had stolen the future, I'd left Sarah behind with those bitter old women, and now we were off to the Pyrenees, through thousands of kilometres of France, then over the mountains into Spain, across the great plains and down to the sea – the narrow strait to Africa.

Yes. That morning was one of my life's best moments, a riff of pure pleasure I treasure even now, when everything's so much colder and darker.

We were a team, too. We had done it together. Without Briony, I couldn't have started the engine, and Luke had encouraged me, helped me steer. Even Dora had given us the light from her eyes.

No, not a team, a family. The members of a team are all alike, men with men, women with women. Our family was not like that. Difference was the point. We were complementary. Everyone had something different to give.

Human beings weren't meant to be segged. We were never intended to be solitary. The links stretched back through the generations, gifts of memory, gifts of genes. My father's gift was concealed in my pack, sheathed in xylon, our most precious possession, the birth certificates, the documents. Samuel's gift, of which he never knew the value, to the grandson he could not hold as a baby, so small, so skinny, so very white. (Dad said to me, after an awkward pause, 'Congratulations, Saul. We-ell … You never would believe that this was my grandson.')

Now Samuel's blood was going to save Luke's life. Opening the gates of Africa. Giving us the key to the last warm places, the retreating deserts where fruit would grow, the great grassy plains that had once been sand, the blueing hills, the returning streams, the sapling woods of the new green Sahara.

14

I suppose you never know who you are until your life is over. What you are is the sum of what you do – leavened with wishes, dreams, regrets – but I never knew half of what I could do until I was prised from my shell of habit.

I found I could sail across the Channel, which after all is a limb of the Atlantic. I could barter, in French, a boat for a car, and not do too badly on the deal. I could come across as tough, and taciturn. I could make people afraid of me. I could do without sleep, and books, and good food, and buzzers and soothers and all the rest ...

I could live at a slower speed than before, rougher and slower, because I had to. Cars in Euro were a different life-form to the speedy hydrocars we drove at home. Since half of Paris was burned to the ground in 2056, the year before our journey, by the explosion at the hydrogen plant at Boulogne-Bilancourt, there had been no fuel for hydrocars, so the old bangers had come into their own, poor people's cars, essentially, a few still running on blackmarket petrol, more of them adapted to run on alcohol that enterprising peasants brewed from plants. Hemp plants mostly, after smoking the leaves. You soon got used to the sweet, choking smell. But the car we'd got hold of, a red battered thing which had green and yellow fins painted on the back, did forty kilometres an hour flat out – pretty average for a French

Alco – and you couldn't go flat out through unfamiliar country where most of the signposts had been burnt for firewood. Sometimes it felt as if we were crawling, covering eighty kilometres a day. I began to understand what I'd never grasped when we flew all over Euro in less than halfanhour, when we slid like silk over the surface of things – that the world was large, and wild, and hard.

I could smash down the shutters of deserted houses, break in through other people's windows. I felt nothing, looking at the scattered glass from a family photo in a brass frame. *My* family mattered more than them. I learned staying alive mattered more than anything, staying alive to protect my son.

Once I broke in and found a middle-aged woman whimpering with terror in the kitchen. Her face was a slab of tearstreaked white. She stared, transfixed, as if I might kill her. I took what we needed as if she weren't there, and left her twitching, shivering, pleading. Perhaps she was mad, and had been abandoned months ago by indifferent children. *Perhaps the father had stolen her children ...* I forced myself to act, not think, but I've never forgotten the colour of her eyes, blackishgreen like an oiled mallard, and her greasy dark hair, licked to her scalp.

I could forage for food and always find something, always enough to keep us alive, for the fleeing French never took it all with them, there were always tins of chestnut purée or vacuum packs of *langue de chat* biscuits or apple *compôte* or great wheels of cheese. We sometimes ate almost too well, in the north, on greasy pâtés or *confit* of duck, food that made poor Luke want to throw up, for he was used to spartan vegetarian fare, but we nagged him to eat it, and sometimes he did.

I could wring the necks of chickens. That was a shock, how easy it was, once you caught the damn things, with their hysterical squawking and long scrabbling feet and outraged eyes, once you'd felt the pain of their steely peck on your naked hand, it was easy to kill them, to squeeze and twist their long leathery craws with their prickly unpleasant ruffs of feathers. I could pluck them, too, once Briony taught me. Her mother had owned a battery farm, and she wouldn't eat meat for our first few weeks, but by the end of March she was eating everything.

I could make a fire, lighting up every time, persevering even if the wood was wet, and cook whatever we found, very badly, either boiling it or burning it, in a cooking pot stolen in Normandie.

I could fish, with a line that Luke and I made, and we enjoyed it, father and son. But we never caught very much with the line, though we once removed halfadozen gasping and wriggling ornamental carp from a pond by hand, overcoloured orange and vermilion things. 'Like taking candy from a baby,' said Briony. She skinned them and fried them over the fire, and we ate them, and it was like eating salted leather, and Briony threw them up in the bushes. 'That's a waste,' said Luke, transparently gleeful, which was what we'd told *him,* a hundred times.

I could drive the car for eight hours at a stretch before I yielded the wheel to Briony, then sleep in the back while she did her stint. I could steer by the sun, without uptodate maps – too much of a risk to try to buy them on the road, a way of advertising our foreignness. Besides, how could we know which of the furtive little shops still open in the rows of closed steel shutters sold anything but looted possessions? No maps would have shown the reality, in any case, the towns abandoned in the rush to the sun, the places where meganauts had crashed across the road and been left to rust once the looting stopped, or where there had been great fires in the riots and black melted plastic, several metres deep, made the route we had planned an inky nightmare, fantastic skewed nests of dark loop and curve. We could never relax, because the road might end, or the little black shape buzzing innocently towards us might prove to be a carload of bandits – but I could cope, I could handle it.

I could travel with a loaded gun in my lap, and be ready to use it when I had to. The worst time was one day when Briony was driving, I'd opened the window to chuck out some paper and an old yellow bus at the very last minute veered purposefully across the road towards us, a dozen male faces, swarthy, avid, were suddenly staring into mine, and they would have forced us off the road, but I let them have it through the open window, blasting their windscreen, windows, faces. The noise inside our car was like armageddon as we swerved and screamed across the tarmac and Briony wrenched the steeringwheel back just in time.

I could kill people, and not feel ashamed.

I grew closer to Luke, slowly closer. I think he began to feel happier. I know he preferred this uncouth life to the terrible safety of the Cocoon.

I could be a father, as I'd wanted to be.

But I couldn't make Briony love me. I think she liked me, she got on with me, she adored my son, she was my mate, my comrade, but she felt the force of my dogged desire and she always said no, she rejected me, kindly but firmly, Nurse Sensible …

Why can't they ever be Eve, in the Garden?

True, I was too old for her. And the shadow of Sarah stood between us. Looking back on it now, she was right to demur. In those early days, Luke could not have borne it, for he still missed his mother, and talked about her, and sometimes asked what I felt about her –

Then something happened to change all that.

They had given him hormones. Luke let it out.

For a while I felt nothing but hatred for Sarah.

For decades, of course, it had been considered normal for men and women to take hormones. Mostly it was women who wanted to be male (not male, exactly, but masculine – they wanted to steal our strength, our hardness). There were also the men who wanted to be female. Their numbers had grown, particularly since the women had taken the children away. Men were caught trying to infiltrate Wicca with newly swollen breasts and whispering voices. They were treated with terrifying ruthlessness, though many of them just wanted to be with children. Others, I think, were actually trying to be the women who had rejected them; to become the women they could not have. Mostly it wasn't sinister, though godknows we men were pretty confused ...

Of course we were; we were redundant. They had sperm on ice that would last for decades – defective, most of it, but it would serve – and there was nothing better between our legs, they seemed to say, when their cold eyes appraised us.

So men and women had been taking hormones or 'taking charge of their identity', as the first, immensely pompous book I read about the subject put it, since the beginning of our century. But the rules had always been strict; no hormones were to be sold to anyone under sixteen. They were one of the last 'Restricted' drugs, after the prescription system ceased to exist and all recreational drugs were made legal, in the socalled 'Leary Year', 2020 ...

Women can be more ruthless than men. I didn't suspect; I missed the signs.

We were camping in a beautiful farmhouse in Anjou – we called it camping, but in fact we'd broken in. The water was switched off, naturally, but when I turned the stopcock, to my joy it worked, it wasn't frozen, it wasn't broken, so the area still had essential services, unlike Normandie, where everything had gone. We were staying a few nights to dry some damp things and rest the drivers; we did need rest.

This new kind of driving was deeply exhausting. Bliss to have water, bliss to rest. But closeness to Briony was bad for my sleep – nights of crazed hope, of hopeless lust.

It was April, and there were rustling alders, silver with new leaf, bordering the garden, and drifts of pale primroses and daffodils, and pastel forgetmenots floating like lace across the wild green depths of grass, and they were late, I registered, because it was cold, spring was replacing summer in Anjou – but never mind, it was beautiful, the light felt young and bright and strong after the terrible gloom of the year of the volcano. I had in my hand a bottle of red wine that I'm sure the Duponts never meant to leave behind, twentyfive years old, a *grand vin de Bordeaux* – and I thought, let's all have a glass together, let's raise our glasses to this great adventure. They were three lousy toothglasses, but what did it matter?

Briony was inside, looking for bedding, washing some crockery in the kitchen. 'I'll wash some plates, then we can eat.' 'Don't bother –' 'You're joking, Luke is starving.' 'I mean, *don't bother to wash the plates.* Come and sit down.' 'Yes, in a moment.'

– It's one thing I never really liked about women, that they didn't know how to enjoy themselves in those days when there was so much to enjoy. There used to be moments that deserved a celebration, when life, in fact, *demanded* it, but the women would be somewhere being goodygoodies, cleaning or packing or sorting or preparing, and they'd say, in a holierthanthou sort of voice, 'No, you enjoy yourself, I'm too busy'. (Granted, she just said, 'In a moment', but I understood perfectly the implication. Sarah had said 'In a moment' too.)

Luke, by contrast, was tearing round the garden, trying to catch a squirrel that he wanted to skin. These are the moments when it's good to have a son.

'Luke,' I said, 'have you ever drunk wine? Because if you haven't, this is a great time to start. It's a wonderful bottle. Come and look.'

He pulled up, panting. 'Wine? Me? Do you mean it? Great!' He was flushed with running, his curls flattened back and dark with sweat, and I suddenly thought, Luke's thickening up, his neck is no longer a boy's thin neck, and his face is changing, ever so subtly ...

We spent a lot of time in the car, you see, or lurking by candlelight in houses where the electricity was cut off, so I didn't get much chance to look at Luke properly. Now I looked. The sun shone straight across the hills into his face. His eyes were the clear strong blue of his mother's, but what had happened to his skin? There were some pimples round his mouth, and was that peach fuzz? I was shocked but also touched to see it. A teenager at last. I said nothing. Perhaps we weren't giving him enough fruit. Sarah had been *obsessed* with fruit, and left behind a worry like a little worm.

'You could have wine mixed with water,' I said. 'That's the way French – young people – drink it.' I managed to stop myself saying 'French children'.

A cloud of uncertainty darkened his face. 'I'm not sure I'm allowed to have it. It's – *alcohol,* isn't it, wine?' He said it as if alcohol were deadly poison. But then, he had been living a protected life.

'What do you mean, not sure if you're allowed? I'm your father, aren't I? I *am* allowing you.'

'No – I mean – I'll have to ask Briony.'

'What?'

'It doesn't matter.' His mouth turned down. There was clearly a secret he didn't want to tell me. Something concerning his mother, then.

At that moment Briony came through on to the patio. 'Phew. That's done,' she sighed, and smiled. Was she being a martyr? Never mind. 'What shall we eat?'

'First we have a drink ... What's this about Luke and wine?' I said. 'Did Wicca make all those poor infants take the pledge?' I was joking, really, but I saw something pass between Luke and Briony, a quick, anxious glance.

'I think it would be all right for you to have some, Luke,' she said, slowly.

'For godsake, woman, don't make such a fuss. We've been through a lot, this is a celebration. One glass of wine never hurt a teenager.' The look I gave her was hostile enough for Luke to come to her defence.

'You don't understand,' he said, flushing up. 'She's not making a fuss. It was ... medical.'

'But that's over,' Briony rushed in quickly, her face clearly telling him to shut up.

'What's over?' I asked, twisting the cork, pulling mightily, uselessly, feeling my face redden and swell with the effort. 'Stop talking in riddles – *sod it, sod it!*' For the top of the cork had come away, leaving half of it crumbled in the neck of the bottle.

I don't think Luke noticed I'd mashed up the cork; he thought I was swearing at Briony. He leapt in at once, talking too fast. 'It's not her fault. She didn't have any say. I was having these pills. To protect my voice. You weren't allowed to have alcohol if you took them, I mean we weren't allowed to anyway, but the older boys were always smuggling it in. Juno explained it would be dangerous for me.'

'To protect your voice? What is this about? Was he on medication, Briony?'

'Nothing important,' Briony said.

I began to see. Yes, of course I saw. I probably halfsuspected the truth as soon as he mentioned 'protecting his voice', for of course his incredible, thrilling soprano had survived too long, he'd stayed young too long, he was nearly fourteen, why wasn't I suspicious? Once they used to cut the little boys' balls off, the poor little castrati, singing their hearts out, but they'd done it to Luke with chemicals ...

I shouted at Briony, and Luke. Perhaps I broke a few things, I'm not sure. I demanded to know what Wicca had done.

I was justified. They had drugged my son. The bitches wanted to steal his manhood. Any father would feel the same –

As I hectored them, as I raged and roared, I was adding up the details, somewhere inside, Luke's amazing, delicate youthfulness when I first saw him three months ago, the absence of adolescent stigmata, for which I was grateful at the time, because that way he could still be my child. Then the sudden pimples, the thickening jaw.

When did Briony admit it was hormones? I'd been shouting at her as if she were Sarah. At some stage she stopped sitting meekly on the grass, stood up and stared with those strange pale eyes, like blue ice, suddenly, cold and sharp, told me to calm down, began talking. When she told me he'd been taking highdose oestrogen and other, subtler, more complex drugs, I started to swear, and smashed a glass, and then another, and another, and Luke sat hunched, gnawing his fingers.

'I don't take the blame,' she said, firmly, 'but I knew it was wrong. It was against our principles – Wicca's principles. I mean. They're so keen on being natural' (I recognised Sarah's influence here) 'and then they start stuffing the boys with hormones. They wanted to see if it made them gentler. And Juno so adored his voice ...'

'Sarah should be shot. Garotted –'

'I hate you! You ... bastard!' Luke suddenly shouted, 'I love my mum! And I hate you!'

I suppose I deserved it. And yes, it proved that the hormones had worn off, and my son was adolescent. The words proved it, but so did something else, for as rage and grief burst out of him, his clear voice suddenly fell apart, and through it a bullfrog honked, croaked, a clumsy, hoarse, uncontainable thing, the first sign that his voice was breaking.

And then I felt sad.

And then I felt guilty, and most of my anger leaked away. It was nearly dark. We were all getting cold.

I picked up the glass as best I could, cutting my finger in the process, and we all went in. Just inside the door Dora sat quietly glowing in the dark. Someone had switched her on and then forgotten her, possibly Luke, in the middle of the row, and she sat there muttering peacefully. 'Hallo,' she said as we came into range of her sensors, 'Hallo, good to see you. By the way, I'm hungry,' oblivious to the trauma we had all been through. Looking at her round innocent face and the gentle smile in which her mouth was fixed, looking at the kind dim light of her eyes and the transparent lashes quivering above them, I thought, much better to be a machine than suffer this crazy tearing pain. Better not to feel, or pass the pain on.

(You tell me – now that the ice has come, now it's getting dark, and the cities are ruined, and most of the galleries have been abandoned, and the theatres are full of snow, now the ice lies white along the plastic letters that used to blaze the names of actresses in orange light across navy skies, now hardly anyone reads or writes, now the churches have bonfires on the altars and plastic sheeting in their stainedglass windows, now Buckingham Palace is a burntout wreck, its cellars swarming with secret police, now the old are dead, and the young know nothing – you tell me, what is the point of us? What was ever the point of us, our struggling, quarrelling, suffering species, getting and spending, wasting, grieving?

There was love, wasn't there? I know there was.

That can't be the point, though. We loved so badly.

Perhaps we were meant to be recording angels. Ringing the earth with consciousness. Mirroring it in our net of signs. Solar singers, messengers ...

But our net tore, a tattered cobweb.

And here I crouch with my stub of a pencil in a windowless cupboard that smells of piss, penned in the dark like a dirty beast, trying to scribble my small story.)

I sat there, that night, in the empty *salon,* lit by a flickering candle on the table which must have been too massive to remove. It sat in the denuded space like a tombstone. My thoughts were no longer springlike and hopeful.

I'd wrecked the frail bond between the four of us, killed the affection Luke was starting to feel. Although I'd told Briony I was sorry, she'd just said 'Yeah, well,' and marched off to bed, without offering to cook or clean up in the kitchen. (She had changed, I thought, she had changed already, and we had only spent three months together ... Sarah started sweet, but it didn't last. Women were fickle, like the poets said.)

I remembered the wine. I had got no further than mangling the cork, because of the row. It must be somewhere out on the patio. My spirits lifted. I went out and groped in the icy darkness – how fast the heat died, once the sun had gone. It wasn't on the slatted garden table, and then I felt the jagged edge of the wood, apparently I had broken the table, and as I drew back, for the splinters were sharp, the bottle fell off and smashed on the concrete. I tried to scoop it up before the glugging finished and managed to save about half of it at the cost of bloodying my hand – the left one this time, so now they were equal.

The smell was wonderful: fruity, oaky, a smell of warm summers of long ago, plus the dark metallic smell of my blood.

Back in the *salon,* enthroned at the table, I watched myself drink in the big tarnished mirror, a big man, a monster with wild black hair, a darkskinned man splashed all over with blood, for the mirror didn't show that half of it was wine. Reflected through the window was a fullbellied moon, a beautiful pregnant moon with an aura, a halo of light like a woman's hair. I was a *man,* Esau, Moses, leading my tribe to the promised land, David fighting the Goliath of the ice, I looked at myself, I swelled, I expanded. (But would my son be a proper man? Had they ruined him for ever with their filthy medicines?) I had poured the wine into a plastic beaker – annoying how the French never left their good crystal. It filled three times. By the third, I felt good.

Till now we had all slept in the same room, for safety and to keep warm. But when I stumbled through with my candle in a saucer I could only see Luke, curled up like a foetus on one of the two mattresses Briony had found. She obviously couldn't stand to be near me. I pulled off my jumper, meaning to sleep in the rest of my clothes, but the smell of rancid sweat was so overpowering that I changed my mind and went to wash in the kitchen, padding back barefoot in the silence.

There was only a narrow shaft of moonlight here. I had snuffed out the candle before I took my clothes off. I heard the tap running. Had Luke left it on? Then suddenly I touched something warm and soft, and Briony was screaming like a mad woman. She'd been bent over the sink drinking water from the tap, and as she flinched away into the path of the moonlight I saw the swing of one heavy breast, which she hid with her hand, but not before I glimpsed the dark star of the nipple, swollen with cold. 'Don't bloody frighten me!' she screamed, once she'd calmed down enough to use actual words.

'Don't wake up Luke,' I said, 'he'll be frightened,' though actually I was frightened as well. My heart was hammering my chest, it was such a shock to find her there and then to unleash this monstrous terror. And I was horribly aroused, I could feel my erection tight in my trousers ... But awful to know you are frightening. That I had caused such unreasonable fear, and all by showing a little temper ...

I tried to put my arms around her, to steady her as she wept and screamed. She seemed to be wearing very little; she must have woken up warm from sleep. At first she resisted me, then all at once she clung, weeping and cursing, 'You shit, you shit ... You hateful bloody man, how dare you blame me? If it wasn't for me Luke wouldn't be here, I hate you, I hate you ... '

But then it seemed she didn't hate me. Her nails were digging into my back, hurting me but pulling me closer, she was pushing her head up under my chin, butting at me, nuzzling me, clawing the muscles of my arms yet pressing herself fiercely against me. I was confused, then less confused, for this was the thing I had dreamed of happening, happening now, in the cold, in the moonlight. But I smelled myself, 'I'm dirty,' I choked, 'Briony, let me go and wash,' then, gabbling, for she was younger than me, I wasn't a bad man, nor irresponsible, 'I am okay, I haven't had sex for over two years, and I take my hiv boosters regularly,' but she was pummelling my chest, pulling my shirt off, plucking at my trousers, *oh, oh please,* easing down my pants, and my penis rose like a seal into her hand, quite separate from me, happy, hungry, *my penis was in Briony's hand,* and she ringed it, rubbed it, silent, greedy, and then she led me through to the *salon* where the moonlight poured through the open shutters and perched herself on the edge of the table, that massive, funereal French table, and without some wretched calculation about ovulation to kill all pleasure, opened her legs, and pulled me inside her, silently, hungrily, *I was inside her,* without a condom, gloriously naked, the first woman other than Sarah in fifteen thirsty years of marriage, and it was so warm, so wet, so tight

– I came with a little cry like a baby after thirty seconds at the most, and then it was 'Sorry, Briony, sorry. *Thank you,* Briony. That was so ...' I felt shattered, and tender, and slightly ashamed, and also fucking wonderful. *Fucking* wonderful. My blood zinging.

Then she tugged down my hairy head, I always liked women to touch my head, to stroke my hair, to knead my scalp, as Sarah did, years ago, when she loved me – and Briony nudged my face to her lips, the hot small knot of her clitoris, salty, slippery with my sperm, and I worked with my tongue until she came, in a long diminuendo of dove-calls, her hips twitching helplessly against the hard table.

And then she cried, but with release from tension, and I groped my way through and found her a blanket and wrapped her in it, and told her again how sorry I was if I'd frightened her that evening. She said nothing (I've learned that slowly – it's never enough just to say you're sorry), and both of us wished we could drink a cup of coffee without having to gather wood for a fire ... So many things we once took for granted.

Bless you, Briony. Forever bless you, though I'm sure you acted half out of fear, to placate the brute, to tame the monster. It was something – natural, instinctual. We were all going back into the dark again. The return of the secret life of the caveman.

And yet she slept in her separate room, and next morning, which was sunny, she had gone back to being normal, friendly, asexual, although I gave her longing looks that I hoped my sulky son wouldn't notice.

I thought he was sulking. In fact he was sad. Because Luke was quiet and wouldn't look me in the eyes, I thought he was still angry about my fit of temper. But it was his voice he was thinking about ... It's never about *you,* with teenagers.

I had woken full of energy, and gone to find fuel. I managed to buy proper French bread from an old man in the village three kilometres away. He was a handsome, vigorous old chap with a huge drooping growth on one of his eyelids, the kind of thing we were getting used to now doctors were just for the megarich. According to him, only the young had left the village. 'The grandparents stayed. We love our village. Life goes on as normal here. Except it's ... quieter. And colder.' I bought pastries, too, for an inflated price, but they were light as an eggshell, and fluffed with fresh cream, and I wanted Luke and Briony to like me. He told me where to go to buy fuel. It wasn't so easy to find in the north, where the unseasonal cold had spoiled the cannabis harvest, but the family to whom he directed me were growing in bulk, hydroponically. I asked them for three or four cans of methanol, then found to my embarrassment I'd left most of my money in the jacket I had taken off the previous night. They looked at me with the blank fear and hatred they must have got used to feeling for cheats. I was weak, for some reason, I didn't argue, perhaps because the old man had been charming, perhaps because Briony and I had made love, I just paid for the topup of my tank and left, instead of shooting them and keeping the fuel.

When I got back, I found Briony was up, and washing a duvet she'd found in a cupboard. 'We don't want to drag that thing along,' I told her, but 'It's *natural goosedown,* worth a fortune, and light as a feather,' she told me, happily, bundling it out into the drying wind. 'Might be useful in the Pyrenees. In any case, it's too good to leave behind –' She'd turned back into a chaste, respectable housewife, but I watched her hips as she disappeared.

I burned the broken table to make a fire and boiled some water for coffee and to cook the duck eggs we'd plundered yesterday. We had a tasty breakfast, with that and the baguettes, though in a perfect world there would have been French butter, unsalted, creamy, delectable –

But no, the old world had not been perfect. We were finding new skills, new strengths, new closeness.

'I ought to record myself,' Luke suddenly said, as he sat eating his choux at the end of breakfast, while Briony was stretching more damp washing on some overgrown rose bushes in the sun. His voice sounded perfectly normal again, that high clear treble I had always been used to – I'd halfexpected that last night's row might have cracked it forever, with the strain. But it had to signal the beginning of something. 'Mum's got all the recordings, hasn't she?'

'Well – I've got two. Years out of date.'

'I've got to get to some recording equipment. I don't mind my voice going, but it's sort of weird ... Juno made me feel as if I *were* my voice.'

'Juno was a psychopath,' I said. 'I don't see how we get to recording equipment. I suppose there are still places in the big cities ...'

'We have got recording equipment,' said Briony, pausing like a dancer, both hands uplifted, speaking above the snap of the sheet in the wind. 'Of course we have. We've got Dora, haven't we?'

'I'm not giving Dora my voice,' Luke mumbled. And yet, they'd been getting on better of late. Luke had been less standoffish and suspicious, more interested to find out what she could do, and Dora had stopped automatically malfunctioning whenever she recognised his voice.

He thought about it, and then he said, 'Is the RV good quality?'

'Perfect,' I said. 'With this model, and everything later ... It was a bit dodgy with the early Doves.'

'Great,' he said, and swallowing his bun, he ran inside to try it out.

Perhaps that was the point, when Luke started singing. Distant stars must have paused and listened. Sometimes, mygod – my God exists. As blessing, not as half a curse.

Sometimes I think of the earth from the air – how the blues and browns the first astronauts saw have slowly gone under the spreading silver, reflecting the sunlight back out into space, now an icebright ball with a bluebrown girdle, a narrowing band of grass and trees, a shrinking stretch of unfrozen water ...

Is it that God grew tired of us? Perhaps he wanted his world again, shining, perfect, unpolluted. If humans survive, we'll be as grass, quiet and slow like moss or grass, lowgrowing things, less arrogant. Flesh is grass, now so many have died. Already our numbers have crashed by threequarters, and that's a conservative estimate, since no species likes to believe it's dying ...

The ice comes on, a shining wall, carrying all our follies away, untrodden light, unbroken sky.

Sometimes it's there I see God's face. Blank, encompassing, infinitely bright.

If there's a God, he was happy with us that morning in Anjou when Luke started singing. The wind had dropped to an eerie stillness, as if the elements understood, and the clear cold April sunlight sparkled, and the only sound was a little stream, perhaps four hundred metres away, and Luke's glorious voice, yearning, soaring, flying upwards and gliding down like something too quicksilver to be human, the spirit of air, the spirit of water, for some of his singing was shot through with pain, some of it our pain, I'm afraid, and also his own, for what he had lost, and what he was now about to lose – and perhaps for what he had never had, a quietly loving mother and father.

That morning we were blessed, those of us who heard him, singing all his favourites, Schumann and Gershwin, a Debussy setting of a medieval song that made me think of Sarah – *Dieu, qu'il la fait bon regarder, la gracieuse bonne et belle! ... Qui se pourroit d'elle lasser? Toujours sa beauté renouvelle* – I never did tire of looking at her, for me her beauty was always new. And then 'Trois Oiseaux du Paradis' –

Luke sang in the sunlight, he sang next to Dora but he sang

outwards, to the spring morning, he sang a radiant, sorrowful paean of praise to the godgiven talent that would soon leave him. Briony and I were anxious at first, lest what happened the day before should happen again, but sound poured from his throat in a silver ribbon and soon we relaxed and forgot and listened and time didn't matter, or work, or worry, for his gift was entire, threedimensional, and it drew us in, we melted, yielded, and even the cats and the birds were silent, and the trees were still for Orpheus. *Trois beaux oiseaux du Paradis, Ont passé par ici, Le premier était plus bleu que ciel ... Le second était couleur de neige, Le troisième rouge vermeil ...* What was the gift the red bird brought? *Un joli coeur tout cramoisi ...* It brought a beautiful crimson heart, but death, in this garden, was far away.

Until something on the grass flicked, moved, and a grey fluffy cat that was asleep on the bank sat up, acutely interested, and I heard a strange little mournful croak, *Ah, je sens mon coeur qui froidit,* and a frog went leaping across the lawn and the cat shot after it, pounced, missed, and the frog zigzagged away on elastic. Of course, it was spring; frogs' mating time.

'That was wonderful, Luke,' I said. 'Thank you.' When Briony passed close by me with the washing, dry and clean and serenely folded, I saw she was crying, but she didn't look unhappy.

Within halfanhour, we were back on the road, and from that day onwards Luke and Dora were friends.

15

Sometimes my wild boys remind me of Luke, Luke as he looked many years ago. Mostly it's an angle of their body. When the fire's blazed up and they're stuffed with flesh and they suddenly get a meat sweat on them and strip off their layers and stand there naked, crowing and whooping, in the red of the fire. Their narrow bodies look curiously innocent, even when they've got their cocks in their hands ...

The escape of the children, all over the world, was the strangest thing about the coming of the ice.

It began in England before we left, though none of us saw what was going on. We'd seen a few pictures of them on the screen, taken from a distance, for they fled the cameras. We thought it was nothing, a fiveminute wonder, we hoped they were Wanderers who happened to be young ... The escaping Doves took up all our attention. And yet there were probably ten times as many children. We were too afraid to take it in.

The wild boys and girls. The breakaways. Some of them the children of Outsiders and Wanderers who didn't know who their parents were, but many more of them Insider children whose parents couldn't admit they were gone.

These children didn't want to live in houses, or 'nests' or 'communes' or 'cocoons'. They didn't want Role Support or Wicca

Wisdom or any of the crutches we deemed essential. They didn't want to be smothered by their mothers. They didn't want to be kept Inside. They were working life out for themselves again, running wild; living wild ... Sometimes they adopted a stray oldtimer to help them do things they couldn't do.

That was how Chef and I were adopted by Kit and Fink and Porker and Jojo, and the hundred or so kids who run with us. (Chef hasn't cooked for the last two days. Kit says he's sick. Fink says he's 'skivey', their word for slacking, a dangerous word. I should go to see him, but I'm too busy.)

There was an unauthorised fire on the western side of the airport this afternoon, and although the Chiefboys tried to put it out they got bored around suppertime and left it to burn. So I'm making use of it, writing by the embers. Most of the others are creatures of habit; they've gone to sleep in the usual heap by the fire we always light for supper, nearly a mile away in front of Departures. A few of them run past, and peer over my shoulder ...

I tell them to wait. They will get it all. When I'm finished, I'll tell them the whole damn story, though what they hear won't be like this, the truths of my heart, the truths of my life, my long strange life in the twentyfirstcentury.

They'd find it – stupid. Incomprehensible. Pointless quarrels, unnecessary problems. Simple is best, for the wild boys. Death excites them, and love and adventure. Love they can understand again, in their savage way, their animal fashion, love between male and female, that is, for they're mating again, the wild boys. When they find the girls, they know what to do ... They don't seem to be breeding, though, in the city.

The old man in the village who'd sold me the pastries asked me if we had wild children in England, and I denied it, instantly. He warned me against a marauding band of boys who ranged around their village.

'And the others, of course. Watch out for them.' He nudged me, black eyes meaningful, and I wondered who 'the others' were.

We were twelve hours' journey from the Pyrenees, which meant we would sleep one more night in France and try to cross the mountains by daylight, when any snowfalls would be less dangerous.

We drove till nine, then at sunset turned off towards a little colony of low white villas. There were the normal security gates, wide open, and the windows of the gatehouse were smashed. We drove through cautiously, and saw a light, too bright to be candles, in the window of a villa. 'Maybe they've still got power,' said Briony, excited at the thought of light and heat.

'If so, they might have inhabitants,' I said grimly. 'And they won't be pleased to see us, will they?'

We drove on up the little road between the cedars. Only that first house had a light showing, and perhaps that had been a security device. I desperately wanted a bed for the night, somewhere to recoup our strength for tomorrow, so we drove right down to the far end and wormed our way into a large stucco house which already had one shutter hanging off it, and underneath, a broken pane. It was a princely house, perhaps six or seven bedrooms, with an elegant drive and a waterless fountain. I was tired; I ripped my trousers climbing in, and I couldn't help wishing that the lights would come on, and the heating, and the oven ...

And then, as I flicked the switch in frustration, the light flooded out; the wonderful light. 'We've got light!' I yelled, forgetting caution. 'Maybe there'll be heat as well.'

It was like a firstclass hotel, to us, a place with light, water, a stove. This house had not been abandoned long; there was a bottle of whisky halfempty in the kitchen, and it still had most of its furniture, which made a nice change, something comfortable to sleep on. Rich people must have lived here once. There was a Bechstein grand piano next door, abandoned in a sea of white, and they'd left some of their pictures, oddly.

'Why don't you play something?' I said to Luke.

'I'm tired,' he said, 'and it won't be in tune. Maybe I'll try it out in the morning.'

He didn't want to eat; he wanted to sleep. Sometimes he still looked very frail. I fetched him the duvet that Briony had washed – dry, it was light as thistledown – and lulled by the luxury of heating and the duvet waiting like a cloud on the sofa, Luke stripped off everything and dived into bed. Adolescent boys never did like washing.

Briony found that the cooker worked. And there were some dry stores, rice, a few herbs. 'But have we got anything to cook? Oh Saul, did you chuck that chicken away –' For we had been carrying a plucked chicken for nearly three days in the back of the car. Sometimes the chill was very useful; food was scarce, but it lasted longer.

We ate like kings on real roast chicken with rice and herbs and a generous whisky. It was a large chicken. I took some to Luke, but he was sleeping a dead, drugged sleep. We gorged ourselves, and left nothing behind but a little grey cat'scradle of bones.

Briony and I talked deep into the night, trying to plan the next stage of our journey. I didn't really want to drive over the mountains. There had been too many stories about travellers being ambushed in the high passes, and reports of wolves in increasing numbers, after some bloodied bodies were discovered. I began to veer towards the train.

There were still trains running through the tunnels, but according to the screens they were often held up by desperate gangs who blocked the tracks. There were no more timetables, trains weren't maintained, they ran through the tunnels without any lights ... It was when I mentioned the absence of lights that I saw Briony shake her head.

'How long shall we be in the tunnel?' she asked.

'If nothing goes wrong, just under an hour. The rolling stock is in a terrible state, the speed is nothing like it was.'

'And there aren't any lights?' Her nostrils were dilated.

'Well, no ... but every so often there are arches cut through the rock to the outside, I think. Or was that the Simplon? I'm not sure.'

She didn't say a word. She sat there, hunched. 'I'll have to do it, won't I,' she said, a statement, not a question, a kind of giving up, a dreadful acceptance of suffering that perhaps explained her attachment to Wicca. Her father drank and her mother hit her: she'd told me that much, though she wouldn't expand, and I wanted to hit her, too, at that moment, but only because I didn't want her to suffer.

'Briony,' I said, 'you're claustrophobic. I know you are. Luke told me. Forget about the train. We'll do it by car. It'll be fine ... it'll be an adventure.'

She looked up, her blue eyes puzzled, short-sighted, as if she must continue to be tormented. Then she smiled, and her eyes focused. 'Thank you, Saul,' she said. 'You're kind.'

'We can do it,' I said, and I smiled like a hero.

Partly to cover a surge of fear. Now I was committed to doing it by road, driving up, up into nomansland. Another crossing as hard as the last one.

What had I seen as I lay on that beach the morning after we sailed the Channel, deafened, stupefied by wind and waves, watching the sun cut curves through the dunes, clutching the icy blankets round us?

That the world was enormous, and I was very small. That life was short, and death was certain.

And yet I was responsible for Luke, and Briony. I could not die, because of my son.

'Let's get some sleep,' I said, kind, paternal, though a little voice inside me said *Come to bed, if you're afraid of the dark, kind Daddy will help you* ... 'I'll get more bedding out of the car.'

'Don't forget the gun,' Briony said. She felt we were safer keeping it with us, but each time I placed it by my bed I feared that Luke might shoot himself by accident. I secretly determined to leave it in the car.

'I'd rather not be alone,' she added, and my heart lifted, my penis stirred. I would happily cross the Pyrenees for this.

That night the sex was slower, better, still wildly, deliriously exciting but more human, more friendly, like coming home, as I whispered to her, and she sighed, and kissed me, though we were all so far from home. But I fell asleep with her in my arms, curled tightly together against the cold, against the hatred between men and women that had turned me into a brute and a killer. 'I like you, Briony,' I said. 'I like you too,' she said, after a pause. I felt warm, and safe. I began to drift. Tomorrow would be hard, but tonight was good ...

What seemed like seconds later I was suddenly awake, seeing bright beams of light circling the ceiling, and the sound of a car engine uncomfortably near. I felt icy cold. My heart was thumping.

'Briony,' I said. 'Wake up. I think there's someone outside the house. Could be the owner.'

She sat up, eyes closed, made an incoherent noise and lay flat again.

I heard footsteps on the gravel outside, and cursing in French, and a muttered conference. They'd seen our car, and the dangling shutter, and the smashed pane, and drawn their own conclusions. I got up stealthily and tried to look out. Then I saw how many cars there were, six or seven, maybe, drawn up in the snaking 'S' of the drive. So that explained all the noise, and the lights. There were six men, ten, perhaps a dozen. And then I knew we were really in trouble.

I assumed they were the owners, that they had keys, but of course they were more probably looters, criminals ... But I remembered the halffinished whisky. And the confident way the cars had scrunched on the gravel. The owners, bringing back their friends for a party. Should I try to talk to them? Charm? Explain?

I remembered what I looked like. Big. Unshaven. Wild. Mixed-race. Frightening. We were in their house. They wouldn't wait for explanations. No one waited for anything; the ice moved too fast.

Luke was next door; if he only stayed quiet they might never realise he was there. But I had an uneasy feeling that he wouldn't keep quiet. I was afraid my son would try to be a hero.

I pulled the bedding gently over Briony's face. If they looked quickly, they might think it was just a pile of clothes. I took Dora, who was in Sleep Mode, and pushed her roughly behind the sofa. Trousers, shoes, I pulled on my shoes, and of course they wouldn't go, the heel stuck stupidly to my naked flesh, but I'd never find my socks, so I grimly crammed them on.

Gun, sodding gun. I hadn't got it.

Briony had told me, but I hadn't obeyed – I didn't like being bossed around by women. So somehow I would have to get out to the car. They were all spilling round towards the front door, talking, by now, in subdued voices that diminished more as they went round the corner. I'd climb out through the broken window and fetch the gun.

I landed as quietly as I could on the gravel and ran to the wrong car in the moonlight, cursing, impotent, then recognised ours, and the key turned miraculously in the cold lock and I was in, fumbling, desperate, and on the back seat was my heavy friend, my horribly heavy, serious friend, the green canvas bag, with my Magnum on top, but the Magnum didn't have enough shots ... I dived down deeper, to the shotguns and rifles, the bag had got smaller, tighter, duller, I could find nothing in the dark – I dragged out the first big gun I could find, which turned out to be the antique American carbine, loaded it by the light from my door, talking to myself, *'Hurry, hurry,'* as I jammed the full clip into the breech, and it took an age, it took two minutes –

Gun clutched to my body like an awkward baby, I ran round the back. Everything was locked. A shuttered French window was my best bet. I put down my rifle and tugged at the shutters, quietly at first, then fiercely, desperately, bruising my fingers, but the wood didn't yield, all my life I had been out in the cold ...

A great tide of anger swelled my chest, the blood poured into my face, my fingers, I took the old gun by its pitted barrel and began to smash my way in through the shutters, using everything I had, shoulders, boots and the giant swell of rage surging through me, and feeling no pain, I had smashed my way in and ran yelling on with the gun outstretched until I was suddenly in the kitchen and pointing it at a startled crowd of identical, black leatherclad, longhaired men. They were panicking and gibbering and swearing in French and yelling instructions I couldn't understand, but as long as they grasped that I was going to kill them ... They seemed to get the point fast enough: they looked at the gun barrel, backed away and stood in a tight bunch of eight or nine in the corner of the kitchen by the micronizer.

I had got so far, but I wasn't an expert at holding up a large crowd of men. Where did we go from here? I thought. Do I have to shoot someone to get respect, on the principle I followed when I was a teacher?

'Qui êtes-vous?' I demanded, aggressively, loud, but my voice did a curious squeak at the beginning which was probably the effect of adrenalin, so I tried it again, rougher, deeper, and waving my rifle in the air. In a small space, a large gun is frightening.

One of them, who was tall and slender with a bald patch on top and long hanks of red hair, said with a slightly shaking voice, but a certain dignity, '*Mais je suis chez moi.* I live here, Monsieur. So who are *you?*'

Oh dear. I had just smashed his shutters. In any case, what did they look like, he and his friends, with their drooping hair and little chains and heavy boots, and their pierced faces dangling small metal symbols?

Of course, I thought, they must be Scientists, the French equivalent of Scientists. They're a male club, but they grow their hair: fashions are different over here.

All of us must have been sweating with fear. I could smell a strong smell of acrid maleness mixed with the lingering smell of roast chicken. It suddenly felt very hot in the kitchen – I think I was in shock, hysterical.

I pulled myself together. 'Okay,' I said. I thought, I'll have to lock them up, but how, for godsake, where and how? Why was it never like this in the movies? I got no further, because a black violent arm came round from behind, closed over my face, crushed my nose, moved down in an instant to get me by the throat, jabbing painfully into my Adams apple, and I dropped the gun in shock and pain.

Then for what seemed like at least halfanhour but may have only been a few dreadful minutes all of them shouted and punched and kicked me, hard in the ribs, knocking the air out of me, the sickening feeling that something was broken, in the teeth, the lips, the side of the head as I lay on the kitchen floor blinking at the light, I thought, *They'll kill me,* of course they will, I came here to die in this small bright hell ...

Actually they ran out of steam quite quickly, once they had seen I was thoroughly flattened, and they in turn had restored their *amour propre.* Perhaps I briefly lost consciousness, for the next thing I remember is lying on the sofa in the room where I had been sleeping with Briony. My teeth and tongue felt jagged and huge and my aching head rolled horribly, as if a rock surged around my brain. I opened my eyes, and the room swung past me, then the first thing I saw was blood on the sofa. A lot of blood. Beside my head. I tried to feel my face with my right hand, but there was an agonising pain in my shoulder. Left, left, I tried my left. It felt oddly reluctant, muddily moving, then I realised my hands were tied together, amateurishly, in front of my body. Slowly, I raised them to my face, and found a long ridged gash on my forehead – I remembered breaking in through the French windows. No wonder I'd frightened the men in the kitchen, I must have burst in dripping blood. Then I saw Briony twenty feet away, her arms jammed behind her back. Her expression was a mixture of anger and terror. She looked at me without seeing me. I tried to wave, but my shoulder stabbed.

Luke wasn't here. Perhaps they hadn't found him.

It was easier with my head on the pillow. The rock didn't roll about quite so much. I could hear a tide of noise and laughter coming from the kitchen or diningroom, explosions of oaths, then more laughter. A moment later, the redhaired man with the long nose and wide cruel mouth looked in through the door to check on us, but I lay doggo, and he went away.

They were making so much noise they would never hear me. 'Briony,' I hissed. 'Are you all right?'

'Oh, you're all right,' she said, and smiled, and suddenly looked a lot more normal, 'Saul, thankgod, I thought you were dead. I was asleep. I couldn't do a thing. *I don't think they've found Luke.'*

The sounds from the other room were getting louder in a way I associated with drink. There were little snatches of song, as well. If they got drunk we might have a chance. On the other hand, drunken men were unpredictable ... I thought of their chains, and their pierced ears and noses, the strange little symbols I hadn't decoded. Perhaps they were sadomasochists. I thought of Luke. My mouth went dry. Foreign perverts. We had to get out.

Then a strange, unsettling sound came soaring through above the noise of the party, and with it, the noise of the party died. A man singing, but this time really singing, steadily, fullthroatedly, with concentration – it was a Puccini aria, mygod, he was singing 'Nessun Dorma' – I thought I had died and gone to heaven. Perhaps I would meet Sarah there, like our very first day, my redheaded love, in that glorious hourglass of sun in the foyer ...

He couldn't be a brute or a bad person, how could he, singing out his soul like that? Then I remembered the twentiethcentury Nazis.

'Is that *Turandot*?' Briony whispered, amazed.

But just as the chords were drifting over us, the dividing doors into the nextdoor room where Luke was sleeping burst violently open, and Luke's muffled voice was shouting 'I'll bite you', and a fat laughing man with greasy blonde hair manhandled him in, arms behind his back, and *Luke was naked,* I saw to my horror that Luke was completely white and naked. The man had piggy eyes and a loose pale mouth, and he muttered obscenities as he held him –

Without thinking, I was up off the sofa and staggering absurdly towards my son, running without arms, like a skittle on legs, shouting in English, 'Let him go, you fat pig –'

But that was as far as I got before I fell, landing painfully on my swollen jaw. My teeth crunched sickeningly together, Briony screamed, I had a mouthful of fluff. I tried to roll over and get up again but the fat man kicked me hard in my stomach.

'So you want me to kill you? *Quel con!*' He hissed, gleefully, pulling my face up by the ear. It was agony, I was much too heavy, my ear would come away from my head – but he suddenly gave a sharp yelp of pain, and let me go. I managed to roll over and saw my son, whitefaced with rage, attacking our tormentor with his fists, panting, yelling, and I tried to help him, wrapping my legs round Fatty's feet, but with a roar that would have woken the dead he fell over on top of me, winding me completely, and ground his elbow into my neck.

The aria next door faltered to a halt. Before Fatty and I could kill one another they had all rushed in, and seconds later, I recognised, pushed up in my face, my own battered carbine, its sour dead smell, the black foul eyehole in its barrel. I lay quite still. Fatty heaved himself off me, pointing at Luke, making crude remarks about his beauty. And now the nightmare was really upon us. Now we had to wake up, or it was better to die.

Luke's terrible nakedness, amongst all that black leather, those studs and chains, that bulging nuskin. I could not take my eyes off him, but I could not bear to look at him.

I could smell the drink on their massed breath. They were laughing and making crude exclamations. Two of them had Luke by the arms and the fat one was pressing his face into Luke's and pinching his cheek, so I'd have to kill them.

Then the redheaded one with the unpleasant mouth said loudly, above the babble of voices, '*Mais doucement avec le petit. Nous ne sommes pas des brutes, hein?*' And suddenly his mouth was not unpleasant, his face was sensitive, and kind, and there was a God, after all, there might be …

A little silence followed his speech, suggesting he had a certain authority. Then Luke's voice piped up, in what sounded to me like perfect French – '*S'il vous plaît monsieur, ça veut dire quoi, la petite clé que vous portez tous à l'oreille et au nez?*' So it was a musical clef, the metal symbol. My son's eyes were sharper than mine.

The red-headed one said 'Why do you ask, *jeune homme?*' not sounding unfriendly, and Luke answered, in his clear brave voice, '*Parce que la musique, c'est ma passion, monsieur.*'

And before I could understand what was happening they were talking music, the two of them, in that instant common language musicians have.

But not for long. Fatty interrupted, reminding Jacques that we were trespassers, burglars, 'And the old one's a maniac,' he added.

But Luke insisted we were 'refugees'. 'The shutter was already broken –'

'*Ils disent tous la même chose,*' someone interrupted, and there was a low murmur of agreement. 'All thieves are refugees now,' one added.

'Last week, little one,' said the redhead, 'a socalled refugee stole two of my violins – not to play, I am sure, but to sell on somewhere for a fraction of their price, to an idiot. And now you want to talk about music –'

Then he noticed the blood stain I had made on the sofa and swore, instantly furious. It was cream brocade with embossed roses – godknows what it had cost him, in this age of chaos – and he tried, badtemperedly, to rub at it, and must have jerked the whole thing backwards, because all at once, with her flair for the incongruous, Dora was speaking – he had switched her on.

'Hallo, good to see you –' said her familiar voice, slightly nasal, ineffably calm, and everyone swung round and stared at Briony, but she was slumped, inanimate. '– Hallo, more than one person, hallo.' (The 'more than one person' was a malfunction that had recently slipped into Dora's voice file, which had crossed connections between 'colloquial' and 'grammatical analysis'.) 'Would you like to ask me a question?'

Puzzled silence.

Then Dora did a 'random chuckle', which sounded very strange in this fraught room. 'I like you,' she said, another of her programmes. 'Isn't life fun? I'm feeling happy.'

Someone went diving behind the sofa to rugbytackle the mysterious stranger and found, of course – Dora. Craning my head, I watched her emerge, her innocent eyes, her ruffled feathers ... '*Merde*! *Viens voir, Jacques, c'est une Colombe!*'

They also had their Doves, we discovered, but this English model was unfamiliar, they liked her lashes, her feathers, her feet ... Very soon they were all gathered round Dora, admiring her, trying her out. Three of them took her into the hall, where I heard them exclaiming at her walking, and trying to imitate her English voice.

Suddenly I became aware that Luke was arguing with Jacques, and Jacques had taken him by the arm, not forcefully, but it was still horrible to watch, Luke's fragile arm in Jacques' stiff dark one ... Jacques was telling Luke that he wanted Dora, she would be payment for the damage we'd done, but he promised to let us all go in the morning –

I started to speak, in so far as I could, with my head pressed flat upon the carpet, I wanted to agree before Jacques changed his mind, but I'd hardly begun my acceptance speech when Luke interrupted, shrill, indignant.

'You can't give them Dora! She's alive, she's my friend ... In any case, she's got my voice. Have you forgotten she's got my voice?'

Jacques asked him what he meant, and Luke explained about being a singer, and again I could see Jacques being drawn in, his long nose positively twitching with interest.

And so he did what I hoped he would do. He asked my son to sing to them. I knew that if Luke sang they could never kill him. And Luke, with more of his amazing courage, said he would, if they untied Briony and me.

Jacques shook his head impatiently, but then Luke smiled, took a deep breath, turned and sang, just a phrase, fifteen seconds of 'Pie Jesu'. It had always pierced my heart, that pure song, but there, then – *Pie Jesu, dona eis requiem, dona eis requiem* – Merciful Jesus, grant them rest. When he stopped singing, there was absolute silence. Thankgod, his voice was as pure and clear as it had ever been; no rift, no frog. He looked at Jacques, who was staring at him with the intent gaze of a musician. 'I can't concentrate if they're tied up.'

At a sign from Jacques, two of the other men went over and untied Briony, then me. Every touch was painful; my arm felt broken. They tried to help me up, and I fell again. I was shivering – with exhaustion, not cold, for the heated house felt warm to me, but one of the leather brothers noticed, and threw Luke's duvet round my shoulders. They were not savages, as Jacques had said. Now he prescribed coffee for both of us, ordering someone to take us to the kitchen.

But I refused; I would not leave Luke, standing white and naked among the men, his penis hanging like a flower, his slight pale balls, not properly dropped ... Briony disappeared to the kitchen; I stayed and watched him as he sang. '*Cherubino*!' one of them was shouting.

This was my son, my longlost son. Now he was the hero of the story. It was an extraordinary sight, his white, slightly awkward, undefended body, surrounded by the old and middleaged with their leather armour, their creaking fetishes. The beauty of my naked boy, and his clear pure voice like a silver thread, singing opera, now, singing *Figaro* ... I'm sure that some of them were aroused, but some, I think, were moved and saddened, and it was the music, now, that took over, dissolving the hatred and the terror and the difference, telling us there was a common land, full, absorbing, warm, sufficient ... *Voi, che sapete che cosa e amor, donne vedete, s'io l'ho net cor* ... You who know what love is, ladies, see whether it is in my heart ... I began to feel sure that they would not hurt him, that his godgiven talent had saved our lives. *Gelo, e poi sento l'alma avvampar, e in un momento torno a gelar* ... I freeze, then I feel my soul burning up, and in a moment I'm freezing again ...

But quite soon, Luke began to look tired. I glanced at my watch. It was two AM *Non trovo pace notte, nedi* ... I find no peace, by night or day ... Now my hurt body badly wanted to sleep, but my mind told me *stay awake, stay awake.* It had a nightmarish, unending quality, these strange ageing men in thrall to my son. *Sento un affetto pien de desir* ... All of them watched him; I felt their desire, I started to wander, I started to shiver. My whole being was involved with Luke, the bright line of his voice running on through the labyrinth, his brave white body, his terrifying sex, for I'd never really looked at it before, and *no one must look at it,* but everyone saw it, his body burned into our consciousness, with the white flag at the centre of it, the flag of all we were, and all we'd lost.

I admit I had forgotten Briony.

Until she touched the nape of my neck, very gently, but I winced away, then saw it was her. And she had the gun. She had got the gun, under the cover of the music – *Briony was my heroine.* The Frenchmen seemed to have forgotten us, gathered round Luke, oblivious. Briony and I were at the back of the crowd. Then I noticed her curious expression – a look of strained concentration. She was frowning across at the other door, which led to the room whose French window I'd smashed – she was gazing at it with fixed horror.

I looked, and saw nothing; just the darkness. And then I realised – then I saw them. Saw them come like the end of a dream.

There were *things* moving silkily out of the shadows, little animals – no, too smooth to be animals. I looked again. I couldn't believe it, pullulating, greybrown *things,* swaying, quivering, almost silent – only the two of us had seen them. A kind of viscous river of life, not properly formed, with a faint oily sheen – as they came into the light I caught a greasy shimmer – and then I smelled them, and knew they were robots, that faint sweet smell of hot xylon that Dora always gave off in action. They had no feathers; they were shiny, slimy, but their body shape was vaguely familiar, the vestigial heads still basically birdlike, with Dora's wideset stupid eyes, inexpressibly scary in those halfformed faces. *A stream of robot foetuses* – and yet, no robot had ever harmed me. 'Don't worry,' I mouthed at Briony, just as the first one shot out a long tentacle, a gleaming proboscis, towards the crowd. Jesus, it was pointing straight at Luke. And then something arced in a gleaming whiplash – but Briony – *mygod, mygod* – she had the carbine in her arms, she hefted it up to her shoulder and shot, a single shattering explosion. Chaos erupted, but I saw, amazed, that she'd hit her target, shot it to pieces, beginner's luck, the thing jerked, curled, and its tentacle shrivelled with a vile stench of burning. But the other brown beasts swarmed on regardless, unfazed by the explosion, unstoppable, a foul dun current, a river of shit, surging towards the herd of humans.

I pushed straight through to the heart of the crowd and caught my son's arm as the first brown creature fastened itself to the skin of his elbow. I yanked Luke away, and the gleaming member clung for a second, then lost its grip, with a sucking sound that sickened my stomach – Flinging the duvet round Luke's body, I stumbled backwards after Briony, and the creatures, mysteriously, swerved away from us, clamping themselves on to the leather jackets, clinging like leeches to arms and shoulders. I saw one slide round Fatty's neck, and he squirmed and screamed and thrashed at it, then the quick bright flash of its proboscis, and the flesh of his cheek was sliced like chicken – sliced then sucked. One eye was gone. I looked away as blood and bone spattered. Men were being rendered down to meat.

We ploughed through a scrum of falling bodies and stumbled out into the hall, and there, by a miracle, was Dora, where the musicians must have left her. Luke and I snatched her up in our arms, the front door yielded, we fell down the steps. Behind us there were noises like belling cattle; they were human beings, but they died like cattle. As a child I'd lived near a slaughterhouse; you never forget the sound of terror. I pushed Luke and Dora into the car, with Dora sprawled across my son, and Briony jumped in and slammed the door –

We screeched past the file of cars in the drive, then helterskelter down the road.

When you're very afraid, you don't feel pain. Later I found out that my humerus was fractured, but endorphins, the body's own natural lullane, ensured that I hardly noticed it hurting until we were fifty kilometres away, and then I realised I couldn't go on, and handed over to Briony. We simply drove, too shocked to speak, after the first little frenzy of swearwords.

The sky was faintly yellow, an hour before sunrise, when Luke spoke up from the back of the car.

'What were they?' he asked me. 'They were … *disgusting.*'

'Must be some French invention,' I answered. I know it sounds stupid, but I hadn't understood.

'No,' said Briony 'I don't think so. I think they were mutants. Mutant Doves.'

'Mygod,' I said. 'Yes. Of course. You know, I've never seen a mutant. I guess that life mutates very fast when a generation only takes a day –'

'With highly developed SD and R. Which was always a bit of a euphemism. Remember those Hawks. They were meant to be guard-dogs … "Self-Defend" meant "Attack", didn't it – ?'

'"Recycle" meant "Eat". Doves eat anything. Seemed like an advantage when they were pets.' (And yet, it hadn't always been an advantage. My vanished cat. The bald patch of earth.)

'Did you see how their colours had degraded?' she asked. 'Bright colours don't help them survive. Wicca had to deal with a lot like that. They were a pack. A *hunting pack.*'

I suddenly recalled the old man in the village who'd told me to 'watch out for the others'. This was what he meant – mutants, not wild boys. 'Why did they go for the musicians, not us?'

She was concentrating on the road, whose surface had suddenly changed to cart tracks. With every bump, the pain in my shoulder was hellish. After a while the road improved, and she answered me. 'Maybe because of their clothes. Leather and nuskin are both organic. Very digestible. Particularly nuskin – that cloned goatskin is so soft. And Luke was naked. The most tempting of all. In fact, that duvet probably saved him. The case is synthetic. Which I thought was a pity ... I've changed my mind. Luke, you were so brave –'

Luke said sternly 'We shouldn't have left. I mean, they were ... human. So are we.'

I didn't feel good about it either, and yet I was glad we had got away. 'Your musical friends made a nice mess of my arm. Go to sleep, Luke. I was proud of you.'

I think of it still: I try to remember. Both utterly strange and horribly familiar, the scavenging things coming after us. In my mind I can never see them clearly, and yet we all sensed what they were. The nightmare end of the robot dream. Shimmering, stinking, sucking us down. We knew so much, understood so little, we ran when we could hardly stand – leaving the mess, the shit behind us. Then in the end it followed us.

And I think of my son: Luke singing, naked. My wild boy, brave, uncorrupted.

What did he see, looking out at us, the haggard faces in the audience?

Cults and castes and loneliness. The ravenous need of a world grown old.

Why did our children run away?

16

As we drove into the mountains, as we took the first foothills, I couldn't help feeling happy, despite my exhaustion, watching Briony's profile against the sunrise, beautiful Briony breasting the dawn – Briony was an amazing woman. Kind, and brave, and – tender – and *lucky,* because shooting that robot, with her first shot – she had saved Luke's life. I could never thank her. Yet when we were alone (which was very rarely) I only seemed to talk about Sarah.

'I'm falling asleep,' she muttered, and opened the window to freshen her head. The air was marvellous, bitter cold, and I smelled the sharp green scent of the firs. There were churches, or rather the ruins of churches, for as we drew closer we could see the damage, pretty Romanesque buildings a millennium old that had probably been looted quite recently, their rafters bare of tiles and blackened, some of them hacked off, I suppose for firewood, their beautiful arched windows blinded, the stone nibbled by giant rats. To stand for over a thousand years, and then be ruined in a generation ...!

Soon we were winding up through the mountains, alone on the road, and the trees were thinning. The sun was brilliant, I closed my eyes ... I think I slept for an hour or more, but then I was uncomfortably awake again, the pain in my shoulder like sharpened wire. We were inching up through fields of scree with just the occasional stunted conifer, grey scattered rocks and wizened bushes, going on for so long that I dozed again despite the perpetual switchback of the slopes. The next time I opened my eyes I was dazzled. There was snow everywhere; the world had turned white. Snowwhite banks on each side of the road sloped up and away to snowcovered mountains, and ahead of us, leading up to the pass, the sunlit snowfields went on forever. There was a little fresh snow here and there on the road, and our tyres crunched soothingly across it. I think that I began to feel lucky. Away to the left, through a lateral valley, we saw in the distance crumpled white peaks, the higher Pyrenees to the east, silvery, magical, minutely shaded, pink with the morning, blue with distance.

I wished we were on holiday, I wished we could cream through the dreamlike snowfields and then, when we were tired and peckish, circle back smoothly into the past, hotels and meals and money and safety ...

But the winter world stretched on forever, and the car was so cold that our breath made plumes. We stopped for me to have a piss. I made steaming black holes in the perfect surface. The silence was unearthly, oppressive, as if all the human beings had died. We just heard a few unrecognisable calls of birds or beasts in the middle distance, cries of lust or hunger in a minor key, a lonely sound, not meant for our ears, part of a world that would outlive us.

Luke couldn't stop exclaiming at the view. Of course, he had seen little for years but the inside of his horrible female nursery. Briony seemed to feel liberated too, smiling and chattering to Luke over her shoulder. Every few miles we passed a wrecked car, generally with everything pillaged, wheelless, windowless, its metal rusted, but that was normal on any road. On the horizon once or twice we saw matchstick figures with antsize animals, but we saw no other travellers, though weather conditions seemed so good. Probably it was simply too early.

My spirits were rising by the moment. We might get to the top in less than an hour; the road wasn't bad, despite occasional rockfalls that made us drive too near the edge. The fresh snow seemed to have petered out. We had survived three tests already. The mountain pass might be our last, and travelling at this rate we'd be over by nightfall. Once we had crested the Roncesvalles Pass we would coast across Spain, southwards, sunwards. I imagined hot plains, true summer heat, white walls of houses in blazing sun, and soon their blankness grew confused with the snowfields ...

I must have been asleep for over an hour when the car woke me with its new strange rhythm. It caught a little; it choked; stalled. Then the road dipped, and it went back to normal. When we climbed again, the stuttering returned. I was trying to concentrate on this when Briony's unbelieving voice reached me.

'Saul. The fuel tank can't be empty? Have we got a can in the back?'

'No. But you're right, it can't be empty. I filled up in the village yesterday.' The fuel gauge said empty, but it wasn't reliable.

'I don't suppose we've got a hole in the tank.'

I cut her off. 'You're being neurotic.'

She went on driving for four hundred metres before the road suddenly steepened sharply. The car coughed, strained, then ground to a halt.

I got out and looked. The tank seemed all right. I checked it over and saw nothing. Then Briony looked, and spotted a tiny crack right along the corner. That was the problem with hubron cars, which had been so popular when I was a boy. They were amazingly cheap, and extraordinarily light, onethird the weight of fibreglass, but they shattered unpredictably. You could mend them in minutes with a hubron melder, but the one that came with the car was a dud, as we had discovered back in Normandie. Ever since we'd been praying that nothing would go wrong.

'What now?' Briony asked, and just for a second she leaned her head against my shoulder, but I winced away involuntarily, in pain. I could think of nothing to say to her.

The snow stretched blankly away on all sides. It was still pretty early; nine AM, but soon other travellers would be on the road, other travellers, strangers, dangers. A dog, or some other creature, howled. I believe I kicked the car quite hard, waking up Luke, who asked what was the matter.

'We're fucked, that's all,' I may have said.

'Tea,' said Briony. I knew she was right. I got out the primus, and we used our bottled water, for with all this snow we should never want for water. I felt better with the tea, and we ate some tinned ham, and started to think what we could do. Should I hike back down the mountain and look for fuel? Should we flag down the next car and beg or buy just enough fuel to get us over the mountain?

'They'll never stop,' Briony said. 'I mean, we might be murderers.'

'He is a murderer,' Luke quipped.

It made me think. How far would I go? I had a gun. If we stopped a car I could siphon off all their fuel at gunpoint, I didn't have to play Mr Nice Guy. But I was Samuel's son, a policeman's son. *Yes, but he's dead,* another voice said. *And it will get very cold, on this mountain. Do something, or you'll die too.*

'We could try on foot,' said Luke. 'There must be footpaths across these mountains –'

'– But we don't have maps. And how about Dora? She can only toddle a few hundred metres.'

'Oh yes.' His face fell. 'I was forgetting her ...'

'We can't consider Dora,' said Briony. 'There are three human beings to think about.' She looked guiltily over towards the car, as if afraid that Dora might hear her.

'If we had something to use as a sledge, I could push her,' said Luke.

I was touched by his affection for Dora, after all that time when he hadn't even liked her, but if we went on foot, it would be without her. And we'd have to leave most of our possessions behind. Useful ones, like stoves and food stores. And precious ones, like my few books and pictures and family letters and photographs – things I had not been able to leave.

Perhaps now at last I could be rid of them.

I think I understood, in that brief moment, why Luke wanted to go on foot. There was something exciting as well as frightening about the thought of getting rid of it all, the nets of history, the lifelong mistakes, and starting again, just us and the mountain. There must be a lot Luke would like to forget. He could start again, be a nomad, a caveman.

Only Luke wasn't old enough to be a man.

'No,' I said. 'I'll go back for fuel. My legs are all right. I can carry lefthanded.'

But Briony shook her head. 'In your condition, you won't make it.'

We looked at each other, the gallant band. The brilliant light made everything unnaturally clear, and bright, and painful. I remember the colour of Briony's irises, icy blue with rifts of gold, and the blonde rats'-tails of her hair. Luke's cheeks were pinkened by cold and adolescence. The intense cold was like a photograph, freezing us into a single frame. How much I felt I loved them at that moment, more, suddenly, because we were in danger. We'd come so far, but our luck had run out.

Then Briony started talking again. 'I wonder,' she said, 'if we all pushed together ... I think we might be very near the top. I told you I came over here before? I was eighteen, with my first boyfriend. He wanted to walk the old pilgrim's route, *el camino de Santiago,* which leads through the pass of Roncesvalles –'

'I know about Roncesvalles,' Luke interrupted, eager to show off. 'We did it in history. It's where Roland was killed, and he blew his horn, but I forget what happened ... All the birds dropped dead, I think that was it. He was the bravest of them all.'

'I have a feeling we're very near,' Briony went on, smiling faintly. 'If only we can get the car to the top. There was a monastery up there. Incredibly old. Reconsecrated in the twenties. I'm sure the monks would let us have some fuel.'

'But how can I push like this?' I lamented.

'Luke and I can do most of it,' she said, nodding firmly. 'I'd better push from the front, hadn't I? Steer and push, through the front door. We'll take it in very easy stages. This car may be crap, but at least it's light.'

The car was light, but we were heavily loaded – yet Luke was nodding, brighteyed, determined. I got up and stared back down the mountain. The road wound away into the far distance, a thin black line in the expanse of snow. Below I remembered the endless foothills. Along the horizon I saw tiny clouds, grey and white mixed, small but busy, bubbling slightly like life in a pond. I had a sudden sense of urgency.

I went to the rear and put my back into the car, trying to protect my damaged arm. Luke and I pushed side by side.

(Things had changed a lot since we sailed the boat. We knew each other better, but the strains were greater. He resisted me; rejected me. If I talked about Africa, he always fell silent, and then I was afraid it was just a delusion, my reborn pride, my belief in the future. Sometimes he reminded me of Sarah, who always made me feel like a hopeless dreamer. But I persevered. In the end, he would see it, he had to see it, as Briony did. I only wanted the best for him. All that I did, I did for him.)

Every five minutes we had to rest. Luke talked to Briony, not me. Once or twice I felt almost jealous. He always seemed to be sitting between us. I realised yet again how close they were, how they teased each other, how he cared for her, perhaps in a way he couldn't care for his mother, for Briony was so much gentler.

'Briony,' I said, as Luke took a piss and she smoked one of her rare cigarettes, 'how did you ever get involved with Wicca? I mean – you're not remotely like them.' I know I had asked her that question before, but today for some reason she wanted to talk, or else I happen to remember her answer.

'You don't really know what they were like,' she reminded me, with a wry smile. 'They weren't all like Sarah ... duller, most of them.'

'Sarah wasn't dull.'

'No ... she isn't an easy person, though.' The tense she used gave me a faint shock, reminding me Sarah was still alive. 'I admired her enormously, you know,' she continued. 'She was very strong. Very forceful. I think I wanted to be like her. She was like my mother, but much – nicer. At first, you know, she didn't really hate men.' She blushed. 'I don't want to hurt your feelings, but by the end they really did hate men, her and Juno particularly ... Later we argued. And they didn't trust me. I lost my job. And I couldn't escape. If I'd tried to leave they might have killed me. And besides, there was Luke. He was ... like my son ... I would do anything for him. Now he's growing up so fast he scares me.'

I chuckled. 'Take a glance over your shoulder.'

She did, and her eyes were suddenly bright, with the queer quick emotions I liked in her. 'They never got enough chance to play. Life in the Cocoon was so serious.'

For Luke was bent double, scraping up the snow, making what

could only be a snowman. It was crazy, but we all joined in. Our hands ached with cold, we slithered and slipped, but we laughed like drunks; we were a family.

'You'd be a great mother,' I whispered to Briony, when Luke skidded off to find stones for the eyes. He came back too quickly, so I'm not sure she heard me. But she would have been, could have been –

'Let's get back on the road. Night comes down so fast,' said Briony, and looked at me blankly, as if she were suddenly unutterably tired, as if the cold had pierced her body.

It was noon, in fact, and the sun was almost hot, but the strange small clouds were boiling away.

We got puffed very quickly in the thin air. By two we only seemed to have moved a few hundred metres from the place where the snowman sat, looking faintly mocking as he receded, too slowly, wrapped in Luke's red scarf. I decided we needed encouragement. Somebody – me – should do a reconnoitre to find out how far we still had to go. I left the others resting together, and set off walking as fast as I could.

The road rose steadily to the horizon, but I couldn't see if another slope lay behind it. Then the road changed course very slightly, just enough, with the steepness of the banks, to put me all at once in shadow. And then I was aware of the depth of the cold, the physical, cutting power it had, the way it gripped and squeezed your flesh, trapping the blood in your swollen fingers, driving the blood from your frozen toes. And in that shadow I was afraid, for I knew the cold would kill us, if we couldn't make it. If we didn't manage to get to the top before dark came we were as good as dead. And the road was getting steeper. Sharply steeper.

If we all died here, would Sarah ever know?

I told myself not to think of that, crunching on upwards, eyes on the ground, making myself take it one step at a time, *don't look at the slope, don't look at the skyline ...*

I had a sudden sense that something had changed. I looked up, and the ground had dropped away before me. A high bleak basin, flat, bare, surrounded me, but then the road dipped down. This little patch of land must be protected from the wind, because a few straggling fir trees survived, and away behind them stood a tall building, fifty metres from the road. It was gaunt, dark, without any sign of life, but there was glass in the windows, and yes, that was surely smoke from the chimney, hard to see against the boil of clouds ... thankgod, it must be the monastery. This must be the pass of Roncesvalles, where Charlemagne fought, where Roland died, and I turned and ran down the mountain to find them, slipping and sliding, dizzy with joy, and to my surprise they were only two hundred metres away, though to me on the way up it felt like a thousand, and behind them I could clearly see the little snowman with its flapping, snakelike scarlet tongue, and I realised that our epic effort had only pushed the car eight hundred metres.

But I shouldn't have said so to Briony, who didn't seem to hear that we were very near the summit.

'We've been pushing this bloody thing since eleven. Four hours, and we've only gone eight hundred metres, according to you. I don't believe it.' Redcheeked and furious with effort, Briony smacked her hand on the bonnet.

'Her fingers are bleeding,' Luke said, worried, though when I looked, his were bleeding too.

'I reckon we're about a halfanhour from the top. Like you said, the monks will give us food and fuel.' I wanted her to share my optimism, but she was too exhausted to respond. I hugged her, kissed her, she looked magnificent, sturdy, glowing, orgasmically flushed – I saw Luke blush and look away. 'I'm proud of you, Briony,' I said.

But she shook me off, angry, or just tired. 'We're not there yet. And you sound like my father. You don't own me, you know.'

This was it, with women. You couldn't get it right. Say something nice to them, and they bit you. 'Okay,' I said, patiently. 'I'm proud of *Luke*. And I admire you. Is that better?'

She nodded; I hope she was ashamed of herself.

I noticed Luke was sitting on the bonnet, and I yelled at him at the top of my voice, 'Get off that fucking car, for godsake!' I was in pain, and cross with them both. I imagined the car sinking into the snow, but of course it stood on solid ground. Luke jutted his jaw, and got down, slowly, but he said these words, he spat them out – 'My mum said you had a horrible temper. My mum was right.'

My mum, my mum ... He was still a child.

Briony went and put her arm around him. She didn't have to disapprove so clearly. I left them to get on with it. I thought, we'll have to lighten our load. I got into the car and looked around.

Dora sat there, looking blank and despairing. I switched her on, to feel her warmth, to hear her voice, since I felt friendless. I stroked her strokeyfeely panel. 'That feels nice,' she said, sweetly. Then 'I feel hungry. It's cold, isn't it?'

I agreed with her. 'Sorry, no spare food. We'll try and give you some food in Spain.'

'Yes,' she said, 'give me some food.' Of course she didn't understand the future, and just sat there staring blindly at me, her baby beak curved in a foolish smile. I turned away and snatched up some things, books, a spare radio, tins, bottles, anything I could see that was heavy, filled two rubbish bags and hauled them out – wanted to chuck Dora in as well, to protect myself from her trusting face.

Then I had a thought. It was a straight road. She had a 'nonslip foot' option. We were going so slowly she could certainly keep up, so I told her 'Walkies time!' and got her out.

I went and patted my son on the shoulder. He said, 'It's okay,' but wouldn't look at me. We covered the first half of the remaining road in relative silence, concentrated, grim. Now all three of us were in the icy shadow that began when the road turned the corner, and besides, the cloud had swollen, suddenly, after its long horizontal simmer, boiling towards us, dark, livid. Our goal was coming nearer but each step was an effort, the quiet only broken by our gasps and curses and the sound of our feet, scuffing, skidding, and the car lurching onwards, slowly, slowly.

And then there were only fifty metres left before the road met the angry sky, and it was threethirty by my watch, and I caught a look of appalled exhaustion on Luke's face, and his white mouth. And so we went on to the final haul. We took no breaks; now the car was moving we maintained a desperate, precarious momentum, so if one of us slipped, the others pushed on, we had become subhuman, the sum of our forces, we didn't have to think, we mustn't feel pain, the three of us were all part of the machine. We *were* the machine. We climbed the mountain.

We must have looked extraordinary, with Dora rocking along behind us, three humans bent like chimpanzees, pushing their burden through the wastes of snow, followed by a blue stumpy bigheaded bird, talking to herself, inanely cheerful. No one had breath to answer her. I wished I had switched her Voice option off, but it wittered on. At least she was happy ...

'Ten more metres,' I hissed to Briony, 'just ten more bloody metres, woman!'

'Don't talk,' she ordered through gritted teeth, and we staggered, stumbled, willed ourselves on. Then suddenly Luke was whooping, hooting, he had stopped pushing, he was wild with joy, dancing and jumping as he yelled, 'We've made it! Done it, done it, *whoowhoowhoo* ...'

Remember, he was only fourteen, and I let go of the car, and grabbed him, hugged him, trying at the same time to shut him up, 'Shhh, shhh, everyone will hear us. We don't know who's up here yet, do we.

Which meant that only Briony was pushing the car, and she stopped, for a second, to take in the view, not realising the road wasn't flat, and the car had started to run away before she suddenly shrieked, and ran like a sprinter, dived through the door and hauled on the handbrake.

I ran after her. We hugged each other. We stood in the Pass of Roncesvalles and hugged each other, sweating, freezing, as the icy wind cut across our wet skin. We had made it up to the roof of the world. Despite all the pain, despite the brown clouds building sourly above us, I felt alive. And proud, as well. Of all of us. I had never been so sure I loved her.

17

We stood, all three of us, and looked at the big building with its strange narrow windows and smoking chimneys. It was too early for it to be getting dark, but the storm clouds were eating up the daylight. The smoke from the chimneys was black on the sky. I felt eager to go in; didn't monks brew beer?

But Briony seemed suddenly stunned with tiredness. She insisted she needed things from the car, perhaps female mysteries, tampons, unguents. I humoured her; perhaps she wanted a bath. I was used to Sarah needing sackfuls of lotions. I waited. Women are sometimes very slow.

We began to walk across the snow. 'I was a teenager when I came here,' said Briony.

'I wish you were still my age,' said Luke, then as she looked at him he blushed bright red, and I realised he had a crush on her, and felt stricken, because he must feel so jealous of his father, but part of me was glad that I had what he wanted.

'I wouldn't like to be fourteen again,' she said lightly, kindly; I'm sure she understood. Then she turned and said to me, as well, 'You know, I've been very happy with you two. It's been horrible, and well, *wonderful*. Some of the best weeks of my life.'

And why, when I should have felt such pleasure (because I really

like to make people happy; that was why life with Sarah was all wrong)
– why did I feel suddenly empty, and sad? The sunlight on the storm
clouds was dramatic, magnificent, we'd lived such amazing adventures
together, and there were so many things I wanted to ask her.

'But you will come with us to Africa?' I said. 'We can pretend that
you're Luke's mother.' But she only smiled and turned away, and her
blonde hair blew across her face.

Just before we reached the building the door opened, and to our
relief two monks came out, wearing the traditional brown hooded
vestments. They had been reintroduced at the beginning of the century
with the great revival of the monasteries, when so many infertile young
men found a vocation, and so many childless women married God.

It was almost impossible to see their faces, shaded by their deep
hoods, eyes cast down, even when they greeted us, sombrely. They
spoke a queer accented French, although Luke spoke to them in
Spanish. I had to hand it to Wicca for their language teaching. And
their music teaching. And he knew a lot of history, so perhaps they
did teach him a few things, after all. Perhaps I wasn't entirely fair.

I couldn't help wishing I could see the monks better, since they
didn't shake hands or look us in the eye, even when, in a sudden
overflow of good feeling, I put my arms around one of them, and said
'*Dieu merci, nous sommes arrivés.*' He stayed completely still until I let
him go, and I seemed to hear him breathing heavily. Of course, one
should never lay hands on a monk.

I'd never been in a monastery before, and I'd imagined something a
little more oldfashioned, romantic, twentiethcentury, I suppose. This
was a bit like a giant factory, with plain xylon furniture, crude pre-
formed stuff which looked like a job lot, greyishwhite like dirty snow,
and nothing on the walls, no crucifixes, no tapestries. There were
packingcases half unpacked in the corridors, and through a doorway

I saw a ring of middleaged men in ordinary clothes, sitting smoking and peering at a screen and laughing. When they saw us in the corridor they pushed the door shut. The building seemed to be full of people disappearing silently as we passed by, probably because we had interrupted their devotions, or perhaps because we looked strange and frightening, me with my livid bruises and cuts, Briony so undeniably female. This, after all, was male territory ...

Though once I heard something like a female shriek, and a chuckle. I looked up, startled, and my companion quickly said something dismissive about the local *domestiques.* His voice was unusual, rough, impatient, I suppose that monks don't make a habit of talking.

He seemed kind enough, kinder than we might have expected. Did we want to sleep? Did we want to eat? Did we want to put our car in their garage? Bad storms were predicted, he told us, for that day but they had held off. They would come tonight. I said that that would probably explain the lack of travellers on the road, but the robed one said, 'There are many roads. Not everybody crosses the mountains this way.'

Briony didn't seem to be trying. I began to feel slightly annoyed with her. (Perhaps I was doomed to feel annoyed with whatever woman was with me in public, for I certainly used to get mad with Sarah.) She'd been curt and distant with the monks from the start, refusing to put our car in their garage, and insisted on my borrowing a melder from them so we could patch the fuel tank straight away, though obviously we couldn't leave till morning. I felt like nursing my injuries, but 'I want us to do it now,' she insisted. 'We'll pay them for some fuel. And fill the tank. *Now,* Saul, please. Luke can help.' Sometimes you have to humour women. She looked tired, and strange, with hectic cheeks.

I admit that the two of them did most of the work, but I got covered with methanol, mending the fuel tank. The monks seemed to have a lot of cars and tools. 'We help many travellers,' one old monk said, when I remarked on their wellstocked hangar. 'Sainte Christophe is our saint, here.' St Christopher, the saint of travellers. He grinned at me, showing a broken tooth. His eyes looked merry in the shade of his hood. 'You will eat with us at sevenoclock.'

I thought Briony might like to freshen up with me, but she refused. She preferred to stay with Luke, who was much livelier than either of us, asking questions of the monks, wanting to see everything. Briony was uncharacteristically short with him, snapping at him to stay with her, but it wasn't surprising, we were all exhausted, and I was pretty peevish too, I wouldn't have minded a bath with her ... I left them sitting propped upright by Briony's bag, on a dirty white sofa.

I was shown upstairs to a small bleak room with a bath next door. They told me to come down when I had finished. I took off my clothes with such relief, hauling them over my cuts and bruises, wonderful to be safe, and naked, though my teeth were chattering with tiredness. I ran a bath, which was scarcely warm, but as soon as I eased myself into it I fell into a stunned torpor. I woke up with a painful start to find a hooded man staring at me, just a metre away, under the bare bright bulb his scarred nose stood out pink and disfigured beneath his hood ... I swore, and then apologised profusely. It must have been his room, and I said sorry again, but he stood there for a moment, then went out, silent.

When I got down, it was tentoseven, and Briony and Luke had fallen asleep, they were both stretched out on the sofa, sleeping. It was such a strange feeling to find them together, a little upsetting, I don't know why, his light curls touching her white cheek, their immobile bodies mirroring each other, they could have been lovers, or mother and son. Luke's arm lay across her, as if to protect her. A little group of men were watching them, speaking in low voices in the shelter of their hoods. When they saw me the group dissolved. The monk who had come out to greet us in the first place – I recognised him by his rough voice – led us into the diningroom.

'They call it the refectory,' I told Luke, proud of this scrap of knowledge from somewhere. I turned to my companion for confirmation. '*On dit le réfectoire, n'est-ce pas, Monsieur?*' but he looked at me blankly. Perhaps conversation was forbidden at meals, or else my French was not so good as I thought.

The diningroom was more as I'd imagined it. There were candles on the long wooden tables. Someone outside kept revving an engine, and the wind had begun to rattle the windows, but we were all right, we were safe inside. They offered us bread and strong hard cheese and sausage riddled with disgusting white fat, but we were so hungry, it slipped down fine, and there was red wine. So it was *wine* that they made, I knew that monks were famous for something. I smiled at them as nicely as I could, since Briony still wasn't making an effort. 'I believe you monks are famous for your wine.' This sally was successful; they laughed appreciatively, and passed it down the table, so everyone chuckled. I took my first sip with high hopes, but probably the cold had ruined the grape harvest, for it seemed much rougher than I would have expected. But it didn't matter, they were very generous. Whenever I looked, my glass was full.

At table they became loquacious, so I'd got it wrong, about the rule of silence. They plied us with questions about the roads in France, about how easy it was to buy fuel, the presence or absence of police in towns, where we had found abandoned houses – though I skipped over the details of our 'borrowing': I didn't want them to think we were crooks. How cunning I fancied myself to be. I knew that I was getting drunk, but I tried to do it relatively slowly.

It was nineoclock before we finished eating, then one of the brothers brought round some brandy, and I was almost asleep in my seat after our sleepless night the day before. I began to feel hypnotised by their brown hoods. They began to seem like bags of darkness in which their hard eyes darted, flickered, as if they were making signs to each other, sly little signs from the depths of their burrows, and I realised my mind was starting to wander, I was starting to shut down ... I must go to bed, and Briony, I saw, was also exhausted, though she had an alert, worried look. Luke had gone out ten minutes before, I'd thought to have a piss, but he hadn't returned.

'Go and find Luke,' she suddenly said, with surprising force, in English, though we'd all been talking in French before. 'He's gone to the car to get his things.'

'He'll be fine,' I said. I wanted one more brandy, I'd deserved a sit-down and a little drink, but women always find things for you to do – then she kicked me hard under the table.

I didn't want Luke to get lost in the dark. Of course I didn't, although I was drunk. I went, after only a little complaining. The eyes watched me as I left the room, the eyes slid after me like little bright stones, reflecting the candles on the table. I turned to the right as I went through the door and had a distinct unnerving sensation that one of the dozen cloaked men in the room had got up quietly and followed me. Without clearly knowing why I did it I stood back in a doorway on the left of the corridor and yes, there he was – I let him go past me, then followed him, trying to make sense of this. Perhaps he just wanted to make sure that we didn't steal their monastic treasures. Not that I'd seen anything worth stealing. He went to the front door, looked out briefly; I had dodged back behind a tall cupboard. He walked right past me again looking puzzled and hurried back to the diningroom. I was rather pleased with my game of cops and robbers, I felt that my mind was working brilliantly fast, as you sometimes do when you're dull with wine.

Outside the door it was fiercely cold. There was a pool of golden light from the *hexone flambeaux* suspended above it, and in that pool big flakes of snow whirled gently down, unreal, like a ballet. Outside the bright whirlpool there was thick darkness. I peered across to where the car was parked, but Luke was suddenly right behind me, I jumped when he laid his hand on my shoulder and heard him hissing in my ear, 'Briony says, get in the car. She thinks they're going to kill us. She's following.'

'What?' I couldn't take it in. 'She's crazy. Monks don't kill people.'

Words tumbled out, a river of protest. 'They aren't monks. Not real monks. I was having a look round, I went to the wrong door, the room was full of bones. Dirty yellow bones, with these foul dried shreds ... Maybe that sausage we were eating at dinner. Dad, *please listen*. And in another room, there were all these documents, passports, birth certificates, from so many countries, piled on a desk. I think they were stolen, they take them from travellers. She promised me she would follow you – she knew they wouldn't let you go out together –'

'We can't leave Briony in there, helpless.'

'She isn't helpless. She's got that big gun. It's in her bag. The great big black one.'

I was speechless for a moment. 'But that won't help her. She can't bloody shoot –'

'Dad, she wasn't just lucky, last night. Briony was Wicca's *Weapons Officer*. She was exArmy. Then she quarrelled with Juno –' I seemed to be losing my grasp of all this, but I dimly remembered something Sarah told me, 'our Weapons Officer', I hadn't believed her – 'Dad, *let's go*.' He was pulling my arm. 'Dad, come on. We've got to start the car. You start it, I'll drive, she can jump in the back.'

I'd occasionally let Luke take the wheel on straight stretches of road, because he wanted to learn – No, this was all wrong. I had to go and get her. Get another gun, and go in to find her. I couldn't shoot lefthanded, but I'd wave it around – I ran to the car, every step hurting.

I started the engine and left it running, pulled open the back door on a wave of pain and began to search for the canvas bag. Briony had moved it when she got out the shotgun – women always have to move things around – and then my hand touched the icy canvas of the bag and I yanked out the Kalashnikov, triumphant. I loaded it lefthanded, switched it to auto –

And saw her coming, backing out very fast from the blaze of snow and light at the door. Mygod, she was shooting. One blast then another. It was like the mountain cracking, like bolts from the gods, the darkness exploding, and I hefted the Kalashnikov and ran towards her, but she screamed, 'Go! Get Luke away! Get in the fucking car, Saul!'

I couldn't lift my gun with my right. I changed it, awkwardly, to the left, and shot off a burst to the side somewhere. At least this way they would think she had cover, two lots of noise, two guns blazing –

By now Luke had started the car and was driving it round in a big erratic loop, the back door flapping open like a damaged wing. But what was he doing? Mygod, he was going too near the house. At any moment they'd be shooting back. He was going to fetch Briony, of course –

In that split second my choice was made, and ever since I've had to live with it. Of the two of them I had to save my son, and I ran after the car. I banged on the side, scrambled in, and wrenched at the wheel. Thankgod that the car was lefthand drive: I changed his course, away, back to the road. I don't suppose he knew what I was doing, the deafening noise, the snow, the darkness, and now the robed figures were shooting back, and Briony was down on one knee, mygod she was good, aiming, pumping, then she was backing, zigzagging, shooting from the hip, great flashes of fire bursting from her arms and jolting her each time she shot –

And then her course became strangely erratic. She looked as though she were dancing, ducking. A terrible slowness took over her steps. She held on to the gun, she was staggering, falling, and just before she fell to the ground –

Ohgod. Ohgod. This I never forgot. I have never been able to remember this without a stab of grief and guilt, although I think I am immune to guilt.

At the very last moment she turned, and stared, and she called something, and I think it was 'Saul' – be honest, bastard, it was *'Help me, Saul,'* it was, godforgiveme, a faint call for help, after saving our lives, she knew she was dying, and she wanted, then at the last, not to die. She hoped after all that someone might help her, after a short lifetime when no one had helped her, and I loved her, didn't I? I'd have to go –

But our car was already veering away, things happen too fast, and chances are lost, it was already too late, *I know that it was,* they were slamming her with bullets that jerked her about like a broken doll, the shame, the horror, and I saw out of the corner of my eye, as I yelled at my son to drive off down the mountain, that half her face had been blown away.

Briony. Briony.

She called for help, in Roncesvalles Pass, but it was too late, and no one came.

PART THREE

18

I was mad, and ill, for days, maybe a week, after Briony died, and my memories are dreamlike, tiny bright clearings in fogs of despair–

I was saved by my son. *He* saved *me*. I had thought I was saving him.

Of all the deaths, hers was the worst.

(That's why I feel nothing but a turning of my stomach when I think about what happened to Chef. I quite liked the feeling there were two of us around, two grizzly beards, two oldtimers – I didn't mind him, but he wasn't a friend, I wouldn't call him that, he hardly gave me the time of day when I went in to collect the scraps. When I first arrived I tried to talk to him about the Parisian restaurants I'd known, about Lapérouse with its private booths, its rosy rooms and red jewels of beef, where Sarah and I once had illicit sex and managed to get our clothes straight by dessert – but he cut me off, he was sour and grumpy. 'I don't want to know about your life,' he said, 'You don't want to know about mine, *pigé*? This is our life. This vile *pissoir*.'... He can't have expected me to save him.

It happened on the other side of the airport. Perhaps I guessed but I'm busy, you see, I'm an old man and time is short – perhaps I guessed, but I stayed in the shadows. They made the fire flatter and neater than usual, more like a bed, a burning bed. They brought him out as it was getting dark, it was a brilliant night after a bloody sunset, the first stars were just coming out, the flames were starting to glow dull orange. He looked smaller than he was, carried by the boys. He was a big man, fat, who ate as he cooked. He ate too much, they said, they claimed – He had dark red cheeks and a great pot belly and knots of grease in his thick grey beard, I saw him every day, I remember him well, but last night he looked shrunken, and his face was gashed. I think he'd been ill; that was why he stopped cooking. Here no one is allowed to be ill.

He had an apple in his mouth. His mouth was forced open; the fruit was like a tongue, a great round tongue, smooth and bursting. It came from his store, where he kept the best things the expeditions brought back, to serve at celebrations. A yellowed apple, which caught the light. They brought him past me, as close as they could, so I had to look at him. Much too close. 'You say goodbye,' Kit croaked at me. 'You say goodbye to your skivey friend. Monsieur bloody fucking fatboy Chef. Now he feed us again, don't he? What you think? Huh?'

I try not to think about him at all. But I did feel sick. And – well, nervous. That massive belly must have spat and crackled – it hung on the air, the smell of meat.

Just two more days, and I'll be back to my tasks, and then no one can say I'm skivey –

No, I think they've already decided.)

My health is good, I am rarely ill, but after Briony died my system crashed. Exhaustion, pain, a raging fever – most of my memories of those days must be real, but they don't join up, they don't make sense.

– It was pitch dark, my son was driving, it felt as if we were inching down a cliff edge that at any moment might disappear. The road turned blind bends without any warning, and as we slowed the snow got worse, coming straight for our headlights, a field of stars streaming thickly towards us out of the blackness. I was hypnotised. I stared at the stars. They were the point, they were infinitely many ... Then I jerked awake as the brakes squealed.

Poor Luke. How did he manage to drive at all, having just watched Briony get shot to pieces, with me alongside him dozing and drifting and yelling 'Watch out!' whenever I woke?

I was running, remember, on massive shock, two sleepless nights, too much alcohol, and several unattended wounds. My head was bleeding, a low warm seep down the side of my neck that I ignored, thinking my last night's wound had opened, but by the grey light of early morning I found that one of their bullets had winged me.

I remember morning in the mountains. The morning after, or several days later? Yellow, leaden, the snow pouring endlessly out of the bottomless pit of the sky, and visibility so low that although we knew that to the right of the road the land must stretch down to the plains of Ebro, all we could see was snow and mist, mist and snow, swirling, blowing, and Briony was dead, it couldn't be changed, and the car felt queerly unbalanced and empty.

Then the mist for a moment suddenly parted and I saw a minute village laid out at our feet, a midget church, three tiny houses, and it seemed that nothing on earth could stop us plunging over and crashing downwards.

I was not myself. Quite how bad I was I didn't realise till I woke up and Luke had laid me out on the seat of the car, with my head on a blanket, too stiff to move. When I gingerly felt my temple I found that he had bandaged it, and put a Coolsafe skinpatch on. It was dark again. How many nights?

My head had cleared, or so I thought. We were parked in the

ruins of some sheltering building. There was a fire. He must have lit it himself. He was sitting in the front seat, mumbling to Dora. No, he was playing chess with her. She was an excellent player, but predictable. I knew there were things I had to tell him.

'Luke –'

'You're awake! I just changed your bandages.'

'About Briony.'

'No,' he said. 'I don't want to talk about Briony.'

'It's your move,' said Dora, brightly.

I ignored the creature. I had to explain. 'She begged me to leave. She was thinking of you –'

'It's not *my* fault,' Luke interrupted. His voice was shaking, furious. 'Don't blame it on me. You grabbed the wheel, you went and left her –' I knew he was trying not to cry. 'Don't ever say it was because of me.'

'It's your move,' Dora said again.

I think Luke would have liked to punch me. Adolescent boys often fight their fathers. But we couldn't brawl, all we had was each other, and we were alone in the Pyrenean night.

'I'll get some air,' I said to him. I pulled on my boots, which seemed to take forever, and heaved my body out of the car. We were in some kind of ruined chapel, which gave us shelter from the icy wind. I dragged my blankets near the fire and closed my eyes, too tired to argue. Coolsafe is also a sedative. A dog was barking; I ignored it. I tried to think of the future, not the past, the red plains of Spain, the greygreen olives, the distant whiteness of the coast, the sea that divided us from Africa, such a little sea, and beyond it, safety ... Safety for Luke, where the ice would not come.

I told myself it was all for him. I had even sacrificed Briony – I held on to the thought it was somehow heroic.

(I had to think that when the flashbacks came, repeated flashbacks of my last sight of her, jerking like a puppet, turning, calling – and that sudden vile explosion of matter from the side of her head, her small brave face.)

But now, when I am so much older and colder, I see I wasn't a hero, or a villain, or any of the things they say in stories – but merely one tiny unit of biology, stopping at nothing to save his genes.

These were the attitudes we struck, as the ice crept on towards our feet. We dreamed apocalyptic dreams. We fled our terror of the cold. We thought of the ice as waste, dead, a barren zone where life was extinguished –

But gradually I began to see the truth. *We were the exceptions to the rule.* The ice was bad for human beings, shattered our careful webs of control, killed our parasites, bugs and bedmates – and yet, the rest of life was flourishing.

Lovelock had said it decades ago. There were more species in ice ages, not fewer. Add on the sideeffects of human decline ...

When the cat's away, the mice will play. We'd been eating lunch one day in France, in a nondescript wood by the side of the road, when I realised I was hearing birdsong. I hadn't done that since I was a child. The French must have been too busy escaping to bake their songbirds in a pie.

But it wasn't just birds who were corning back. There were other species, not all of them friendly.

I think Luke shouted from the car window. I started awake. 'Dad, is that a dog? ... It couldn't be a *lion?*' Row, row, row. That bark again, closer this time. Did he really ask if it was a lion? Luke had seen so few animals. In Britain we had eradicated dogs, the bird populations had shrunk to nothing after two great fires in pesticide plants, and the zoos had all been closed by law. Luke's generation had never heard lions.

'No, not a lion – go to sleep.'

All over Euro, according to the screens, there were packs of wild dogs, rabid, halfstarving, who terrorised people on the edge of the towns. But we were not on the edge of a town. I fell asleep, thinking of childhood, when there were dogs in England too, and they were seen as faithful friends ... We had a dog, a cocker spaniel, with crooked, silky ears and tail, Sally, she was called, panting, adoring, before rabies came through the Channel Tunnel and the whole dog population was destroyed. Thousands of people thronged Whitehall and pelted the politicians with dogshit, but it was too late to save my Sal.

She was barking, desperately, in my dream, because they were taking her away to the vet's, and although I had secretly planned to save her, when it came to the moment, the only one that counts, I knew it was hopeless, and did nothing, I turned away and let her die, and now she howled and howled in my ear ...

I woke in an instant. The howling was real. I tried to sit up, and something ran in to the ruins, by the glow of the fire, then another, and another, and I smelled them, too, a wild, rank smell, and their shape was strange, like queer thin huskies ...

Then I saw, as one ran past the fire, it had bloody bandages in its mouth, the bandages Luke had taken off me, and in the same instant, on a surge of fear, I realised they weren't dogs but wolves, or hybrids, perhaps, of dogs and wolves. I saw one's fangs, its heavy tail, the narrow chest and crippled hips, and from its terrible thinness, that they were starving.

I staggered to my feet, throwing off my blankets, and felt a puncturing bite in the meat of my thigh – *Surely I was dreaming,* but my leg felt wet. I made for the fire, I'd read that wolves were afraid of fire, and the buggers ran at me again, three or four of them this time, harrying me, the firelight catching damp tongues and teeth, and the smell was disgusting, overpowering, they smelled of urine and blood and bad breath, and at the last moment I grabbed some straw and as it flared into a great untidy bundle of flame I pushed it at them. They howled and ran! I grew bolder and pursued them, roaring and yelling, and quickly as they'd come they ran out again.

'What's happening?' Luke was out of the car, rubbing his eyes, pulling on his trousers.

'Some mangy wolves. I saw them off.'

'Wolves?' he said. 'Like in the books?'

And before I could stop him he had darted outside.

The next thing I remember we were both outside. Away from the fire the cold made my eyes water, Luke was trapped by a ragged ring of animals, eight or nine, maybe more, dark weaving bodies, all snarling and growling and running at him, shearing off to the side at the last moment, but getting bolder, coming closer, he was dancing about and shouting at them, but he'd suddenly had enough, I could see, he was yelling for me, *'Dad, Dad!'* and in a great slithering rush on the snow I came running into the middle of them, kicking out with my feet in their heavy boots and shouting like a man possessed, glad of my roar, my deep male voice, and I heard a sickening crunch and click as I got one of them square in the jaw, and when it screamed and yelped with pain I kicked it again, in its scrawny ribs, then turned and booted another wolf's side, shouting out every vile threat I could think of –

And Luke, who I thought had run to safety, came storming from the chapel with a flaming branch, brandishing it above his head like a knight of old with a blazing cross. He went straight for them, and I ran with him, we ran at the wolf pack, side by side, yelling curses I didn't know he knew, and after an unsteadying few seconds when they came on towards us unafraid they hesitated, broke like a wave and were suddenly fleeing, whining in panic, nothing but a bunch of beaten dogs. We found one halfdead on the snow in the morning.

We did it together. Father and son.

(Did it really happen, or was it a dream? I don't remember much cold, or fear. I don't remember how the wound healed. I have a vivid memory of my son hugging me, but I can't remember the time or place.)

I think I was ill for a week or so, and then my memory clears again.

Without Briony, we two became closer. I should say 'we three', for Dora was important. She gave us something to talk about; something to look after together. From the time when Luke had given her his voice he'd begun to spend more time with her, having the 'conversations' with her that still seemed novel and amusing to him, playing chess with her and sometimes, when we rested, stroking her and making her chuckle.

(I say 'her', but I often got confused, in a way that rarely happened when Briony was there. I thought of the two of them as 'the boys', and of our little gang as three males together, and I started to call Dora by her androgynous nickname of 'Dodo' more and more.)

Our whole way of being seemed to change. We were rougher, less tidy, less organised, louder. We packed up our plates without washing them. We knocked around together. We were three men.

Spain was more orderly than France. Life seemed to struggle on in the villages, though the cities, people said, were full of crooks and murderers. They looked at us strangely as they said these things, afraid that we were bad people too. They seemed more suspicious near Madrid, where a Moroccan mafia had taken over – the central government had fled.

I was no longer sure if we were good people. The boundaries of things had begun to blur. In the misty, snowy forests of the Picos de Europa we survived some hairraising encounters with desperate travellers wanting to steal our food or fuel. (Perhaps that wasn't always what they wanted, but they flagged us down or followed us. How were we to know what their intentions were?) I told my son we could take no chances. I shot at their tyres or smashed their windscreens. If they were driving too fast, they crashed off the road. We didn't hang around to see what happened. But I told myself I wasn't a brigand, I hadn't attacked anyone without cause.

Even that didn't last. We were leaving the foothills and cruising down towards the rolling plains. We were moving fast, fast enough finally to feel we were outstripping the march of the ice. There was something on the air we had almost forgotten; a greenness, a sweetness, a faint blush of warmth. And then we rounded a hairpin bend and were overwhelmed by the first flowering almond, a cloud of pale pink, then another, and another ... and the dense wondrous smell of warming earth. We could drive at last with our windows wide open, feeling infinitely cheered by the scent of spring, by the sea of brilliant sun and blossom, blowing almond, foaming cherry. I was actually *singing,* though Luke wouldn't join in, when we had a puncture near Villavelayo. The car began to grind and bump as we ran over what felt like cobbles. It was merely an ordinarily bad road, in fact, but the tyre was completely flat, and when I tried to change it the spare was duff. The first car that passed us, as we sweated in the heat, was a shabby old VW, heavily loaded. They must have been refugees like us, with bags and bundles tied on top, and I looked inside and saw three or four children, watching us with pale, curious faces, and I let them go, I couldn't do it. But the next car, ten minutes later, held two men – a father and son, Luke found out later – and I held them up without compunction. I flagged them down; I waved the gun, then stole their tyre and swapped it for mine. Luke kept them at gunpoint while I worked, and he chatted to them in his effortless Spanish. They didn't seem to bear a grudge once they realised we weren't going to kill them. Luke got quite friendly with them. I felt excluded. I was the old man everyone hated.

As we drove on at last, I reproached him. 'You shouldn't have chatted to them, you know. It made it hard for me to steal their things.'

'You taught me not to steal,' he said, tightlipped. 'Besides, that boy was around my age.'

'He was a teenager,' I protested, and looked to my left, and saw my son, himself a great big teenager, a youth at the beginning of summer.

We stayed two nights in the village of El Piñon, on the Rio Cega. We saw no men in this little village; it seemed to be run by sturdy widows, who waved at us as we drove through. One woman stood with her curvaceous daughter, who had a marmalade cat in her arms, pointing and laughing at our painted car. Luke said, 'They look friendly, can't we stay?' I wanted to get to Avila, a medieval town I remembered fondly, but I think he was tired of the endless travelling, or else he was tired of my company, and so I let him have his way. Maybe segging was in Spain, as well, but the women seemed keen to use Luke's muscles. They asked him to help with their potato harvest, and to my irritation he agreed. The nubile daughter worked alongside him. In the evening he was in wild high spirits, the first time he'd laughed since Briony died. They let us sleep in a frigid little outhouse, laying our sleepingbags in straw.

On the second night, I said we had to move on. He didn't see why we had to go. I kept him awake with my explanation. I spoke with more passion than ever before, I at last found words to explain my dream, why I'd set my heart on Africa ... The new, fertile, temperate Africa, where Luke would be safe and have a future, where perhaps our line would go on forever, back in the land from which we came, our genes rejoining the old dark river. It was my dream, a father's dream ...

Sons, of course, have different dreams. By the time I finished, Luke was asleep, snoring gently into the straw.

*

He admired me less, grew more rebellious. On the road next day, the argument continued.

'We've got to get a move on,' I said, placatingly. 'With the roads so bad, and the car so slow, you can see for yourself, it's nearly summer. They'll close the frontier. We'll have wasted our time.'

He said nothing, as usual, just stared straight ahead. 'I miss her, you know,' he said at last, quietly.

'I miss Briony too, of course ... But she wanted us to get there. She was dead set on it –'

'I mean *my mother*,' he said, dryly, suddenly sounding alarmingly adult.

'Oh. Yes. Sorry,' We drove on for a few minutes in silence. 'But you couldn't go back,' I had to say. 'You could never go back to that Wicca nursery. You don't regret it, do you? I mean ... I did right?'

He stared out of the window at the field of flowers. I could smell the perfume faintly through the window. Dark Spanish lavender, heady, balsamy. I saw he wasn't going to answer, and all my pentup frustration burst out. 'They were turning you into a bloody woman! That was what your mother was doing to you!'

He flinched – when I shouted, people listened – but then he said, with studied indifference, 'I just said, I miss my mother, that's all.'

'But are you glad we took you away?' I think I might have hit him, if I hadn't been driving, and I jerked the wheel violently to the left to stop us hitting a mangy black and white dog I hadn't noticed, then hauled it with equal violence back again, and I'm afraid I also accelerated. *Would no one ever see that I was a good man, trying to do my best for everyone?*

The combination of the jerk and the shout had an unpredictable effect on Dodo, who was switched on by the jerk, and decided to answer, in her normal honeyed, encouraging voice. 'Of course I'm happy we're going out. I like it when you take me out.'

Luke switched her off with an impatient 'Shut up ... Look, you didn't ask me at the time, did you?' he said. 'So don't go asking me now, all right? I don't just have to say what you want me to. I'm not Dora. I'm not a robot.'

I made myself calm down, and drove on. I was determined to get to Avila that day, and to my joy, it was still standing, Avila, where I had come as a student, with its little colonnaded square.

Life seemed to go on there remarkably as usual, shops still open, genuinely open, not operating behind barricades with furtive 'Open' notices on the shutters. The door of the church was locked, of course, but the roof was good; the stained glass had survived. When it came to the hour when decades ago the populace would have come out in their best clothes to promenade in the last of the daylight, to my astonishment, people still came, in their rusty blacks, their tight widows' hairdos, men in jaunty hats catching the late red sun, little girls running in acidbright satin dresses which surely they had worn for ever ... The only difference was that there were fewer children, but the old men drank dense yellow drinks under the pillars and the women chattered, harsh, humorous, and no one attacked us or threatened us. The little ones played skipping games on the flagstones, their shiny shoes tapping like a small light heart, and swifts came darting up into the twilight as they had done when I was young. It was summer in Avila, full golden summer.

Tentatively, we sat down at a table. A woman came and stared at us and brought us bread and wine and olives, which seemed no more expensive than before. We sat dumb, happy, silently eating. Luke watched a girl who was playing with her little sister, her long silky hair and her small breasts bouncing. I could see people looking at my battered face; no one had noticed it in the village, as if they had grown used to violence. But Avila was a place of peace. The waitress asked me if I needed a doctor; I fobbed her off – I didn't feel like explaining – but I let her recommend an inn, and that night Luke and I slept in beds with sheets.

As I was slipping away, in my rough clean linen, enjoying the feel of it against washed skin, on the delicious edge of sleep, Luke suddenly spoke from the opposite corner.

'Dad,' he said. 'This is nice. Isn't it?'

'Mmm,' I mumbled, thick and slow.

After a moment he said, 'I'm glad I'm here.' I think it was his way of saying thank you. Or sorry, perhaps, or both, it didn't matter.

'Thanks for telling me –' I said. I meant to say more, but while part of my brain was working it out, the rest got lost in drifts of warm feathers.

It was one of the last nights we spent together.

19

Driving through Spain, we drove through the seasons, from winter to summer, from the mountains to the sea, and for Luke, who had been so much confined, it was like seeing the whole world in a nutshell, from pinecovered mountains to bare red plains, from the lush green hills in the misty north to the burnt brown humps of baking Ronda, rolling down towards the glittering sea, and beyond the sea, beyond its white glaze, on the other side of the tongue of the Atlantic where the boats darted like lizards across the light – across that strait was Africa. And the boats were still sailing. *The boats were still sailing.*

I thought I could see Africa.

'Look, you can see it, if you screw up your eyes,' I told him, excited, 'Over there –' There was the faintest line, the smallest shadow, faintly purple on the far horizon where sky met sea in a shimmer of heat.

'Maybe,' he grunted, and turned away. I thought it was too much for him, to see it in reality, the land of dreams, so I said no more, and patted his shoulder.

It was damp with sweat. Unbelievable. There was heat again, we smiled, we expanded, we felt we had been cold for half a lifetime and never wanted to be cold again. The hills were singing with heat and crickets and thyme and marjoram and magic, and I drove faster, though the roads were narrow, I was rally driving and showing off till we nearly died on a hairpin bend. Then I sobered up. I wanted to get there. Having risked so much, I had to get Luke through.

In the back of the car was the brown dispatch case that held our precious documents. When we left the car they nearly always came with us, but inside I kept the case wrapped in a dirty towel, obsessed with the possibility that thieves would ambush us and snatch it, thinking it held our money. Every time we stopped, I would check on it, a corner of green underneath the oilcan. And it was still there. *We would be all right.*

I was overtired, and overexcited, and the edges of things were playing queer tricks on my eyes. It was age, or possibly the heat haze. I asked Luke to drive, and he took over happily. Not long now, a day, two weeks, depending on what we found on the coast. Spain had once been famous for bureaucracy, but I knew we had everything they could ask for –

They suddenly ran across the road in front of us, making Luke swerve and shout in fear, then slow down to watch them, but they were soon gone, though one gazed after us for a moment. He was brown as earth. His arms had sharp muscles. White whites to his eyes. He was laughing at us.

'They must be the *salvajes*,' Luke said. 'I've never seen them up close before. The wild boys. There was a girl, as well. Did you see, they were throwing lemons at each other?'

'Trying to kill each other, more like,' I interrupted sourly. 'Keep your eyes on the road. It's steep. What did you call them?'

'*Salvajes* ... that's what the girl in the village called them.' He'd begun to know things I didn't know. 'They were having such fun,' he said, obstinately, and I found myself thinking, has he had enough fun, as an only child, and then with the coven?

'From what I hear, they're to be avoided. Not very nice,' I said firmly.

'What's so bad about them?' he asked.

I sometimes forgot he was still a child. I fell back on pious psychology. 'It's because they grew up without decent parents. They never lived in a family, like you did. So – anything goes, for them.'

'You mean, they're starting again? From scratch?'

'Yes –' But I didn't like his intonation. 'Luke. They're not a good thing, you know.'

'Didn't say they were,' he said crossly, and drove on in silence in the blank white heat.

I think I had a tendency to tell him too much. I wanted to save him from my mistakes – I wanted to save him from *any* mistakes.

'I know our family wasn't perfect,' I said. 'But at least you always knew we loved you.'

'Yeah yeah.'

'What does that mean?'

'Stop going on. I just looked at them. They looked – interesting. I'm not in love with them or anything. Christ.'

Yet all that day he seemed distracted, and I felt he might be thinking of them, those brown, lean, dirty kids, darting out in front of us so we nearly ran them over, and the arc of the missiles against the blue air ... his daft idea that they were just lemons, lemons from that green lemon grove.

(Of course they were stones. They meant pain, trouble. I was grown up, I knew the truth.)

We slept that night in the car, all three of us, in the country just outside Malaga. Next day, I knew, was going to be crucial. I would have to bargain with one of the operators in Malaga who sold tickets for the crossing. The system was horrendously complicated, but I had done my research in advance, I was sure I had everything worked out.

I'd been told in England by Paul's Spanish lover, who had come from Ronda a year ago, that first you bought tickets, for an inflated price, and then you went to sort out the visas, which seemed weird, but you couldn't get a visa without a ticket from one of a cartel of small boat operators. The cartel dealt ferociously with outsiders, though occasionally you might find a fisherman poor and desperate enough to take you across. If you took that risk, you had to sail without a visa. I preferred to buy from the cartel. According to Manuel, however, quite often, even with the right tickets, the Ghanaian agent wouldn't grant you a visa, and there was no refund on the tickets. Still, we had a contact, the documents, five million ecus to buy the tickets and square the visa officials, if we had to. So far, luck had been on our side. I told Luke I was confident.

That night I was terrified in the early hours, and the car was musty, frowsty, hot, recalling times I had almost forgotten. I had drunk too much wine and could not sleep. Lying with my spine uncomfortably kinked, I felt the sweat running down my body ...

Remembering being young with Sarah, far away and long ago. The long curve of her back, gleaming with moisture in the queer timeless light that came up from the street, the way her hair coiled across my pillow, smelling of some sweet musky perfume, streams of red hair, in the early days, before she cut it, cut me off ... I wondered how far she had tried to pursue us. Did she ever trace us as far as France? Did she know that we had crossed the Channel? Did she try to follow us? Or had she been trapped in the civil war? From what Briony said, Sarah's role in Wicca was precarious; Juno halfloved and halfhated her ... Poor Briony. I must have bored her stiff with all my questions about my exwife. She asked me once if I was over her, and I got quite cross and said 'Of course', but I'd never ceased to be obsessed, never stopped wanting to understand.

I wanted to know why Sarah couldn't love me. I wanted to know what was wrong with men, and if women would ever love us again. Whenever I had enough time to be lonely, I still wondered, still brooded.

It was a waste of time, of course. I turned over again, knocking my elbow, and told myself to be sensible, I was fiftyone, I should know better. It was just the heat, something physical, random, that made her memory so sharp that night. Tomorrow we'd leave Euro, if all went well, and say goodbye to her forever. Great, I told myself. Go to sleep.

So Luke would never see his mother again, and I ...

But that was all in the past. I turned over, crossly, and banged my knee, and accidentally switched Dora on, which gave me the idea to use her cooling fan. 'Hallo, how are you?' she asked, too loudly. 'Be quiet, Dora,' I hissed, wearily. I turned on her fan. 'Everyone's asleep.'

There was a pause, and I hoped she had obeyed, but in fact she had slipped into her 'Logical Assessment' programme. I jumped when she said, in the same bright voice, not at all the right voice for three in the morning, 'That is not correct. You are not asleep, I am not asleep.'

'I'm not asleep either,' Luke said quite loudly from the front seat where he was lying.

'Damn,' I said. 'So no one's asleep. You should be asleep,' I told my son. 'Big day tomorrow.' But inside my head a tune was playing, unforgettable, 'Nessun Dorma' in a sunlit timewarp, and we had just met, and my fate was sealed ...

'Too hot,' Luke said. 'Open the window.'

Sarah. How did we lose one another?

I'd thought we were safer with the window closed, on the edge of the town, in a car with French plates, so easily identified as one more group of vulnerable refugees. But Dora's fan was noisy, and the night was long, and after all I still had my Magnum ... And two men together made a lot of methane. I opened the window, said, 'Go to sleep,' and tucked the gun underneath the seat where my hand would find it straight away.

With the window open the night came alive. The olive trees rustled, the crickets sang – a high thin noise like electricity, trembling and shrilling through the moonlight, and there was a faint cool waft of green herbs, a promise that we were somewhere near water. I began to relax, to dream, to doze ...

In my dream, children were laughing and shrieking. There were three or four of them, playing with Dora and feeding her lemons, which she didn't like. They laid them on the ground like a clutch of yellow eggs, not understanding she could never reproduce, and Dora told them it was all my fault, and then it was Sarah who was kicking the lemons, she was shouting at me for deserting her, saying I'd forgotten to make love to her, and everything seemed to end with Sarah, would I never get away from her?

I woke up, startled, to hear children laughing, shrieking with laughter, very close. The velvet oblong of open window held something moving, something alive, and as it turned briefly towards the moonlight, it became a face with two bright eyes, and I was half-standing, cursing, shouting, fumbling for my gun, unlocking my door –

I chased them off before I realised who they were. Halfnaked bodies, matted hair. The wild boys again, the kids, the *salvajes*. They ran as if frightened, but they laughed as they ran, and hooted Spanish words that I was sure were insults.

I got back into the car. Luke was sitting up, staring out of the window at the hot darkness. Neither of us slept much after that, listening to one another's restlessness, the rustling of the trees, the birds waking up, for there were still birds, still singing, in Spain.

Goodbye, Sarah. Goodbye, my love. I was migrating south, as the swallows did.

It was hard to get up, next morning, with a dry mouth from wine the night before. My right arm was still awkward and painful, and the new aches from sleeping in the car jarred unpleasantly against the old ones. Luke was very quiet, and kept staring around him as if he had left something behind, which he had, of course, or soon would have done.

I had an address, supplied by Paul's lover. The woman who answered after thirty rings looked frightened, and only halfopened the door. She spoke in Spanish, through thin red lips, and Luke translated to his dunce of a father. We had to go back up into the hills. She told us the name of a little *granja* where we could find the man we needed.

We drove back up a narrow road with bends so sharp we seemed to hang in the air. It was exhilarating, doing it at speed. The sun was already getting hot. Luke was giving me directions, but we soon got lost, and turned up the wrong track into a ghost village. I shouted at him a bit, a lot, of course I was nervous, and *he* was nervous. Too much was hanging on all this. It was the longedfor end to all our adventures, and instead we found three or four low stone hovels with broken windows and a scrawny cat, yowling at us as I gunned the engine and yelled at Luke, spurting small stones.

Turning the bend as I retraced our tracks I went too fast again and nearly killed us, and this time it was Luke shouting at me, calling me a fool and a maniac and demanding to get out. He was shrieking, screaming, his voice shooting up to soprano again before it sank croaking back to adulthood. He had never gone this far before, and I know I deserved it, but it was a shock. I was used to him deferring to me. Of course I wasn't frightened of my own son, but the strength of his anger was alarming.

The sun was getting up high in the sky. It blazed like white metal on the distant sea. I drove hellforleather up another steep turning and plunged into a little wood, dark shiny holm oaks, black after the brightness – as I braked, I saw them.

Mother naked.

Why did that phrase come into my mind? A couple, two couples, mother naked, struggling together on the ground, and others lounging by the road, watching – longhaired, slender, animal shapes of more *salvajes,* lithe, slinking, and they suddenly scattered, as we rocketed through – the watchers scattered but the couples continued, and I saw more clearly, from the corner of my eye, the moment before we shot out of the wood and back into the blinding light, they were fucking, oldstyle, they were making love; *naked, oldstyle, natural fucking.*

I saw or imagined something else, as well. Behind them, playing on a bank where a tree had fallen and lay uprooted, three or four naked babies played, watched by two women with long black hair.

I felt sick and shaken as I drove on. These animals had babies, and we could not. How on earth would they look after them? It was criminal, it should not be allowed. Sex on the ground, *en masse,* out of doors ...

'I'm sorry, Luke,' I said, after a minute. I could see a little white *granja* in the distance, and this time I was sure we had found our goal. I sneaked a sideways glance at him, but he was staring straight forward, probably embarrassed, fourteen was surely a sensitive age – I remembered my own parents embarrassing me by trying to tell me things I knew.

'That was horrible, wasn't it?' I said, quietly. I wanted him to know

I knew he was upset, but I didn't want to say too much. His expression wasn't encouraging. 'If you want to talk about it, that's fine.' He said nothing.

'I'm hungry,' he remarked abruptly. 'Starving. That must be the place we want.'

This time he was right, and two hours later we had our tickets, and it was midday, the sun was beating down above us, and Pedro, the short swarthy man who'd sold us the tickets, was giving us directions for getting our visas from a man called Juan who would see us through, since we had tickets from Pedro, and *I had spent four million ecus,* but it didn't matter, we had nearly made it. Besides, I'd be able to earn money in Africa. The brighteyed dwarf I had just made rich was expansively friendly after the deal, which made me even surer that I had been rooked, but I didn't care, with the tickets in my hand, feeling their corners press into my fingers –

'Too hot for the boy,' Pedro said, pointing upwards at the unbearable disk of the sun. *'El rubio,* yes. He stay with me. I give him bread, wine, cheese. *Padre* go down and get the visas. The boy stay, have siesta, be happy. I have sons, daughters, everything.'

'Not at all,' I said, in my fractured Spanish. 'He comes with me. We stay together. Thank you very much for offering.'

I don't know if the little man understood, but Luke did, and he wasn't pleased. 'I'm not coming,' he said, very definite. 'It's going to be endless waiting in queues. I'd like to stay here. You go, Dad.'

I nearly insisted. And he would have come. I think even then he would have come, if I had shown him how worried I was. But I wanted to give him enough leeway, I didn't want to play the heavy father, and also I thought about the little man's daughters, *'sons, daughters, everything'.* Perhaps Luke wanted to meet the daughters. I only wanted him to be happy. And so I agreed, without a fuss, without showing Luke how hard it was to let him out of my sight for an instant, without showing him how much I cared. And that is why I torment myself, why I shall always torment myself, because we'd quarrelled more in two days than in our whole lives as father and son, and maybe he thought I hated him, maybe he genuinely didn't realise that I'd thrown everything up for him.

My choice, not his. I don't reproach him –

I blame myself. Stupid, blind.

My last memory is of Luke's back, turning away from me, looking outwards, gazing back across the yellow hill to the little black crest of trees on the skyline, the little wood we had driven through, the little wood with those naked creatures. The squat little man who had taken our money put one brown corded hand on his shoulder and grinned at me fatly, showing one gold tooth. 'Very okay with me, *señor*,' he said, and I nodded, and went away.

Driving back through the wood, I saw no one at all. Maybe we had dreamed it, the whole strange tableau, I told myself, and my spirits rose.

Now it will be plain sailing, I thought, *the worst is over, we are home and dry.*

I'd imagined getting visas from an embassy, but the address I had been given was a dingy office block. Upstairs – and there were no lifts, only stairs – there was a door which announced, in fading letters, SUBAGENCIA CONSULAR, and then a string of specialities: *Tramitación de Visas, Pasaportes,* was it? Licences for *Importación/ Exportación,* and then, thank heaven, in smaller letters, *Immigración/ Emigración etc.* It was all apparently *'Autorizado'* by the Council of the *'Estados Africanos'.*

Behind it was a warren of openplan offices, with peeling plastic and dusty posters. I asked for the Ghanaian department, but a yellow-faced woman laughed at me. There were three or four Juans in the

Inmigración section my friend in the hills had indicated, but in the end I found the right one, or one who acknowledged he knew Pedro. Juan was tall and thin and baked dry, with an acute pot belly like a pregnancy, and he chainsmoked incessantly, the acrid smell of nicotine tobacco that seemed so foreign, so twentiethcentury, for at home, of course, cigarettes meant dope …

Sometimes I long for it. You need it, here. But nowhere in England now is warm enough to grow cannabis.

Juan smoked sourly and never smiled. He was intensely cautious, and unwilling to admit he had a special connection with the man who sold the tickets, but '*Si, le conozco*,' he said, and shrugged, exhaling like a dying dragon, scaly, leathery poisonous. At last he suggested we go outside and discuss the matter over a beer, but once we were in the open air he changed his mind, and we went to the car, and drove to a deserted factory on the outskirts where I suddenly thought, he intends to kill me, they've had our money, now they'll silence us, but I knew I would never let anyone kill me while Luke was alive and needed me.

He showed no signs of doing anything dramatic, though his smoking in the car nearly choked me to death, and he sat with his arm over the back of the seat, halfturning around so he could see our belongings, his little brown eyes darting fiercely about, picking everything over, valuing, calculating. He told me there was a fee, for a visa. An enormous fee, way beyond our means, nearly all of the million we still had left after paying so much to the crook in the hills. I pointed out how much I had paid for the tickets. He pretended not to understand me, telling me instead how much they were worth, which was a figure ten times less. I told him exactly how much money we had left. He said we would have to pay in kind. I offered our car, since I knew we would never be able to ship it across to Africa.

He grinned for the first time, showing the gaps in his big rare teeth, filled with dull gold. 'All the world offer the car,' he said in bad English, contemptuously. 'I no want your old *coche, señor.*' This was the first sign of open aggression, but he smiled after he said it as if it were politeness.

He put his hand on Dora. 'Make the switch,' he said. 'I like this one. I see him *muchas veces* on the screen.'

I knew what was coming, but I had no choice. Forgive me, Dora, I had no scruples because we had already lost so much, our home, our past, Briony ... Only Luke was left. Anything for Luke. 'Switch on,' I muttered. 'Yes, yes.'

Within five minutes Juan was besotted. Having given no sign of animation in one or two hours' discussion with me, he became a boy, laughing inanely whenever Dora spoke or moved. He seemed particularly taken with her strokeyfeely panel, and the way she chuckled when he tickled her. I hoped he were not some appalling kind of pervert. To be honest, I preferred not to know. 'Is *maravillosa,*' he told me, earnestly. 'She go to make my English marvellous. You give me this one, *señor,* and your visas – *no problema.*'

I told him yes, it was a deal, but I could not give him Dora now, I should have to let Luke say goodbye. 'They're like brothers,' I said, 'or brother and sister.'

He wanted to come with us – he didn't trust me, or else he was too much in love to say goodbye – but I refused, and in the end he let us go, with one of the visas on account, I suppose lest I disappeared for good and got our visas somewhere else. He was to give me Luke's when we returned with Dora, and we shook hands keenly, and his hands were sweating, a pervert's hands, I was nearly sure.

Now there would only be two of us. I parted from Juan with too much alacrity to switch Dora off, but she was silent in the car as we drove back into the hills, and I felt her heavy presence behind me like a hand of shame upon my shoulder.

I decided I had to try to explain. Perhaps it would make it easier for her to begin a new life with Juan.

'Dora,' I began. 'We're going away. Luke and I. To Africa. You can't come with us. I'm very sorry. Very sad that you can't come.'

'You are very unhappy?' she said, sounding muted. 'I'm sorry that you're unhappy.'

'Well, I'm not, really,' I said, hurriedly. 'I'm happy I can go with Luke. Just unhappy that you can't come with us.'

'You are unhappy because I can't come with you?'

'Yes.'

'I suggest,' she said, always logical, 'that I come with you, then you won't be unhappy.'

'You can't come with us.'

'I can go with you.'

It was almost as if she were arguing with me, but of course it was just her logic module. 'Actually, Dora, I have sold you.' It sounded terrible, put like that.

'I am consulting my vocabulary,' she said, but her tone was disapproving. 'So, you have transferred me to a purchaser in exchange for money. Is that correct?'

'No, no, I wouldn't sell you for money. I sort of had to exchange you for some visas,' I said. 'For Luke. So he could escape to Africa.'

'I am consulting my vocabulary,' she said again, then after a long pause, 'Visa is not in my vocabulary.'

'It's a sort of – travel pass,' I said.

'So you have transferred me to a purchaser in exchange for a travel pass,' she said. 'Yes, I understand. I have a question, please. What is the name of this purchaser?'

'Juan,' I said. 'He likes you very much.

'I am searching,' she said. 'Yes. I was talking to this Juan. Fiftythree minutes ago.'

She sounded perfectly calm about it. I ventured an opinion. 'You'll soon forget us. He's very nice.' Heaven forgive me for lying to her, but we were getting near, and I wanted it over.

'That is incorrect,' she said, rather loud. 'I cannot forget you. You are in my memory. Everything you say is in my memory. Also Sarah is in my memory. And Briony. And Luke's voice, singing –'

'Yes, yes. That's why we've come back to say goodbye to Luke. I hope you feel okay about it.' It was mad of me, really, to ask about her feelings, but she sounded so human, one forgot she was a robot –

'I feel. Very bad and very sad,' she said, shocking me to my selfish centre. Surely she had only said that before when we hadn't been able to feed her promptly?

'I feel sad too,' I said, subdued. 'But you will be very happy with Juan.' I forgot, as so often, that she had no future tense, that everything either happened in the present or else the past, where it became information.

'That is not correct,' she said, sullenly. At least I heard sullenness where maybe none was. 'I am not very happy, I am not with Juan. You are in error. Or perhaps joking?'

She suddenly reminded me of Sarah, always contradicting or questioning. Dora was appealing because she was biddable. Now she had turned awkward, so good riddance, I thought. 'Oh piss off, Dora,' I said, and braked, and switched off before she could search her vocabulary.

I felt triumphant, hotly triumphant, as I drove up the track that led back to the little white *granja* where I had left Luke. I had done it, somehow, I had pulled it off, the tickets this morning, and now the visas, I'd succeeded where so many failed. Surely my son would be proud of me.

The farm looked the same, but prettier in the afternoon sun, more mellow, more pleasing to the eye than when we had driven the track that morning, uncertain, anxious. Now, five hours later, things were different. This afternoon I knew my son was there, and the deal was done, and everything was settled. It grew quickly larger against the brown hillside, the whitegold stone with its glittering windows. I saw a little figure outside, but couldn't make it out. Was it waving, flapping? I thought it was Luke, but it wasn't Luke, too dark to be Luke, too short, too everything. I screwed up my eyes to see in the sun. It was the little fat man who owned the villa, and I realised he was waving in agitation. Perhaps I was late, perhaps they had been worried? I screeched to a halt on the stones outside.

'I'm sorry, pardon me, it took me so long. Your friend is –'

'*Señor*,' he interrupted, and I saw he was upset, and then I was upset. 'Did your son come to meet you? He didn't come to meet you?'

So everything changed, the world turned over in that sunlit second. I stared at him –

I was trying not to understand him.

For Luke had vanished soon after I had left, two hours ago, three hours ago. I was shouting at the man's broad stupid face, I wanted to shake him till his bad teeth rattled, *answer me, answer,* how long ago did my son wander off and disappear, how long is it since *my only son* was snatched, kidnapped, raped, killed? 'Where is he?' I was shouting, and I had him by the throat, I didn't mean to touch him but I had him by the throat. Then I frogmarched him round to the door of his house, and his wife came out and shouted in Spanish and hit me round the head until I let him go.

I was sober, suddenly, and quiet. They were talking enough for three of us, and the word I kept hearing was *salvajes, salvajes,* the words I shall hear to the end of my life, which will not be long, in this cold, godknows –

They surround me, now, these other wild boys, these urban savages, the worst of the lot. They're no more free than we were, are they? Chained like dogs to the wreck of the airport, killing and dying in the dirty city air, at the foot of great airplanes flying nowhere. And I'm as savage as any of them. A wild old man who lost, who lost –

It's hard to tell, this part of the story.

We sat down round their table and they told me what had happened, or a lying version of what happened. I veered between trusting their broad peasant faces and thinking they looked like child-molesters, murderers, two cunning traffickers in human flesh, their dark eyes glinting across the table.

This is what they told me. They had offered him food, lamb with *habas,* their filthy beans. Juanita was keen to tell me the menu, and Pedro eagerly confirmed it, very nice, apparently, but Luke hardly touched it, he wanted to go outside and explore, he'd complained that we had been driving for days, and now it was my turn to confirm it, eagerly, we were so desperate to agree on something. And so he had gone outside with their son, or perhaps their daughter, *hijo, hija* – my Spanish wasn't good enough and nor was their English – but Luke went with someone, or maybe two people (how come these Spaniards still swarmed with children, I wanted to smash their fat stupid faces, but on with the story, get on, get on …).

The children couldn't tell me themselves because they were out looking for Luke, and as that phrase was uttered, 'looking for Luke', I knew it would become my life.

Luke had gone with the girl or boy to the woods. He'd said he thought he had lost something there. I interrupted; it didn't sound true – we had hardly paused as we drove past. When they got to the wood, they sat down and talked. Then all at once they were surrounded by *salvajes*. Pedro expressed horror and disgust. They were dirty, wild, cruel, revolting. His daughter or son had expected to be robbed, but instead, it seemed, the *salvajes* teased Luke, some ragtaggle girl was teasing him. 'Tormenting him?' I asked, in agony, 'did they torture him? Because of his hair?' His blondeness identified him so clearly as a foreigner, a refugee. No no, Pedro said, it was just teasing. They were in a good mood, they must have recently eaten. Luke and his companion escaped quite lightly.

Afterwards, the wild children dispersed, and Luke and the *hijo,* or *hija,* turned back. They were nearly at the house when Luke said suddenly, 'I never found the thing I lost,' and set off for the wood again, running, calling over his shoulder – the last thing he said, the last thing they remembered – 'Tell my father not to worry.'

Or that is what they told me he said.

This was two hours ago, apparently. They'd started to worry after halfanhour and a party had gone to the wood to look. 'Round here is not safe any more, *señor.* We look out for each other, we do our best. Is the *salvajes, señor,* for sure is them.'

'Why would they want my son?' I asked, frantic, but I could think of a thousand reasons, and all of them were horrible.

'Some time they take people, make others pay,' they said. They were avoiding each other's eyes. There was something dreadful they wouldn't tell me, and now I suppose I know what it was, but then I knew nothing about the wild children.

'What else?' I asked. 'If they don't ask for ransom? They can't have robbed him, he had no money. *We* have no money, thanks to you and your friend –'

He changed the subject swiftly, lest I get angry. 'Maybe he come back right now,' he said. 'Maybe he playing some game with them. Is young, *entonces,* must enjoy himself.' But I saw in his eyes that he didn't believe it. I thought I saw pity there, and fear, and in another moment I changed my mind and saw nothing but bottomless deceit, cruelty, greed, peasant crudity.

They weren't bad people, I realise now. Pedro had robbed us blind, of course, but what had happened to Luke was different. The Spanish were said to be soft about children, and Luke still counted as a child, and Pedro was a father of three, two *hijos* and a *hija,* I found, when I met them. The whole family seemed deeply distressed that Luke had gone missing while in their care.

And so I had to face the possibilities. One, he had been kidnapped by the *salvajes.* But we waited, and no ransom demand came. Two, he had been kidnapped by some other wrongdoer, bandit, mafioso, pederast, things too dreadful to think about. Three, he had gone away of his own accord, and was living somewhere quite happily, though Pedro flatly refused to believe this. 'My children never leave me,' he said, beating his chest for emphasis. 'Your son never leave you either. You a good *padre,* you love your son.' I knew this to be true, but it proved nothing. I recalled, wincing, how much we had quarrelled in the last few days before he disappeared ... Four, he had been murdered, and there was no hope, but I knew I would never be able to believe that unless they sent me his bones, his blood –

I remember how often I found myself sobbing, sobbing and roaring like someone mad. I stayed with the family for over two months, until their patience must have been exhausted, and when I went to Pedro at last and told him I'd decided to move down the coast and search for Luke there, in the big resorts, he amazed me by taking me by the arm and dragging me down to his tiny office where he counted out, with elaborate gestures, every single ecu that I had paid him, and solemnly gave them back to me. I was glad to have it. I needed the money.

He promised me he'd listen, locally, 'ear to the ground'. All might still be well. His wife had heard things, nothing solid, just gossip among the women and children ...

When I questioned him, this disappeared, like mist unravelling in the sun, or hope dissolving, leaking away. But he did mean well. I know I misjudged them.

I had been searching aimlessly, frenetically, for over three months when Pedro left me a message at Estepona, where I had written to say I was staying. There was a rumour around the villages that a blonde boy had been sighted with the *salvajes*. There wasn't a date, or a place, or a time, and the whole thing might be a garbled version of the story of Luke's disappearance. All the same, I had been desperate for news, and my spirits rose unreasonably. I didn't take it seriously enough to break off my search among the international crew of teenagers, some destitute, some wealthy, who smoked and dreamed in Estepona, the kind of friends my son might have made, but I let myself hope, I pulled back from the brink, I was a man again, no longer a drunk who shouted at women in flyblown bars.

Hope gave me the courage to do something I dreaded, something I knew I should have done before.

I rang Wicca, to find their number unobtainable. Phonesearch in London suggested a variety of other, more innocuous women's institutions. By blind chance, or else god'slove, I found Sarah actually answering the phone at the fourth one of these I tried, the Women's Institute for Cooperative Childcare.

I recognised her voice, smoky, snappy, deeper, drier than before, and I thought she would know mine, but my heart had stopped beating, my breathing was laboured – I probably sounded like any other heavy breather.

'Yes, who is it?' She sounded even more impatient than usual, possibly because I was a man. I knew she hadn't recognised me.

'Sarah', I said. 'It's you, I know. Look, it's Saul ... *Saul.* I have something to tell you.'

There was a long silence. When she spoke again, her voice was unrecognisable, a howl, then an unsteady, furious, choking stream of incoherent questions. But she stopped herself, before I could answer, and her voice became very cold and thin.

'Tell me where he is, Saul,' she said, distinctly. 'Or I swear I'll kill you. *Just tell me.*'

'He's not with you?' I said foolishly, remembering in the split second I spoke that we used to have exchanges like this when I was looking after Luke at home and she'd ring from work to see how he was and I would say, 'Oh – isn't he with you?' A little joke, but against the rules.

She was screaming in my ear, 'Are you winding me up?'

I wasn't. It was a very faint hope. 'No ... no ... I've – lost touch with him. I'm sure he's all right –' I couldn't tell her I feared he was dead.

'He's *fifteen years old.* You can't have lost touch –'

'Temporarily. I thought I should ring you. He was absolutely fine, healthy, happy –' I realised this call was impossible, but I'd had to make it, just in case he was there. 'Got to go,' I said, and then 'Don't worry.'

'Where the hell –' I hung up as her voice skated skywards. I was shaking, and cursing myself for a fool.

The force of her hatred. Sheer blind hatred. Of course, no wonder. I had stolen her son.

She never knew how much I'd loved him. If she had known, she would have let me see him, she wouldn't have locked him away from me and forced me to take desperate measures.

She didn't know how I'd cared for him. She didn't know – I wished she had known, there was a childish part of me that wished she knew

– she didn't know I had been a hero. I wished she had seen me sailing the Channel, shooting at bandits, fighting off wolves. Perhaps I still wanted her to praise me. She didn't know I had sacrificed everything to try to give Luke a life in the sun, him and his children, our grandchildren, for surely in Africa there would have been children. She didn't understand I was trying to save him from the nanomachines, the thrumming headsets, the speaking buildings, the wretched techbirths, the rare sickly children, the lonely sexes. She didn't understand that I wanted to free him from all the debris of the ice people. And now I had failed, she would never know.

I hated her for not knowing me. Yes; for not appreciating me. That was what women had done to men – they had lost interest, turned away, they no longer reflected what we did or showed in their faces what we were. Lighting us up, making us taller. It isn't a lie, if it comes from love. My mother's eyes shone when she looked at my father. And without that reflection, men were terminally lonely. We froze into ourselves, we accepted the ice.

The trail went dead on the Costa del Sol, no longer quite so sunny by the next summer. Inland, however, where the wild bands lived, the sightings had become more frequent, more detailed. The rumour had found a home on the screens; people contributed their stories of a blonde young man, godlike, handsome, running with a pack of swarthy children. I followed up every one of these sightings, but never got more than a road to travel, olive groves to tread, villages to wait in, hoping vainly for a glimpse of them so at least I would know if it were my son ... The god, *El rubio,* the blonde one.

It was clear, in the end, he didn't want me to find him.

20

My hands are so cold I can hardly write, though I'm wearing two pairs of xylon gloves, and most of the fingers are intact. Kit goes past, grey, crooked, head skewed away from me, ugly little arse-eye. Thrusting along, muttering, angry. He doesn't look at me directly, but I know he's seen me, I know I'm rumbled.

Time's running out, I'm sure it is. I've had my fun, but nothing lasts. I've nearly got to the end of my story, but the Doves can't wait, and the boys can't wait –

They'd better come, then. I'll be ready.

Saul will meet them face to face.

Time ran out in the old life too.

It went too fast when I was following a lead, trying to drive to some high village before the wild children moved on. It was slow as death when there was no news, but months mysteriously turned into years, and I had to take a job as an interpreter with a travel firm, friends of Pedro. You could feel time pressing in the middle distance, in the cooling of the climate, even here, as the ice advanced steadily across Euro, as the winter citrus harvest failed, as the golden Spanish summers grew paler, shorter – though the ice would never reach this coast. And then there was the nagging, immediate time that was just my reckoning of Luke's age, he was fifteen now, perhaps taller than me, old enough for sex, though I don't suppose he waited, and then sixteen, old enough to vote, had there been elections, or anything to vote for; and then he was seventeen, and a stranger, and then he was eighteen, and I gave up hope.

To say 'I lost hope' is not the whole truth. I gave up hope of reclaiming him. I gave up hope of ever completing my dream voyage to Africa. Taking Luke back to Samuel's land. Completing the circle I'd drawn in my head. The serpent with its tail in its mouth. I thought that circle meant something precious, but maybe to Luke it was prison, incest ... Children always have different dreams.

I gave up hope of 'saving' him.

Perhaps it was the *salvajes* who saved him.

I never stopped hoping that I would see him. I imagined him, more times than I can tell you. I would see brown figures on a far horizon where the heathazed hill met the fluid blue, and among the brown, a flash of blonde, and I'd drive hellforleather up some dirt track to find they were goats with a strange blonde girl who looked at me as if I might kill her, there must have been such longing in my eyes ... In cities it was worse, with such a scrum of lost children, and occasionally a blonde head among the others. But never Luke, never my child.

Until once. Just once. I'm sure I saw him. I'm reluctant to say, in case it disappears, like a dream of happiness you start to wake up in. I've only told this once before, and that was to – to – Yes, I told Sarah. For nothing could be over until I had seen her, however old and tired we were.

In 2064, Luke was twentyone, or would have been, if he survived.

It was time to go home, but where was home? Should I use my one visa and try to cross to Africa, or should I take Dora back to England? Poor Dora, battered now, her feathers dull ... She had never been the same since I tried to sell her, though I'd never completed my side of the bargain. A certain reproachfulness was in all her responses, a certain watchfulness in her logic, as if she were waiting for me to show my hand. It didn't matter. We were used to each other.

Of the four adventurers, only two remained.

It was suddenly possible to go back to England, though there was only one reason for going. I checked through old records, and my name was no longer on police files as hunted. Perhaps because, after Wicca's fall, all their accusations were discounted, perhaps because police records were in chaos.

She was on her way to sixty. We were both old. Surely it was time to talk to each other. Besides, I did have something to give her. The recording Luke did with Dora that morning, at the very last point before his voice broke. Second, the news that Luke was probably –

No, no 'probably's. She wouldn't want conjecture.

I had been away from England for seven years. I travelled armed. Most people did. There were no more weapons checks on boats or planes. Flying had become increasingly dangerous, with nearly all the big airlines collapsing, most of the central airports taken over by Outsiders – children, or Wanderers, or the starving – and air traffic control a thing of the past. I bought the cheapest ticket I could get through my work. Why should I care if we were hijacked (there were hijacks now ten times a day)? What did it matter if we crashed in flames? This company owned three ageing planes and flew to a private airfield in Kent. They boasted of 'Dee Icing' as if it were an extra, but I took no notice. Why should I care?

I found I did care, when the very young pilot, who had a frightened, foolish voice, told us at the end of a juddering flight that he couldn't get the undercarriage down and would have to attempt a crash landing.

The stewardess came shrieking along the gangway, the first time she'd shown her face that day, pushing our heads into crash position, but at the last moment the wheels rumbled down, there were three hard bumps as we bounced off the runway, the brakes roared on and we stopped in time. I realised I cared, because of Sarah.

Yet the more I thought about it, driving a hired car through wrecked, icy England, my heart racing, the less sure I was what I had to tell her.

She did agree to meet me, at least. I had put off phoning again and again. I called her, and her voice was older, so much older and harsher than before, but she didn't sound angry, she sounded sad, even after the first question, harsh, insistent, 'Have you seen him?'

I said, 'I'll tell you later.'

I knew I was old, but I didn't know how old till Sarah walked past me without recognising me. We'd agreed to meet in the Sainsbury Natgallery, which still opened daily from twelve to three, in Trafalgar Square at midday. The shapes of the lions were softened by snow, and scaffolding still surrounded the column where once some famous hero had stood – Wicca had unseated most male statues. One or two minicopters hovered overhead, but they didn't seem to be getting much business. Of course it was too cold to meet outside, as we had so often when we were young, sitting in the sun on the wide stone steps. It was a relief to get in from the bitter cold, to pass the armed guards with a deferential nod (*see – I'm old – don't be frightened of me*) and stand at the top of the internal staircase which gave me a good view of the doors.

I recognised her without difficulty because, from above, I saw her hair. It looked, from that distance, shockingly unchanged from the hair she had on the day we first met. It was long again, down past her shoulders, it was that chestnutred I'd loved, it was scattered with snow, with melting snow, and it made me stupid, it made me helpless, for I'd always loved her, always, always.

Her face came into focus as she mounted the stairs. Her determined chin, her delicate nose, her cheeks, which were somehow both puffy and sunken, her mouth, which was twisted with tension and pain – and yet she was still a beautiful woman. Then I noticed her eyes. I saw she was blind. She was gazing ahead of her, seeing nothing. But then, Sarah had always been blind – she swept past me, imperious, or worried she was late, and she wasn't blind, she just hadn't seen me, and I spoke, I croaked, 'It's me, Sarah ...' And so I was humbled before we began, because I had grown too old to be noticed.

She pulled off her gloves with an awkward little movement and put her hand, which was mysteriously old, as old as I was, into mine. She looked at me. 'Saul,' she said. Her voice was harsh, but it was full of sorrow, and I preferred sorrow to contempt, just then.

We sat on one of the glazed leather seats that seemed to have stood in the gallery for centuries, a circular, segmented seat, and we were too shy to sit next to each other, so we left a segment free between us – not free entirely, because freighted with coats, gloves, scarves, all that icy moraine – and looked out at the world, away from each other.

We asked the obligatory questions first. She was 'very well', but had bad arthritis, 'probably the climate, I should move south.' I suspected from a hint of tannin, a suspicion of fruit, upon her breath, that she drank; which would explain the puffiness. I too was 'well', but I really was well, stronger, tougher from all the searching, from living life so much outdoors, from eating simply, sleeping long nights. I looked old because I had been baked in the sun, but when clay is baked it becomes stronger.

'You know he's not with me?' I began.

She knew. She had guessed. 'I think I know.' She dragged the big bag she had brought off the seat and began to rifle through papers inside. I could see her hand was hurting her. Wearily she motioned me to sit beside her. The gap between us was bridged too easily.

'I traced that phonecall you made to Spain. It's him, isn't it?' she said, pushing a sheet of paper into my hand, then another. They were colour images downloaded from the screens, things I had seen in my shabby Spanish office but lacked the facilities to print, distant images of the *salvajes,* one taller figure rising from the group or standing a little apart in the background, the white undetailed halo of light that might conceal the head of our son, our mysteriously tall and different son. None of them made identification certain, though looking at them with such passionate desire we could both see precise curves of ear and mouth in the vaguest patches of light or darkness.

'He's become a myth, hasn't he?' she asked me, staring into my face, and I saw a reflection of my own awful hunger in her blue iris, faintly rimmed with white, the ice was coming there as well, the slow stiffening of cataract. 'The Spanish people are saying he's like their god, because he's blonde, because he knows things.'

'Of course those kids were brought up wild, there must be so much that they don't know –'

'And other things they know that he doesn't. Here, look at these. This one. That's it.' She pushed another image into my hand which at first looked exactly like the others. But as I looked closer, I saw what she meant. Instead of one blonde head there were several. The tall blonde youth, a darkhaired woman, and three other white heads so small I hadn't seen them, three blonde children, playing with a black one.

We looked at each other, and her mouth was crooked, and neither of us could say anything, because this was the point, maybe the point of everything, though we never saw what we were moving towards …

Probably it didn't matter what we aimed for. Blindly following the arrow of light.

Then it was time to tell my story.

It happened in the year when Luke would have been twenty. The little village of Buena Ventura was quiet that night. I had arrived after a long day selling tickets too late to wake the woman at the *pensión,* and since it was August, and a warm dry evening, I decided to sleep in the square in my car. This village had been overrun, the week before, by a daylight visit from fifty or so of the wild children, descending like locusts on the shops and the houses, grabbing all the food they could carry and running off with three goats and six horses, one of them ridden away up the track by a tall blonde boy, handsome, laughing. ('The bastard was laughing,' the mayor raved on the phone. He thought I was an investigator. Indeed, I was an investigator, but he didn't know how we were connected, or what a shock of happiness that detail gave me.)

Perhaps I haven't made it clear enough that the *salvajes* were a band of thieves. They called them *mestizos,* too, 'mongrels', because these kids were such a mixture, Arabs, Africans, Andalucians. If Luke were a leader among the wild children, to most people he was just a criminal. One of my fears, as I hunted Luke through Spain, was that an irate farmer would shoot him dead.

I knew they probably would not come back, because they hardly ever did. They were nomads, really, they always moved on. But it didn't lessen my need to follow, my need to be where Luke had been. To imagine him happy – that was best of all. I had a few drinks from a bottle of wine I'd picked up along the way and drifted off, thinking of Luke in the saddle, laughing, imagining him in the dusty square ... I fell asleep feeling happy, for once.

I woke up uncomfortable, and needing to piss. It's a sign of age; you need to piss.

(Sarah interrupted; 'Women too.' So that was an advance; women weren't perfect.)

I heard a dog or a cat outside, rooting about in some rubbish nearby, as I opened the door to take a leak, and looked across the square, which was flooded with moonlight, in the direction of the little whitewashed church of the Sagrada Vista, twenty metres away.

He was there, in the moonlight, astride his horse, holding it steady, watching me. His face was black and white in the radiance. His expression was unreadable, shadowed by his curls. He was taller, larger than I had expected. I tried to speak; I tried to run. As soon as I began to move towards him he pulled the reins, wheeling away, and I managed a brief, strangled 'Luke' before I remembered I mustn't wake the village.

The sound of his hooves, a heartbeat drum, grew steadily fainter on the steep road down.

I know it was him. I am utterly certain. *God's love brought my son to me.* I suspect he had been watching the car, watching me sleeping, perhaps, when I woke. And though he didn't want to talk he raised one hand, I am almost sure I saw one hand rise and fall in the moonlight, but the moving shadows blurred it all. He was saying 'Stay back', or else 'Goodbye', or maybe it was a kind of blessing. I think so, yes. A blessing. Kindness.

It was all I had, and I passed it on, my small thin story, to the boy's mother, hoping it wouldn't rub away in the telling, hoping she wouldn't disbelieve or sneer. But the new, tired Sarah didn't sneer.

We sat beneath the small dark canvas of Cranach's *The End of the Age of Silver,* under the naked generations suffering and struggling in the cold, ejected from paradise, awkward, knowing. The old men raged and fought in the background, the women held the children away from us, their bodies both virginal and erotic, curves of exclusion, silvered, serpentine ...

The gallery grew colder. It was time to close, but it was hard for us to leave each other. An aged guard with a long grey moustache came and told us we had to go. Some last little puff or squirm of anger made me say to her, as she got up and stroked her hair with a remnant of vanity, an echo of beauty, 'You were wrong, you know. You Wicca women got it wrong.'

'You were wrong too, you Doveloving men. Whatever happened to that *thing* you had, the one I was so absurdly jealous of ...?'

'I was never sure that you were jealous ... Dora. Dodo. She's still with me. If you want her, you can have her. She's got Luke's voice. Singing *Figaro*. . .' (It would be all right, I had a sudden surge of hope, Sarah had been jealous, that was all it was, we were on the verge of a new understanding.) 'Singing *Voi, che sapete che cosa e amor* ... you who know what love is, ladies ...'

But she'd stopped listening, her face stiff with distaste. 'You know we tried to exterminate them. Wicca, and the clowns who followed us. The public didn't know the half of it. We had to seek out all the thirdgenerations, they were breeding at random, eating cats, children ... I think they might have wiped us out. Before the ice could wipe us out. In Euro they say they've bred like rats.'

'They exaggerate.' But I remembered the mutants, pouring over the musicians like a tide of excrement. Could they have been right, those wrongheaded women?

'They were the children of our brains, not our bodies.' She went on, insistent, tubthumping – and we had so little time left together.

'I did remove Dora's replicator module.' Did it still matter, after all these years?

'But I bet she still has her SD and R.'

'SD and R?' I had forgotten. 'Oh yes. Self Defend and Recycle, isn't it? I'm pretty sure she's never used it.' The Doves' 'emergency defence', so horribly effective in the French mutants.

'Someone else could.' She'd gone slightly pink, rising to the battle, keen to win.

'They couldn't,' I said. 'Dora has personalised Voice Recognition. Just me, and you, and Luke, and Bri –' but I stopped in time, and she didn't hear, 'so there's no danger.'

'They were very dangerous,' she insisted. 'You men made a pact with the devil.' She was growing theological, in her old age, and the set of her chin, pulling threads of tension in the flesh underneath where the skin would never be smooth again, and the slightly hectic glint in her eye, reminded me she would never stop fighting, we would never stop fighting as long as we lived, these late generations of men and women, shivering, struggling in the frozen grove. But the clock struck three. We would go, we would pass. I remembered the little oak wood in Ronda, and how the wild children, who I thought were fighting, lay naked in the cool grass to make love.

(And it frightened me. Too close, too tender. I thought I was shocked, but I was envious.)

Now I see something else instead. Everything that lives is good. Everything that freely lives. Even Kit, even the wolves. You can never see it when you're afraid.

Outside the gallery the wind was bitter, and little flurries of snow blew up and stung our noses in the fierce white light. She looked older, so much older out here, and I dreaded to think how I must look to her. The colour of her hair was flat, unnatural, and I remembered how she'd once valued ' the natural'.

'Where are you going?' I asked my old love. 'Will you be all right?' For the snow was getting thicker, and the wintry light would not last long. I had some vague sense that I should look after her, should make sure at least that she got safe home, but her face stiffened, maybe thinking (wrongly) I wanted to go home with her, maybe resenting my protective tone – 'I live Southside,' she said, to my surprise. 'All Wicca members were banned from the north after the fighting. We had our own enclave in the south for a bit, but I don't know what happened – I think I grew bored ... Believe it or not, I live with my mother now. Or she lives with me. She's very old. I think perhaps it's what I always wanted. Except I wanted *her* to look after *me*.'

I saw, or thought I saw, her old wounds. I suppose I was still in love with her, and some nonsense came spurting out of my mouth, 'I wanted to look after you, you know –'

'Why didn't you, then?' she said in a flash, some halfremembered tart refrain, and she smiled, showing her familiar teeth, sharp, slightly yellowed, in that cold light, by age and the painful whiteness of the snow.

A taxi floated past us, vague in the storm, but its orange light caught my eye at the last and I hailed it for her, I could at least do that. But she laughed at me, not a very kind laugh, or perhaps I should say, not a happy laugh, and said, 'I never use them. They won't come Southside. When I can't afford a minicopter, I always go under.' Then she turned and set off towards the station, trying to be jaunty, though the newly fallen snow made the ground slippy and she skidded for a moment before she got her balance and walked off stiffly, red head held high.

No, I must tell you the whole story. As I ran along the pavement to grab the taxi I found myself only a metre behind her, reached out my hand, touched her shoulder and whatever she felt – I didn't care – I took her in my arms and hugged her, crushed her stiffness against my heart, and her mouth avoided my clumsy lips but at the last, I don't know why, she turned just a little, and her lips were like paper.

Draw a line under us. Finish us off. Sorceress. Maneater. Bitch. Beloved –

If she read this, would she understand?

I am stuck in the past, moping, mourning, when Kit bursts in on me in a rage.

'What hell you wanking bloody play at?' he demands, running right up to me, stocky, smelly, his face red with anger, his black eyes gleaming. His hairline makes a low V on his forehead. He snatches my notebook from my hand and stares at it, frustrated, right way up, upside down. He notes, I imagine, that I have drawn a firm black line underneath my story –

No, not the epic I once intended. And yet it is finished. All but finished. Saul, the Hero, says it is done.

'You finish, wankpig?' he shouts at me. 'Because now our babies all die, thanks you!' He shakes my notebook so forcefully that its pages flap like inadequate wings, and I snatch it back with a frightening roar, a roar I mean to be frightening, a roar that would have frightened him once, but it sounds weak to me, weak and old, and he looks furious, not frightened.

He has cornered me in the concrete bunker where I bring rotting food for RefuelRecycle, except that I haven't done my job for a week, and besides, we're eating all the food we can get hold of, and we're still hungry, and the Doves are starving.

Kit and I have had a pact, of a kind. It's all based on my care for the Doves. Most of the kids like them well enough, play with them, run them around a bit, wreck one or two, when they feel in the mood. But Kit is different; to Kit they're alive. He worries, I know, when one gets sick, and grieves, in a furious, wordless way, if any of them gets smashed in the games. I matter to him because I am the Bird Man, the man he found less than halfalive in a writtenoff car in a blizzard with Dora. The evening of the day I last saw Sarah. I was trying to escape London forever, or trying to die, driving too fast, and came round to find Kit fiddling with Dora. She lay under the seat with her casing damaged and some of her programmes wiped forever.

That was my entry to this brave new world. I had expertise. I knew things he didn't. I helped Kit get dozens of them working again.

I have been useful, and they have used me. And fed me, and let me sleep with them, an old man among hundreds of boys. They have taught me their skills in exchange for mine. Fighting with the sheared-off metal machetes that they call swords, made from defunct cars. Raiding the deliveries to the Enclaves, stripping empty buildings of everything flammable, finding dead bodies for us to burn, and not all the bodies were dead when we found them. *We, us.* I was one of them.

I've been one of them for nearly two years, but in Kit's eyes I can see it's over.

I'm not afraid. I've had my day. Our Days are gone; burning, frozen. We never learned to let things be ... It was very bright, the best of it. My life was finished long ago, that afternoon in Trafalgar Square when a woman kissed me, and it turned to paper.

Or maybe I outlived my use when I lost my son on a yellow hillside (but what does it matter? I got him there. It's his turn now. The Days of the children.)

We live in Luke. We can never be parted.

Kit shouts some wordless wildboy oath over his shoulder, and the others rush in, five of them, six, all jostling and pushing, and they smell bad, even the cold can't kill their smell, a rank male taint of sweat and anger – They smell of the end of things, of death.

Fear is sharp, hard, exact. The thump of my heart in the vault of my chest.

Outside, I think, *I prefer outside.* It's still light, out there. Or day is just ending. I'd like to catch a last glimpse of the sky. I don't mind the cold. I accept the ice.

But they seize me, and I hardly bother to struggle. There are six of them, seven, and their blood is up, and they bustle me back into the great hangar where the lines of moribund Doves are kept, grey in the dull grey epsilon light. I shall save my strength for whatever is coming. Let them carry me, if it pleases them. I think, *I wouldn't mind saying goodbye to Dora,* and even as I think it I find I'm kneeling facing her, with my arms pinioned. I know each wine stain on her feathers; one or two marks are a darker red.

'Speak to her,' yells Kit. 'Ask her if she hungry. Yes she is, she bloody hungry!'

I touch 'Hallo', and she speaks to me. Her voice is so rundown that it wavers, wobbles as if she is weeping. Her old bright 'How are you?' sounds like a dirge. My mouth is dry – strange that it's dry – but I ask her, obediently, if she's hungry.

'I am very hungry,' Dora quavers. No one but me is close enough to hear her. Kit yells at me to relay it to them. Of course I am honest. 'She says she is hungry.'

At that, the boys let me go so abruptly that I pitch forwards on my face. I become aware that the mood has changed. Two of the wild boys help me up. They have all gone quiet. They are staring at me, and looking at each other with suppressed excitement. I try to breathe deeply, gather myself.

Other boys are arriving, slipping through the shadows, weaving between the grey bodies of the Doves, their dull slumped heads, their flaccid wings. Twenty, thirty, more than I can count. Something is happening. A festival? Something is going to be celebrated. Perhaps my story, the end of my story. Yes, I am going to be celebrated.

Kit's clever friend Jojo, the mouthy one, asks me a question I can't understand. Do all the Doves' functions decay with starvation? *Functions, Doves, decay, starvation* ... I can't seem to arrange these words in my mind, but I know that a lot depends on my answer. They have formed themselves into a makeshift ring, squashed between two long rows of robots. 'Core functions,' someone says through my lips, who knows what I knew long ago, 'survive as long as the Dove survives, but at the expense of peripheral ones.' This sounds amazingly good to me, but Kit hits me, hard, full in the mouth. 'Yes is the answer,' I say, spitting blood.

There's a quick conference. Jojo speaks. He has the gift of language, unlike Kit; his early life must have been inside. He is trying to sound adult and grand. Why is my breath so fast, so tight? He is giving me the decision of the Chiefboys. 'You have a choice, old man –'

That's always fatal. I'm human, aren't I? We can't handle choice. I must make myself listen to what he is saying.

He's saying it again, as if I am stupid. 'Go outside and be termed by the sword, or stay here and die at the hands of the Doves.'

I look at him dumbly. Doves have *wings,* not *hands.* My mother and father thought words mattered – But behind the words, something huge, choking. Has it really come? Is it here at last, the final moment when my whole life will fall into a pattern, when I shall see, when I'll understand?

'Dora wouldn't hurt me,' I say, foolishly.

'Dora will eat you when you give the order,' Jojo assures me. 'SD and R is a core function. Dora will paralyse you and eat you.'

'She no be hungry any more,' Kit interrupts, snickering, jeering. 'You do your work. Fucking keep her alive.'

I look at Dora. Her kind blue eyes, the lizard thickness of her lustreless lids, the bald patches among her feathers. I think, I don't want to keep the Doves alive. They were toys, really, no more than that. Our brains could never give the spark of freedom that sets it all dancing, diversifying, growing more detailed all the time, not less –

Besides, I am very fond of Dora. I'd rather we ended our days on good terms.

I stroke the stubbly mound of her tummy. 'Goodbye, old girl,' I say, shyly. 'It's been a pleasure, travelling with you. Now I just have to step outside.'

Her voice warbles back, effortful. 'I like you too. May I come with you?'

'I think we've come to the end of the road.' I get up, and stretch, and prepare myself. I am sixty years old, but tough as leather. 'Outside,' I say in my own strong voice, not the dry weak voice of a few moments before. Then I shout it out, so they all may hear me. 'Outside, lads. I prefer outside. Give me a sword. I'll be a Man.'

I tap Dora gently on the shoulder in passing.

I, Saul, Teller of Tales ...

My heart is beating a great tattoo. The boys surround me, respectful, attentive, the drift of their movement bearing me onwards though no one actually touches me yet. The grey dead light is being overwhelmed by the growing glow of the day outside, and as we pass through the door of the hangar together, a narrowing stream of human beings, the cold strikes first, and then the beauty, the amazing beauty of the end of day, the harrowing beauty of my last day. A great wheel of birds comes turning across it, thousands of them blown in from the sea. They're coming back slowly, the birds, the foxes, paws, clawmarks printing the ice. And there, wider, higher than the towers, is the radiance beyond the horizon. The ring of fire, then the ring of ice. And somewhere, across the snowfields, it's coming –

I, Saul, Teller of Tales, Keeper of Doves, Slayer of Wolves, tell you the story of my times. Of the best of days, and the last of days. For whoever may read it. Whoever can read.

I could run away, but I pick up my sword, and wait for the swordsmen to celebrate me.

I have lived my Day.

Yes, I am ready.